BERNARD CORNWELL

Sharpe's Triumph

Richard Sharpe and
the Battle of Assaye,
September 1803

HarperCollins*Publishers*

HarperCollins*Publishers*
77–85 Fulham Palace Road,
Hammersmith, London W6 8JB

www.harpercollins.co.uk

This paperback edition 2006
1

First published in Great Britain by
HarperCollins*Publishers* 1998

Copyright © Bernard Cornwell 1998

Map by Ken Lewis

The author asserts the moral right to
be identified as the author of this work

A catalogue record for this book is
available from the British Library

ISBN-13: 978 0 00 723506 3
ISBN-10: 0 00 723506 2

Set in Baskerville by Rowland Phototypesetting Ltd,
Bury St Edmunds, Suffolk

Printed and bound in Great Britain by
Clays Ltd, St Ives plc

Sharpe's Triumph is for
Joel Gardner,
who walked Ahmednuggur
and Assaye with me

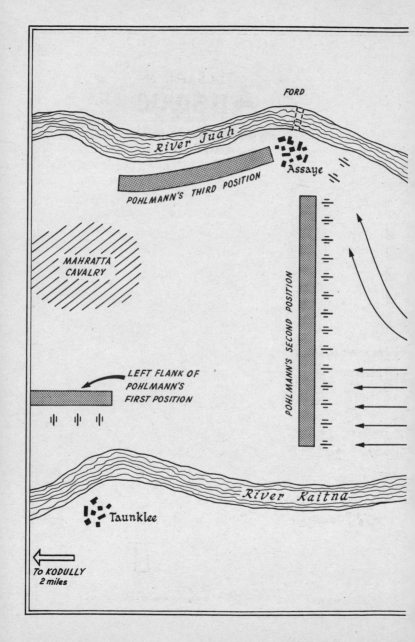

FORD

River Juah

POHLMANN'S THIRD POSITION

Assaye

MAHRATTA
CAVALRY

POHLMANN'S SECOND POSITION

LEFT FLANK OF
POHLMANN'S
FIRST POSITION

River Kaitna

Taunklee

To KODULLY
2 miles

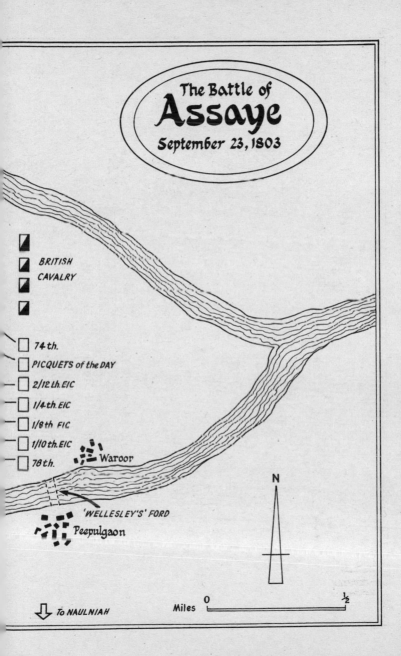

The Battle of Assaye
September 23, 1803

■ BRITISH

◩ CAVALRY

□ 74th.
□ PICQUETS of the DAY
□ 2/12 th. EIC
□ 1/4 th. EIC
□ 1/8 th EIC
□ 1/10 th. EIC
□ 78 th.

Waroor

'WELLESLEY'S' FORD

Peepulgaon

N

To NAULNIAH

Miles 0 ½

CHAPTER 1

It was not Sergeant Richard Sharpe's fault. He was not in charge. He was junior to at least a dozen men, including a major, a captain, a subadar and two jemadars, yet he still felt responsible. He felt responsible, angry, hot, bitter and scared. Blood crusted on his face where a thousand flies crawled. There were even flies in his open mouth.

But he dared not move.

The humid air stank of blood and of the rotted egg smell made by powder smoke. The very last thing he remembered doing was thrusting his pack, haversack and cartridge box into the glowing ashes of a fire, and now the ammunition from the cartridge box exploded. Each blast of powder fountained sparks and ashes into the hot air. A couple of men laughed at the sight. They stopped to watch it for a few seconds, poked at the nearby bodies with their muskets, then walked on.

Sharpe lay still. A fly crawled on his eyeball and he forced himself to stay absolutely motionless. There was blood on his face and more blood had puddled in his right ear, though it was drying now. He blinked, fearing that the small motion would attract one of the killers, but no one noticed.

Chasalgaon. That's where he was. Chasalgaon: a miserable, thorn-walled fort on the frontier of Hyderabad, and because the Rajah of Hyderabad was a British ally the fort had been garrisoned by a hundred sepoys of the East India

Company and fifty mercenary horsemen from Mysore, only when Sharpe arrived half the sepoys and all of the horsemen had been out on patrol.

Sharpe had come from Seringapatam, leading a detail of six privates and carrying a leather bag stuffed with rupees, and he had been greeted by Major Crosby who commanded at Chasalgaon. The Major proved to be a plump, red-faced, bilious man who disliked the heat and hated Chasalgaon, and he had slumped in his canvas chair as he unfolded Sharpe's orders. He read them, grunted, then read them again. 'Why the hell did they send you?' he finally asked.

'No one else to send, sir.'

Crosby frowned at the order. 'Why not an officer?'

'No officers to spare, sir.'

'Bloody responsible job for a sergeant, wouldn't you say?'

'Won't let you down, sir,' Sharpe said woodenly, staring at the leprous yellow of the tent's canvas a few inches above the Major's head.

'You'd bloody well better not let me down,' Crosby said, pushing the orders into a pile of damp papers on his camp table. 'And you look bloody young to be a sergeant.'

'I was born late, sir,' Sharpe said. He was twenty-six, or thought he was, and most sergeants were much older.

Crosby, suspecting he was being mocked, stared up at Sharpe, but there was nothing insolent on the Sergeant's face. A good-looking man, Crosby thought sourly. Probably had the *bibbis* of Seringapatam falling out of their saris, and Crosby, whose wife had died of the fever ten years before and who consoled himself with a two-rupee village whore every Thursday night, felt a pang of jealousy. 'And how the devil do you expect to get the ammunition back to Seringapatam?' he demanded.

'Hire ox carts, sir.' Sharpe had long perfected the way to address unhelpful officers. He gave them precise answers, added nothing unnecessary and always sounded confident.

'With what? Promises?'

'Money, sir.' Sharpe tapped his haversack where he had the bag of rupees.

'Christ, they trust you with money?'

Sharpe decided not to respond to that question, but just stared impassively at the canvas. Chasalgaon, he decided, was not a happy place. It was a small fort built on a bluff above a river that should have been overflowing its banks, but the monsoon had failed and the land was cruelly dry. The fort had no ditch, merely a wall made of cactus thorn with a dozen wooden fighting platforms spaced about its perimeter. Inside the wall was a beaten-earth parade ground where a stripped tree served as a flagpole, and the parade ground was surrounded by three mud-walled barracks thatched with palm, a cookhouse, tents for the officers and a stone-walled magazine to store the garrison's ammunition. The sepoys had their families with them, so the fort was overrun with women and children, but Sharpe had noted how sullen they were. Crosby, he thought, was one of those crabbed officers who were only happy when all about them were miserable.

'I suppose you expect me to arrange the ox carts?' Crosby said indignantly.

'I'll do it myself, sir.'

'Speak the language, do you?' Crosby sneered. 'A sergeant, banker and interpreter, are you?'

'Brought an interpreter with me, sir,' Sharpe said. Which was over-egging the pudding a bit, because Davi Lal was only thirteen, an urchin off the streets of Seringapatam. He was a smart, mischievous child whom Sharpe had found stealing from the armoury cookhouse and, after giving the starving boy a clout around both ears to teach him respect for His Britannic Majesty's property, Sharpe had taken him to Lali's house and given him a proper meal, and Lali had talked to the boy and learned that his parents were dead, that he had no relatives he knew of, and that he lived by his wits. He was also covered in lice. 'Get rid of him,' she had advised Sharpe, but Sharpe had seen something of his own childhood in Davi Lal and so he had dragged him down to the River Cauvery and given him a decent scrubbing. After that Davi Lal had become Sharpe's errand boy. He learned to pipeclay belts, blackball boots and speak his own version of English which, because it came from the lower ranks, was liable to shock the gentler born.

'You'll need three carts,' Crosby said.

'Yes, sir,' Sharpe said. 'Thank you, sir.' He had known exactly how many carts he would need, but he also knew it was stupid to pretend to knowledge in the face of officers like Crosby.

'Find your damn carts,' Crosby snapped, 'then let me know when you're ready to load up.'

'Very good, sir. Thank you, sir.' Sharpe stiffened to attention, about-turned and marched from the tent to find Davi Lal and the six privates waiting in the shade of one of the barracks. 'We'll have dinner,' Sharpe told them, 'then sort out some carts this afternoon.'

'What's for dinner?' Private Atkins asked.

'Whatever Davi can filch from the cookhouse,' Sharpe said, 'but be nippy about it, all right? I want to be out of this damn place tomorrow morning.'

Their job was to fetch eighty thousand rounds of prime musket cartridges that had been stolen from the East India Company armoury in Madras. The cartridges were the best quality in India, and the thieves who stole them knew exactly who would pay the highest price for the ammunition. The princedoms of the Mahratta Confederation were forever at war with each other or else raiding the neighbouring states, but now, in the summer of 1803, they faced an imminent invasion by British forces. The threatened invasion had brought two of the biggest Mahratta rulers into an alliance that now gathered its forces to repel the British, and those rulers had promised the thieves a king's ransom in gold for the cartridges, but one of the thieves who had helped break into the Madras armoury had refused to let his brother join the band and share in the profit, and so the aggrieved brother had betrayed the thieves to the Company's spies and, two weeks later, the caravan carrying the cartridges across India had been ambushed by sepoys not far from Chasalgaon. The thieves had died or fled, and the recaptured ammunition had been brought back to the fort's small magazine for safekeeping. Now the eighty thousand cartridges were to be taken to the armoury at Seringapatam, three days to the south, from where they would be issued to the British troops who were readying themselves for the war against the Mahrattas. A simple job, and Sharpe, who had spent the last four years as a sergeant in the Seringapatam armoury, had been given the responsibility.

Spoilage, Sharpe was thinking while his men boiled a cauldron of river water on a bullock-dung fire. That was the key to the next few days, spoilage. Say seven thousand cartridges lost to damp? No one in Seringapatam would argue with that, and Sharpe reckoned he could sell the seven thousand cartridges on to Vakil Hussein, so long, of course, as there were eighty thousand cartridges to begin with. Still, Major Crosby had not quibbled with the figure, but just as Sharpe was thinking that, so Major Crosby appeared from his tent with a cocked hat on his head and a sword at his side. 'On your feet!' Sharpe snapped at his lads as the Major headed towards them.

'Thought you were finding ox carts?' Crosby snarled at Sharpe.

'Dinner first, sir.'

'Your food, I hope, and not ours? We don't get rations to feed King's troops here, Sergeant.' Major Crosby was in the service of the East India Company and, though he wore a red coat like the King's army, there was little love lost between the two forces.

'Our food, sir,' Sharpe said, gesturing at the cauldron in which rice and kid meat, both stolen from Crosby's stores, boiled. 'Carried it with us, sir.'

A havildar shouted from the fort gate, demanding Crosby's attention, but the Major ignored the shout. 'I forgot to mention one thing, Sergeant.'

'Sir?'

Crosby looked sheepish for a moment, then remembered he was talking to a mere sergeant. 'Some of the cartridges were spoiled. Damp got to them.'

'I'm sorry to hear that, sir,' Sharpe said straight-faced.

'So I had to destroy them,' Crosby said. 'Six or seven thousand as I remember.'

'Spoilage, sir,' Sharpe said. 'Happens all the time, sir.'

'Exactly so,' Crosby said, unable to hide his relief at Sharpe's easy acceptance of his tale, 'exactly so,' then he turned towards the gate. 'Havildar?'

'Company troops approaching, sahib!'

'Where's Captain Leonard? Isn't he officer of the day?' Crosby demanded.

'Here, sir, I'm here.' A tall, gangling captain hurried from a tent, tripped on a guy rope, recovered his hat, then headed for the gate.

Sharpe ran to catch up with Crosby who was also walking towards the gate. 'You'll give me a note, sir?'

'A note? Why the devil should I give you a note?'

'Spoilage, sir,' Sharpe said respectfully. 'I'll have to account for the cartridges, sir.'

'Later,' Crosby said, 'later.'

'Yes, sir,' Sharpe said. 'And sod you backwards, you miserable bastard,' he added, though too softly for Crosby to hear.

Captain Leonard clambered up to the platform beside the gate where Crosby joined him. The Major took a telescope from his tail pocket and slid the tubes open. The platform overlooked the small river that should have been swollen by the seasonal rains into a flood, but the failure of the monsoon had left only a trickle of water between the flat grey rocks. Beyond the shrunken river, up on the skyline behind a grove of trees, Crosby could see red-coated troops led by a European officer mounted on a black horse, and his first thought was that it must be Captain Roberts returning from patrol, but Roberts had a piebald horse and, besides, he had only taken fifty sepoys whereas this horseman led a company almost twice that size. 'Open the gate,' Crosby ordered, and wondered who the devil it was. He decided it was probably Captain Sullivan from the Company's post at Milladar, another frontier fort like Chasalgaon, but what the hell was Sullivan doing here? Maybe he was marching some new recruits to toughen the bastards, not that the skinny little brutes needed any toughening, but it was uncivil of Sullivan not to warn Crosby of his coming. 'Jemadar,' Crosby shouted, 'turn out the guard!'

'Sahib!' The Jemadar acknowledged the order. Other sepoys were dragging the thorn gates open.

He'll want dinner, Crosby thought sourly, and wondered what his servants were cooking for the midday meal. Kid, probably, in boiled rice. Well, Sullivan would just have to endure the stringy meat as a price for not sending any warning, and damn the man if he expected Crosby to feed his sepoys as well. Chasalgaon's cooks had not expected visitors and would not have enough rations for a hundred more hungry sepoys. 'Is that Sullivan?' he asked Leonard, handing the Captain the telescope.

Leonard stared for a long time at the approaching horseman. 'I've never met Sullivan,' he finally said, 'so I couldn't say.'

Crosby snatched back the telescope. 'Give the bastard a salute when he arrives,' Crosby ordered Leonard, 'then tell him he can join me for dinner.' He paused. 'You too,' he added grudgingly.

Crosby went back to his tent. It was better, he decided, to let Leonard welcome the stranger, rather than look too eager himself. Damn Sullivan, he thought, for not sending warning, though there was a bright side, inasmuch as Sullivan might have brought news. The tall, good-looking Sergeant from Seringapatam doubtless could have told Crosby the latest rumours from Mysore, but it would be a chill day in hell before Crosby sought news from a sergeant. But undoubtedly something was changing in the wider world, for it had been nine weeks since Crosby last saw a Mahratta raider, and that was decidedly odd. The purpose of the fort at Chasalgaon was to keep the Mahratta horse raiders out of the Rajah of Hyderabad's wealthy territory, and Crosby fancied he had done his job well, but even so he found the absence of any enemy marauders oddly worrying. What were the bastards up to? He sat behind his table and shouted for his clerk. He would write the damned armoury Sergeant a note explaining that the loss of seven thousand cartridges was due to a leak in the stone roof of Chasalgaon's magazine. He certainly could not admit that he had sold the ammunition to a merchant.

'What the bastard did,' Sharpe was saying to his men, 'was sell the bloody stuff to some heathen bastard.'

'That's what you were going to do, Sergeant,' Private Phillips said.

'Never you bleeding mind what I was going to do,' Sharpe said. 'Ain't that food ready?'

16

'Five minutes,' Davi Lal promised.

'A bloody camel could do it faster,' Sharpe grumbled, then hoisted his pack and haversack. 'I'm going for a piss.'

'He never goes anywhere without his bleeding pack,' Atkins commented.

'Doesn't want you thieving his spare shirt,' Phillips answered.

'He's got more than a shirt in that pack. Hiding something he is.' Atkins twisted round. 'Hey, Hedgehog!' They all called Davi Lal 'Hedgehog' because his hair stuck up in spikes; no matter how greasy it was or how short it was cut, it still stuck up in unruly spikes. 'What does Sharpie keep in the pack?'

Davi Lal rolled his eyes. 'Jewels! Gold. Rubies, diamonds, emeralds, sapphires and pearls.'

'Like sod he does.'

Davi Lal laughed, then turned back to the cauldron. Out by the fort's gate Captain Leonard was greeting the visitors. The guard presented arms as the officer leading the sepoys rode through the gate. The visitor returned the salute by touching a riding crop to the brim of his cocked hat which, worn fore and aft, shadowed his face. He was a tall man, uncommonly tall, and he wore his stirrups long so that he looked much too big for his horse, which was a sorry, sway-backed beast with a mangy hide, though there was nothing odd in that. Good horses were a luxury in India, and most Company officers rode decrepit nags. 'Welcome to Chasalgaon, sir,' Leonard said. He was not certain he ought to call the stranger 'sir', for the man wore no visible badge of rank on his red coat, but he carried himself like a senior officer and he reacted to Leonard's greeting with a lordly nonchalance. 'You're invited to dine with us, sir,' Leonard added, hurrying after the horseman who, having tucked his riding crop under his belt, now led his sepoys straight onto the parade ground. He stopped his horse under the flagpole from which the

British flag drooped in the windless air, then waited as his company of red-coated sepoys divided into two units of two ranks each that marched either side of the flagpole. Crosby watched from inside his tent. It was a flamboyant entrance, the Major decided.

'Halt!' the strange officer shouted when his company was in the very centre of the fort. The sepoys halted. 'Outwards turn! Ground firelocks! Good morning!' He at last looked down at Captain Leonard. 'Are you Crosby?'

'No, sir. I'm Captain Leonard, sir. And you, sir?' The tall man ignored the question. He scowled about Chasalgaon's fort as though he disapproved of everything he saw. What the hell was this? Leonard wondered. A surprise inspection? 'Shall I have your horse watered, sir?' Leonard offered.

'In good time, Captain, all in good time,' the mysterious officer said, then he twisted in his saddle and growled an order to his company. 'Fix bayonets!' The sepoys pulled out their seventeen-inch blades and slotted them onto the muzzles of their muskets. 'I like to offer a proper salute to a fellow Englishman,' the tall man explained to Leonard. 'You are English, aren't you?'

'Yes, sir.'

'Too many damned Scots in the Company,' the tall man grumbled. 'Have you ever noticed that, Leonard? Too many Scots and Irish. Glib sorts of fellow, they are, but they ain't English. Not English at all.' The visitor drew his sword, then took a deep breath. 'Company!' he shouted. 'Level arms!'

The sepoys brought their muskets to their shoulders and Leonard saw, much too late, that the guns were aimed at the troops of the garrison. 'No!' he said, but not loudly, for he still did not believe what he saw.

'Fire!' the officer shouted, and the parade ground air was murdered by the double ripple of musket shots, heavy coughing explosions that blossomed smoke across the sun-crazed mud and slammed lead balls into the unsuspecting garrison.

'Hunt them now!' the tall officer called. 'Hunt them! Fast, fast, fast!' He spurred his horse close to Captain Leonard and, almost casually, slashed down with his sword, ripping the blade hard back once it had bitten into the Captain's neck so that its edge sawed fast and deep through the sinew, muscle and flesh. 'Hunt them! Hunt them!' the officer shouted as Leonard fell. He drew a pistol from his saddle holster and rode towards the officers' tents. His men were screaming their war cries as they spread through the small fort to chase down every last sepoy of Chasalgaon's garrison. They had been ordered to leave the women and children to the last and hunt down the men first.

Crosby had been staring in horror and disbelief, and now, with shaking hands, he started to load one of his pistols, but suddenly the door of his tent darkened and he saw that the tall officer had dismounted from his horse. 'Are you Crosby?' the officer demanded.

Crosby found he could not speak. His hands quivered. Sweat was pouring down his face.

'Are you Crosby?' the man asked again in an irritated voice.

'Yes,' Crosby managed to say. 'And who the devil are you?'

'Dodd,' the tall man said, 'Major William Dodd, at your service.' And Dodd raised his big pistol so that it pointed at Crosby's face.

'No!' Crosby shouted.

Dodd smiled. 'I assume you're surrendering the fort to me, Crosby?'

'Damn you,' Crosby riposted feebly.

'You drink too much, Major,' Dodd said. 'The whole Company knows you're a sot. Didn't put up much of a fight, did you?' He pulled the trigger and Crosby's head was snatched back in a mist of blood that spattered onto the canvas. 'Pity you're English,' Dodd said. 'I'd much rather shoot a Scotsman.' The dying Major made a terrible gurgling sound, then his body jerked uncontrollably and was finally still. 'Praise the Lord, pull down the flag and find the pay chest,' Dodd said to himself, then he stepped over the Major's corpse to see that the pay chest was where he expected it to be, under the bed. 'Subadar!'

'Sahib?'

'Two men here to guard the pay chest.'

'Sahib!'

Major Dodd hurried back onto the parade ground where a small group of redcoats, British redcoats, were offering defiance, and he wanted to make sure that his sepoys took care of them, but a havildar had anticipated Dodd's orders and was leading a squad of men against the half-dozen soldiers. 'Put the blades in!' Dodd encouraged them. 'Hard in! Twist them in! That's the way! Watch your left! Left!' His voice was urgent, for a tall sergeant had suddenly appeared from behind the cookhouse, a white man with a musket and bayonet in his hands, but one of the sepoys still had a loaded musket of his own and he twisted, aimed and fired and Dodd saw another mist of bright blood sparkle in the sunlight. The sergeant had been hit in the head. He stopped, looked surprised as the musket fell from his hands and as blood streamed down his face, then he fell backwards and was still.

'Search for the rest of the bastards!' Dodd ordered, knowing that there must still be a score of the garrison hidden in the barracks. Some of the men had escaped over the thorn wall, but they would be hunted down by the Mahratta horsemen who were Dodd's allies and who should by now have spread either side of the fort. 'Search hard!' He himself went to look at the horses of the garrison's officers and decided that one of them was marginally better than his own. He moved his saddle to the better horse, then led it into the sunlight and picketed it to the flagpole. A woman ran past him, screaming as she fled from the red-coated killers, but a sepoy caught and tripped her and another pulled the sari off her shoulder. Dodd was about to order them away from the woman, then he reckoned that the enemy was well beaten and so his men could take their pleasure in safety. 'Subadar?' he shouted.

'Sahib?'

'One squad to make sure everyone's dead. Another to open the armoury. And there are a couple of horses in the stable. Pick one for yourself, and we'll take the other back to Pohlmann. And well done, Gopal.'

'Thank you, sahib,' Subadar Gopal said.

Dodd wiped the blood from his sword, then reloaded his pistol. One of the fallen redcoats was trying to turn himself over, so Dodd crossed to the wounded man, watched his feeble efforts for a moment, then put a bullet into the man's head. The man jerked in spasm, then was still. Major Dodd scowled at the blood that had sprayed his boots, but he spat, stooped and wiped the blood away. Sharpe watched the tall officer from the corner of his eye. He felt responsible, angry, hot, bitter and scared. The blood had poured from the wound in his scalp. He was dizzy, his head throbbed, but he was alive. There were flies in his mouth. And then his ammunition began to explode and the tall officer whipped round, thinking it was trouble, and a couple of men laughed at the sight of the ashes bursting into the air with each small crack of powder.

Sharpe dared not move. He listened to women screaming and children crying, then heard hooves and he waited until some horsemen came into view. They were Indians, of course, and all wild-looking men with sabres, matchlocks, spears, lances and even bows and arrows. They slid out of their saddles and joined the hunt for loot.

Sharpe lay like the dead. The crusting blood was thick on

his face. The blow of the musket ball had stunned him, so that he did not remember dropping his own musket or falling to the ground, but he sensed that the blow was not deadly. Not even deep. He had a headache, and the skin of his face felt taut with the crusted blood, but he knew head wounds always bled profusely. He tried to make his breathing shallow, left his mouth open and did not even gag when a fly crawled down to the root of his tongue, and then he could smell tobacco, arrack, leather and sweat and a horseman was bending over him with a horrid-looking curved knife with a rusty blade and Sharpe feared his throat was about to be cut, but instead the horseman began slashing at the pockets of Sharpe's uniform. He found the big key that opened Seringapatam's main magazine, a key that Sharpe had ordered cut in the bazaar so that he would not always have to fill in the form in the armoury guardhouse. The man tossed the key away, slit another pocket, found nothing valuable and so moved on to another body. Sharpe stared up at the sun.

Somewhere nearby a garrison sepoy groaned, and almost immediately he was bayoneted and Sharpe heard the hoarse exhalation of breath as the man died and the sucking sound as the murderer dragged the blade back from the constricting flesh. It had all happened so fast! And Sharpe blamed himself, though he knew it was not his fault. He had not let the killers into the fort, but he had hesitated for a few seconds to throw his pack, pouches and cartridge box onto the fire, and now he chided himself because maybe he could have used those few seconds to save his six men. Except most of them had already been dead or dying when Sharpe had first realized there was a fight. He had been pissing against the back wall of the cookhouse store hut when a musket ball ripped through the reed-mat wall and for a second or two he had just stood there, incredulous, hardly believing the shots and screams his ears registered, and he had not bothered to button his

22

trousers, but just turned and saw the dying campfire and had thrown his pack onto it, and by the time he had cocked the musket and run back to where his men had been expecting dinner the fight was almost over. The musket ball had jerked his head back and there had been a stabbing pain either side of his eyes, and the next he knew he was lying with blood crusting on his face and flies crawling down his gullet.

But maybe he could have snatched his men back. He tortured himself with the thought that he could have saved Davi Lal and a couple of the privates, maybe he could have crossed the cactus-thorn wall and run into the trees, but Davi Lal was dead and all six privates were dead and Sharpe could hear the killers laughing as they carried the ammunition out of the small magazine.

'Subadar!' the tall officer shouted. 'Fetch that bloody flag down! I wanted it done an hour ago!'

Sharpe blinked again because he could not help himself, but no one noticed, and then he closed his eyes because the sun was blinding him, and he wanted to weep out of anger and frustration and hatred. Six men dead, and Davi Lal dead, and Sharpe had not been able to do a damned thing to help them, and he wondered who the tall officer was, and then a voice provided the answer.

'Major Dodd, sahib?'

'Subadar?'

'Everything's loaded, sahib.'

'Then let's go before their patrols get back. Well done, Subadar! Tell the men there'll be a reward.'

Sharpe listened as the raiders left the fort. Who the hell were they? Major Dodd had been in East India Company uniform, and so had all his men for that matter, but they sure as hell were not Company troops. They were bastards, that's what they were, bastards from hell and they had done a thorough piece of wicked work in Chasalgaon. Sharpe

23

doubted they had lost a single man in their treacherous attack, and still he lay silent as the sounds faded away. A baby cried somewhere, a woman sobbed, and still Sharpe waited until at last he was certain that Major Dodd and his men were gone, and only then did Sharpe roll onto his side. The fort stank of blood and buzzed with flies. He groaned and got to his knees. The cauldron of rice and kid had boiled dry and so he stood and kicked it off its tripod. 'Bastards,' he said, and he saw the surprised look on Davi Lal's face and he wanted to weep for the boy.

A half-naked woman, bleeding from the mouth, saw Sharpe stand from among the bloodied heap of the dead and she screamed before snatching her child back into a barracks hut. Sharpe ignored her. His musket was gone. Every damn weapon was gone. 'Bastards!' he shouted into the hot air, then he kicked at a dog that was sniffing at Phillips's corpse. The smell of blood and powder and burned rice was thick in his throat. He gagged as he walked into the cookhouse and there found a jar of water. He drank deep, then splashed the water onto his face and rubbed away the clotted blood. He wet a rag and flinched as he cleaned the shallow wound in his scalp, then suddenly he was overcome with horror and pity and he fell onto his knees and half sobbed. He swore instead. 'Bastards!' He said the word again and again, helplessly and furiously, then he remembered his pack and so he stood again and went into the sunlight.

The ashes of the fire were still hot and the charred canvas remnants of his pack and pouches glowed red as he found a stick and raked through the embers. One by one he found what he had hidden in the fire. The rupees that had been for hiring the carts, then the rubies and emeralds, diamonds and pearls, sapphires and gold. He fetched a sack of rice from the cookhouse and he emptied the grains onto the ground and filled the sack with his treasure. A king's ransom, it was, and it had been taken from a king four years before in the Water Gate at Seringapatam where Sharpe had trapped the Tippoo Sultan and shot him down before looting his corpse.

Then, with the treasure clutched to his midriff, he knelt in the stench of Chasalgaon and felt guilty. He had survived a massacre. Anger mingled with his guilt, then he knew he had duties to do. He must find any others who had survived, he must help them, and he must work out how he could take his revenge.

On a man called Dodd.

Major John Stokes was an engineer, and if ever a man was happy with his avocation, it was Major John Stokes. There was nothing he enjoyed so much as making things, whether it was a better gun carriage, a garden or, as he was doing now, improvements to a clock that belonged to the Rajah of Mysore. The Rajah was a young man, scarcely more than a boy indeed, and he owed his throne to the British troops who had ejected the usurping Tippoo Sultan and, as a result, relations between the palace and Seringapatam's small British garrison were good. Major Stokes had found the clock in one of the palace's antechambers and noted its appalling accuracy, which is why he had brought it back to the armoury where he was happily taking it apart. 'It isn't signed,' he told his visitor, 'and I suspect it's local work. But a Frenchman had his hand in it, I can tell that. See the escapement? Typical French work, that.'

The visitor peered at the tangle of cogwheels. 'Didn't know the Frogs had it in them to make clocks, sir,' he said.

'Oh, indeed they do!' Stokes said reprovingly. 'And very fine clocks they make! Very fine. Think of Lépine! Think of Berthoud! How can you ignore Montandon? And Breguet!' The Major shook his head in mute tribute to such great craftsmen, then peered at the Rajah's sorry timepiece. 'Some rust on the mainspring, I see. That don't help. Soft metal, I suspect. It's catch as catch can over here. I've noticed that. Marvellous decorative work, but Indians make shoddy mechanics. Look at that mainspring! A disgrace.'

'Shocking, sir, shocking.' Sergeant Obadiah Hakeswill did not know a mainspring from a pendulum, and could not have cared less about either, but he needed information from Major Stokes so it was politic to show an interest.

'It was striking nine when it should have struck eight,' the Major said, poking a finger into the clock's entrails, 'or perhaps it was striking eight when it ought to have sounded nine. I don't recall. One to seven it copes with admirably, but somewhere about eight it becomes wayward.' The Major, who was in charge of Seringapatam's armoury, was a plump, cheerful fellow with prematurely white hair. 'Do you understand clocks, Sergeant?'

'Can't say as I does, sir. A simple soldier, me, sir, who has the sun as his clock.' The Sergeant's face twitched horribly. It was an uncontrollable spasm that racked his face every few seconds.

'You were asking about Sharpe,' Major Stokes said, peering into the clock. 'Well, I never! This fellow has made the bearings out of wood! Good Lord above. Wood! No wonder she's wayward! Harrison once made a wooden clock, did you know? Even the gearings! All from timber.'

'Harrison, sir? Is he in the army, sir?'

'He's a clockmaker, Sergeant, a clockmaker. A very fine clockmaker too.'

'Not a Frog, sir?'

'With a name like Harrison? Good Lord, no! He's English, and he makes a good honest clock.'

'Glad to hear it, sir,' Hakeswill said, then reminded the Major of the purpose of his visit to the armoury. 'Sergeant Sharpe, sir, my good friend, sir, is he here?'

'He is here,' Stokes said, at last looking up from the clock, 'or rather he was here. I saw him an hour ago. But he went to his quarters. He's been away, you see. Involved in that dreadful business in Chasalgaon.'

'Chiseldown, sir?'

'Terrible business, terrible! So I told Sharpe to clean himself up. Poor fellow was covered in blood! Looked like a pirate. Now that is interesting.'

'Blood, sir?' Hakeswill asked.

'A six-toothed scapewheel! With a bifurcated locking piece! Well, I never! That is enriching the pudding with currants. Rather like putting an Egg lock on a common pistol! I'm sure if you wait, Sergeant, Sharpe will be back soon. He's a marvellous fellow. Never lets me down.'

Hakeswill forced a smile, for he hated Sharpe with a rare and single-minded venom. 'He's one of the best, sir,' he said, his face twitching. 'And will he be leaving Seringapatam soon, sir? Off on an errand again, would he be?'

'Oh no!' Stokes said, picking up a magnifying glass to look more closely into the clock. 'I need him here, Sergeant. That's it, you see! There's a pin missing from the strike wheel. It engages the cogs here, do you see, and the gearing does the rest. Simple, I suppose.' The Major looked up, but saw that the strange Sergeant with the twitching face was gone. Never mind, the clock was far more interesting.

Sergeant Hakeswill left the armoury and turned left towards the barracks where he had temporary accommodation. The King's 33rd was quartered now in Hurryhur, a hundred and fifty miles to the north, and their job was to keep the roads of western Mysore clear of bandits and so the regiment ranged up and down the country and, finding themselves close to Seringapatam where the main armoury was located, Colonel Gore had sent a detachment for replacement ammunition. Captain Morris of the Light Company had drawn the duty, and he had brought half his men and Sergeant Obadiah Hakeswill to protect the shipment which would leave the city next morning and be carried on ox carts to Arrakerry where the regiment was currently camped. An easy task, but one that had offered Sergeant Hakeswill an opportunity he had long sought.

The Sergeant stopped in one of the grog shops and demanded arrack. The shop was empty, all but for himself, the owner and a legless beggar who heaved himself towards the Sergeant and received a kick in the rump for his trouble. 'Get out of here, you scabby bastard!' Hakeswill shouted. 'Bringing the flies in, you are. Go on! Piss off.' The shop thus emptied to his satisfaction, Hakeswill sat in a dark corner contemplating life. 'I chide myself,' he muttered aloud, worrying the shop's owner who feared the look of the twitching man in the red coat. 'Your own fault, Obadiah,' Hakeswill said. 'You should have seen it years ago! Years! Rich as a Jew, he is. Are you listening to me, you heathen darkie bastard?' The shop's owner, thus challenged, fled into the back room, leaving Hakeswill grumbling at the table. 'Rich as a Jew, Sharpie is, only he thinks he hides it, which he don't, on account of me having tumbled to him. He don't even live in barracks! Got himself some rooms over by the Mysore Gate. Got a bleeding servant boy. Always got cash on him, always! Buys drinks.' Hakeswill shook his head at the injustice of it all. The 33rd had spent the last four years patrolling Mysore's roads and Sharpe, all that while, had been living in Seringapatam's comforts. It was not right, not fair, not just. Hakeswill had worried about it, wondering why Sharpe was so rich. At first he had assumed that Sharpe had been fiddling the armoury stores, but that could not explain Sharpe's apparent wealth. 'Only so much milk in a cow,' Hakeswill muttered, 'no matter how hard you squeeze the teats.' Now he knew why Sharpe was rich, or he thought he knew, and what he had learned had filled Obadiah Hakeswill with a desperate jealousy. He scratched at a mosquito bite on his neck, revealing the old dark scar where the hangman's rope had burned and abraded his skin. Obadiah Hakeswill had survived that hanging, and as a result he fervently believed that he could not be killed. Touched by God, he claimed he was, touched by God.

But he was not rich. Not rich at all, and Richard Sharpe was rich. Rumour had it that Richard Sharpe used Lali's house, and that was an officers-only brothel, so why was Sergeant Sharpe allowed inside? Because he was rich, that was why, and Hakeswill had at last discovered Sharpe's secret. 'It was the Tippoo!' he said aloud, then thumped the table with his tin mug to demand more drink. 'And hurry up about it, you black-faced bastard!'

It had to be the Tippoo. Had not Hakeswill seen Sharpe lurking about the area where the Tippoo had been killed? And no soldier had ever claimed the credit for killing the Tippoo. It was widely thought that one of those Suffolk bastards from the 12th had caught the King in the chaos at the siege's end, but Hakeswill had finally worked it out. It had been Sharpe, and the reason Sharpe had kept quiet about the killing was because he had stripped the Tippoo of all his gems and he did not want anyone, least of all the army's senior officers, to know that he possessed the jewels. 'Bloody Sharpe!' Hakeswill said aloud.

So all that was needed now was an excuse to have Sharpe brought back to the regiment. No more clean and easy duty for Sharpie! No more merry rides in Lali's house for him. It would be Obadiah Hakeswill's turn to live in luxury, and all because of a dead king's treasure. 'Rubies,' Hakeswill said aloud, lingering over the word, 'and emeralds and sapphires, and diamonds like stars, and gold thick as butter.' He chuckled. And all it would need, he reckoned, was a little cunning. A little cunning, a confident lie and an arrest. 'And that will be your end, Sharpie, that will be your end,' Hakeswill said, and he could feel the beauty of his scheme unfold like a lotus blossoming in Seringapatam's moat. It would work! His visit to Major Stokes had established that Sharpe was in the town, which meant that the lie could be told and then, just like Major Stokes's clockwork, everything would go right. Every cog and gear and wheel and spike would slot and click and tick and tock, and Sergeant Hakeswill's face twitched and his hands contracted as though the tin mug in his grip were a man's throat. He would be rich.

It took Major William Dodd three days to carry the ammunition back to Pohlmann's *compoo* which was camped just outside the Mahratta city of Ahmednuggur. The *compoo* was an infantry brigade of eight battalions, each of them recruited from among the finest mercenary warriors of north India and all trained and commanded by European officers. Dowlut Rao Scindia, the Maharajah of Gwalior, whose land stretched from the fortress of Baroda in the north to the fastness of Gawilghur in the east and down to Ahmednuggur in the south, boasted that he led a hundred thousand men and that his army could blacken the land like a plague, yet this *compoo*, with its seven thousand men, was the hard heart of his army.

One of the *compoo*'s eight battalions was paraded a mile outside the encampment to greet Dodd. The cavalry that had accompanied the sepoys to Chasalgaon had ridden ahead to warn Pohlmann of Dodd's return and Pohlmann had organized a triumphant reception. The battalion stood in white coats, their black belts and weapons gleaming, but Dodd, riding at the head of his small column, had eyes only for the tall elephant that stood beside a yellow-and-white-striped marquee. The huge beast glittered in the sunlight, for its body and head were armoured with a vast leather cape onto which squares of silver had been sewn in intricate patterns. The silver covered the elephant's body, continued across its face and then, all but for two circles that had been cut for its eyes, cascaded on down the length of its trunk. Gems gleamed between the silver plates while ribbons of purple silk fluttered from the crown of the animal's head. The last few inches of the animal's big curved tusks were sheathed in silver, though the actual points of the tusks were tipped with needle-sharp points of steel. The elephant driver, the mahout, sweated in a coat of old-fashioned chain mail that had been burnished to the same gleaming polish as his animal's silver armour, while behind him was a howdah made of cedarwood on which gold panels had been nailed and above which fluttered a fringed canopy of yellow silk. Long files of purple-jacketed infantrymen stood to attention on either flank of the elephant. Some of the men carried muskets, while others had long pikes with their broad blades polished to resemble silver.

The elephant knelt when Dodd came within twenty paces and the occupant of the howdah stepped carefully down onto a set of silver-plated steps placed there by one of his purple-coated bodyguards then strolled into the shade of the striped marquee. He was a European, a tall man and big, not fat, and though a casual glance might think him overweight, a second glance would see that most of that weight was solid muscle. He had a round sun-reddened face, big black moustaches and eyes that seemed to take delight in everything he saw. His uniform was of his own devising: white silk breeches tucked into English riding boots, a green coat festooned with gold lace and aiguillettes and, on the coat's broad shoulders, thick white silk cushions hung with short golden chains. The coat had scarlet facings and loops of scarlet braid about its turned-back cuffs and gilded buttons. The big man's hat was a bicorne crested with purple-dyed feathers held in place by a badge showing the white horse of Hanover; his sword's hilt was made of gold fashioned into the shape of an elephant's head, and gold rings glinted on his big fingers. Once in the shade of the open-sided marquee he settled himself on a divan where his aides gathered about him. This was Colonel Anthony Pohlmann and he commanded the *compoo*, together with five hundred cavalry and twenty-six field guns. Ten years before, when Scindia's army had been nothing but a horde of ragged troopers on half-starved horses, Anthony Pohlmann had been a sergeant in a Hanoverian regiment of the East India Company; now he rode an elephant and needed two other beasts to carry the chests of gold coin that travelled everywhere with him.

Pohlmann stood as Dodd climbed down from his horse. 'Well done, Major!' the Colonel called in his German-accented English. 'Exceedingly well done!' Pohlmann's aides, half of them European and half Indian, joined their commander in applauding the returning hero, while the body-guard made a double line through which Dodd could advance to meet the resplendent Colonel. 'Eighty thousand cartridges,' Pohlmann exulted, 'snatched from our enemies!'

'Seventy-three thousand, sir,' Dodd said, beating dust off his breeches.

Pohlmann grinned. 'Seven thousand spoiled, eh? Nothing changes.'

'Not spoiled by me, sir,' Dodd growled.

'I never supposed so,' Pohlmann said. 'Did you have any difficulties?'

'None,' Dodd answered confidently. 'We lost no one, sir, not even a scratch, while not a single enemy soldier survived.' He smiled, cracking the dust on his cheeks. 'Not one.'

'A victory!' Pohlmann said, then gestured Dodd into the tent. 'We have wine, of sorts. There is rum, arrack, even water! Come, Major.'

Dodd did not move. 'My men are tired, sir,' he pointed out.

'Then dismiss them, Major. They can take refreshment at my cook tent.'

Dodd went to dismiss his men. He was a gangling Englishman with a long sallow face and a sullen expression. He was also that rarest of things, an officer who had deserted from the East India Company, and deserted moreover with one hundred and thirty of his own sepoy troops. He had come to Pohlmann just three weeks before and some of Pohlmann's European officers had been convinced that Lieutenant Dodd was a spy sent by the British whose army was readying to attack the Mahratta Confederation, but Pohlmann had not been so sure. It was true that no other British officer had ever deserted like Dodd, but few had reasons like Dodd, and Pohlmann had also recognized Dodd's hunger, his awkwardness, his anger and his ability. Lieutenant Dodd's record showed he was no mean soldier, his sepoys liked him, and he had a raging ambition, and Pohlmann had believed the Lieutenant's defection to be both wholehearted and real. He had made Dodd into a major, then given him a test. He had sent him to Chasalgaon. If Dodd proved capable of killing his old comrades then he was no spy, and Dodd had passed the test triumphantly and Scindia's army was now better off by seventy-three thousand cartridges.

Dodd came back to the marquee and was given the chair of honour on the right side of Pohlmann's divan. The chair on the left was occupied by a woman, a European, and Dodd could scarcely keep his eyes from her, and no wonder, for she was a rare-looking woman to discover in India. She was young, scarce more than eighteen or nineteen, with a pale face and very fair hair. Her lips were maybe a trifle too thin and her forehead perhaps a half inch too wide, yet there was something oddly attractive about her. She had a face, Dodd decided, in which the imperfections added up to attractiveness, and her appeal was augmented by a timid air of vulnerability. At first Dodd assumed the woman was Pohlmann's mistress, but then he saw that her white linen dress was frayed at the hem and some of the lace at its modest collar was crudely darned, and he decided that Pohlmann would never allow his mistress to appear so shabbily.

'Let me introduce Madame Joubert to you,' Pohlmann said, who had noticed how hungrily Dodd had stared at the woman. 'This is Major William Dodd.'

'Madame Joubert?' Dodd stressed the 'Madame', half rising and bowing from his chair as he acknowledged her.

'Major,' she said in a low voice, then smiled nervously before looking down at the table that was spread with dishes of almonds.

Pohlmann snapped his fingers for a servant, then smiled at Major Dodd. 'Simone is married to Captain Joubert, and that is Captain Joubert.' He pointed into the sunlight where a short captain stood to attention in front of the paraded battalion that stood so stiff and still in the biting sun.

'Joubert commands the battalion, sir?' Dodd asked.

'No one commands the battalion,' Pohlmann answered. 'But until three weeks ago it was led by Colonel Mathers. Back then it had five European officers; now it has Captain Joubert and Lieutenant Sillière.' He pointed to a second European, a tall thin young man, and Dodd, who was observant, saw Simone Joubert blush at the mention of Sillière's name. Dodd was amused. Joubert looked at least twenty years older than his wife, while Sillière was only a year or two her senior. 'And we must have Europeans,' Pohlmann went on, stretching back on the divan that creaked under his weight. 'The Indians are fine soldiers, but we need Europeans who understand European tactics.'

'How many European officers have you lost, sir?' Dodd asked.

'From this *compoo*? Eighteen,' Pohlmann said. 'Too many.' The men who had gone were the British officers, and all had possessed contracts with Scindia that excused them from fighting against their own countrymen, and to make matters worse the East India Company had offered a bribe to any British officer who deserted the Mahrattas and, as a result, some of Pohlmann's best men were gone. It was true that he still had some good officers left, most of them French, with a handful of Dutchmen, Swiss and Germans, but Pohlmann knew he could ill afford the loss of eighteen European officers. At least none of his artillerymen had deserted and Pohlmann put great faith in the battle-winning capacity of his guns. Those cannon were served by Portuguese, or by half-breed Indians from the Portuguese colonies in India, and those professionals had stayed loyal and were awesomely proficient.

Pohlmann drained a glass of rum and poured himself another. He had an extraordinary capacity for alcohol, a capacity Dodd did not share, and the Englishman, knowing his propensity for getting drunk, restrained himself to sips of watered wine. 'I promised you a reward, Major, if you succeeded in rescuing the cartridges,' Pohlmann said genially.

'Knowing I've done my duty is reward enough,' Dodd said. He felt shabby and ill-uniformed among Pohlmann's gaudy aides and had decided that it was best to play the bluff soldier, a role he thought would appeal to a former sergeant. It was said that Pohlmann kept his old East India Company uniform as a reminder of just how far he had risen.

'Men do not join Scindia's army merely for the pleasures of doing their duty,' Pohlmann said, 'but for the rewards such service offers. We are here to become rich, are we not?' He unhooked the elephant-hilted sword from his belt. The scabbard was made of soft red leather and was studded with small emeralds. 'Here.' Pohlmann offered the sword to Dodd.

'I can't take your sword!' Dodd protested.

'I have many, Major, and many finer. I insist.'

Dodd took the sword. He drew the blade from the scabbard and saw that it was finely made, much better than the drab sword he had worn as a lieutenant these last twenty years. Many Indian swords were made of soft steel and broke easily in combat, but Dodd guessed this blade had been forged in France or Britain, then given its beautiful elephant hilt in India. That hilt was of gold, the elephant's head made the pommel, while the handguard was the beast's curved trunk. The grip was of black leather bound with gold wire. 'Thank you, sir,' he said feelingly.

'It is the first of many rewards,' Pohlmann said airily, 'and those rewards will shower on us when we beat the British. Which we shall, though not here.' He paused to drink rum. 'The British will attack any day now,' he went on, 'and they doubtless hope I'll stay and fight them here, but I don't have a mind to oblige them. Better to make the bastards march after us, eh? The rains may come while they pursue us and the rivers will hold them up. Disease will weaken them. And once they are weak and tired, we shall be strong. All Scindia's *compoos* will join together and the Rajah of Berar has promised his army, and once we are all gathered we shall crush the British. But that means I have to give up Ahmednuggur.'

'Not an important city,' Dodd commented. He noticed that Simone Joubert was sipping wine. She kept her eyes lowered, only occasionally glancing up at her husband or at Lieutenant Sillière. She took no notice of Dodd, but she would, he promised himself, she would. Her nose was too small, he decided, but even so she was a thing of pale and fragile wonder in this hot, dark-skinned land. Her blonde hair, which was hung with ringlets in a fashion that had prevailed ten years before in Europe, was held in place by small mother-of-pearl clips.

'Ahmednuggur is not important,' Pohlmann agreed, 'but

36

Scindia hates losing any of his cities and he stuffed Ahmednuggur full of supplies and insisted I post one regiment inside the city.' He nodded towards the white-coated troops. 'That regiment, Major. It's probably my best regiment, but I am forced to quarter it in Ahmednuggur.'

Dodd understood Pohlmann's predicament. 'You can't take them out of the city without upsetting Scindia,' he said, 'but you don't want to lose the regiment when the city falls.'

'I can't lose it!' Pohlmann said indignantly. 'A good regiment like that? Mathers trained it well, very well. Now he's gone to join our enemies, but I can't lose his regiment as well, so whoever takes over from Mathers must know how to extricate his men from trouble.'

Dodd felt a surge of excitement. He liked to think that it was not just for the money that he had deserted the Company, nor because of his legal troubles, but for the long overdue chance of leading his own regiment. He could do it well, he knew that, and he knew what Pohlmann was leading up to.

Pohlmann smiled. 'Suppose I give you Mathers's regiment, Major? Can you pull it out of the fire for me?'

'Yes, sir,' Dodd said simply. Simone Joubert, for the first time since she had been introduced to Dodd, looked up at him, but without any friendliness.

'All of it?' Pohlmann asked. 'With its cannon?'

'All of it,' Dodd said firmly, 'and with every damned gun.'

'Then from now it is Dodd's regiment,' Pohlmann said, 'and if you lead it well, Major, I shall make you a colonel and give you a second regiment to command.'

Dodd celebrated by draining his cup of wine. He was so overcome with emotion that he hardly dared speak, though the look on his face said it all. His own regiment at last! He had waited so long for this moment and now, by God, he would show the Company how well their despised officers could fight.

37

Pohlmann snapped his fingers so that a servant girl brought him more rum. 'How many men will Wellesley bring?' he asked Dodd.

'No more than fifteen thousand infantry,' the new commander of Dodd's regiment answered confidently. 'Probably fewer, and they'll be split into two armies. Boy Wellesley will command one, Colonel Stevenson the other.'

'Stevenson's old, yes?'

'Ancient and cautious,' Dodd said dismissively.

'Cavalry?'

'Five or six thousand? Mostly Indians.'

'Guns?'

'Twenty-six at most. Nothing bigger than a twelve-pounder.'

'And Scindia can field eighty guns,' Pohlmann said, 'some of them twenty-eight-pounders. And once the Rajah of Berar's forces join us, we'll have forty thousand infantry and at least fifty more guns.' The Hanoverian smiled. 'But battles aren't just numbers. They're also won by generals. Tell me about this Major General Sir Arthur Wellesley.'

'Boy Wellesley?' Dodd responded scathingly. The British General was younger than Dodd, but that was not the cause of the derisory nickname. Rather it was envy, for Wellesley had connections and wealth, while Dodd had neither. 'He's young,' Dodd said, 'only thirty-four.'

'Youth is no barrier to good soldiering,' Pohlmann said chidingly, though he well understood Dodd's resentment. For years Dodd had watched younger men rise up through the ranks of the King's army while he had been stuck in the Company's hidebound ranks. A man could not buy promotion in the Company, nor were promotions given by merit, but only by seniority, and so forty-year-old men like Dodd were still lieutenants while, in the King's army, mere boys were captains or majors. 'Is Wellesley good?' Pohlmann asked.

'He's never fought a battle,' Dodd said bitterly, 'not unless you count Malavelly.'

'One volley?' Pohlmann asked, half recalling stories of the skirmish.

'One volley and a bayonet charge,' Dodd said, 'not a proper battle.'

'He defeated Dhoondiah.'

'A cavalry charge against a bandit,' Dodd said scornfully. 'My point, sir, is that Boy Wellesley has never faced artillery and infantry on a real battlefield. He was jumped up to major general solely because his brother is Governor General. If his name had been Dodd instead of Wellesley he'd be lucky to command a company, let alone an army.'

'He's an aristocrat?' Pohlmann enquired.

'Of course. What else?' Dodd asked. 'His father was an earl.'

'So . . .' Pohlmann put a handful of almonds in his mouth and paused to chew them. 'So,' he went on, 'he's the younger son of a nobleman, sent into the army because he wasn't good for anything else, and his family purchased him up the ranks?'

'Exactly, sir, exactly.'

'But I hear he is efficient?'

'Efficient?' Dodd thought about it. 'He's efficient, sir, because his brother gives him the cash. He can afford a big bullock train. He carries his supplies with him, so his men are well fed. But he still ain't ever seen a cannon's muzzle, not facing him, not alongside a score of others and backed by steady infantry.'

'He did well as Governor of Mysore,' Pohlmann observed mildly.

'So he's an efficient governor? Does that make him a general?'

'A disciplinarian, I hear,' Pohlmann said.

39

'He sets a lovely parade ground,' Dodd agreed sarcastically. 'But he isn't a fool?'

'No,' Dodd admitted, 'not a fool, but not a general either. He's been promoted too fast and too young, sir. He's beaten bandits, but he took a beating himself outside Seringapatam.'

'Ah, yes. The night attack.' Pohlmann had heard of that skirmish, how Arthur Wellesley had attacked a wood outside Seringapatam and there been roundly thrashed by the Tippoo's troops. 'Even so,' he said, 'it never serves to underestimate an enemy.'

'Overestimate him as much as you like, sir,' Dodd said stoutly, 'but the fact remains that Boy Wellesley has never fought a proper battle, not with more than a thousand men under his command, and he's never faced a real army, not a trained field army with gunners and disciplined infantry, and my guess is that he won't stand. He'll run back to his brother and demand more men. He's a careful man.'

Pohlmann smiled. 'So let us lure this careful man deep into our territory where he can't retreat, eh? Then beat him.' He smiled, then hauled a watch from his fob and snapped open the lid. 'I have to be going soon,' he said, 'but some business first.' He took an envelope from his gaudy coat's pocket and handed the sealed paper to Dodd. 'That is your authority to command Mathers's regiment, Major,' he said, 'but remember, I want you to bring it safely out of Ahmednuggur. You can help the defence for a time, but don't be trapped there. Young Wellesley can't invest the whole city, he doesn't have enough men, so you should be able to escape easily enough. Bloody his nose, Dodd, but keep your regiment safe. Do you understand?'

Dodd understood well enough. Pohlmann was setting Dodd a difficult and ignoble task, that of retreating from a fight with his command intact. There was little glory in such a manoeuvre, but it would still be a difficult piece of soldiering and Dodd knew he was being tested a second time. The first test had been Chasalgaon, the second would be Ahmednuggur. 'I can manage it,' he said dourly.

'Good!' Pohlmann said. 'I shall make things easier for you by taking your regiment's families northwards. You might march soldiers safely from the city's fall, but I doubt you can manage a horde of women and children too. And what about you, Madame?' He turned and laid a meaty hand on Simone Joubert's knee. 'Will you come with me?' He talked to her as though she were a child. 'Or stay with Major Dodd?'

Simone seemed startled by the question. She blushed and looked up at Lieutenant Sillière. 'I shall stay here, Colonel,' she answered in English.

'Make sure you bring her safe home, Major,' Pohlmann said to Dodd.

'I shall, sir.'

Pohlmann stood. His purple-coated bodyguards, who had been standing in front of the tent, hurried to take their places on the elephant's flanks while the mahout, who had been resting in the animal's capacious shade, now mounted the somnolent beast by gripping its tail and clambering up its backside like a sailor swarming up a rope. He edged past the gilded howdah, took his seat on the elephant's neck and turned the beast towards Pohlmann's tent. 'Are you sure' – Pohlmann turned back to Simone Joubert 'that you would not prefer to travel with me? The howdah is so comfortable, as long as you do not suffer from seasickness.'

'I shall stay with my husband,' Simone said. She had stood and proved to be much taller than Dodd had supposed. Tall and somewhat gawky, he thought, but she still possessed an odd attraction.

'A good woman should stay with her husband,' Pohlmann said, 'or someone's husband, anyway.' He turned to Dodd.

'I shall see you in a few days, Major, with your new regiment. Don't let me down.'

'I won't, sir, I won't,' Dodd promised as, holding his new sword, he watched his new commander climb the silver steps to the howdah. He had a regiment to save and a reputation to make, and by God, Dodd thought, he would do both things well.

CHAPTER 2

Sharpe sat in the open shed where the armoury stored its gun carriages. It had started to rain, though it was not the shooting downpour of the monsoon, just a miserable steady grey drizzle that turned the mud in the yard into a slippery coating of red slime. Major Stokes, beginning the afternoon in a clean red coat, white silk stock and polished boots, paced obsessively about a newly made carriage. 'It really wasn't your fault, Sharpe,' he said.

'Feels like it, sir.'

'It would, it would!' Stokes said. 'Reflects well on you, Sharpe, 'pon my soul, it does. But it weren't your fault, not in any manner.'

'Lost all six men, sir. And young Davi.'

'Poor Hedgehog,' Stokes said, squatting to peer along the trail of the carriage. 'You reckon that timber's straight, Sharpe? Bit hog-backed, maybe?'

'Looks straight to me, sir.'

'Ain't tight-grained, this oak, ain't tight-grained,' the Major said, and he began to unbuckle his sword belt. Every morning and afternoon his servant sent him to the armoury in carefully laundered and pressed clothes, and within an hour Major Stokes would be stripped down to breeches and shirtsleeves and have his hands full of spokeshaves or saws or awls or adzes. 'Like to see a straight trail,' he said. 'There's a number four spokeshave on the wall, Sharpe, be a good fellow.'

43

'You want me to sharpen it, sir?'

'I did it last night, Sharpe. I put a lovely edge on her.' Stokes unpeeled his red jacket and rolled up his sleeves. 'Timber don't season here properly, that's the trouble.' He stooped to the new carriage and began running the spokeshave along the trail, leaving curls of new white wood to fall away. 'I'm mending a clock,' he told Sharpe while he worked, 'a lovely-made piece, all but for some crude local gearing. Have a look at it. It's in my office.'

'I will, sir.'

'And I've found some new timber for axletrees, Sharpe. It's really quite exciting!'

'They'll still break, sir,' Sharpe said gloomily, then scooped up one of the many cats that lived in the armoury. He put the tabby on his lap and stroked her into a contented purr.

'Don't be so doom-laden, Sharpe! We'll solve the axletree problem yet. It's only a question of timber, nothing but timber. There, that looks better.' The Major stepped back from his work and gave it a critical look. There were plenty of Indian craftsmen employed in the armoury, but Major Stokes liked to do things himself, and besides, most of the Indians were busy preparing for the feast of Dusshera which involved manufacturing three giant-sized figures that would be paraded to the Hindu temple and there burned. Those Indians were busy in another open-sided shed where they had glue bubbling on a fire, and some of the men were pasting lengths of pale cloth onto a wicker basket that would form one of the giants' heads. Stokes was fascinated by their activity and Sharpe knew it would not be long before the Major joined them. 'Did I tell you a sergeant was here looking for you this morning?' Stokes asked.

'No, sir.'

'Came just before dinner,' Stokes said, 'a strange sort of

44

fellow.' The Major stooped to the trail and attacked another section of wood. 'He twitched, he did.'

'Obadiah Hakeswill,' Sharpe said.

'I think that was his name. Didn't seem very important,' Stokes said. 'Said he was just visiting town and looking up old companions. D'you know what I was thinking?'

'Tell me, sir,' Sharpe said, wondering why in holy hell Obadiah Hakeswill had been looking for him. For nothing good, that was certain.

'Those teak beams in the Tippoo's old throne room,' Stokes said, 'they'll be seasoned well enough. We could break out a half-dozen of the things and make a batch of axletrees from them!'

'The gilded beams, sir?' Sharpe asked.

'Soon have the gilding off them, Sharpe. Plane them down in two shakes!'

'The Rajah may not like it, sir,' Sharpe said.

Stokes's face fell. 'There is that, there is that. A fellow don't usually like his ceilings being pulled down to make gun carriages. Still, the Rajah's usually most obliging if you can get past his damned courtiers. The clock is his. Strikes eight when it should ring nine, or perhaps it's the other way round. You reckon that quoin's true?'

Sharpe glanced at the wedge which lowered and raised the cannon barrel. 'Looks good, sir.'

'I might just plane her down a shade. I wonder if our templates are out of true? We might check that. Isn't this rain splendid? The flowers were wilting, wilting! But I'll have a fine show this year with a spot of rain. You must come and see them.'

'You still want me to stay here, sir?' Sharpe asked.

'Stay here?' Stokes, who was placing the quoin in a vice, turned to look at Sharpe. 'Of course I want you to stay here, Sergeant. Best man I've got!'

'I lost six men, sir.'

'And it wasn't your fault, not your fault at all. I'll get you another six.'

Sharpe wished it was that easy, but he could not chase the guilt of Chasalgaon out of his mind. When the massacre was finished he had wandered about the fort in a half-daze. Most of the women and children still lived, but they had been frightened and had shrunk away from him. Captain Roberts, the second in command of the fort, had returned from patrol that afternoon and he had vomited when he saw the horror inside the cactus-thorn wall.

Sharpe had made his report to Roberts who had sent it by messenger to Hurryhur, the army's headquarters, then dismissed Sharpe. 'There'll be an enquiry, I suppose,' Roberts had told Sharpe, 'so doubtless your evidence will be needed, but you might as well wait in Seringapatam.' And so Sharpe, with no other orders, had walked home. He had returned the bag of rupees to Major Stokes, and now, obscurely, he wanted some punishment from the Major, but Stokes was far more concerned about the angle of the quoin. 'I've seen screws shatter because the angle was too steep, and it ain't no good having broken screws in battle. I've seen Frog guns with metalled quoins, but they only rust. Can't trust a Frog to keep them greased, you see. You're brooding, Sharpe.'

'Can't help it, sir.'

'Doesn't do to brood. Leave brooding to poets and priests, eh? Those sorts of fellows are paid to brood. You have to get on with life. What could you have done?'

'Killed one of the bastards, sir.'

'And they'd have killed you, and you wouldn't have liked that and nor would I. Look at that angle! Look at that! I do like a fine angle, I declare I do. We must check it against the templates. How's your head?'

'Mending, sir.' Sharpe touched the bandage that wrapped his forehead. 'No pain now, sir.'

'Providence, Sharpe, that's what it is, providence. The good Lord in His ineffable mercy wanted you to live.' Stokes released the vice and restored the quoin to the carriage. 'A touch of paint on that trail and it'll be ready. You think the Rajah might give me one roof beam?'

'No harm in asking him, sir.'

'I will, I will. Ah, a visitor.' Stokes straightened as a horseman, swathed against the rain in an oilcloth cape and with an oilcloth cover on his cocked hat, rode into the armoury courtyard leading a second horse by the reins. The visitor kicked his feet from the stirrups, swung down from the saddle, then tied both horses' reins to one of the shed's pillars. Major Stokes, his clothes just in their beginning stage of becoming dirty and dishevelled, smiled at the tall newcomer whose cocked hat and sword betrayed he was an officer. 'Come to inspect us, have you?' the Major demanded cheerfully. 'You'll discover chaos! Nothing in the right place, records all muddled, woodworm in the timber stacks, damp in the magazines and the paint completely addled.'

'Better that paint is addled than wits,' the newcomer said, then took off his cocked hat to reveal a head of white hair.

Sharpe, who had been sitting on one of the finished gun carriages, shot to his feet, tipping the surprised cat into the Major's wood shavings. 'Colonel McCandless, sir!'

'Sergeant Sharpe!' McCandless responded. The Colonel shook water from his cocked hat and turned to Stokes. 'And you, sir?'

'Major Stokes, sir, at your service, sir. John Stokes, commander of the armoury and, as you see, carpenter to His Majesty.'

'You will forgive me, Major Stokes, if I talk to Sergeant Sharpe?' McCandless shed his oilskin cape to reveal his East

India Company uniform. 'Sergeant Sharpe and I are old friends.'

'My pleasure, Colonel,' Stokes said. 'I have business in the foundry. They're pouring too fast. I tell them all the time! Fast pouring just bubbles the metal, and bubbled metal leads to disaster, but they won't listen. Ain't like making temple bells, I tell them, but I might as well save my breath.' He glanced wistfully towards the happy men making the giant's head for the Dusshera festival. 'And I have other things to do,' he added.

'I'd rather you didn't leave, Major,' McCandless said very formally. 'I suspect what I have to say concerns you. It is good to see you, Sharpe.'

'You too, sir,' Sharpe said, and it was true. He had been locked in the Tippoo's dungeons with Colonel Hector McCandless and if it was possible for a sergeant and a colonel to be friends, then a friendship existed between the two men. McCandless, tall, vigorous and in his sixties, was the East India Company's head of intelligence for all southern and western India, and in the last four years he and Sharpe had talked a few times whenever the Colonel passed through Seringapatam, but those had been social conversations and the Colonel's grim face suggested that this meeting was anything but social.

'You were at Chasalgaon?' McCandless demanded.

'I was, sir, yes.'

'So you saw Lieutenant Dodd?'

Sharpe nodded. 'Won't ever forget the bastard. Sorry, sir.' He apologized because McCandless was a fervent Christian who abhorred all foul language. The Scotsman was a stern man, honest as a saint, and Sharpe sometimes wondered why he liked him so much. Maybe it was because McCandless was always fair, always truthful and could talk to any man, rajah or sergeant, with the same honest directness.

'I never met Lieutenant Dodd,' McCandless said, 'so describe him to me.'

'Tall, sir, and thin like you or me.'

'Not like me,' Major Stokes put in.

'Sort of yellow-faced,' Sharpe went on, 'as if he'd had the fever once. Long face, like he ate something bitter.' He thought for a second. He had only caught a few glimpses of Dodd, and those had been sideways. 'He's got lank hair, sir, when he took off his hat. Brown hair. Long nose on him, like Sir Arthur's, and a bony chin. He's calling himself Major Dodd now, sir, not Lieutenant. I heard one of his men call him Major.'

'And he killed every man in the garrison?' McCandless asked.

'He did, sir. Except me. I was lucky.'

'Nonsense, Sharpe!' McCandless said. 'The hand of the Lord was upon you.'

'Amen,' Major Stokes intervened.

McCandless stared broodingly at Sharpe. The Colonel had a hard-planed face with oddly blue eyes. He was forever claiming that he wanted to retire to his native Scotland, but he always found some reason to stay on in India. He had spent much of his life riding the states that bordered the land administered by the Company, for his job was to explore those lands and report their threats and weaknesses to his masters. Little happened in India that escaped McCandless, but Dodd had escaped him, and Dodd was now McCandless's concern. 'We have placed a price on his head,' the Colonel said, 'of five hundred guineas.'

'Bless me!' Major Stokes said in astonishment.

'He's a murderer,' McCandless went on. 'He killed a goldsmith in Seedesegur, and he should be facing trial, but he ran instead and I want you, Sharpe, to help me catch him. And I'm not pursuing the rogue because I want the reward money; in fact I'll refuse it. But I do want him, and I want your help.'

Major Stokes began to protest, saying that Sharpe was his best man and that the armoury would go to the dogs if the Sergeant was taken away, but McCandless shot the amiable Major a harsh look that was sufficient to silence him.

'I want Lieutenant Dodd captured,' McCandless said implacably, 'and I want him tried, and I want him executed, and I need someone who will know him by sight.'

Major Stokes summoned the courage to continue his objections. 'But I need Sergeant Sharpe,' he protested. 'He organizes everything! The duty rosters, the stores, the pay chest, everything!'

'I need him more,' McCandless snarled, turning on the hapless Major. 'Do you know how many Britons are in India, Major? Maybe twelve thousand, and less than half of those are soldiers. Our power does not rest on the shoulders of white men, Major, but on the muskets of our sepoys. Nine men out of every ten who invade the Mahratta states will be sepoys, and Lieutenant Dodd persuaded over a hundred of those men to desert! To desert! Can you imagine our fate if the other sepoys follow them? Scindia will shower Dodd's men with gold, Major, with lucre and with spoil, in the hope that others will follow them. I have to stop that, and I need Sharpe.'

Major Stokes recognized the inevitable. 'You will bring him back, sir?'

'If it is the Lord's will, yes. Well, Sergeant? Will you come with me?'

Sharpe glanced at Major Stokes who shrugged, smiled, then nodded his permission. 'I'll come, sir,' Sharpe said to the Scotsman.

'How soon can you be ready?'

'Ready now, sir.' Sharpe indicated the newly issued pack and musket that lay at his feet.

'You can ride a horse?'

Sharpe frowned. 'I can sit on one, sir.'

'Good enough,' the Scotsman said. He pulled on his oil-cloth cape, then untied the two reins and gave one set to Sharpe. 'She's a docile thing, Sharpe, so don't saw on her bit.'

'We're going right now, sir?' Sharpe asked, surprised by the suddenness of it all.

'Right now,' McCandless said. 'Time waits for no man, Sharpe, and we have a traitor and a murderer to catch.' He pulled himself into his saddle and watched as Sharpe clumsily mounted the second horse.

'So where are you going?' Stokes asked McCandless.

'Ahmednuggur first, and after that God will decide.' The Colonel touched his horse's flanks with his spurs and Sharpe, his pack hanging from one shoulder and his musket slung on the other, followed.

He would redeem himself for the failure at Chasalgaon. Not with punishment, but with something better: with vengeance.

Major William Dodd ran a white-gloved finger down the spoke of a gunwheel. He inspected his fingertip and nearly nine hundred men, or at least as many of the nine hundred on parade who could see the Major, inspected him in return.

No mud or dust on the glove. Dodd straightened his back and glowered at the gun crews, daring any man to show pleasure in having achieved a near perfect turn-out. It had been hard work, too, for it had rained earlier in the day and the regiment's five guns had been dragged through the muddy streets to the parade ground just inside Ahmednuggur's southern gate, but the gunners had still managed to clean their weapons meticulously. They had removed every scrap of mud, washed the mahogany trails, then polished the barrels until their alloy of copper and tin gleamed like brass.

Impressive, Dodd thought, as he peeled off the glove. Pohlmann had left Ahmednuggur, retreating north to join his *compoo* to Scindia's gathering army, and Dodd had ordered this surprise inspection of his new command. He had given the regiment just one hour's notice, but so far he had found nothing amiss. They were impressive indeed; standing in four long white-coated ranks with their four cannon and single howitzer paraded at the right flank. The guns themselves, despite their gleam, were pitiful things. The four field guns were mere four-pounders, while the fifth was a five-inch howitzer, and not one of the pieces fired a ball of real weight. Not a killing ball. 'Peashooters!' Dodd said disparagingly.

'Monsieur?' Captain Joubert, the Frenchman who had desperately hoped to be given command of the regiment himself, asked.

'You heard me, Monsewer. Peashooters!' Dodd said as he lifted a limber's lid and hoisted out one of the four-pounder shots. It was half the size of a cricket ball. 'You might as well spit at them, Monsewer!'

Joubert, a small man, shrugged. 'At close range, Monsieur . . .' he began to defend the guns.

'At close range, Monsewer, close range!' Dodd tossed the shot to Joubert who fumbled the catch. 'That's no use at close range! No more use than a musket ball, and the gun's ten times more cumbersome than a musket.' He rummaged through the limber. 'No canister? No grape?'

'Canister isn't issued for four-pounder guns,' Joubert said. 'It isn't even made for them.'

'Then we make our own,' Dodd said. 'Bags of scrap metal, Monsewer, strapped to a sabot and a charge. One and a half pounds of powder per round. Find a dozen women in the town and have them sew up the bags. Maybe your wife can help, Monsewer?' He leered at Joubert who showed no reaction. Dodd could smell a man's weakness, and the oddly attractive Simone Joubert was undoubtedly her husband's weakness, for she clearly despised him and he, just as clearly, feared losing her. 'I want thirty bags of grape for each gun by this time tomorrow,' Dodd ordered.

'But the barrels, Major!' Joubert protested.

'You mean they'll be scratched?' Dodd jeered. 'What do you want, Monsewer? A scratched bore and a live regiment? Or a clean gun and a row of dead men? By tomorrow, thirty rounds of canister per gun, and if there ain't room in the limbers then throw out that bloody round shot. Might as well spit cherrystones as fire those pebbles.' Dodd slammed down the limber's lid. Even if the guns fired makeshift grapeshot he was not certain that they were worth keeping. Every battalion in India had such close-support artillery, but in Dodd's opinion the guns only served to slow down a regiment's manoeuvres. The weapons themselves were cumbersome, and the livestock needed to haul them was a nuisance, and if he were ever given his own *compoo* he would strip the regiments of field guns, for if a battalion of infantry could not defend itself with firelocks, what use was it? But he was stuck with the five guns, so he would use them as giant shotguns and open fire at three hundred yards. The gunners would moan about the damage to their barrels, but damn the gunners.

Dodd inspected the howitzer, found it as clean as the other guns, and nodded to the gunner-subadar. He offered no compliment, for Dodd did not believe in praising men for merely doing their duty. Praise was due to those who exceeded their duty, punishment for those who fell short, and silence must serve the rest.

Once the five guns had been inspected Dodd walked slowly down the white-jacketed infantry ranks where he looked every man in the eye and did not change his grim expression once, even though the soldiers had taken particular care to be well turned out for their new commanding officer. Captain Joubert followed a pace behind Dodd and there was something ludicrous about the conjunction of the tall, long-legged Dodd and the diminutive Joubert who needed to scurry to keep up with the Englishman. Once in a while the Frenchman would make a comment. 'He's a good man, sir,' he might say as they passed a soldier, but Dodd ignored all the praise and, after a while, Joubert fell silent and just scowled at Dodd's back. Dodd sensed the Frenchman's dislike, but did not care.

Dodd showed no reaction to the regiment's appearance, though all the same he was impressed. These men were smart and their weapons were as clean as those of his own sepoys who, reissued with white jackets, now paraded as an extra company at the regiment's left flank where, in British regiments, the skirmishers paraded. East India Company battalions had no skirmishers, for it was believed that sepoys were no good at the task, but Dodd had decided to make his loyal sepoys into the finest skirmishers in India. Let them prove the Company wrong, and in the proving they could help destroy the Company.

Most of the men looked up into Dodd's eyes as he walked by, although few of them looked at him for long, but instead glanced quickly away. Joubert saw the reaction, and sympathized with it, for there was something distinctly unpleasant about the Englishman's long sour face that edged on the frightening. Probably, Joubert decided, this Englishman was a flogger. The English were notorious for using the whip on their own men, reducing redcoats' backs to welters of broken flesh and gleaming blood, but Joubert was quite wrong about Dodd. Major Dodd had never flogged a man in his life, and that was not just because the Company forbade it in their army, but because William Dodd disliked the lash and hated to see a soldier flogged. Major Dodd liked soldiers. He hated most officers, especially those senior to him, but he liked soldiers. Good soldiers won battles, and victories made officers famous, so to be successful an officer needed soldiers who liked him and who would follow him. Dodd's sepoys were proof of that. He had looked after them, made sure they were fed and paid, and he had given them victory. Now he would make them wealthy in the service of the Mahratta princes who were famous for their generosity.

He broke away from the regiment and marched back to its colours, a pair of bright-green flags marked with crossed *tulwars*. The flags had been the choice of Colonel Mathers, the Englishman who had commanded the regiment for five years until he resigned rather than fight against his own countrymen, and now the regiment would be known as Dodd's regiment. Or perhaps he should call it something else. The Tigers? The Eagles? The Warriors of Scindia? Not that the name mattered now. What mattered now was to save these nine hundred well-trained men and their five gleaming guns and take them safely back to the Mahratta army that was gathering in the north. Dodd turned beneath the colours. 'My name is Dodd!' he shouted, then paused to let one of his Indian officers translate his words into Marathi, a language Dodd did not speak. Few of the soldiers spoke Marathi either, for most were mercenaries from the north, but men in the ranks murmured their own translation and so Dodd's message was relayed up and down the files. 'I am a soldier! Nothing but a soldier! Always a soldier!' He paused again. The parade was being held in the open space inside the gate and a crowd of townsfolk had gathered to gape at the troops, and among the crowd was a scatter of the robed Arab mercenaries who were reputed to be the fiercest of all the Mahratta troops. They were wild-looking men, armed with every conceivable weapon, but Dodd doubted they had the discipline of his regiment. 'Together,' he shouted at his men, 'you and I shall fight and we shall win.' He kept his words simple, for soldiers always liked simple things. Loot was simple, winning and losing were simple ideas, and even death, despite the way the damned preachers tried to tie it up in superstitious knots, was a simple concept. 'It is my intent,' he shouted, then waited for the translation to ripple up and down the ranks, 'for this regiment to be the finest in Scindia's service! Do your job well and I shall reward you. Do it badly, and I shall let your fellow soldiers decide on your punishment.' They liked that, as Dodd had known they would.

'Yesterday,' Dodd declaimed, 'the British crossed our frontier! Tomorrow their army will be here at Ahmednuggur, and soon we shall fight them in a great battle!' He had decided not to say that the battle would be fought well north of the city, for that might discourage the listening civilians. 'We shall drive them back to Mysore. We shall teach them that the army of Scindia is greater than any of their armies. We shall win!' The soldiers smiled at his confidence. 'We shall take their treasures, their weapons, their land and their women, and those things will be your reward if you fight well. But if you fight badly, you will die.' That phrase sent a shudder through the four white-coated ranks. 'And if any of you prove to be cowards,' Dodd finished, 'I shall kill you myself.'

He let that threat sink in, then abruptly ordered the regiment back to its duties before summoning Joubert to follow him up the red stone steps of the city wall to where Arab guards stood behind the merlons ranged along the firestep. Far to the south, beyond the horizon, a dusky cloud was just visible. It could have been mistaken for a distant rain cloud, but Dodd guessed it was the smear of smoke from the British campfires. 'How long do you think the city will last?' Dodd asked Joubert.

The Frenchman considered the question. 'A month?' he guessed.

'Don't be a fool,' Dodd snarled. He might want the loyalty of his men, but he did not give a fig for the good opinion of its two European officers. Both were Frenchmen and Dodd had the usual Englishman's opinion of the Frogs. Good dancing masters, and experts in tying a stock or arranging lace to fall prettily on a uniform, but about as much use in a fight as spavined lapdogs. Lieutenant Sillière, who had followed Joubert to the firestep, was tall and looked strong, but Dodd mistrusted a man who took such care with his uniform and he could have sworn he detected a whiff of lavender water coming from the young Lieutenant's carefully brushed hair. 'How long are the city walls?' he asked Joubert.

The Captain thought for a moment. 'Two miles?'

'At least, and how many men in the garrison?'

'Two thousand.'

'So work it out, Monsewer,' Dodd said. 'One man every two yards? We'll be lucky if the city holds for three days.' Dodd climbed to one of the bastions from where he could stare between the crenellations at the great fort which stood close to the city. That two-hundred-year-old fortress was an altogether more formidable stronghold than the city, though its very size made it vulnerable, for the fort's garrison, like the city's, was much too small. But the fort's high wall was faced by a big ditch, its embrasures were crammed with cannon and its bastions were high and strong, although the fort was worth nothing without the city. The city was the prize, not the fort, and Dodd doubted that General Wellesley would waste men against the fort's garrison. Boy Wellesley would attack the city, breach the walls, storm the gap and send his men to slaughter the defenders in the rat's tangle of alleys and courtyards, and once the city had fallen the redcoats would hunt for supplies that would help feed the British army. Only then, with the city in his possession, would Wellesley turn his guns against the fort, and it was possible that the fort would hold the British advance for two or three weeks and thus give Scindia more time to assemble his army, and the longer the fort held the better, for the overdue rains might come and hamper the British advance. But of one thing Dodd was quite certain: as Pohlmann had said, the war would not be won here, and to William Dodd the most important thing was to extricate his men so that they could share that victory. 'You will take the regiment's guns and three hundred men and garrison the north gate,' Dodd ordered Joubert.

The Frenchman frowned. 'You think the British will attack in the north?'

'I think, Monsewer, that the British will attack here, in the south. Our orders are to kill as many as we can, then escape to join Colonel Pohlmann. We shall make that escape through the north gate, but even an idiot can see that half the city's inhabitants will also try to escape through the north gate and your job, Joubert, is to keep the bastards from blocking our way. I intend to save the regiment, not lose it with the city. That means you open fire on any civilian who tries to leave the city, do you understand?' Joubert wanted to argue, but one look at Dodd's face persuaded him into hasty agreement. 'I shall be at the north gate in one hour,' Dodd said, 'and God help you, Monsewer, if your three hundred men are not in position.'

Joubert ran off. Dodd watched him go, then turned to Sillière. 'When were the men last paid?'

'Four months ago, sir.'

'Where did you learn English, Lieutenant?'

'Colonel Mathers insisted we speak it, sir.'

'And where did Madame Joubert learn it?'

Sillière gave Dodd a suspicious glance. 'I would not know, sir.'

Dodd sniffed. 'Are you wearing perfume, Monsewer?'

'No!' Sillière blushed.

'Make sure you never do, Lieutenant. And in the meantime take your company, find the Killadar, and tell him to break open the city treasury. If you have any trouble, break the damn thing open yourself with one of our guns. Give every man three months' pay and load the rest of the money on pack animals. We'll take it with us.'

Sillière looked astonished at the order. 'But the Killadar, Monsieur . . .' he began.

'The Killadar, Monsewer, is a wretched little man with the balls of a mouse! You are a soldier. If we don't take the money, the British will get it. Now go!' Dodd shook his head in exasperation as the Lieutenant went. Four months without pay! There was nothing unusual in such a lapse, but Dodd disapproved of it. A soldier risked his life for his country, and the least his country could do in return was pay him promptly.

He walked eastwards along the firestep, trying to anticipate where the British would site their batteries and where they would make a breach. There was always a chance that Wellesley would pass by Ahmednuggur and simply march north towards Scindia's army, but Dodd doubted the enemy would choose that course, for then the city and fort would lie athwart the British supply lines and the garrison could play havoc with the convoys carrying ammunition, shot and food to the redcoats.

A small crowd was gathered on the southernmost ramparts to gaze towards the distant cloud that betrayed the presence of the enemy army. Simone Joubert was among them, sheltering her face from the westering sun with a frayed parasol. Dodd took off his cocked hat. He always felt oddly awkward with women, at least white women, but his new rank gave him an unaccustomed confidence. 'I see you have come to observe the enemy, Ma'am,' he said.

'I like to walk about the walls, Major,' Simone answered,

'but today, as you see, the way is blocked with people.'

'I can clear a path for you, Ma'am,' Dodd offered, touching the gold hilt of his new sword.

'It is not necessary, Major,' Simone said.

'You speak good English, Ma'am.'

'I was taught it as a child. We had a Welsh governess.'

'In France, Ma'am?'

'In the Île de France, Monsieur,' Simone said. She was not looking at Dodd as she spoke, but staring into the heat-hazed south.

'Mauritius,' Dodd said, giving the island the name used by the British.

'The Île de France, Monsieur, as I said.'

'A remote place, Ma'am.'

Simone shrugged. In truth she agreed with Dodd. Mauritius was remote, an island four hundred miles east of Africa and the only decent French naval base in the Indian Ocean. There she had been raised as the daughter of the port's captain, and it was there, at sixteen, that she had been wooed by Captain Joubert who was on passage to India where he had been posted as an adviser to Scindia. Joubert had dazzled Simone with tales of the riches that a man could make for himself in India, and Simone, bored with the small petty society of her island, had allowed herself to be swept away, only to discover that Captain Joubert was a timid man at heart, and that his impoverished family in Lyons had first claim on his earnings, and whatever was left was assiduously saved so that the Captain could retire to France in comfort. Simone had expected a life of parties and jewels, of dancing and silks, and instead she scrimped, she sewed and she suffered. Colonel Pohlmann had offered her a way out of poverty, and now she sensed that the lanky Englishman was clumsily attempting to make the same offer, but Simone was not minded to become a man's mistress just because she was bored. She might for love, and in the absence of any love in her life she was fighting an attraction for Lieutenant Sillière, although she knew that the Lieutenant was almost as worthless as her husband and the dilemma was making her think that she was going mad. She wept about it, and the tears only added to her self-diagnosis of insanity. 'When will the British come, Major?' she asked Dodd.

'Tomorrow, Ma'am. They'll establish batteries the next day, knock at the wall for two or three days, make their hole and then come in.'

She looked at Dodd beneath the hem of her parasol. Although he was a tall man, Simone could still look him in the eye. 'They'll take the city that quickly?' she asked, showing a hint of worry.

'Nothing to hold them, Ma'am. Not enough men, too much wall, not enough guns.'

'So how will we escape?'

'By trusting me, Ma'am,' Dodd said, offering Simone a leering smile. 'What you must do, my dear, is pack your luggage, as much as can be carried on whatever packhorses your husband might possess, and be ready to leave. I shall send you warning before the attack, and at that time you go to the north gate where you'll find your husband. It would help, of course, Ma'am, if I knew where you were lodged?'

'My husband knows, Monsieur,' Simone said coldly. 'So once the *rosbifs* arrive I need do nothing for three days except pack?'

Dodd noted her use of the French term of contempt for the English, but chose to make nothing of it. 'Exactly, Ma'am.'

'Thank you, Major,' Simone said, and made a gesture so that two servants, whom Dodd had not noticed in the press of people, came to escort her back to her house.

'Cold bitch,' Dodd said to himself when she was gone, 'but she'll thaw, she'll thaw.'

61

The dark fell swiftly. Torches flared on the city ramparts, lighting the ghostly robes of the Arab mercenaries who patrolled the bastions. Small offerings of food and flowers were piled in front of the garish gods and goddesses in their candlelit temples. The inhabitants of the city were praying to be spared, while to the south a faint glow in the sky betrayed where a red-coated army had come to bring Ahmednuggur death.

Lieutenant-Colonel Albert Gore had taken command of the King's 33rd in succession to Sir Arthur Wellesley and it had not been a happy battalion when Gore arrived. That unhappiness was not Sir Arthur's fault for he had long left the battalion for higher responsibilities, but in his absence the 33rd had been commanded by Major John Shee who was an incompetent drunk. Shee had died, Gore had received command, and now he was slowly mending the damage. That mending could have been a great deal swifter if Gore had been able to rid himself of some of the battalion's officers, and of all those officers it was the lazy and dishonest Captain Morris of the Light Company whom he would have most liked to dismiss, but Gore was helpless in the matter. Morris had purchased his commission, he was guilty of no offences against the King's regulations and thus he had to stay. And with him stayed the malevolent, unsettling, yellow-faced and perpetually twitching Sergeant Obadiah Hakeswill.

'Sharpe was always a bad man, sir. A disgrace to the army, sir,' Hakeswill told the Colonel. 'He should never have been made into a sergeant, sir, 'cos he ain't the material of what sergeants are made, sir. He's nothing but a scrap of filth, sir, what shouldn't be a corporal, let alone a sergeant. It says so in the scriptures, sir.' The Sergeant stood rigidly at attention, his right foot behind his left, his hands at his sides and his elbows straining towards the small of his back. His voice boomed in the small room, drowning out the sound of the pelting rain. Gore wondered whether the rain was the late beginning of the monsoon. He hoped so, for if the monsoon failed utterly then there would be a lot of hungry people in India the following year.

Gore watched a spider crawl across the table. The house belonged to a leather dealer who had rented it to the 33rd while they were based in Arrakerry and the place seethed with insects that crawled, flew, slunk and stung, and Gore, who was a fastidious and elegant man, rather wished he had used his tents. 'Tell me what happened,' Gore said to Morris, 'again. If you would be so kind.'

Morris, slouching in a chair in front of Gore's table with a thick bandage on his head, seemed surprised to be asked, but he straightened himself and offered the Colonel a feeble shrug. 'I don't really recall, sir. It was two nights ago, in Seringapatam, and I was hit, sir.'

Gore brushed the spider aside and made a note. 'Hit,' he said as he wrote the word in his fine copperplate hand. 'Where exactly?'

'On the head, sir,' Morris answered.

Gore sighed. 'I see that, Captain. I meant where in Seringapatam?'

'By the armoury, sir.'

'And this was at night?'

Morris nodded.

'Black night, sir,' Hakeswill put in helpfully, 'black as a blackamoor's backside, sir.'

The Colonel frowned at the Sergeant's indelicacy. Gore was resisting the urge to push a hand inside his coat and scratch his belly. He feared he had caught the Malabar Itch, a foul complaint that would condemn him to weeks of living with a salve of lard on his skin, and if the lard failed he would be reduced to taking baths in a solution of nitric acid. 'If it

63

was dark,' he said patiently, 'then surely you had no chance to see your assailant?'

'I didn't, sir,' Morris replied truthfully.

'But I did, sir,' Hakeswill said, 'and it was Sharpie. Saw him clear as daylight, sir.'

'At night?' Gore asked sceptically.

'He was working late, sir,' Hakeswill said, 'on account of him not having done his proper work in the daylight like a Christian should, sir, and he opened the door, sir, and the lantern was lit, sir, and he came out and hit the Captain, sir.'

'And you saw that?'

'Clear as I can see you now, sir,' Hakeswill said, his face racked with a series of violent twitches.

Gore's hand strayed to his coat buttons, but he resisted the urge. 'If you saw it, Sergeant, why didn't you have Sharpe arrested? There were sentries present, surely?'

'More important to save the Captain's life, sir. That's what I deemed, sir. Get him back here, sir, into Mister Mickle-white's care. Don't trust other surgeons, sir. And I had to clean up Mister Morris, sir, I did.'

'The blood, you mean?'

Hakeswill shook his head. 'The substances, sir.' He stared woodenly over Colonel Gore's head as he spoke.

'Substances?'

Hakeswill's face twitched. 'Begging your pardon, sir, as you being a gentleman as won't want to hear it, sir, but Sergeant Sharpe hit Captain Morris with a jakes pot, sir. A full jakes pot, sir, liquid and solids.'

'Oh, God,' Gore said, laying down his pen and trying to ignore the fiery itch across his belly. 'I still don't understand why you did nothing in Seringapatam,' the Colonel said. 'The Town Major should have been told, surely?'

'That's just it, sir,' Hakeswill said enthusiastically, 'on account of there not being a Town Major, not proper, seeing as Major Stokes does the duties, sir, and the rest is up to the Rajah's Killadar and I don't like seeing a redcoat being arrested by a darkie, sir, not even Sharpe. It ain't right, that. And Major Stokes, he won't help, sir. He likes Sharpe, see? He lets him live comfortable, sir. Off the fat of the land, sir, like it says in the scriptures. Got himself a set of rooms and a *bibbi*, he has, and a servant, too. Ain't right, sir. Too comfortable, sir, whiles the rest of us sweats like the soldiers we swore to be.'

The explanation made some sort of sense, or at least Gore appreciated that it might convince Sergeant Hakeswill, yet there was still something odd about the whole tale. 'What were you doing at the armoury after dark, Captain?'

'Making certain the full complement of wagons was there, sir,' Morris answered. 'Sergeant Hakeswill informed me that one was missing.'

'And was it?'

'No, sir,' Morris said.

'Miscounted, sir,' Hakeswill said, 'on account of it being dark, sir.' Hakeswill had indeed summoned Morris to the armoury after dark, and there he had hit the Captain with a baulk of timber and, for good measure, had added the contents of a chamber pot that Major Stokes had left outside his office. The sentries had been sheltering from the rain in the guardhouse and none had questioned the sight of Hakeswill dragging the recumbent Morris back to his quarters, for the sight of drunken officers being taken home by sergeants or privates was too common to be remarkable. The important thing was that Morris had not seen who assaulted him and was quite prepared to believe Hakeswill's version, for Morris relied utterly on Hakeswill in everything. 'I blames myself, sir,' Hakeswill went on, 'on account of not chasing Sharpie, but I thought my duty was to look after my Captain, sir, on account of him being drenched by a slop pot.'

'Enough, Sergeant!' Gore said.

'It ain't a Christian act, sir,' Hakeswill muttered resentfully. 'Not with a jakes pot, sir. Says so in the scriptures.'

Gore rubbed his face. The rain had taken the edge off the damp heat, but not by much, and he found the atmosphere horribly oppressive. Maybe the itch was just a reaction to the heat. He rubbed his hand across his belly, but it did not help. 'Why would Sergeant Sharpe assault you without warning, Captain?' he asked.

Morris shrugged. 'He's a disagreeable sort, sir,' he offered weakly.

'He never liked the Captain, sir, Sharpie didn't,' Hakeswill said, 'and it's my belief, sir, that he thought the Captain had come to summon him back to the battalion, where he ought to be soldiering instead of living off the fat of the land, but he don't want to come back, sir, on account of being comfortable, sir, like he's got no right to be. He never did know his place, sir, not Sharpe, sir. Got above himself, sir, he has, and he's got cash in his breeches. On the fiddle, I dare say.'

Gore ignored the last accusation. 'How badly are you hurt?' he asked Morris.

'Only cuts and bruises, sir.' Morris straightened in the chair. 'But it's still a court-martial offence, sir.'

'A capital offence, sir,' Hakeswill said. 'Up against the wall, sir, and God have mercy on his black soul, which I very much doubts God will, God having better things to worry about than a sorry piece of scum like Sharpie.'

Gore sighed. He suspected there was a great deal more to the story than he was hearing, but whatever the real facts Captain Morris was still right. All that mattered was that Sergeant Sharpe was alleged to have struck an officer, and no excuse in the world could explain away such an offence. Which meant Sergeant Sharpe would have to be tried and very probably shot, and Gore would regret that for he had heard some very good things of the young Sergeant Sharpe. 'I had great hopes of Sergeant Sharpe,' the Colonel said sadly.

'Got above himself, sir,' Hakeswill snapped. 'Just 'cos he blew the mine at Seringapatam, sir, he thinks he's got wings and can fly. Needs to have his feathers clipped, sir, says so in the scriptures.'

Gore looked scornfully at the twitching Sergeant. 'And what did you do at the assault of the city, Sergeant?' he asked.

'My duty, sir, my duty,' Hakeswill answered. 'What is all I ever expects any other man to do, sir.'

Gore shook his head regretfully. There really was no way out of this dilemma. If Sharpe had struck an officer, then Sharpe must be punished. 'I suppose he'll have to be fetched back here,' Gore admitted.

'Of course,' Morris agreed.

Gore frowned in irritation. This was all such a damned nuisance! Gore had desperately hoped that the 33rd would be attached to Wellesley's army, which was about to plunge into Mahratta territory, but instead the battalion had been ordered to stay behind and guard Mysore against the bandits who still plagued the roads and hills. Now, it seemed, over-stretched as the battalion was, Gore would have to detach a party to arrest Sergeant Sharpe. 'Captain Lawford could go for him,' he suggested.

'Hardly a job for an officer, sir,' Morris said. 'A sergeant could do the thing just as well.'

Gore considered the matter. Sending a sergeant would certainly be less disruptive to the battalion than losing an officer, and a sergeant could surely do the job as well as anyone. 'How many men would he need?' Gore asked.

'Six men, sir,' Hakeswill snapped. 'I could do the job with six men.'

'And Sergeant Hakeswill's the best man for the job,' Morris

urged. He had no particular wish to lose Hakeswill's services for the few days that it would take to fetch Sharpe, but Hakeswill had hinted that there was money in this business. Morris was not sure how much money, but he was in debt and Hakeswill had been persuasive. 'By far the best man,' he added.

'On account of me knowing the little bugger's cunning ways, sir,' Hakeswill explained, 'if you'll excuse my Hindi.'

Gore nodded. He would like nothing more than to rid himself of Hakeswill for a while, for the man was a baleful influence on the battalion. Hakeswill was hated, that much Gore had learned, but he was also feared, for the Sergeant declared that he could not be killed. He had survived a hanging once, indeed the scar of the rope was still concealed beneath the stiff leather stock, and the men believed that Hakeswill was somehow under the protection of an evil angel. The Colonel knew that was a nonsense, but even so the very presence of the Sergeant made him feel distinctly uncomfortable. 'I'll have my clerk write the orders for you, Sergeant,' the Colonel said.

'Thank you, sir!' Hakeswill said. 'You won't regret it, sir. Obadiah Hakeswill has never shirked his duty, sir, not like some as I could name.'

Gore dismissed Hakeswill who waited for Captain Morris under the building's porch and watched the rain pelt onto the street. The Sergeant's face twitched and his eyes held a peculiar malevolence that made the single sentry edge away. But in truth Sergeant Obadiah Hakeswill was a happy man. God had put Richard Sharpe into his grasp and he would pay Sharpe back for all the insults of the last few years and especially for the ghastly moment when Sharpe had hurled Hakeswill among the Tippoo Sultan's tigers. Hakeswill had thought the beasts would savage him, but his luck had held and the tigers had ignored him. It seemed they had been fed not an hour before and thus the guardian angel who preserved Hakeswill had once again come to his rescue.

So now Obadiah Hakeswill would have his revenge. He would choose six men, six bitter men who could be trusted, and they would take Sergeant Sharpe, and afterwards, somewhere on the road home from Seringapatam where there were no witnesses, they would find Sharpe's money and then finish him. Shot while attempting to escape, that would be the explanation, and good riddance too. Hakeswill was happy and Sharpe was condemned.

Colonel McCandless led Sharpe north towards the wild country where the frontiers of Hyderabad, Mysore and the Mahratta states met. 'Till I hear otherwise,' McCandless told Sharpe, 'I'm assuming our traitor is in Ahmednuggur.'

'What's that, sir? A city?'

'A city and a fort next to each other,' the Colonel said. McCandless's big gelding seemed to eat up the miles, but Sharpe's smaller mare offered a lumpy ride. Within an hour of leaving Seringapatam Sharpe's muscles were sore, within two he felt as though the backs of his thighs were burning, and by late afternoon the stirrup leathers had abraded through his cotton trousers to grind his calves into bloody patches. 'It's one of Scindia's frontier strongholds,' the Colonel went on, 'but I doubt it can hold out long. Wellesley plans to capture it, then strike on north.'

'So we're going to war, sir?'

'Of course.' McCandless frowned. 'Does that worry you?'

'No, sir,' Sharpe said, nor did it. He had a good life in Seringapatam, maybe as good a life as any soldier had ever had anywhere, but in the four years between the fall of Seringapatam and the massacre at Chasalgaon Sharpe had not heard a shot fired in anger, and a part of him was envious of his old colleagues in the 33rd who fought brisk skirmishes against the bandits and rogues who plagued western Mysore.

'We're going to fight the Mahrattas,' McCandless said. 'You know who they are?'

'I hear they're bastards, sir.'

McCandless frowned at Sharpe's foul language. 'They are a confederation of independent states, Sharpe,' he said primly, 'that dominate much of western India. They are also warlike, piratical and untrustworthy, except, of course, for those which are our allies, who are romantic, gallant and heroic.'

'Some are on our side, sir?'

'A few. The Peshwa, for one, and he's their titular leader, but small notice they take of him. Others are staying aloof from this war, but two of the biggest princes have decided to make a fight of it. One's called Scindia, and he's the Maharajah of Gwalior, and the other's called Bhonsla, and he's the Rajah of Berar.'

Sharpe tried standing in the stirrups to ease the pain in his seat, but it only made the chafing of his calves worse. 'And what's our quarrel with those two, sir?'

'They've been much given to raiding into Hyderabad and Mysore lately, so now it's time to settle them once and for all.'

'And Lieutenant Dodd's joined their army, sir?'

'From what we hear, he's joined Scindia's army. But I haven't heard much.' The Colonel had already explained to Sharpe how he had been keeping his ears open for news of Dodd ever since the Lieutenant had persuaded his sepoys to defect, but then had come the terrible news of Chasalgaon, and McCandless, who had been travelling north to join Wellesley's army, had seen Sharpe's name in the report and so had turned around and hurried south to Seringapatam. At the same time he had sent some of his own Mahratta agents north to discover Dodd's whereabouts. 'We should meet those fellows today,' the Colonel said, 'or tomorrow at the latest.'

The rain had not stopped, but nor was it heavy. Mud spattered up the horses' flanks and onto Sharpe's boots and white trousers. He tried sitting half sideways, he tried leaning forward or tipping himself back, but the pain did not stop. He had never much liked horses, but now decided he hated them. 'I'd like to meet Lieutenant Dodd again, sir,' he told McCandless as the two men rode under dripping trees.

'Be careful of him, Sharpe,' McCandless warned. 'He has a reputation.'

'For what, sir?'

'A fighter, of course. He's no mean soldier. I've not met him, of course, but I've heard tales. He's been up north, in Calcutta mostly, and made a name for himself there. He was first over the *pettah* wall at Panhapur. Not much of a wall, Sharpe, just a thicket of cactus thorn really, but it took his sepoys five minutes to follow him, and by the time they reached him he'd killed a dozen of the enemy. He's a tall man who can use a sword and is a fine pistol shot too. He is, in brief, a killer.'

'If he's so good, sir, why is he still a lieutenant?'

The Colonel sighed. 'I fear that is the way of the Company's army, Sharpe. A man can't buy his way up the ladder as he can in the King's army, and there's no promotion for good service. It all goes by seniority. Dead men's shoes, Sharpe. A fellow must wait his turn in the Company, and there's no way round it.'

'So Dodd has been waiting, sir?'

'A long time. He's forty now, and I doubt he'd have got his captaincy much before he was fifty.'

'Is that why he ran, sir?'

'He ran because of the murder. He claimed a goldsmith cheated him of money and had his men beat the poor fellow so badly that he died. He was court-martialled, of course, but the only sentence he got was six months without pay. Six months without pay! That's sanctioning murder, Sharpe! But Wellesley insisted the Company discharge him, and he planned to have Dodd tried before a civilian court and condemned to death, so Dodd ran.' The Colonel paused. 'I wish I could say we're pursuing him because of the murder, Sharpe,' he went on, 'but that isn't so. We're pursuing him because he persuaded his men to defect. Once that rot starts, it might never stop, and we have to show the other sepoys that desertion will always be punished.'

Just before nightfall, when the rain had stopped and·Sharpe thought his sore muscles and bleeding calves would make him moan aloud in agony, a group of horsemen came cantering towards them. To Sharpe they looked like *silladars*, the mercenary horsemen who hired themselves, their weapons and their horses to the British army, and he pulled his mare over to the left side of the road to give the heavily armed men room to pass, but their leader slowed as he approached, then raised a hand in greeting. 'Colonel!' he shouted.

'Sevajee!' McCandless cried and spurred his horse towards the oncoming Indian. He held out his hand and Sevajee clasped it.

'You have news?' McCandless asked.

Sevajee nodded. 'Your fellow is inside Ahmednuggur, Colonel. He's been given Mathers's regiment.' He was pleased with his news, grinning broadly to reveal red-stained teeth. He was a young man dressed in the remnants of a green uniform Sharpe did not recognize. The jacket had European epaulettes hung with silver chains, and over it was strapped a sword sling and a sash, both of white silk and both stained brown with dried blood.

'Sergeant Sharpe,' McCandless made the introductions, 'this is Syud Sevajee.'

Sharpe nodded a wary greeting. 'Sahib,' he said, for there was something about Syud Sevajee that suggested he was a man of rank.

'The Sergeant has seen Lieutenant Dodd,' McCandless explained. 'He'll make sure we capture the right man.'

'Kill all the Europeans,' Sevajee suggested, 'and you'll be sure.' The suggestion, it seemed to Sharpe, was not entirely flippant.

'I want him captured alive,' McCandless said irritably. 'Justice must be seen to be done. Or would you rather that your people believe a British officer can beat a man to death without any punishment?'

'They believe that anyway,' Sevajee said carelessly, 'but if you wish to be scrupulous, McCandless, then we shall capture Mister Dodd.' Sevajee's men, a dozen wild looking warriors armed with everything from bows and arrows to lances, had fallen in behind McCandless.

'Syud Sevajee is a Mahratta, Sharpe,' McCandless explained.

'One of the romantic ones, sir?'

'Romantic?' Sevajee repeated the word in surprise.

'He's on our side, if that's what you mean,' McCandless said.

'No,' Sevajee hurried to correct the Colonel 'I am opposed to Beny Singh, and so long as he lives I help the enemies of my enemy.'

'Why's this fellow your enemy, sir, if you don't mind me asking?' Sharpe asked.

Sevajee touched the hilt of his *tulwar* as if it was a fetish. 'Because he killed my father, Sergeant.'

'Then I hope you get the bastard, sir.'

'Sharpe!' McCandless said in reprimand.

Sevajee laughed. 'My father,' he explained to Sharpe, 'led one of the Rajah of Berar's *compoos*. He was a great warrior,

Sergeant, and Beny Singh was his rival. He invited my father to a feast and served him poison. That was three years ago. My mother killed herself, but my younger brother serves Beny Singh and my sister is one of his concubines. They too will die.'

'And you escaped, sir?' Sharpe asked.

'I was serving in the East India Company cavalry, Sergeant,' Sevajee answered. 'My father believed a man should know his enemy, so sent me to Madras.'

'Where we met,' McCandless said brusquely, 'and now Sevajee serves me.'

'Because in return,' Sevajee explained, 'your British bayonets will hand Beny Singh to my revenge. And with him, of course, the reward for Dodd. Four thousand, two hundred rupees, is it not?'

'So long as he's taken alive,' McCandless said dourly, 'and it might be increased once the Court of Directors hears what he did at Chasalgaon.'

'And to think I almost caught him,' Sevajee said, and described how he and his few men had visited Ahmednuggur posing as *brindarries* who were loyal to Scindia.

'*Brindarrie?*' Sharpe asked.

'Like *silladars*,' McCandless told him. 'Freelance horsemen. And you saw Dodd?' he asked Sevajee.

'I heard him, Colonel, though I never got close. He was lecturing his regiment, telling them how they would chase you British out of India.'

McCandless scoffed. 'He'll be lucky to escape from Ahmednuggur! Why has he stayed there?'

'To give Pohlmann a chance to attack?' Sevajee suggested. 'His *compoo* was still close to Ahmednuggur a few days ago.'

'Just one *compoo*, sir?' Sharpe suggested. 'One *compoo* won't beat Wellesley.'

Sevajee gave him a long, speculative look. 'Pohlmann,

Sergeant,' he said, 'is the best infantry leader in Indian service. He has never lost a battle, and his *compoo* is probably the finest infantry army in India. It already outnumbers Wellesley's army, but if Scindia releases his other *compoos*, then together they will outnumber your Wellesley three to one. And if Scindia waits until Berar's troops are with him, he'll outnumber you ten to one.'

'So why are we attacking, sir?'

'Because we're going to win,' McCandless said firmly. 'God's will.'

'Because, Sergeant,' Sevajee said, 'you British think that you are invincible. You believe you cannot be defeated, but you have not fought the Mahrattas. Your little army marches north full of confidence, but you are like mice waking an elephant.'

'Some mice,' McCandless snorted.

'Some elephant,' Sevajee said gently. 'We are the Mahrattas, and if we did not fight amongst ourselves we would rule all India.'

'You've not faced Scottish infantry yet,' McCandless said confidently, 'and Wellesley has two Scottish regiments with him. Besides, you forget that Stevenson has an army too, and he's not so very far away.' Two armies, both small, were invading the Mahratta Confederation, though Wellesley, as the senior officer, had control of both. 'I reckon the mice will startle you yet,' McCandless said.

They spent that night in a village. To the north, just beyond the horizon, the sky glowed red from the reflection of flames on the smoke of thousands of campfires, the sign that the British army was just a short march away. McCandless bargained with the headman for food and shelter, then frowned when Sevajee purchased a jar of fierce local arrack, Sevajee ignored the Scotsman's disapproval, then went to join his men who were gaming in the village's tavern. McCandless shook his head. 'He fights for mercenary reasons, Sharpe, nothing else.'

'That and vengeance, sir.'

'Aye, he wants vengeance, I'll grant him that, but once he's got it he'll turn on us like a snake.' The Colonel rubbed his eyes. 'He's a useful man, all the same, but I wish I felt more confident about this whole business.'

'The war, sir?'

McCandless shook his head. 'We'll win that. It doesn't matter by how many they outnumber us, they won't outfight us. No, Sharpe, I'm worried about Dodd.'

'We'll get him, sir,' Sharpe said.

The Colonel said nothing for a while. An oil lamp flickered on the table, attracting huge winged moths, and in its dull light the Colonel's thin face looked more cadaverous than ever. McCandless finally grimaced. 'I've never been one for believing in the supernatural, Sharpe, other than the providences of Almighty God. Some of my countrymen claim they see and hear signs. They tell of foxes howling about the house when a death is imminent, or seals coming ashore when a man's to be lost at sea, but I never credited such things. It's mere superstition, Sharpe, pagan superstition, but I can't chase away my dread about Dodd.' He shook his head slowly. 'Maybe it's age.'

'You're not old, sir.'

McCandless smiled. 'I'm sixty-three, Sharpe, and I should have retired ten years ago, except that the good Lord has seen fit to make me useful, but the Company isn't so sure of my worth now. They'd like to give me a pension, and I can't blame them. A full colonel's salary is a heavy item on the Company's accounts.' McCandless offered Sharpe a rueful look. 'You fight for King and country, Sharpe, but I fight and die for the shareholders.'

'They'd never replace you, sir!' Sharpe said loyally.

'They already have,' McCandless admitted softly, 'or Wellesley has. He has his own head of intelligence now, and the Company knows it, so they tell me I am a "supernumerary upon the establishment".' He shrugged. 'They want to put me out to pasture, Sharpe, but they did give me this one last errand, and that's the apprehension of Lieutenant William Dodd, though I rather think he's going to be the death of me.'

'He won't, sir, not while I'm here.'

'That's why you are here, Sharpe,' McCandless said seriously. 'He's younger than I am, he's fitter than I am and he's a better swordsman than I am, and that's why I thought of you. I saw you fight at Seringapatam and I doubt Dodd can stand up to you.'

'He won't, sir, he won't,' Sharpe said grimly. 'And I'll keep you alive, sir.'

'If God wills it.'

Sharpe smiled. 'Don't they say God helps those who help themselves, sir? We'll do the job, sir.'

'I pray you're right, Sharpe,' McCandless said, 'I pray you're right.' And they would start at Ahmednuggur, where Dodd waited and where Sharpe's new war would begin.

CHAPTER 3

Colonel McCandless led his small force into Sir Arthur Wellesley's encampment late the following afternoon. For most of the morning they had been shadowed by a band of enemy horsemen who sometimes galloped close as if inviting Sevajee's men to ride out and fight, but McCandless kept Sevajee on a tight leash and at midday a patrol of horsemen in blue coats with yellow facings had chased the enemy away. The blue-coated cavalry were from the 19th Light Dragoons and the Captain leading the troop gave McCandless a cheerful wave as he cantered after the enemy who had been prowling the road in hope of finding a laggard supply wagon. Four hours later McCandless topped a gentle rise to see the army's lines spread across the countryside while, four miles farther north, the red walls of Ahmednuggur stood in the westering sun. From this angle the fort and the city appeared as one continuous building, a vast red rampart studded with bastions. Sharpe cuffed sweat from his face. 'Looks like a brute, sir,' he said, nodding at the walls.

'The wall's big enough,' the Colonel said, 'but there's no ditch, no glacis and no outworks. It'll take us no more than three days to punch a hole.'

'Then pity the poor souls who must go through the hole,' Sevajee commented.

'It's what they're paid to do,' McCandless said brusquely. The area about the camp seethed with men and animals.

Every cavalry horse in the army needed two lascars to gather forage, and those men were busy with sickles, while nearer to the camp's centre was a vast muddy expanse where the draught bullocks and pack oxen were picketed. *Puckalees*, the men who carried water for the troops and the animals, were filling their buckets from a tank scummed with green. A thorn hedge surrounded six elephants that belonged to the gunners, while next to the great beasts was the artillery park with its twenty-six cannon, and after that came the sepoys' lines where children shrieked, dogs yapped and women carried patties of bullock dung on their heads to build the evening fires. The last part of the journey took them through the lines of the 78th, a kilted Highland regiment, and the soldiers saluted McCandless and then looked at the red facings on Sharpe's coat and called out the inevitable insults. 'Come to see how a real man fights, Sergeant?'

'You ever done any proper fighting?' Sharpe retorted.

'What's a Havercake doing here?'

'Come to teach you boys a lesson.'

'What in? Cooking?'

'Where I come from,' Sharpe said, 'it's the ones in skirts what does the cooking.'

'Enough, Sharpe,' McCandless snapped. The Colonel liked to wear a kilt himself, claiming it was a more suitable garment for India's heat than trousers. 'We must pay our respects to the General,' McCandless said, and turned towards the larger tents in the centre of the encampment.

It had been two years since Sharpe had last seen his old Colonel and he doubted that Major-General Sir Arthur Wellesley would prove any friendlier now than he ever had. Sir Arthur had always been a cold fish, sparing with approval and frightening in his disapproval, and his most casual glance somehow managed to make Sharpe feel both insignificant and inadequate, and so, when McCandless dismounted outside the General's tent, Sharpe deliberately hung back. The General, still a young man, was standing beside a line of six picketed horses and was evidently in a blazing temper. An orderly, in the blue-and-yellow coat of the 19th Dragoons, was holding a big grey stallion by its bridle and Wellesley was alternately patting the horse and snapping at the half-dozen aides who cowered nearby. A group of senior officers, majors and colonels, stood beside the General's tent, suggesting that a council of war had been interrupted by the horse's distress. The grey stallion was certainly suffering. It was shivering, its eyes were rolling white and sweat or spittle was dripping from its drooping head.

Wellesley turned as McCandless and Sevajee approached. 'Can you bleed a horse, McCandless?'

'I can put a knife in it, sir, if it helps,' the Scotsman answered.

'It does not help, damn it!' Wellesley retorted savagely. 'I don't want him butchered, I want him bled. Where is the farrier?'

'We're looking for him, sir,' an aide replied.

'Then find him, damn it! Easy, boy, easy!' These last three words were spoken in a soothing tone to the horse which had let out a feeble whinny. 'He's fevered,' Wellesley explained to McCandless, 'and if he ain't bled, he'll die.'

A groom hurried to the General's side carrying a fleam and a blood stick, both of which he mutely offered to Wellesley. 'No good giving them to me,' the General snapped, 'I can't bleed a horse.' He looked at his aides, then at the senior officers by the tent. 'Someone must know how to do it,' Wellesley pleaded. They were all men who lived with horses and professed to love them, though none knew how to bleed a horse, for that was a job left to servants, but finally a Scottish major averred that he had a shrewd idea of how the thing was done, and so he was given the fleam and its hammer. He took off his red coat, chose a fleam blade at random and stepped up to the shivering stallion. He placed the blade on the horse's neck and drew back the hammer with his right hand.

'Not like that!' Sharpe blurted out. 'You'll kill him!' A score of men stared at him while the Scottish Major, the blade unhit, looked rather relieved. 'You've got the blade the wrong way round, sir,' Sharpe explained. 'You have to line it up along the vein, sir, not across it.' He was blushing for having spoken out in front of the General and all the army's senior officers.

Wellesley scowled at Sharpe. 'Can you bleed a horse?'

'I can't ride the things, sir, but I do know how to bleed them. I worked in an inn yard,' Sharpe added as though that was explanation enough.

'Have you actually bled a horse?' Wellesley demanded. He showed not the slightest surprise at seeing a man from his old battalion in the camp, but in truth he was far too distracted by his stallion's distress to worry about mere men.

'I've bled dozens, sir,' Sharpe said, which was true, but those horses had been big heavy carriage beasts, and this white stallion was plainly a thoroughbred.

'Then do it, damn it,' the General said. 'Don't just stand there, do it!'

Sharpe took the fleam and the blood stick from the Major. The fleam looked like a mis-shapen penknife, and inside its brass case were folded a dozen blades. Two of the blades were shaped as hooks, while the rest were spoon-shaped. He selected a middle-sized spoon, checked that its edge was keen, folded the other blades away and then approached the horse 'You'll have to hold him hard,' he told the dragoon orderly.

'He can be lively, Sergeant,' the orderly warned in a low voice, anxious not to provoke another outburst from Wellesley.

81

'Then hang on hard,' Sharpe said to the orderly, then he stroked the horse's neck, feeling for the jugular.

'How much are you going to let out?' Wellesley asked.

'Much as it takes, sir,' Sharpe said, who really had no idea how much blood he should spill. Enough to make it look good, he reckoned. The horse was nervous and tried to pull away from the orderly. 'Give him a stroke, sir,' Sharpe said to the General. 'Let him know it ain't the end of the world.'

Wellesley took the stallion's head from the orderly and gave the beast's nose a fondling. 'It's all right, Diomed,' he said, 'we're going to make you better. Get on with it, Sharpe.'

Sharpe had found the jugular and now placed the sharp curve of the spoon-blade over the vein. He held the knife in his left hand and the blood stick in his right. The stick was a small wooden club that was needed to drive the fleam's blade through a horse's thick skin. 'All right, boy,' he murmured to the horse, 'just a prick, nothing bad,' and then he struck the blade hard with the stick's blunt head.

The fleam sliced through hair and skin and flesh straight into the vein, and the horse reared up, but Sharpe, expecting the reaction, held the fleam in place as warm blood spurted out over his shako. 'Hold him!' he snapped at Wellesley, and the General seemed to find nothing odd in being ordered about by a sergeant and he obediently hauled Diomed's head down. 'That's good,' Sharpe said, 'that's good, just keep him there, sir, keep him there,' and he skewed the blade slightly to open the slit in the vein and so let the blood pulse out. It ran red down the white horse's flank, it soaked Sharpe's red coat and puddled at his feet.

The horse shivered, but Sharpe sensed that the stallion was calming. By relaxing the pressure on the fleam he could lessen the blood flow and after a while he slowed it to a trickle and then, when the horse had stopped shivering, Sharpe pulled the blade free. His right hand and arm were drenched in blood.

He spat on his clean left hand, then wiped the small wound. 'I reckon he'll live, sir,' he told the General, 'but a bit of ginger in his feed might help.' That was another trick he had learned at the coaching tavern.

Wellesley stroked Diomed's nose and the horse, suddenly unconcerned by the fuss all about him, lowered his head and cropped at a miserable tuft of grass. The General smiled, his bad mood gone. 'I'm greatly obliged to you, Sharpe,' Wellesley said, relinquishing the bridle into the orderly's grasp. ''Pon my soul, I'm greatly obliged to you,' he repeated enthusiastically. 'As neat a blood-letting as ever I did see.' He put a hand into his pocket and brought out a *haideri* that he offered to Sharpe. 'Well done, Sergeant.'

'Thank you, sir,' Sharpe said, taking the gold coin. It was a generous reward.

'Good as new, eh?' Wellesley said, admiring the horse. 'He was a gift.'

'An expensive one,' McCandless observed drily.

'A valued one,' Wellesley said. 'Poor Ashton left him to me in his will. You knew Ashton, McCandless?'

'Of course, sir.' Henry Ashton had been Colonel of the 12th, a Suffolk regiment posted to India, and he had died after taking a bullet in the liver during a duel.

'A damned shame,' Wellesley said, 'but a fine gift. Pure Arab blood, McCandless.'

Most of the pure Arab blood seemed to be on Sharpe, but the General was delighted with the horse's sudden improvement. Indeed, Sharpe had never seen Wellesley so animated. He grinned as he watched the horse, then he told the orderly to walk Diomed up and down, and he grinned even more widely as he watched the horse move. Then, suddenly aware that the men about him were taking an amused pleasure from his own delight, his face drew back into its accustomed cold mask. 'Obliged to you, Sharpe,' he said yet again, then he turned and walked towards his tent. 'McCandless! Come and give me your news!'

McCandless and Sevajee followed the General and his aides into the tent, leaving Sharpe trying to wipe the blood from his hands. The dragoon orderly grinned at him. 'That's a six-hundred-guinea horse you just bled, Sergeant,' he said.

'Bloody hell!' Sharpe said, staring in disbelief at the dragoon. 'Six hundred!'

'Must be worth that. Best horse in India, Diomed is.'

'And you look after him?' Sharpe asked.

The orderly shook his head. 'He's got grooms to look after his horses, and the farrier to bleed and shoe them. My job is to follow him into battle, see? And when one horse gets tired I give him another.'

'You drag all those six horses around?' Sharpe asked, astonished.

'Not all six of them,' the dragoon said, 'only two or three. But he shouldn't have six horses anyway. He only wants five, but he can't find anyone to buy the spare. You don't know anyone who wants to buy a horse, do you?'

'Hundreds of the buggers,' Sharpe said, gesturing at the encampment. 'Every bleeding infantryman over there for a start.'

'It's theirs if they've got four hundred guineas,' the orderly said. 'It's that bay gelding, see?' He pointed. 'Six years old and good as gold.'

'No use looking at me,' Sharpe said. 'I hate the bloody things.'

'You do?'

'Lumpy, smelly beasts. I'm happier on my feet.'

'You see the world from a horse's back,' the dragoon said, 'and catch women's eyes.'

'So they're not entirely useless,' Sharpe said and the orderly grinned. He was a happy, round-faced young man with tousled brown hair and a ready smile. 'How come you're the General's orderly?' Sharpe asked him.

The dragoon shrugged. 'He asked my Colonel to give him someone and I was chosen.'

'You don't mind?'

'He's all right,' the orderly said, jerking his head towards Wellesley's tent. 'Don't crack a smile often, leastwise not with the likes of you and me, but he's a fair man.'

'Good for him.' Sharpe stuck out his bloodied hand. 'My name's Dick Sharpe.'

'Daniel Fletcher,' the orderly said, 'from Stoke Poges.'

'Never heard of it,' Sharpe said. 'Where can I get a scrub?'

'Cook tent, Sergeant.'

'And riding boots?' Sharpe asked

'Find a dead man in Ahmednuggur,' Fletcher said. 'It'll be cheaper than buying them off me.'

'That's true,' Sharpe said, then he limped to the cook tent. The limp was caused by the sore muscles from long hours in the saddle. He had purchased a length of cotton cloth in the village where they had spent the night, then torn the cloth into strips that he had wrapped about his calves to protect them from the stirrup leathers, but his calves still hurt. God, he thought, but he hated bloody horses.

He washed the worst of Diomed's blood from his hands and face, diluted what was on his uniform, then went back to wait for McCandless. Sevajee's men still sat on their horses and stared at the distant city that was topped by a smear of smoke. Sharpe could hear the murmur of voices inside the General's tent, but he paid no attention. It wasn't his business. He wondered if he could scrounge a tent for his own use, for it had already rained earlier in the day and Sharpe suspected it might rain again, but Colonel McCandless was not a man much given to tents. He derided them as women's luxuries, preferring to seek shelter with local villagers or, if no peasant house or cattle byre was available, happily sleeping beneath the stars or in the rain. A pint of rum, Sharpe thought, would not go amiss either.

'Sergeant Sharpe!' Wellesley's familiar voice broke into his thoughts and Sharpe turned to see his old commanding officer coming from the big tent.

'Sir!' Sharpe stiffened to attention.

'So Colonel McCandless has borrowed you from Major Stokes?' Wellesley asked.

'Yes, sir,' Sharpe said. The General was bareheaded and Sharpe saw that his temples had turned prematurely grey. He seemed to have forgotten Sharpe's handiwork with his horse, for his long-nosed face was as unfriendly as ever.

'And you saw this man Dodd at Chasalgaon?'

'I did, sir.'

'Repugnant business,' Wellesley said, 'repugnant. Did he kill the wounded?'

'All of them, sir. All but me.'

'And why not you?' Wellesley asked coldly.

'I was covered in blood, sir. Fair drenched in it.'

'You seem to be in that condition much of the time, Sergeant,' Wellesley said with just a hint of a smile, then he turned back to McCandless. 'I wish you joy of the hunt, Colonel. I'll do my best to help you, but I'm short of men, woefully short.'

'Thank you, sir,' the Scotsman said, then watched as the General went back into his big tent which was crammed with red-coated officers. 'It seems,' McCandless said to Sharpe when the General was gone, 'that we're not invited to supper.'

'Were you expecting to be, sir?'

'No,' McCandless said, 'and I've no business in that tent tonight either. They're planning an assault for first light tomorrow.'

Sharpe thought for a moment that he must have misheard. He looked northwards at the big city wall. 'Tomorrow, sir? An assault? But they only got here today and there isn't a breach!'

'You don't need a breach for an escalade, Sergeant,' McCandless said. 'An escalade is nothing but ladders and murder.'

Sharpe frowned. 'Escalade?' He had heard the word, but was not really sure he knew what it meant.

'March straight up to the wall, Sharpe, throw your ladders against the ramparts and climb.' McCandless shook his head. 'No artillery to help you, no breach, no trenches to get you close, so you must accept the casualties and fight your way through the defenders. It isn't pretty, Sharpe, but it can work.' The Scotsman still sounded disapproving. He was leading Sharpe away from the General's tent, seeking a place to spread his blanket. Sevajee and his men were following, and Sevajee was walking close enough to listen to McCandless's words. 'Escalades can work well against an unsteady enemy,' the Colonel went on, 'but I'm not at all convinced the Mahrattas are shaky. I doubt they're shaky at all, Sharpe. They're dangerous as snakes and they usually have Arab mercenaries in their ranks.'

'Arabs, sir? From Arabia?'

'That's where they usually come from,' McCandless confirmed. 'Nasty fighters, Sharpe.'

'Good fighters,' Sevajee intervened. 'We hire hundreds of them every year. Hungry men, Sergeant, who come from their bare land with sharp swords and long muskets.'

'Doesn't serve to underestimate an Arab,' McCandless agreed. 'They fight like demons, but Wellesley's an impatient man and he wants the business over. He insists they won't be expecting an escalade and thus won't be ready for one, and I pray to God he's right.'

'So what do we do, sir?' Sharpe asked.

'We go in behind the assault, Sharpe, and beseech Almighty God that our ladder parties do get into the city. And once we're inside we hunt for Dodd. That's our job.'

'Yes, sir,' Sharpe said.

'And once we have the traitor we take him to Madras, put him on trial and have him hanged,' McCandless said with satisfaction, as though the job was as good as done. His gloomy forebodings of the previous night seemed to have vanished. He had stopped at a bare patch of ground. 'This looks like a fair billet. No more rain in the offing, I think, so we should be comfortable.'

Like hell, Sharpe thought. A bare bed, no rum, a fight in the morning, and God only knew what kind of devils waiting across the wall, but he slept anyway.

And woke when it was still dark to see shadowy men straggling past with long ladders across their shoulders. Dawn was near and it was time for an escalade. Time for ladders and murder.

Sanjit Pandee was Killadar of the city, which meant that he commanded Ahmednuggur's garrison in the name of his master, Dowlut Rao Scindia, Maharajah of Gwalior, and in principle every soldier in the city, though not in the adjacent fortress, was under Pandee's command. So why had Major Dodd ejected Pandee's troops from the northern gatehouse and substituted his own men? Pandee had sent no orders, but the deed had been done anyway and no one could explain why, and when Sanjit Pandee sent a message to Major Dodd and demanded an answer, the messenger was told to wait and, so far as the Killadar knew, was still waiting.

Sanjit Pandee finally summoned the courage to confront the Major himself. It was dawn, a time when the Killadar was not usually stirring, and he discovered Dodd and a group of his white-coated officers on the southern wall from where the Major was watching the British camp through a heavy telescope mounted on a tripod. Sanjit Pandee did not like to disturb the tall Dodd who was being forced to stoop awkwardly because the tripod was incapable of raising the glass to the level of his eye. The Killadar cleared his throat, but that had no effect, and then he scraped a foot on the firestep, and still Dodd did not even glance at him, so finally the Killadar demanded his explanation, though in very flowery terms just in case he gave the Englishman offence. Sanjit Pandee had already lost the battle over the city treasury which Dodd had simply commandeered without so much as a by-your-leave, and the Killadar was nervous of the scowling foreigner.

'Tell the bloody man,' Dodd told his interpreter without taking his eye from the telescope, 'that he's wasting my bloody time. Tell him to go and boil his backside.'

Dodd's interpreter, who was one of his younger Indian officers, courteously suggested to the Killadar that Major Dodd's attention was wholly consumed by the approaching enemy, but that as soon as he had a moment of leisure, the Major would be delighted to hold a conversation with the honoured Killadar.

The Killadar gazed southwards. Horsemen, British and Indian, were ranging far ahead of the approaching enemy column. Not that Sanjit Pandee could see the column properly, only a dark smudge among the distant green that he supposed was the enemy. Their feet kicked up no dust, but that was because of the rain that had fallen the day before. 'Are the enemy truly coming?' he enquired politely.

'Of course they're not bloody coming,' Dodd said, standing

upright and massaging the small of his back. 'They're running away in terror.'

'The enemy are indeed approaching, sahib,' the interpreter said deferentially.

The Killadar glanced along his defences and was reassured to see the bulk of Dodd's regiment on the firestep, and alongside them the robed figures of his Arab mercenaries. 'Your regiment's guns,' he said to the interpreter, 'they are not here?'

'Tell the interfering little bugger that I've sold all the bloody cannon to the enemy,' Dodd growled.

'The guns are placed where they will prove most useful, sahib,' the interpreter assured the Killadar with a dazzling smile, and the Killadar, who knew that the five small guns were at the north gate where they were pointing in towards the city rather than out towards the plain, sighed in frustration. Europeans could be so very difficult.

'And the three hundred men the Major has placed at the north gate?' Sanjit Pandee said. 'Is it because he expects an attack there?'

'Ask the idiot why else they would be there,' Dodd instructed the interpreter, but there was no time to tell the Killadar anything further because shouts from the ramparts announced the approach of three enemy horsemen. The emissaries rode beneath a white flag, but some of the Arabs were aiming their long-barrelled matchlocks at the approaching horsemen and the Killadar quickly sent some aides to tell the mercenaries to hold their fire. 'They've come to offer us *cowle*,' the Killadar said as he hurried towards the south gate. *Cowle* was an offer of terms, a chance for the defenders to surrender rather than face the horrors of assault, and the Killadar hoped he could prolong the negotiations long enough to persuade Major Dodd to bring the three hundred men back from the north gate.

The Killadar could see that the three horsemen were riding towards the south gate which was topped by a squat tower from which flew Scindia's gaudy green and scarlet flag. To reach the tower the Killadar had to run down some stone steps because the stretch of wall just west of the gate possessed no firestep, but was simply a high, blank wall of red stone. He hurried along the foot of the wall, then climbed more steps to reach the gate tower just as the three horsemen reined in beneath.

Two of the horsemen were Indians while the third was a British officer, and the three men had indeed come to offer the city *cowle*. If the Killadar surrendered, one of the Indians shouted, the city's defenders would be permitted to march from Ahmednuggur with all their hand weapons and whatever personal belongings they could carry. General Wellesley would guarantee the garrison safe passage as far as the River Godavery, beyond which Pohlmann's *compoo* had withdrawn. The officer finished by demanding an immediate answer.

Sanjit Pandee hesitated. The *cowle* was generous, surprisingly generous, and he was tempted to accept because no man would die if he took the terms. He could see the approaching column clearly now, and it looked to him like a red stain smothering the plain. There would be guns there, and the gods alone knew how many muskets. Then he glanced to his left and right and he saw the reassuring height of his walls, and he saw the white robes of his fearsome Arabs, and he contemplated what Dowlut Rao Scindia would say if he meekly surrendered Ahmednuggur. Scindia would be angry, and an angry Scindia was liable to put whoever had angered him beneath the elephant's foot. The Killadar's task was to delay the British in front of Ahmednuggur while Scindia gathered his allies and so prepared the vast army that would crush the invader. Sanjit Pandee sighed. 'There can be no *cowle*,' he called down to Wellesley's three messengers, and the horsemen did not try to change his mind. They just tugged on their reins, spurred their horses and rode away. 'They want battle,' the Killadar said sadly, 'they want loot.'

'That's why they come here,' an aide replied. 'Their own land is barren.'

'I hear it is green,' Sanjit Pandee said.

'No, sahib, barren and dry. Why else would they be here?'

News spread along the walls that *cowle* had been refused. No one had expected otherwise, but the Killadar's reluctant defiance cheered the defenders whose ranks thickened as townsfolk climbed to the firestep to see the approaching enemy.

Dodd scowled when he saw that women and children were thronging the ramparts to view the enemy. 'Clear them away!' he ordered his interpreter. 'I want only the duty companies up here.' He watched as his orders were obeyed. 'Nothing's going to happen for three days now,' he assured his officers. 'They'll send skirmishers to harass us, but skirmishers can't hurt us if we don't show our heads above the wall. So tell the men to keep their heads down. And no one's to fire at the skirmishers, you understand? No point in wasting good balls on skirmishers. We'll open fire after three days.'

'In three days, sahib?' a young Indian officer asked.

'It will take the bastards one day to establish batteries and two to make a breach,' Dodd forecast confidently. 'And on the fourth day the buggers will come, so there's nothing to get excited about now.' The Major decided to set an example of insouciance in the face of the enemy. 'I'm going for breakfast,' he told his officers. 'I'll be back when the bastards start digging their breaching batteries.'

The tall Major ran down the steps and disappeared into the city's alleys. The interpreter looked back at the approaching column, then put his eye to the telescope. He was looking for guns, but at first he could see only a mass of men in red coats with the odd horseman among their ranks, and then he saw something odd. Something he did not comprehend.

Some of the men in the front ranks were carrying ladders. He frowned, then saw something more familiar beyond the red ranks and tilted the glass so that he could see the enemy's cannon. There were only five guns, one being hauled by men and the four larger by elephants, and behind the artillery were more redcoats. Those redcoats wore patterned skirts and had high black hats, and the interpreter was glad that he was behind the wall, for somehow the men in skirts looked fearsome.

He looked back at the ladders and did not really understand what he saw. There were only four ladders, so plainly they did not mean to lean them against the wall. Maybe, he thought, the British planned to make an observation tower so that they could see over the defences, and that explanation made sense and so he did not comprehend that there was to be no siege at all, but an escalade. The enemy was not planning to knock a hole in the wall, but to swarm straight over it. There would be no waiting, no digging, no saps, no batteries and no breach. There would just be a charge, a scream, a torrent of fire, and then death in the morning sun.

'The thing is, Sharpe,' McCandless said, 'not to get yourself killed.'

'Wasn't planning on it, sir.'

'No heroics, Sharpe. It's not your job. We just follow the heroes into the city, look for Mister Dodd, then go back home.'

'Yes, sir.'

'So stay close to me, and I'm staying close to Colonel Wallace's party, so if you lose me, look for him. That's Wallace there, see him?' McCandless indicated a tall, bareheaded officer riding at the front of the 74th.

'I see him, sir,' Sharpe said. He was mounted on McCandless's spare horse and the extra height allowed him to see over the heads of the King's 74th who marched in front of him. Beyond the Highlanders the city wall looked dark red in the early sun, and on its summit he could see the occasional glint of a musket showing between the dome-shaped merlons that topped the wall. Big round bastions stood every hundred yards and those bastions had black embrasures which Sharpe assumed hid the defenders' cannon. The brightly coloured statues of a temple's tower showed above the rampart while a slew of flags drooped over the gate. No one fired yet. The British were within cannon range, but the defenders were keeping their guns quiet.

Most of the British force now checked a half-mile from the walls while the three assault parties organized themselves. Two of the attacking groups would escalade the wall, one to the left of the gate and the other to the right, and both would be led by Scottish soldiers with sepoys in support. The King's 78th, the kilted regiment, would attack the wall to the left while their fellow Highlanders of the 74th would assault to the right. The third attack was in the centre and would be led by the 74th's Colonel, William Wallace, who was also commander of one of the two infantry brigades and evidently an old friend of McCandless for, seeing his fellow Scot, Wallace rode back through his regiment's ranks to greet him with a warm familiarity. Wallace would be leading men of the 74th in an assault against the gate itself and his plan was to run a six-pounder cannon hard up against the big timber gates then fire the gun to blast the entrance open. 'None of our gunners have ever done it before,' Wallace told McCandless, 'and they've insisted on putting a round shot down the gun, but I swear my mother told me you should never load shot to open gates. A double powder charge, she instructed me, and nothing else.'

94

'Your mother told you that, Wallace?' McCandless asked.

'Her father was an artilleryman, you see, and he brought her up properly. But I can't persuade our gunners to leave out the ball. Stubborn fellows, they are. English to a man, of course. Can't teach them anything.' Wallace offered McCandless his canteen. 'It's cold tea, McCandless, nothing that will send your soul to perdition.'

McCandless took a swig of the tea, then introduced Sharpe. 'He was the fellow who blew the Tippoo's mine in Seringapatam,' he told Wallace.

'I heard about you, Sharpe!' Wallace said. 'A damn fine day's work, Sergeant, well done.' And the Scotsman leaned across to give Sharpe his hand. He was a middle-aged man, balding, with a pleasant face and a quick smile. 'I can tempt you to some cold tea, Sharpe?'

'I've got water, sir, thank you,' Sharpe said, patting his canteen which was filled with rum, a gift from Daniel Fletcher, the General's orderly.

'You'll forgive me if I'm about my business,' Wallace said to McCandless, retrieving his canteen. 'I'll see you inside the city, McCandless. Joy of the day to you both.' Wallace spurred back to the head of his column.

'A very good man,' McCandless said warmly, 'a very good man indeed.'

Sevajee and his dozen men cantered up to join McCandless. They all wore red jackets, for they planned to ride into the city with McCandless and none wanted to be mistaken for the enemy, yet somehow the unbuttoned jackets, which had been borrowed from a sepoy battalion, made them look more piratical than ever. They all carried naked *tulwars*, curved sabres that they had honed to a razor's edge at dawn. Sevajee reckoned there would be no time for aiming firelocks once they were inside Ahmednuggur. Ride in, charge whoever still put up a fight and cut down hard.

95

The two escalade parties started forward. Each had a pair of ladders, and each party was led by those men who had volunteered to be first up the rungs. The sun was fully above the horizon now and Sharpe could see the wall more plainly. He reckoned it was twenty foot high, give or take a few inches, and the glint of guns in every embrasure and loophole showed that it would be heavily defended. 'Ever seen an escalade, Sharpe?' McCandless asked.

'No, sir.'

'Risky business. Frail things, ladders. Nasty being first up.'

'Very nasty, sir.'

'And if it fails it gives the enemy confidence.'

'So why do it, sir?'

'Because if it succeeds, Sharpe, it lowers the enemy's spirits. It will make us seem invincible. *Veni, vidi, vici.*'

'I don't speak any Indian, sir, not proper.'

'Latin, Sharpe, Latin. I came, I saw, I conquered. How's your reading these days?'

'It's good, sir, very good,' Sharpe answered enthusiastically, though in truth he had not read very much in the last four years other than lists of stores and duty rosters and Major Stokes's repair orders. But it had been Colonel McCandless and his nephew, Lieutenant Lawford, who had first taught Sharpe to read when they shared a cell in the Tippoo Sultan's prison. That was four years ago now.

'I shall give you a Bible, Sharpe,' McCandless said, watching the escalade parties march steadily forward. 'It's the one book worth reading.'

'I'd like that, sir,' Sharpe said straight-faced, then saw that the picquets of the day were running ahead to make a skirmish line that would pepper the wall with musket fire. Still no one fired from the city wall, though by now both the picquets and the two ladder parties were well inside musket range. 'If you don't mind me asking, sir,' Sharpe said to McCandless, 'what's to stop that bugger – sorry, sir – what's to stop Mister Dodd from escaping out the other side of the city, sir?'

'They are, Sharpe,' McCandless said, indicating the cavalry that now galloped off on both sides of the city. The British 19th Dragoons rode in a tight squadron, but the other horsemen were Mahratta allies or else *silladars* from Hyderabad or Mysore, and they rode in a loose swarm. 'Their job is to harass anyone leaving the city,' McCandless went on. 'Not the civilians, of course, but any troops.'

'But Dodd's got a whole regiment, sir.'

McCandless dismissed the problem. 'I doubt that two whole regiments will serve him. In a minute or two there'll be sheer panic inside Ahmednuggur, and how's Dodd to get away? He'll have to fight his way through a crowd of terrified civilians. No, we'll find him inside the place if he's still there.'

'He is,' Sevajee put in. He was staring at the wall through a small telescope. 'I can see the uniforms of his men on the firestep. White jackets.' He pointed westwards, beyond the stretch of wall that would be attacked by the 78th.

The picquets suddenly opened fire. They were scattered along the southern edge of the city, and their musketry was sporadic and, to Sharpe, futile. Men firing at a city? The musket balls smacked into the red stone of the wall which echoed back the crackle of the gunfire, but the defenders ignored the threat. Not a musket replied, not a cannon fired. The wall was silent. Shreds of smoke drifted from the skirmish line which went on chipping the big red stones with lead.

Colonel Wallace's assault party was late in starting, while the kilted men of the 78th, who were assaulting the wall to the left of the gate, were now far in advance of the other attackers. They were running across open ground, their two ladders in plain sight of the enemy, but still the defenders ignored them. A regiment of sepoys was wheeling left, going to add their musket fire to the picquet line. A bagpiper was playing, but he must have been running for his instrument kept giving small ignominious hiccups. In truth it all seemed ignominious to Sharpe. The battle, if it could even be called a battle, had begun so casually, and the enemy was not even appearing to regard it as a threat. The skirmishers' fire was scattered, the assault parties looked under strength and there seemed to be no urgency and no ceremony. There ought to be ceremony, Sharpe considered. A band should be playing, flags should be flying, and the enemy should be visible and threatening, but instead it was ramshackle and almost unreal.

'This way, Sharpe,' McCandless said, and swerved away to where Colonel Wallace was chivvying his men into formation. A dozen blue-coated gunners were clustered about a six-pounder cannon, evidently the gun that would be rammed against the city gate, while just beyond them was a battery of four twelve-pounder cannon drawn by elephants and, as Sharpe and McCandless urged their horses towards Wallace, the four mahouts halted their elephants and the gunners hurried to unharness the four guns. Sharpe guessed the battery would spray the wall with canister, though the silence of the defenders seemed to suggest that they had nothing to fear from these impudent attackers. Sir Arthur Wellesley, mounted on Diomed who seemed no worse for his blood-letting, rode up behind the guns and called some instruction to the battery commander who raised a hand in acknowledgement. The General was accompanied by three scarlet-coated aides and two Indians who, from the richness of their robes, had to be commanders of the allied horsemen who had ridden to stop the flight of fugitives from the city's northern gate.

The attackers from the 78th were just a hundred paces from the wall now. They had no packs, only their weapons. And still the enemy treated them with lordly disdain. Not a gun fired, not a musket flamed, not a single rocket slashed out from the wall.

'Looks like it will be easy, McCandless!' Wallace called.

'I pray as much!' McCandless said.

'The enemy has been praying too,' Sevajee said, but McCandless ignored the remark.

Then, suddenly and appallingly, the silence ended.

The enemy was not ignoring the attack. Instead, from serried loopholes in the wall and from the bastions' high embrasures and from the merlons along the parapet, a storm of gunfire erupted. One moment the wall had been clear in the morning sun, now it was fogged by a thick screen of powder smoke. A whole city was rimmed white, and the ground about the attacking troops was pitted and churned by the strike of bullets. 'Ten minutes of seven,' McCandless shouted over the noise, as though the time was important. Rockets, like those Sharpe had seen at Seringapatam, scared out from the walls to stitch their smoke trails in crazy tangles above the assaulting parties' heads, yet, despite the volume of fire, the defenders' opening volley appeared to do little harm. One redcoat was staggering, but the assault parties still went forward, and then a pain-filled squeal made Sharpe look to his right to see that an elephant had been struck by a cannonball. The beast's mahout was dragging on its tether, but the elephant broke free and, maddened by its wound, charged straight towards Wallace's men. The Highlanders scattered. The gunners had begun to drag their loaded six-pounder forward, but they were right in the injured beast's path and now sensibly abandoned the gun to flee from the crazed animal's charge. The wrinkled skin of the elephant's left flank was sheeted in red. Wallace shouted incoherently, then spurred his horse out of the way. The elephant, trunk raised and eyes white, thumped past McCandless and Sharpe. 'Poor girl,' McCandless said.

'It's a she?' Sharpe asked.

'All draught animals are female, Sharpe. More docile.'

'She ain't docile, sir,' Sharpe said, watching the elephant burst free of the army's rear and trample through a field of stubble pursued by her mahout and an excited crowd of small skinny children who had followed the attacking troops from the encampment and now whooped shrilly as they enjoyed the chase. Sharpe watched them, then involuntarily ducked as a musket ball whipped just over his shako and another ricocheted off the six-pounder's barrel with a surprisingly musical note.

'Not too close now, Sharpe,' McCandless warned, and Sharpe obediently reined in his mare.

Colonel Wallace was calling his men back into formation. 'Damned animals!' he snarled at McCandless.

'Your mother had no advice on elephants, Wallace?'

'None I'd repeat to a godly man, McCandless,' Wallace said, then spurred his horse towards the six-pounder's disordered gunners. 'Pick up the traces, you rogues. Hurry!'

The 78th had reached the wall to the left of the gate. They rammed the foot of their two ladders into the soil, then swung the tops up and over onto the wall's parapet. 'Good boys,' McCandless shouted warmly, though he was far too distant for the attackers to hear his encouragement. 'Good boys!' The first kilted Highlanders were already scrambling up the rungs, but then a man was hit by a bullet from the flanking bastion and he stopped, clung to the ladder, then slowly toppled sideways. A crowd of Highlanders jostled at the bottom of the ladders to be the next up the rungs. Poor bastards, Sharpe thought, so eager to climb to death, and he saw that the leading men on both ladders were officers. They had swords. The men climbed with their bayonet-tipped muskets slung over their shoulders, but the officers climbed sword in hand. One of them was struck and the man behind unceremoniously shoved him off the ladder and hurried up to the parapet and there, inexplicably, he stopped.

His comrades shouted at him to get a bloody move on and scramble over the wall, but the man did nothing except to unsling his musket, and then he was hurled backwards in a misting spray of blood. Another man took his place, and the same happened to him. The officer at the top of the second ladder was crouching on the top rung, occasionally peering over the coping of the wall between two of the dome-shaped merlons, but he was making no attempt to cross the parapet. 'They should have more than two ladders, sir,' Sharpe grumbled.

'Wasn't time, laddie, wasn't time,' McCandless said. 'What's holding them?' he asked as he stared with an agonized expression at the stalled men. The Arab defenders in the nearest bastion were being given a fine target and their musketry was having a terrible effect on the crowded ladders. The noise of the defenders' fire was continuous; a staccato crackle of musketry, the hiss of rockets and the thunderous crash of cannon. Men were blasted off the ladders, and their place was immediately taken by others, but still the men at the top of the rungs did not try to cross the wall, and still the defenders fired and the dead and injured heaped up at the foot of the ladders and the living pushed them aside to reach the rungs and so offer themselves as targets to the unending gunfire. One man at last heaved himself onto the wall and straddled the coping where he unslung his musket and fired a shot down into the city, but almost immediately he was hit by a blast of musket fire. He swayed for a second, his musket clattered down the wall's red face, then he followed it to the ground. The new man at the top of the ladder heaved himself up, then, just like the rest, he checked and ducked back.

'What's holding them?' McCandless cried in frustration. 'In God's name! Col'

'There's no bloody firestep,' Sharpe said grimly.

McCandless glanced at him. 'What?'

'Sorry, sir. Forgot not to curse, sir.'

But McCandless was not worried about Sharpe's language. 'What did you say, man?' he insisted.

'There's no firestep there, sir.' Sharpe pointed at the wall where the Scotsmen were dying. 'There's no musket smoke on the parapet, sir.'

McCandless looked back. 'By God, you're right.'

The wall had merlons and embrasures, but not a single patch of musket smoke showed in those defences, which meant that the castellation was false and there was no firestep on the wall's far side where defenders could stand. From the outside the stretch of wall looked like any other part of the city's defences, but Sharpe guessed that once the Highlanders reached the wall's summit they were faced with a sheer drop on the far side, and doubtless there was a crowd of enemies waiting at the foot of that inner wall to massacre any man who survived the fall. The 78th were attacking into thin air and being bloodied mercilessly by the jubilant defenders.

The two ladders emptied as the officers at last realized their predicament and shouted at their men to come down. The defenders cheered the repulse and kept firing as the two ladders were carried back from the ramparts.

'Dear God,' McCandless said, 'dear God.'

'I warned you,' Sevajee said, unable to conceal his pride in the fighting qualities of the Mahratta defenders.

'You're on our side!' McCandless snarled, and the Indian just shrugged.

'It ain't over yet, sir,' Sharpe tried to cheer up the Scotsman.

'Escalades work by speed, Sharpe,' McCandless said, 'and we've lost surprise now.'

'It will have to be done properly,' Sevajee remarked smugly, 'with guns and a breach.'

But the escalade was not defeated yet. The assault party

of the 74th had now reached the wall to the right of the gate and their two ladders were swung up against the high red stones, but this stretch of wall did possess a firestep and it was crowded with eager defenders who rained a savage fire down onto the attackers. The British twelve-pounders had opened fire, and their canister was savaging the defenders, but the dead and wounded were dragged away to be replaced by reinforcements who quickly learned that if they let the attackers come up the two ladders then the cannon would cease fire, and so they let the Scots climb the rungs and then hurled down baulks of wood that could scrape a ladder clear in seconds. Then a cannon in one of the flanking bastions hammered a barrel load of stones and scrap iron into the men crowding about the foot of the ladders. 'Oh, dear God,' McCandless prayed again, 'dear God.' More men began to climb the ladders while the wounded crawled and limped back from the walls, pursued by the musket fire of the defenders. A Scottish officer, claymore in hand, ran up one of the ladders with the facility of a sailor swarming up rigging. He cut the claymore at a lunging bayonet, somehow survived a musket blast, put a hand on the coping, but then a spear took him in the throat and he seemed to shake like a gaffed fish before tumbling backwards and carrying two men down to the ground with him. The sound of the defenders' musketry was punctuated by the deeper crash of the small cannon that were mounted in the hidden galleries of the bastions. One of those cannon now struck a ladder in the flank and Sharpe watched appalled as the whole flimsy thing buckled and broke, carrying seven men down to the ground in its wreckage. The 78th had been repulsed and the 74th had lost one of their two ladders. 'This is not good,' McCandless said grimly, 'not good at all.'

'Fighting Mahrattas,' Sevajee said smugly, 'is not like fighting men from Mysore.'

Colonel Wallace's party was still a good hundred yards from the gate, slowed by the weight of their six-pounder cannon. It seemed to Sharpe that Wallace needed more men to handle the cumbersome gun and the enemy's musket fire was taking its toll of the few men he did have shoving at the wheels or dragging at the traces. Wellesley was not far behind Wallace, and just behind the General, mounted on one of his spare horses and with a second on a leading rein, was Daniel Fletcher. The musket fire spurted scraps of dried mud all around Wellesley and his aides, but the General seemed to have a charmed life.

The 78th returned to the attack on the left, only this time they ran their two ladders directly at the bastion which flanked the wall where their first attempt had failed. The threatened bastion reacted with an angry explosion of musket fire. One of the ladders fell, its carriers hard hit by the volley, but the other swung on up and as soon as its top struck the bastion's summit a kilted officer climbed the rungs. 'No!' McCandless cried, as the officer was hit and fell. Other men took his place, but the defenders tipped a basket of stones over the parapet and the tumbling rocks scoured the ladder clear. A volley of musketry made the defenders duck and when the smoke cleared Sharpe saw that the kilted officer was again ascending the ladder, this time without his tall hat. He carried his claymore in his right hand and the big sword hampered him. An Arab fleetingly appeared at the top of the ladder with a lump of timber that he hurled down at the attacker, and the officer was thrown back a second time. 'No!' McCandless lamented again, but then the same officer appeared a third time. He was determined to have the honour of being first into the city, and this time he had tied his red waist-sash to his wrist and let his claymore hang by its hilt from a loop of the silk, thus leaving both hands free and allowing him to climb much faster. He kept climbing, and his men crowded behind him in their big bearskin hats, and the loopholes in the bastion's galleries spat flame and smoke as they scrambled past the bastion's storeys, but magically the officer survived the fusillade and Sharpe had his heart in his mouth as the man drew nearer and nearer to the top. He expected to see a defender appear at any moment, but the attackers who were not queuing at the foot of the ladder were now hammering the bastion's summit with musket fire and under its cover the bare-headed officer scrambled up the last few rungs, paused to take hold of his claymore's hilt, then leaped over the top of the wall. Someone cheered, and Sharpe caught a distinct view of the officer's claymore rising and falling above the red wall's coping. More Highlanders were clambering up the ladder and though some were blasted off by musket fire from the bastion's loopholes, others were at last reaching the high parapet and following their officer onto the defences. The second ladder was swung into place and the trickle of attackers became a stream. 'Thank God,' McCandless said fervently, 'thank God indeed.'

The 78th were in the bastion, and now the 74th, which had been reduced to just one ladder, also made their lodgement. An officer had organized two companies to give the parapet a blast of musketry just as a sergeant reached the top of the ladder, and the fusillade cleared the embrasures as the sergeant clambered over the wall. His bayonet stabbed down, then he reeled backwards as a defender slashed at him with a *tulwar*, but a lieutenant was behind him and he hacked down with his claymore and then kicked the defender in the face. A third man crossed, the fourth was killed, and then another man was on the wall and the Scotsmen screamed their war cries as they began the grim job of clearing the defenders off the firestep. Sharpe could hear the clash of blades on the wall, and see a cloud of powder smoke above the crenellations where the Scots of the 74th were fighting their way along the parapet, but he could see nothing on the bastion where the kilted 78th were fighting. He guessed they were clearing the bastion floor by floor, charging down the steep stone steps and carrying their bayonets to the gunners and infantrymen who manned the lower galleries.

The Scots at last reached the bastion's ground floor where they killed one last defender and then burst out of the tower's inner doorway to be faced by a horde of Arabs who poured a volley of matchlock fire into the attackers' ranks. 'Charge the bastards! Charge them!' The same young officer who had led the assault now rallied his men and led them against the robed defenders who were reloading their long-barrelled muskets. The Highlanders attacked with bayonets and a ferocity born of desperation.

The Scots were inside the city, but so far the only route to reinforce them was up the three remaining ladders, and one of those was bending dangerously after being struck by a small round shot. Wellesley was shouting at Wallace to get the gate open, and Colonel Wallace was bellowing at his gunners to get their damned weapon into place. The defenders above the gate did their best to stop the advancing cannon, but Wallace ordered a company of infantry to help the gunners roll the cannon forward and those men cheered as they bounced and rattled the heavy gun towards the gate. 'Give them fire,' Wallace shouted, 'give them fire!' and his remaining infantrymen blasted a ragged volley up at the gate's defenders. The flags above the rampart twitched as the balls snatched at the silk. The six-pounder rumbled forward, thumping over the uneven road surface that was being pocked by musket balls spat from the gatehouse loopholes. A bagpipe was playing and the savage music made a fine accompaniment to the gun's wild charge. 'Keep firing,' Wallace shouted at his infantry, 'keep firing!' His men's musket balls struck tiny puffs of dust and flakes of stone from the gate that was wreathed in smoke, smoke so thick that the gun seemed to disappear in fog as it rolled the last few yards, but then Sharpe heard the resounding thump as the gun's muzzle was rammed hard against the big wooden gate. 'Get back,' the gun commander shouted, 'get back!' and the men who had hauled the gun scrambled clear.

'Make ready!' Wallace shouted, and his men stopped their firing and dragged out bayonets that they slotted over their blackened musket muzzles. 'Fire the gun!' Wallace shouted. 'Fire it! For God's sake, fire!' A rocket seethed out of the smoke, trailing sparks, and for a second Sharpe thought it would plunge into the heart of Wallace's waiting men, but then it arced up into the clear blue sky and blazed safely away.

Inside the city the Arabs who had tried to defend the bastion now retreated in front of the battle-maddened Scots who swarmed out of the bastion's inner door. The Arabs might come from a hard, warlike country, but so did the kilted men who came snarling into the city. Sepoys were climbing the ladders now and they joined the Highlanders. Their instinct was to charge across the cleared space inside the wall and so reach the cover of the city's alleyways, but the young officer who led the attack knew that the defenders could still rally if he did not open the gate and so let in a flood of attackers. 'To the gate!' he shouted, and led his men along the inner face of the wall to reach the south gate. The Arabs waiting just inside the arch turned and fired as the Scots approached, but the young officer seemed invincible. He screamed as he charged, then his reddened claymore slashed down, and his men's bayonets lunged forward. Two sepoys joined them, stabbing and screaming, and the outnumbered Arabs died or fled. 'Open the gate!' the young officer shouted, and one of the sepoys ran forward to lift the heavy locking bar out of its iron brackets.

'Fire!' Colonel Wallace shouted on the gate's far side.

The gun captain touched his portfire to the priming reed. There was a fizz of spark, a wisp of smoke and then the double-charged gun leaped back and the sound of its massive discharge was magnified by the echo that bounced deafeningly off the gate's high archway. The doors splintered, and the sepoy who had been lifting the bar was cut in two by the six-pound ball and by the wicked-edged scraps of shattered timber that exploded into the city. The other attackers on the inner side of the gate reeled away from the smoke and flame of the blast, but the bar was lifted and the cannon's discharge swung the gates open.

'Charge!' Wallace shouted, and his men screamed as they ran into the smoke-shrouded arch and pushed past the gun and trampled over the bloody halves of the slaughtered sepoy.

'Come on, Sharpe, come on!' McCandless had his own claymore drawn and the old man's face was alight with excitement as he spurred his horse towards the doomed city. The assault troops who had been waiting to climb the ladders now joined the surge of men running towards the broken gates.

For Ahmednuggur had fallen, and from the first shot until the opening of the gate it had taken just twenty minutes. And now the redcoats went for their reward and the suffering inside the city could begin.

Major William Dodd had never reached his breakfast. Instead he had hurried back to the walls the moment he heard the first muskets fire and, once on the firestep, he had stared appalled at the ladder parties, for he had never once anticipated that the British would attempt an escalade. Of all the methods of taking a city, an escalade was the riskiest, but Dodd realized he should have foreseen it. Ahmednuggur had no ditch, nor any glacis, indeed the city had no obstacle outside its ramparts and that made it a prime candidate for escalade, though Dodd had never believed that Boy Wellesley would dare try such a stratagem. He thought Wellesley too cautious.

None of the assaults was aimed at the stretch of wall where Dodd's men were positioned, so all they could do was fire their muskets obliquely at the advancing British, but the distance was too great for their fire to be effective and the thick powder smoke of their muskets soon obscured their aim and so Dodd ordered them to cease fire. 'I can only see four ladders,' his interpreter said.

'Must have more than four,' Dodd remarked. 'Can't do it with just four.'

For a time it seemed the Major must be right for the defence was making a mockery of the attack, while Dodd's men were troubled by nothing more threatening than a scatter of sepoy skirmishers who fired ineffectually at his stretch of the wall. He showed his derision of the skirmishers' fire by standing openly in an embrasure from where he could watch the enemy's cavalry ride about the city's flank to cut off any escape from the northern gate. He could deal with a few cavalrymen, he decided. A scrap of stone was driven from the coping beside him by a musket ball. The stone flake rapped against the leather swordbelt that was buckled round Dodd's new white coat. He did not like wearing white. It showed the dirt, but worse, it made any wound look much worse than it really was. Blood on a red coat hardly showed, but even a small amount of blood on a white coat could make a nervous man terrified. He wondered if Pohlmann or Scindia would agree to the cost of new jackets. Brown, maybe, or dark blue.

The interpreter came to where the Major stood in the embrasure. 'The Killadar requests that we form up behind the gate, sir.'

'Noted,' Dodd said curtly.

'He says the enemy are approaching the gate with a gun, sahib.'

'Sensible of them,' Dodd said, but otherwise ignored the request. Instead he stared eastwards and saw a Scottish officer suddenly appear at the summit of a bastion. Kill him, he silently urged the Arabs in the bastion, but the young officer jumped down and began laying about him with his claymore, and suddenly there were more kilted Scotsmen crossing the wall. 'I do hate the bloody Scots,' he said.

'Sahib?' The interpreter asked.

'Priggish bastards, they are,' Dodd said, but the priggish bastards looked as if they had just captured the city and Dodd knew it would be madness to get involved in a doomed fight to save it. That way he would lose his regiment.

'Sahib?' the interpreter interrupted Dodd nervously. 'The Killadar was insistent, sir.'

'Bugger the Killadar,' Dodd said, jumping down from the embrasure. 'I want the men off the wall,' he ordered, 'and formed in companies on the inner esplanade.' He pointed down to the wide space just inside the wall. 'Now,' he added and, with one last glance at the attackers, he ran down the steps. 'Jemadar!' he shouted to Gopal, whom he had promoted as a reward for loyalty.

'Sahib!'

'Form up! March by companies to the north gate! If any civilians block your path, open fire!'

'Kill them?' the Jemadar asked.

'I don't want you to bloody tickle them, Gopal. Slaughter them!'

The interpreter had listened to this exchange and stared appalled at the tall Englishman. 'But, sir . . .' he began to plead.

'The city's lost,' Dodd growled, 'and the second rule of war is not to reinforce failure.'

The interpreter wondered what the first rule was, but knew this was not the time to ask. 'But the Killadar, sir . . .'

'Is a lily-livered mouse and we are men. Our orders are to save the regiment so it can fight again. Now, go!'

Dodd saw the first redcoats burst out of the inner door of the bastion, heard the Arab volley that threw some of the attackers down into the bloodied dust, but then he turned away from the fight and followed his men into the city's streets. It went against the grain to abandon a fight, but Dodd knew his duty. The city might die, but the regiment must live. Captain Joubert should be holding the north gate safe where Dodd's guns waited, and where his own saddle horses and pack mule were ready, and so he called for his other French officer, the young Lieutenant Sillière, and told him to take a dozen men to rescue Simone Joubert from the panic that he knew was about to engulf the city. Dodd had rather hoped he could fetch Simone himself, posing as her protector, but he knew that the fall of the city was imminent and there would be no time for such gallantries. 'Bring her safe, Lieutenant.'

'Of course, sir,' Sillière said and, glad to be given such a duty, he ordered a dozen men to follow him into the alleys.

Dodd gave one backward glance towards the south, then marched away from the sight. There was nothing for him here but failure. It was time to go north, for it was there, Dodd knew, beyond the wide rivers and among the far hills and a long way from their supplies, that the British would be lured to their deaths.

But Ahmednuggur, and everything inside it, was doomed.

CHAPTER 4

Sharpe followed McCandless into the gatehouse's high archway, using the weight of his mare to push through the sepoys
and Highlanders who jostled in the narrow roadway that was
still half blocked by the six-pounder cannon. The mare shied
from the thick powder smoke that hung in the air between
the scorched and smoking remnants of the two gates and
Sharpe, gripping the mane to keep in the saddle, kicked his
heels back so that the horse shot forward and trampled
through the fly-blown intestines of the sepoy who had been
struck in the belly by the six-pound shot. He hauled on the
reins, checking the mare's fright among the sprawled bodies
of the Arabs who had died trying to defend the gate. The
fight here had been short and brutal, but there was no resistance left in the city by the time Sharpe caught up with
McCandless who was staring in disapproval at the victorious
redcoats who hurried into Ahmednuggur's alleyways. The
first screams were sounding. 'Women and drink,' McCandless
said disapprovingly. 'That's all they'll be thinking of, women
and drink.'

'Loot too, sir,' Sharpe corrected the Scotsman. 'It's a
wicked world, sir,' he added hastily, wishing he could be let
off the leash himself to join the plunderers. Sevajee and his
men were through the gate now, wheeling their horses behind
Sharpe, who glanced up at the walls to see, with some surprise,
that many of the city's defenders were still on the firestep,

though they were making no effort to fire at the red-coated enemy who flooded through the broken gate. 'So what do we do, sir?' he asked.

McCandless, usually so sure of himself, seemed at a momentary loss, but then he saw a wounded Mahratta crawling across the cleared space inside the wall and, throwing his reins to Sharpe, he dismounted and crossed to the casualty. He helped the wounded man into the shelter of a doorway and there propped him against a wall and gave him a drink from his canteen. He spoke to the wounded man for a few seconds. Sevajee, his *tulwar* still drawn, came alongside Sharpe. 'First we kill them, then we give them water,' the Indian said.

'Funny business, war, sir,' Sharpe said.

'Do you enjoy it?' Sevajee asked.

'Don't rightly know, sir. Haven't seen much.' A short skirmish in Flanders, the swift victory of Malavelly, the chaos at the fall of Seringapatam, the horror of Chasalgaon and today's fierce escalade: that was Sharpe's full experience of war and he harboured all the memories and tried to work out from them some pattern that would tell him how he would react when the next violence erupted in his life. He thought he enjoyed it, but he was dimly aware that perhaps he ought not to enjoy it. 'You, sir?' he asked Sevajee.

'I love it, Sergeant,' the Indian said simply.

'You've never been wounded?' Sharpe guessed.

'Twice. But a gambler does not stop throwing dice because he loses.'

McCandless came running back from the wounded man. 'Dodd's heading for the north gate!'

'This way,' Sevajee said, sawing his reins and leading his cut-throats off to the right where he reckoned they would avoid the press of panicked people crowding the centre of the city.

'That wounded man was the Killadar,' McCandless said as he fiddled his left boot into the stirrup, then hauled himself into the saddle. 'Dying, poor fellow. Took a bullet in the stomach.'

'Their chief man, eh?' Sharpe said, looking up at the gatehouse where a Highlander was ripping down Scindia's flags.

'And he was bitterly unhappy with our Lieutenant Dodd,' McCandless said as he spurred his horse after Sevajee. 'It seems he deserted the defences.'

'He's in a hurry to get away, sir,' Sharpe suggested.

'Then let us hurry to stop him,' McCandless said, quickening his horse so that he could push through Sevajee's men to reach the front ranks of the pursuers. Sevajee was using the alleyways beneath the eastern walls and for a time the narrow streets were comparatively empty, but then the crowds increased and their troubles began. A dog yapped at the heels of McCandless's horse, making it rear, then a holy cow with blue painted horns wandered into their path and Sevajee insisted they wait for the beast, but McCandless angrily banged the cow's bony rump with the flat of his claymore to drive it aside, then his horse shied again as a blast of musketry sounded just around the corner. A group of sepoys were shooting open a locked door, but McCandless could not spare the time to stop their depredations. 'Wellesley will have to hang some of them,' he said, spurring on. Refugees were fleeing into the alleys, hammering on locked doors or scaling mud walls to find safety. A woman, carrying a vast bundle on her head, was knocked to the ground by a sepoy who began slashing at the bundle's ropes with his bayonet. Two Arabs, both armed with massive matchlock guns with pearl-studded stocks, appeared ahead of them and Sharpe unslung his musket, but the two men were not disposed to continue a lost fight and so vanished into a gateway. The street was littered with discarded uniform jackets, some green, some blue, some brown, all thrown off by panicking defenders who now tried to pass themselves off as civilians. The crowds thickened as they neared the city's northern edge and the air of panic here was palpable. Muskets sounded constantly in the city and every shot, like every scream, sent a shudder through the crowds that eddied in hopeless search of an escape.

McCandless was shouting at the crowds, and using the threat of his sword to make a passage. There were plenty of men in the streets who might have opposed the Colonel's party, and some of those men still had weapons, but none made any threatening move. Ahmednuggur's surviving defenders only wanted to live, while the civilians had been plunged into terror. A crowd had invaded a Hindu temple where the women swayed and wailed in front of their garlanded idols. A child carrying a birdcage scurried across the road and McCandless wrenched his horse aside to avoid trampling the toddler, and then a loud volley of musketry sounded close ahead. There was a pause, and Sharpe imagined the men tearing open new cartridges and ramming the bullets into their muzzles, and then, exactly at the moment he expected it, the second volley sounded. This was not the ragged noise of plundering men blasting open locked doors, but a disciplined infantry fight. 'I warrant that fight's at the north gate!' McCandless called back excitedly.

'Sounds heavy, sir,' Sharpe said.

'It'll be panic, man, panic! We'll just ride in and snatch the fellow!' McCandless, so close to his quarry, was elated. A third volley sounded, and this time Sharpe heard the musket balls smacking against mud walls or ripping through the thatched roofs. The crowds were suddenly thinner and McCandless drove back his spurs to urge his big gelding closer to the firefight. Sevajee was alongside him, *tulwar* shining, and his men just behind. The city walls were close to their right-hand side, and ahead, over a jumble of thatched and slate roofs, Sharpe could see a blue-and-green-striped flag flying over the ramparts of a square tower like the bastion that crowned the south gate. The tower had to be above the north gate, and he kicked his horse on and hauled back the cock of his musket.

The horsemen cleared the last buildings and the gate was now only thirty yards ahead on the far side of an open, paved space, but the moment McCandless saw the gate he wrenched his reins to swerve his horse aside. Sevajee did the same, but the men behind, Sharpe included, were too late. Sharpe had thought that the disciplined volleys must be being fired by redcoats or sepoys, but instead two companies of white-jacketed soldiers were barring the way to the gate and it was those men who were firing to keep the space around the gate clear for other white-coated companies who were marching in double-quick time to escape the city. The volleys were being fired indiscriminately at civilians, redcoats and fugitive defenders alike, their aim solely to keep the gate free for the white-coated companies that were under the command of an unnaturally tall man mounted on a gaunt black horse. And just as Sharpe saw the man, and recognized him, so the left-hand company aimed at the horsemen and fired.

A horse screamed. Blood spurted fast and warm over the cobbles as the beast fell, trapping its rider and breaking his leg. Another of Sevajee's men was down, his *tulwar* ringing as it skittered across the stones. Sharpe heard the whistle of musket balls all about him and he tugged on the reins, wrenching the mare back towards the alley, but she protested his violence and turned back towards the enemy. He kicked her. 'Move, you bitch!' he shouted. 'Move!' He could hear ramrods rattling in barrels and he knew it would only be seconds before another volley came his way, but then McCandless was beside him and the Scotsman leaned over, seized Sharpe's bridle and hauled him safely into the shelter of an alley.

'Thank you, sir,' Sharpe said. He had lost control of his horse and felt ashamed. The mare was quivering and he patted her neck just as Dodd's next volley hammered its huge noise through the city. The balls thumped into the mud-brick walls, shattered tiles and tore handfuls out of the palm thatch. McCandless had dismounted, so Sharpe now kicked his feet from the stirrups, dropped from the saddle and ran to join the Colonel at the mouth of the alley. Once there, he looked for Dodd through the clearing smoke, found him and aimed the musket.

McCandless hurriedly pushed the musket down. 'What are you doing, man?'

'Killing the bugger, sir,' Sharpe snarled, remembering the stench of blood at Chasalgaon.

'You'll do no such thing, Sergeant,' McCandless growled. 'I want him alive!'

Sharpe cursed, but did not shoot. Dodd, he saw, was very calm. He had caused another massacre here, but this time he had been killing Ahmednuggur's civilians to prevent them from crowding the gateway, and his killers, the two white-coated companies, still stood guard on the gate even though the remaining companies had all vanished into the sunlit country beyond the archway's long dark tunnel. So why were those two companies lingering? Why did Dodd not extricate them before the rampaging sepoys and Highlanders caught up with him? The ground ahead of the two rearguard companies was littered with dead and dying fugitives and a horrid number of those corpses and casualties were women and children, while more weeping and shrieking people, terrified by the volley fire and equally frightened of the invaders spreading into the city behind them, were crammed into every street or alley that opened onto the cleared space by the gate.

'Why doesn't he leave?' McCandless wondered aloud.

'He's waiting for something, sir,' Sharpe said.

'We need men,' McCandless said. 'Go and fetch some. I'll keep an eye on Dodd.'

'Me, sir? Fetch men?'

'You're a sergeant, aren't you?' McCandless snapped. 'So behave like one. Get me an infantry company. Highlanders, preferably. Now go!'

Sharpe cursed under his breath, then sprinted back into the city. How the hell was he expected to find men? There were plenty of redcoats in sight, but none was under discipline, and demanding that looters abandon their plunder to go into another fight would like as not prove a waste of time if not downright suicidal. Sharpe needed to find an officer, and so he bullied his way through the terrified crowd in hope of discovering a company of Highlanders that was still obeying orders.

A splintering crash directly above his head made him duck into a doorway just seconds before a flimsy balcony collapsed under the weight of three sepoys and a dark wooden trunk they had dragged from a bedroom. The trunk split apart when it hit the street, spilling out a trickle of coins, and the three injured sepoys screamed as they were trampled by a rush of soldiers and civilians who plunged in to collect the loot. A tall Scottish sergeant used his musket butt to clear a space about the broken trunk, then knelt and began scooping the coins into his upturned bearskin. He snarled at Sharpe, thinking him a rival for the plunder, but Sharpe stepped over the Sergeant, tripped on the broken leg of one of the sepoys, and shoved on. Bloody chaos!

A half-naked girl ran out of a potter's shop, then suddenly stopped as her unwinding sari jerked her to a halt. Two redcoats hauled her back towards the shop. The girl's father, blood on his temple, was slumped just outside the doorway amidst the litter of his wares. The girl stared into Sharpe's eyes and he saw her mute appeal, then the door of the shop was slammed shut and he heard the bar dropping into place. Whooping Highlanders had discovered a tavern and were setting up shop, while another Highlander was calmly reading his Bible while sitting on a brass-bound trunk he had pulled from a goldsmith's shop. 'It's a fine day, Sergeant,' he said equably, though he took care to keep his hand on his musket until Sharpe had safely gone past.

Another woman screamed in an alley, and Sharpe instinctively headed towards the terrible sound. He discovered a riotous mob of sepoys fighting with a small squad of white-jacketed soldiers who had to be among the very last of the city's defenders still in recognizable uniforms. They were led by a very young European officer who flailed a slender sword from his saddle, but just as Sharpe caught sight of him, the officer was caught from behind by a bayonet. He arched his back, and his mouth opened in a silent scream as his sword faltered, then a mass of dark hands reached up and hauled him down from his white-eyed horse. Bayonets plunged down, then the officer's blood-soaked uniform was being rifled for money.

Beyond the dead officer, and also on horseback, was a woman. She was wearing European clothes and had a white net veil hanging from the brim of her straw hat, and it was her scream that Sharpe had heard. Her horse had been trapped against a wall and she was clinging to a roof beam that jutted just above her head. She was sitting side-saddle, facing the street and screaming as excited sepoys clawed at her. Other sepoys were looting a pack mule that had been following her horse, and she turned and shouted at them to stop, then gasped as two men caught her legs. 'No!' she shouted. A small riding whip hung from a loop about her right wrist and she tried letting go of the roof beam and slashing down with the leather thong, but the defiance only made her predicament worse.

Sharpe used his musket butt to hammer his way through the sepoys. He was a good six inches taller than any of them, and much stronger, and he used his anger as a weapon to drive them aside. He kicked a man away from the slaughtered officer, stepped over the body, and swung the musket butt into the skull of one of the men trying to pull the woman from her horse. That man went down and Sharpe turned the musket and drove its muzzle into the belly of the second sepoy. That man doubled over and staggered backwards, but just then a third man seized the horse's bridle and yanked it out from the wall so fast that the woman fell back onto the roadway. The sepoys, seeing her upended with her long legs in the air, shouted in triumph and surged forward and Sharpe whirled the musket like a club to drive them backwards. One of them aimed his musket at Sharpe who stared him in the eyes. 'Go on, you bastard,' Sharpe said, 'I dare you.'

The sepoys decided not to make a fight of it. There were other women in the city and so they backed away. A few paused to plunder the dead European officer, while others finished looting the woman's pack mule which had been stripped of its load and grinning sepoys now tore apart her linen dresses, stockings and shawls. The woman was kneeling behind Sharpe, shaking and sobbing, and so he turned and took her by the elbow. 'Come on, love,' he said, 'you're all right now. Safe now.'

She stood. Her hat had come off when she fell from her horse and her dishevelled golden hair hung about her pale face. Sharpe saw she was tall, had an impression that she was pretty even though her blue eyes were wide with shock and she was still shaking. He stooped for her hat. 'You look like you've been dragged through a hedge backwards, you do,' he said, then shook the dust off her hat and held it out to her. Her horse was standing free in the street, so he grabbed the beast's bridle then led woman and animal to a nearby gateway that opened into a courtyard. 'Have to look after your horse,' he said, 'valuable things, horses. You know how a trooper gets a replacement mount?' He was not entirely sure why he was talking so much and he did not even know if the woman understood him, but he sensed that if he stopped talking she would burst into tears again and so he kept up his chatter. 'If a trooper loses his horse he has to prove it's died, see? To show he hasn't sold it. So he chops off a hoof. They carry little axes for that, some of them do. Can't sell a three-footed horse, see? He shows the hoof to his officers and they issue a new horse.'

There was a rope bed in the courtyard and he led the woman to it. She sat and cuffed at her face. 'They said you wouldn't come for three more days,' she said bitterly in a strong accent.

'We were in a hurry, love,' Sharpe said. She had still not taken the hat so he crouched and held it close to her. 'Are you French?'

She nodded. She had begun to cry again and tears were running down her cheeks. 'It's all right,' he said, 'you're safe now.' Then he saw the wedding ring on her finger and a terrible thought struck him. Had the white-coated officer been her husband? And had she watched him hacked down in front of her? 'That officer,' he said, jerking his head towards the street where sepoys were kicking at doors and forcing shuttered windows with their firelocks, 'was he your husband, love?'

She shook her head. 'Oh, no,' she said, 'no. He was a lieutenant. My husband is a captain.' She at last took the hat, then sniffed. 'I'm sorry.'

'Nothing to be sorry about,' Sharpe said, 'except you had a nasty fright. It's all right now.'

She took a deep breath, then wiped her eyes. 'I seem to be crying always.' She looked into Sharpe's eyes. 'Life is always tears, isn't it?'

'Not for me, love, no. Haven't had a weep since I was a kid, not that I can remember.'

She shrugged. 'Thank you,' she said, gesturing towards the street where she had been assailed by the sepoys. 'Thank you.'

Sharpe smiled. 'I didn't do anything, love, 'cept drive the buggers off. A dog could have done that as well as me. Are you all right? You weren't hurt?'

'No.'

He patted her hand. 'Your husband went without you, did he?'

'He sent Lieutenant Sillière to fetch me. No, he didn't. Major Dodd sent Sillière.'

'Dodd?' Sharpe asked.

The woman heard the interest in Sharpe's voice. 'You know him?' she asked.

'I know of him,' Sharpe said carefully. 'Ain't met him, not properly.'

She studied Sharpe's face. 'You don't like him?'

'I hate him, Ma'am.'

'I hate him too.' She shrugged. 'I am called Simone. Simone Joubert.'

'It's a pretty name, Ma'am. Simone? Very pretty.'

She smiled at his clumsy gallantry. 'You have a name?'

'Richard Sharpe, Ma'am, Sergeant Richard Sharpe, King's 33rd.'

'Richard,' she said, trying it out, 'it suits you. Richard the Lion-Heart, yes?'

'He was a great one for fighting, Ma'am.'

'For fighting the French, Sergeant,' she said reprovingly.

'Someone has to,' Sharpe said with a grin, and Simone

122

Joubert laughed and at that moment Sharpe thought she was the prettiest girl he had seen in years. Maybe not really pretty, but vivacious and blue-eyed and golden-haired and smiling. But an officer's woman, Sharpe told himself, an officer's woman.

'You must not fight the French, Sergeant,' Simone said. 'I won't let you.'

'If it looks like it's going to happen, Ma'am, then I'll let you know and you'll have to hold me down.'

She laughed again, then sighed. A fire had broken out not far away and scraps of burning thatch were floating in the warm air. One of the smuts landed on Simone's white dress and she brushed at it, smearing the black ash into the weave. 'They have taken everything,' she said sadly. 'I had little enough, but it is gone. All my clothes! All!'

'Then you get more,' Sharpe said.

'What with? This?' She showed him a tiny purse hanging from her waist. 'What will happen to me, Sergeant?'

'You'll be all right, Ma'am. You'll be looked after. You're an officer's wife, aren't you? So our officers will make sure you're all right. They'll probably send you back to your husband.'

Simone gave him a dutiful smile and Sharpe wondered why she was not overjoyed at the thought of being reunited with her captain, then he forgot the question as a ragged volley of shots sounded in the street and he turned to see an Arab staggering in the gateway, his robes bright with blood, and an instant later a half-dozen Highlanders leaped onto the twitching body and began to tear its clothing apart. One of them slit the victim's robes with his bayonet and Sharpe saw that the dying man had a fine pair of riding boots.

'There's a woman!' one of the looters shouted, seeing Simone in the courtyard, but then he saw Sharpe's levelled musket and he raised a placatory hand. 'All yours, eh? No trouble, Sergeant, no trouble.' Then the man twisted to look down the street and shouted a warning to his comrades and the six men took to their heels. A moment later a file of sepoys showed in the gateway under the command of a mounted officer. They were the first disciplined troops Sharpe had seen in the city and they were restoring order. The officer peered into the courtyard, saw nothing amiss, and so ordered his men onwards. A half company of kilted redcoats followed the sepoys and Sharpe assumed that Wellesley had ordered the picquets of the day into the city. The picquets, who provided the sentries for the army, were made up of half companies from every battalion.

There was a well in the corner of the yard and Sharpe hauled up its leather bucket to give himself and Simone a drink. He brought up more water for the Frenchwoman's horse, and just then heard McCandless shouting his name through the streets. 'Here, sir!' he called back. 'Here!'

It took a moment or two for McCandless to find him, and when he did the Scotsman was furious. 'Where were you, man?' the Colonel demanded querulously. 'He got away! Clean away! Marched away like a toy soldier!' He had remounted his gelding and stared imperiously down on Sharpe from his saddle. 'Got clean away!'

'Couldn't find men, sir, sorry, sir,' Sharpe said.

'Just one company! That's all we needed!' McCandless said angrily, then he noticed Simone Joubert and snatched off his hat. 'Ma'am,' he said, nodding his head.

'This is Colonel McCandless, Ma'am,' Sharpe made the introduction. 'And this is Simone, sir.' He could not recall her surname.

'Madame Joubert,' Simone introduced herself.

McCandless scowled at her. He had ever been awkward in the presence of women, and he had nothing to say to this young woman so he just glowered at Sharpe instead. 'All I needed was one company, Sharpe. One company!'

'He was rescuing me, Colonel,' Simone said.

'So I surmised, Madame, so I surmised,' the Colonel said unhappily, implying that Sharpe had been wasting his time. More smuts swirled in the smoke down to the yard, while in the street beyond the gateway the picquets were hauling looters from the shops and houses. McCandless stared irritably at Simone who gazed placidly back. The Scotsman was a gentleman and knew the woman was now his responsibility, but he resented the duty. He cleared his throat, then found he still had nothing to say.

'Madame Joubert's husband, sir,' Sharpe said, 'serves in Dodd's regiment.'

'He does, does he?' McCandless asked, showing sudden interest.

'My husband hoped to take command of the regiment when Colonel Mathers left,' Simone explained, 'but, alas, Major Dodd arrived.' She shrugged.

The Colonel frowned. 'Why didn't you leave with your husband?' he demanded sternly.

'That is what I was trying to do, Colonel.'

'And you were caught, eh?' The Colonel patted his horse which had been distracted by one of the burning scraps of straw. 'Tell me, Ma'am, do you have quarters in the city?'

'I did, Colonel, I did. Though if anything is left now . . . ?' Simone shrugged again, implying that she expected to find the quarters ransacked.

'You have servants?'

'The landlord had servants and we used them. My husband has a groom, of course.'

'But you have somewhere to stay, Ma'am,' McCandless demanded.

'I suppose so, yes.' Simone paused. 'But I am alone, Colonel.'

'Sergeant Sharpe will look after you, Ma'am,' McCandless

said, then a thought struck him forcibly. 'You don't mind doing that, do you, Sharpe?' he enquired anxiously.

'I'll manage, sir,' Sharpe said.

'And I am just to stay here?' Simone demanded fiercely. 'Nothing else? That is all you propose, Colonel?'

'I propose, Ma'am, to reunite you with your husband,' McCandless said, 'but it will take time. A day or two. You must be patient.'

'I am sorry, Colonel,' Simone said, regretting the tone of the questions she had shot at McCandless.

'I'm sorry to give you so unfortunate a duty, Sharpe,' McCandless said, 'but keep the lady safe till we can arrange things. Send word to me where you are, and I'll come and find you when everything's arranged.'

'Yes, sir.'

The Colonel turned and spurred out of the courtyard. His spirits, which had collapsed when Dodd had marched out of the city's northern gate, were reviving again, for he saw in Simone Joubert a God-sent opportunity to ride into the heart of his enemy's army. Restoring the woman to her husband might do nothing to visit the vengeance of the Company on Dodd, but it would surely be an unparalleled opportunity to scout Scindia's forces and so McCandless rode to fetch Wellesley's permission for such an excursion, while Simone led Sharpe through the exhausted streets to find her house. On their way they passed an ox cart that had been tipped backwards and weighted down with stones so that its single shaft pointed skywards. A sepoy hung from the shaft's tip by his neck. The man was not quite dead yet and so made small spasmodic motions, and officers, both Scottish and Indian, were forcing sheepish and half-drunken men to stare at the dying sepoy as a reminder of the fate that awaited plunderers. Simone shuddered and Sharpe hurried her past, her horse's reins in his left hand.

'Here, Sergeant,' she said, leading him into an alley that was littered with discarded plunder. Above them smoke drifted across a city where women wept and redcoats patrolled the walls. Ahmednuggur had fallen.

Major Dodd had misjudged Wellesley, and that misjudgement shook him. An escalade seemed too intrepid, too headstrong, for the man Dodd derided as Boy Wellesley. It was neither what Dodd had expected nor what he had wanted from Wellesley. Dodd had wanted caution, for a cautious enemy is more easily defeated, but instead Wellesley had shown a scathing contempt for Ahmednuggur's defenders and launched an assault that should have been easily beaten back. If Dodd's men had been on the ramparts directly in the path of the assault then the attack would have been defeated, of that Dodd had no doubt, for there had only been four ladders deployed and that small number made the ease and swiftness of the British victory even more humiliating. It suggested that General Sir Arthur Wellesley possessed a confidence that neither his age nor experience should have provided, and it also suggested that Dodd might have underestimated Wellesley, and that worried him. Dodd's decision to desert to Pohlmann's army had been forced on him by circumstance, but he had not regretted the decision, for European officers who served the Mahratta chiefs were notorious for the riches they made, and the Mahratta armies far outnumbered their British opponents and were thus likely to be the winners of this war, but if the British were suddenly to prove invincible there would be no riches and no victory. There would only be defeat and ignominious flight.

And so, as he rode away from the fallen city, Dodd was inclined to ascribe Wellesley's sudden success to beginner's luck. Dodd persuaded himself that the escalade must have been a foolish gamble that had been unfairly rewarded with victory. It had been a rash strategy, Dodd told himself, and though it had succeeded, it could well tempt Wellesley into rashness again, and next time the rashness would surely be punished. Thus Dodd attempted to discover good news within the bad.

Captain Joubert could find no good news. He rode just behind Dodd and continually turned in his saddle for a glimpse of Simone's white dress among the fugitives that streamed from the northern gate, but there was no sign of her, nor of Lieutenant Sillière, and each disappointment made Pierre Joubert's loss harder to bear. He felt a tear prickle at the corner of his eye, and then the thought that his young Simone might be raped made the tear run down his cheek.

'What the hell are you blubbing about?' Dodd demanded.

'Something in my eye,' Joubert answered. He wished he could be more defiant, but he felt belittled by the Englishman and unable to stand up to his bullying. In truth Pierre Joubert had felt belittled for most of his life. His small stature and timid nature made him a target, and he had been the obvious choice when his regiment in France had been ordered to find one officer who could be sent as an adviser to Scindia, the Maharajah of Gwalior. They had chosen Joubert, the one officer no one would miss, but the unpopular posting had brought Joubert the one stroke of good fortune that had ever come his way when the ship bringing him to India had stopped at the Île de France. He had met Simone, he had wooed her, he had won her, and he was proud of her, intensely proud, for he knew other men found her attractive and Joubert might have enjoyed that subtle flattery had he not known how desperately unhappy she was. He put her unhappiness down to the vagaries of a newly married woman's temperament and to the heat of India. He consoled himself with the thought that in a year or two he would be summoned back to France and there Simone would learn contentment in the company of his huge family. She would become a mother, learn to keep house and so accept her comfortable fate. So long, that was, as she had survived Ahmednuggur's fall. He spurred his horse alongside Dodd's. 'You were right, Colonel,' the Frenchman said grudgingly. 'There was nothing to be gained by fighting.' He was making conversation in order to keep his mind away from his fears for Simone.

Dodd acknowledged the compliment with a grunt. 'I'm sorry about Madame Joubert,' he forced himself to say.

'The British will send news, I'm sure,' Joubert said, clinging to a hope that Simone would have been rescued by some gallant officer.

'But a soldier's best off without a woman,' Dodd said, then twisted in his saddle to look at the rearguard. 'Sikal's company is lagging,' he told Joubert. 'Tell the buggers to hurry up!' He watched Joubert ride away, then spurred to the head of the column where his vanguard marched with fixed bayonets and charged muskets.

The regiment might have escaped from Ahmednuggur, but it was not yet clear of all danger. British and Mahratta cavalry had ridden around the city to harass any of the garrison who might succeed in escaping, and those horsemen now threatened both flanks of Dodd's column, but their threat was small. Scores of other men were fleeing the city, and those fugitives, because they were not marching in disciplined formations, made much easier targets for the horsemen who gleefully swooped and circled about the refugees. Dodd watched as lances and sabres slashed into the scattered fugitives, but if any of the horsemen came too close to his own white-jacketed ranks he called a company to halt, turned it outwards and made them level their muskets. The threat of a volley was usually enough to drive the horsemen to search for easier pickings, and not one of the enemy came within pistol shot of Dodd's ranks. Once, when the column was some two miles north of the city, a determined squadron of British dragoons tried to head off the regiment's march, but Dodd ordered two of his small cannon to be unlimbered and their paltry round shots, bouncing across the flat, dry ground, were sufficient to make the blue-coated horsemen veer away to find another angle of attack. Dodd reinforced the threat by having his lead company fire one volley of musketry which, even though it was at long range, succeeded in unhorsing one dragoon. Dodd watched the defeated horsemen ride away and felt a surge of pride in his new regiment. This was the first time he had observed them in action, and though the excited cavalry was hardly a worthy foe, the men's calmness and efficiency were entirely praiseworthy. None of them hurried, none shot a ramrod out in panic, none seemed unsettled by the sudden, savage fall of the city and none had shown any reluctance to fire on the civilians who had threatened to obstruct their escape through the north gate. Instead they had bitten the enemy like a cobra defending itself, and that gave Dodd an idea. The Cobras! That was what he would call his regiment, the Cobras! He reckoned the name would inspire his men and put fear into an enemy. Dodd's Cobras. He liked the thought.

Dodd soon left his pursuers far behind. At least four hundred other men, most of them Arabs, had attached themselves to his regiment and he welcomed them, for the more men he brought from the disaster, the higher his reputation would stand with Colonel Pohlmann. By early afternoon his Cobras had reached the crest of the escarpment that looked across the vast Deccan plain to where, far in the hazy distance, he could see the brown River Godavery snaking through the dry land. Beyond that river was safety. Behind him the road was empty, but he knew it would not be long before the pursuing cavalry reappeared. The regiment had paused on the escarpment's edge and Dodd let them rest for a while. Some of the fugitive Arabs were horsemen and Dodd sent those men ahead to find a village that would yield food for his regiment. He guessed he would need to camp short of the Godavery, but tomorrow he would find a way to cross, and a day or so later he would march with flying colours into Pohlmann's camp. Ahmednuggur might have fallen like a rotted tree, but Dodd had brought his regiment out for the loss of only a dozen men. He regretted those twelve men, though not the loss of Sillière, but he particularly regretted that Simone Joubert had failed to escape from the city. Dodd had sensed her dislike of him, and he had taken a piquant delight in the thought of cuckolding her despised husband in spite of that dislike, but it seemed that pleasure must be forgotten or at least postponed. Not that it mattered. He had saved his regiment and saved his guns and the future promised plenty of profitable employment for both.

So William Dodd marched north a happy man.

Simone led Sharpe to three small rooms on an upper floor of a house that smelt as though it belonged to a tanner. One room had a table and four mismatched chairs, two of which had been casually broken by looters, the second had been given over to a huge hip bath, while the third held nothing but a straw mattress that had been slit open and its stuffing scattered over the floorboards. 'I thought men joined Scindia to become rich,' Sharpe said in wonderment at the cramped, ill-furnished rooms.

Simone sat on one of the undamaged chairs and looked close to tears. 'Pierre is not a mercenary,' she said, 'but an adviser. His salary is paid by France, not by Scindia, and what money he makes, he saves.'

'He certainly doesn't spend it, does he?' Sharpe asked,

looking about the small grubby rooms. 'Where are the servants?'

'Downstairs. They work for the house owner.'

Sharpe had spotted a broom in the stable where they had put Simone's horse, so now he went and fetched it. He drew a pail of water from the well and climbed the steps that ran up the side of the house to discover that Simone had not moved, except to hide her face in her hands, and so he set about cleaning up the mess himself. Whichever men had searched the rooms for loot had decided to use the bath as a lavatory, so he began by dragging it to the window, throwing open the shutters and pouring the contents into the alley. Then he sloshed the bath with water and scrubbed it with a dirty towel.

'The landlord is very proud of the bath' – Simone had come to the door and was watching him – 'and makes us pay extra.'

'I've never had a proper bath.' Sharpe gave the zinc tub a slap. He assumed it must have been brought to India by a European, for the outside was painted with square-rigged ships. 'How do you fill it?'

'The servants do it. It takes a long time, and even then it's usually cold.'

'I'll have them fill it for you, if you want.'

Simone shrugged. 'We need food first.'

'Who cooks? Don't tell me, the servants downstairs?'

'But we have to buy the food.' She touched the purse at her waist.

'Don't worry about money, love,' Sharpe said. 'Can you sew?'

'My needles were on the packhorse.'

'I've got a sewing kit,' Sharpe said, and he took the broom through to the bedroom and swept up the straw and stuffed it into the slit mattress. Then he took the sewing kit from his pack, gave it to Simone, and told her to sew the mattress together. 'I'll find some food while you do that,' he said, and went out with his pack. The city was silent now, its survivors cowering from their conquerors, but he managed to barter a handful of cartridges for some bread, some lentil paste and some mangoes. He was stopped twice by patrolling redcoats and sepoys, but his sergeant's stripes and Colonel McCandless's name convinced the officers he was not up to mischief. He found the body of the Arab who had been shot just outside the courtyard where he had sheltered Simone and dragged the riding boots off the corpse. They were fine boots of red leather with hawk-claw steel spurs, and Sharpe hoped they would fit. Nearby, in an alley, he discovered a pile of silk saris evidently dropped by a looter and he gathered up the whole bundle before hurrying back to Simone's rooms.

He pushed open the door. 'Even got you some sheets,' he called, then dropped the bundle of silks because Simone had screamed from the bedroom. Sharpe ran to the door to see her facing three Indians who now turned to confront him. One was an older man dressed in a dark tunic richly embroidered with flowers, while the younger two were in simple white robes. 'You got trouble?' Sharpe asked Simone.

The older man snarled at Sharpe, letting loose a stream of words in Marathi.

'Shut your face,' Sharpe said, 'I was talking to the lady.'

'It is the house owner,' Simone said, gesturing to the man in the embroidered tunic.

'He wants you out?' Sharpe guessed, and Simone nodded. 'Reckons he can get a better rent from a British officer, is that it?' Sharpe asked. He put his food on the floor, then walked to the landlord. 'You want more rent? Is that it?'

The landlord stepped back from Sharpe and said something to his two servants who closed in on either side of the redcoat. Sharpe slammed his right elbow into the belly of one and stamped his left foot onto the instep of the other, then grabbed both men's heads and brought them together with a crack. He let go of them and they staggered away in a daze as Sharpe pulled the bayonet from its sheath and smiled at the landlord. 'She wants a bath, you understand? Bath.' He pointed at the room where the bath stood. 'And she wants it hot, you greedy bastard, hot and steaming. And she needs food.' He pointed at the miserable pile of food. 'You cook it, we eat it, and if you want to make any other changes, you bastard, you talk to me first. Understand?'

One of the servants had recovered enough to intervene and was unwise enough to try to tug Sharpe away from his master. The servant was a big and young man, but he had none of Sharpe's ferocity. Sharpe hit him hard, hit him again, kneed him in the crotch, and by then the servant was halfway across the living-room floor and Sharpe pursued him, hauled him upright, hit him again and that last blow took the servant onto the small balcony at the top of the outside stairs. 'Go and break a leg, you sod,' Sharpe said, and tipped the man over the balustrade. He heard the man cry out as he fell into the alley, but Sharpe had already turned back towards the bedroom. 'Have we still got a problem?' he demanded of the landlord.

The man did not understand a word of English, but he understood Sharpe by now. There was no problem. He backed out of the rooms, followed by his remaining servant, and Sharpe went with them to the stairs. 'Food,' he said, pushing the bread, lentils and fruit into the hands of the cowed landlord. 'And Madame's horse needs cleaning and watering. And feeding. Horse, there, see?' He pointed into the courtyard. 'Feed the bugger,' he ordered. The servant he had pushed over the balcony had propped himself against the alley's far wall where he was gingerly touching his bleeding nose. Sharpe spat on him for good measure, then went back inside. 'I never did like landlords,' he said mildly.

Simone was half laughing and half afraid that the landlord would exact a terrible vengeance. 'Pierre was afraid of him,' she explained, 'and he knows we are poor.'

'You're not poor, love, you're with me,' Sharpe said.

'Rich Richard?' Simone said, pleased to have made a joke in a foreign language.

'Richer then you know, love. How much thread is left?

'Thread? Ah, for the needle. You have plenty, why?'

'Because, my love, you can do me a favour,' he said, and he stripped off his pack, his belt and his jacket. 'I'm not that handy with a needle,' he explained. 'I can patch and darn, of course, but what I need now is some fine needlework. Real fine.' He sat, and Simone, intrigued, sat opposite and watched as he tipped out the contents of his pack. There were two spare shirts, his spare foot cloths, a blacking ball, a brush and the tin of flour he was supposed to use on his clubbed hair, though ever since he had ridden from Seringapatam with McCandless he had let his hair go unpowdered. He took out his stock, which he had similarly abandoned, then the copy of *Gulliver's Travels* that Mister Lawford had given him so he could practise his reading. He had neglected that lately, and the book was damp and had lost some of its pages. 'You can read?' Simone asked, touching the book with a tentative finger.

'I'm not very good.'

'I like to read.'

'Then you can help me get better, eh?' Sharpe said, and he pulled out the folded piece of leather that was for repairing his shoes, and beneath that was a layer of sacking. He took that out, then tipped the rest of the pack's contents onto the table. Simone gasped. There were rubies and emeralds and pearls, there was gold and more emeralds and sapphires and diamonds and one great ruby half the size of a hen's egg.

'The thing is,' Sharpe said, 'that there's bound to be a battle before this Scindia fellow learns his lesson, and as like as not we won't wear packs in a battle, on account of them being too heavy, see? So I don't want to leave this lot in my pack to be looted by some bastard of a baggage guard.'

Simone touched one of the stones, then looked up at Sharpe with wonderment in her eyes. He was not sure that it was wise to show her the treasure, for such things were best kept very secret, but he knew he was trying to impress her, and it was evident that he had. 'Yours?' she asked.

'All mine,' he said.

Simone shook her blonde head in amazement, then began arranging the stones into ranks and files. She formed platoons of emeralds, platoons of rubies and another of pearls, there was a company of sapphires and a skirmish line of diamonds, and all of them were commanded by the great ruby. 'That belonged to the Tippoo Sultan,' Sharpe said, touching the ruby. 'He wore it in his hat.'

'The Tippoo? He's dead, isn't he?' Simone asked.

'And me it was who killed him,' Sharpe said proudly. 'It wasn't really a hat, it was a cloth helmet, see? And the ruby was right in the middle, and he reckoned he couldn't die because the hat had been dipped in the fountain of Zum-Zum.'

Simone smiled. 'Zum-Zum?'

'It's in Mecca. Wherever the hell Mecca is. Didn't work, though. I put a bullet in his skull, right through the bloody hat. Might as well have dunked it in the Thames for all the good it did him.'

'You are rich!' Simone said.

The problem was how to stay rich. Sharpe had not had time to make false compartments in the new pack and pouch that had replaced those he had burned at Chasalgaon, and so he had kept the stones loose in his pack. He had a layer of emeralds at the bottom of his new cartridge pouch, where they would be safe enough, but he needed secure hiding places for the other jewels. He gave a file of diamonds to Simone and she tried to refuse, then shyly accepted the stones and held one against the side of her nose where fashionable Indian women often wore just such a jewel. 'How does it look?' she asked.

'Like a piece of expensive snot.'

She stuck her tongue out at him. 'It's beautiful,' she said. She peered at the diamond that still had its black velvet backing so that the stone would shine more brightly, then she opened her purse. 'Are you sure?'

'Go on, girl, take them.'

'How do I explain them to Pierre?'

'You say you found them on a dead body after the fight. He'll believe that.' He watched her put the diamonds in the purse. 'I have to hide the rest,' he explained to her. He reckoned some of the stones could go in his canteen, where they would rattle a bit when it was dry, and he would have to take care when drinking in case he swallowed a fortune, but that still left a mound of gems unhidden. He used his knife to slit open a seam of his red coat and began feeding the small rubies into the slot, but the stones bunched along the bottom hem and the bulge was an advertisement to every soldier that he was carrying plunder. 'See what I mean?' He showed Simone the bulging seam.

She took the coat, fetched Sharpe's sewing kit from the bedroom, and then began to trap each gem in its own small pouch of the opened seam. The job took her all afternoon, and when she was finished the red coat was twice as heavy. The most difficult stone to hide was the huge ruby, but Sharpe solved that by unwinding his long hair from the shot-weighted bag that clubbed it, then slitting open the bag and emptying the shot. He filled the bag with the ruby and with whatever small stones were left, then Simone rewound his hair about the bag. By nightfall the jewels had vanished.

They ate by lamplight. The bath had never been filled, but Simone said she had taken one a week before so it did not matter. Sharpe had made a brief excursion in the dusk and had returned with two clay bottles filled with arrack, and they drank the liquor in the gloom. They talked, they laughed, and at last the oil in the lamp ran dry and the flame flickered out to leave the room lit by shafts of moonlight coming through the filigree shutters. Simone had fallen silent and Sharpe knew she was thinking of bed. 'I brought you some sheets.' He pointed to the saris.

She looked up at him from under her fringe. 'And where will you sleep, Sergeant Sharpe?'

'I'll find a place, love.'

It was the first time he had slept in silk, not that he noticed, so showing her the gems had not been such a bad idea after all.

He woke to the crowing of cockerels and the bang of a twelve-pounder gun, a reminder that the world and the war went on.

Major Stokes had decided that the real problem with the Rajah's clock was its wooden bearings. They swelled in damp weather, and he was happily contemplating the problem of making a new set of bearings out of brass when the twitching Sergeant reappeared in his office. 'You again,' the Major greeted him. 'Can't remember your name.'

'Hakeswill, sir. Sergeant Obadiah Hakeswill.'

'Punishment on Edom, eh?' the Major said, wondering whether to cast or drill the brass.

'Edom, sir? Edom?'

'The prophet Obadiah, Sergeant, foretells punishment on Edom,' the Major said. 'He threatened it with fire and captivity, as I recall.'

'He doubtless had his reasons, sir,' Hakeswill said, his face jerking in its uncontrollable spasms, 'like I have mine. It's Sergeant Sharpe I'm after, sir.'

'Not here, Sergeant, alas. The place falls apart!'

'He's gone, sir?' Hakeswill demanded.

'Summoned away, Sergeant, by higher authority. Not my doing, not my doing at all. If it was up to me I'd keep Sharpe here for ever, but a Colonel McCandless demanded him and when colonels demand, mere majors comply. So far as I know, which isn't much, they went to join General Wellesley's forces.' The Major was now rummaging through a wooden chest. 'We had some fine augers, I know. Same ones we use on touch-holes. Not that we ever did. Haven't had to rebore a touch-hole yet.'

'McCandless, sir?'

'A Company colonel, but still a colonel. I'll need a round-file too, I suspect.'

'I knows Colonel McCandless, sir,' Hakeswill said gloomily. He had shared the Tippoo's dungeons with McCandless and Sharpe, and he knew the Scotsman disliked him. Which did not matter by itself, for Hakeswill did not like McCandless either, but the Scotsman was a colonel and, as Major Stokes had intimated, when colonels demand, other men obey. Colonel McCandless, Hakeswill decided, could be a problem. But a problem that could wait. The urgent need was to catch up with Sharpe. 'Do you have any convoys going north, sir? To the army, sir?'

'One leaves tomorrow,' Stokes said helpfully, 'carrying ammunition. But have you authority to travel?'

'I have authority, sir, I have authority.' Hakeswill touched the pouch where he kept the precious warrant. He was angry that Sharpe had gone, but knew there was little point in displaying the anger. The thing was to catch up with the quarry, and then God would smile on Obadiah Hakeswill's fortunes.

He explained as much to his detail of six men as they drank in one of Seringapatam's soldiers' taverns. So far the six men only knew that they were ordered to arrest Sergeant Sharpe, but Hakeswill had long worked out that he needed to share more information with his chosen men if they were to follow him enthusiastically, especially if they were to follow him northwards to where Wellesley was fighting the Mahrattas. Hakeswill considered them all good men, by which he meant that they were all cunning, violent and biddable, but he still had to make sure of their loyalty. 'Sharpie's rich,' he told them. 'Drinks when he likes, whores when he likes. He's rich.'

'He works in the stores,' Private Kendrick explained. 'Always on the fiddle, the stores.'

'And he never gets caught? He can't be fiddling that much,' Hakeswill said, his face twitching. 'You want to know the truth of Dick Sharpe? I'll tell you. He was the lucky bugger what caught the Tippoo at Seringapatam.'

''Course he weren't!' Flaherty said.

'So who was it?' Hakeswill challenged them. 'And why was Sharpie made up into a sergeant after the battle? He shouldn't be a sergeant! He ain't experienced.'

'He fought well. That's what Mister Lawford says.'

'Mister bloody Lawford,' Hakeswill said scathingly. 'Sharpie didn't get noticed for fighting well! Bleeding hell, boys, I'd be a major-general if that's all it took! No, it's my belief he paid his way up to the stripes.'

'Paid?' The privates stared at Hakeswill.

'Stands to reason. No other way. Says so in the scriptures! Bribes, boys, bribes, and I knows where he got the money. I know 'cos I followed him once. Here in Seringapatam. Down to the goldsmiths' street he went, and he did his business and after he done it I went to see the fellow he did it with. He didn't want to tell me what the business was, but I thumped him a bit, friendly like, and he showed me a ruby. Like this it was!' The Sergeant held a finger and thumb a quarter-inch apart. 'Sharpie was selling it, see? And where does Sharpie get a prime bit of glitter?'

'Off the Tippoo?' Kendrick said wonderingly.

'And do you know how much loot the Tippoo had? Weighed down with it, he was! Had more stones on him than a Christmas whore, and you know where those stones are?'

'Sharpe,' Flaherty breathed.

'Right, Private Flaherty,' Hakeswill said. 'Sewn into his uniform seams, in his boots, hidden in his pouches, tucked away in his hat. A bloody fortune, lads, which is why when we gets him, we don't want him to get back to the battalion, do we?'

The six men stared at Hakeswill. They knew they were his favourites, and all of them were in his debt, but now they realized he was giving them even more reason to be grateful. 'Equal shares, Sergeant?' Private Lowry asked.

'Equal shares?' Hakeswill exclaimed. 'Equal? Listen, you horrid toad, you wouldn't have no chance of any share, not one, if it wasn't for my loving kindness. Who chose you to come on this parish outing?'

'You did, Sergeant.'

'I did. I did. Kindness of my heart, and you repays it by wanting equal shares?' Hakeswill's face shuddered. 'I've half a mind to send you back, Lowry.' He looked aggrieved and the privates were silent. 'Ingratitude,' Hakeswill said in a hurt voice, 'sharp as a serpent's tooth, it is. Equal shares! Never heard the like! But I'll see you right, don't you worry.' He took out the precious orders for Sharpe's arrest and smoothed the paper on the table, carefully avoiding the spills of arrack. 'Look at that, boys,' he breathed, 'a fortune. Half for me, and you leprous toads get to share the other half. Equally.' He paused to prod Lowry in the chest. 'Equally. But I gets one half, like it says in the scriptures.' He folded the paper and put it carefully in his pouch. 'Shot while escaping,' Hakeswill said, and grinned. 'I've waited four years for this chance, lads, four bloody years.' He brooded for a few seconds. 'Put me in among the tigers, he did! Me! In a tigers' den!' His face contorted in a rictus at the memory. 'But they spared me, they spared me. And you know why? Because I can't die, lads! Touched by God, I am! Says so in the scriptures.'

The six privates were silent. Mad, he was, mad as a twitching hatter, and no one knew why hatters were mad either, but they were. Even the army was reluctant to recruit a hatter because they dribbled and twitched and talked to themselves, but they had taken on Hakeswill and he had survived; malevolent, powerful and apparently indestructible. Sharpe had put him among the Tippoo's tigers, yet the tigers were dead and Hakeswill still breathed. He was a bad man to have as an enemy, and now the piece of paper in Hakeswill's pouch put Sharpe into his power and Obadiah could taste the money already. A fortune. All that was needed was to travel north, join the army, produce the warrant and skin the victim. Obadiah shuddered. The money was so near he could almost spend it already. 'Got him,' he said to himself, 'got him. And I'll piss on his rotten corpse, I will. Piss on it good. That'll learn him.'

The seven men left Seringapatam in the morning, travelling north.

CHAPTER 5

Sharpe was curiously relieved when Colonel McCandless found him next morning, for the mood in the small upper rooms was awkward. Simone seemed ashamed by what had happened in the night and, when Sharpe tried to speak to her, she shook her head abruptly and would not meet his eye. She did try to explain to him, mumbling about the arrack and the jewels, and about her disappointment in marriage, but she could not frame her words in adequate English, though no language was needed to show that she regretted what had happened, which was why Sharpe was glad to hear McCandless's voice in the alley beyond the staircase. 'I thought I told you to let me know where you were!' McCandless complained when Sharpe appeared at the top of the steps.

'I did, sir,' Sharpe lied. 'I told an ensign of the 78th to find you, sir.'

'He never arrived!' McCandless said as he climbed the outside stairs. 'Are you telling me you spent the night alone with this woman, Sergeant?'

'You told me to protect her, sir.'

'I didn't tell you to risk her honour! You should have sought me out.'

'Didn't want to bother you, sir.'

'Duty is never a bother, Sharpe,' McCandless said when he reached the small balcony at the stair head. 'The General expressed a wish to dine with Madame Joubert and I had to explain she was indisposed. I lied, Sharpe!' The Colonel thrust an indignant finger at Sharpe's chest. 'But what else could I do? I could hardly admit I'd left her alone with a sergeant!'

'I'm sorry, sir.'

'There's no harm done, I suppose,' McCandless said grudgingly, then took off his hat as he followed Sharpe into the living room where Simone sat at the table. 'Good morning, Madame,' the Colonel boomed cheerfully. 'I trust you slept well?'

'Indeed, Colonel,' Simone said, blushing, but McCandless was far too obtuse to see or to interpret the blush.

'I have good news, Madame,' the Scotsman went on. 'General Wellesley is agreeable that you should rejoin your husband. There is, however, a difficulty.' It was McCandless's turn to blush. 'I can provide no chaperone, Madame, and you do not possess a maid. I assure you that you may rely utterly upon my honour, but your husband might object if you lack a female companion on the journey.'

'Pierre will have no objection, Colonel,' Simone said meekly.

'And I warrant Sergeant Sharpe will behave like a gentleman,' McCandless said with a fierce look at Sharpe.

'He does, Colonel, he does,' Simone said, offering Sharpe a very shy glance.

'Good!' McCandless said, relieved to be done with such a delicate topic. He slapped his cocked hat against his leg. 'No rain again,' he declared, 'and I dare say it'll be a hot day. You can be ready to ride in an hour, Madame?'

'In less, Colonel.'

'One hour will suffice, Madame. You will do me the honour, perhaps, of meeting me by the north gate? I'll have your horse ready, Sharpe.'

They left promptly, riding northwards past the battery that had been dug to hammer the fort's big walls. The battery's four guns were mere twelve-pounders, scarce big enough to dent the fort's wall, let alone break it down, but General Wellesley reckoned the garrison would be so disheartened by the city's swift defeat that even a few twelve-pound shots might persuade them into surrender. The four guns had opened fire at dawn, but their firing was sporadic until McCandless led his party out of the city when they suddenly all fired at once and Simone's horse, startled by the unexpected noise, skittered sideways. Simone rode side-saddle just behind the Colonel, while Sevajee and his men brought up the rear. Sharpe was wearing boots at last; the tall red leather boots with steel spurs that he had dragged from the body of an Arab.

He glanced back as they rode away. He saw the huge jet of smoke burst from a twelve-pounder's muzzle and a second later heard the percussive thump of the exploding charge and, just as that sound faded, a crack as the ball struck the wall of the fort. Then the other three guns fired and he imagined the steam hissing into the air as the gunners poured water on the overheated barrels. The fort's red walls blossomed with smoke as the defenders' cannon replied, but the pioneers had dug the gunners a deep battery and protected it with a thick wall of red earth, and the enemy's fire wasted itself in those defences. Then Sharpe rode past a grove of trees and the distant fight was hidden and the sound of the guns grew fainter and fainter as they rode farther north until, at last, the sound of the cannonade was a mere grumbling on the horizon. Then they dropped down the escarpment and the noise of the guns faded away altogether.

It was a disconsolate expedition. Colonel McCandless had nothing to say to Simone who was still withdrawn. Sharpe tried to cheer her up, but his clumsy attempts only made her more miserable and after a time he too fell silent. Women were a mystery, he thought. During the night Simone had

145

clung to him as though she were drowning, but since the dawn it had seemed as if she would prefer to be drowned.

'Horsemen on our right, Sergeant!' McCandless said, his tone a reproof that Sharpe had not spotted the cavalry first. 'Probably ours, but they could be enemy.'

Sharpe stared eastwards. 'They're ours, sir,' he called, kicking his horse to catch up with McCandless. One of the distant horsemen carried the new Union flag and Sharpe's good eyes had spotted the banner. The flag was easier to recognize at a distance these days, for since the incorporation of Ireland into the United Kingdom a new red diagonal cross had been added to the flag, and though the new-fangled design looked odd and unfamiliar, it did make the banner stand out.

The cavalry left a plume of dust as they rode to intercept McCandless's party. Sevajee and his men cantered to meet them and Sharpe saw the two groups of horsemen greet each other warmly. The strangers turned out to be *brindarries* from the Mahratta states who, like Sevajee, had sided with the British against Scindia. These mercenaries were under the command of a British officer and, like Sevajee's men, they carried lances, *tulwars*, matchlock guns, flintlocks, pistols and bows and arrows. They wore no uniform, but a handful of the sixty men possessed breastplates and most had metal helmets that were crested with feathers or horsehair plumes. Their officer, a dragoon captain, fell in alongside McCandless and reported seeing a white-coated battalion on the far side of the River Godavery. 'I didn't try and cross, sir,' the Captain said, 'for they weren't exactly friendly.'

'But you're sure they had white coats?'

'No doubts at all, sir,' the Captain said, thus confirming that Dodd must have crossed the river already. He added that he had questioned some grain merchants who had travelled south across the Godavery and those men had told him that Pohlmann's *compoo* was camped close to Aurungabad.

That city belonged to Hyderabad, but the merchants had seen no evidence that the Mahrattas were preparing to besiege the city walls. The Captain tugged his reins, turning his horse southwards so he could carry his news to Wellesley. 'Bid you good day, Colonel. Your servant, Ma'am.' The dragoon officer touched his hat to Simone, then led his brigands away.

McCandless decreed that they would camp that night on the south bank of the River Godavery where Sharpe rigged two horse blankets as a tent for Simone. Sevajee and his men made their beds on the bluff above the river, a score of yards from the tent, and McCandless and Sharpe spread their blankets alongside. The river was high, but it had still not filled the steep-sided ravine that successive monsoons had scarred into the flat earth and Sharpe guessed that the river was only at half flood. If the belated monsoon did arrive the Godavery would swell into a swirling torrent a full quarter-mile wide, but even half full the river looked a formidable obstacle as it surged westwards with its burden of flotsam. 'Too deep to wade,' McCandless said as the sun fell.

'Current looks strong, sir.'

'It'll sweep you to your death, man.'

'So how's the army to cross it, sir?'

'With difficulty, Sharpe, with difficulty, but discipline always overcomes difficulty. Dodd got across, so we surely can.' McCandless had been reading his Bible, but the falling dark now obscured the pages and so he closed the book. Simone had eaten with them, but she had been uncommunicative and McCandless was glad when she withdrew behind her blankets. 'Women upset matters,' the Scotsman said unhappily.

'They do, sir?'

'Perturbations,' McCandless said mysteriously, 'perturbations.' The small flames of the campfire made his already gaunt face seem skeletal. He shook his head. 'It's the heat, Sharpe, I'm convinced of it. The further south you travel, the more sin is provoked among womankind. It makes sense, of course. Hell is a hot place, and hell is sin's destination.'

'So you think that heaven's cold, sir?'

'I like to think it's bracing,' the Colonel answered seriously. 'Something like Scotland, I imagine. Certainly not as hot as India, and the heat here has a very bad effect on some women. It releases things in them.' He paused, evidently deciding he risked saying too much. 'I'm not at all convinced India is a place for European women,' the Colonel went on, 'and I shall be very glad when we're rid of Madame Joubert. Still, I can't deny that her predicament is propitious. It enables us to take a look at Lieutenant Dodd.'

Sharpe poked a half-burned scrap of driftwood into the hottest part of the fire, provoking an updraught of sparks. 'Are you hoping to capture Lieutenant Dodd, sir? Is that why we're taking Madame back to her husband?'

McCandless shook his head. 'I doubt we'll get the chance, Sharpe. No, we're using a heaven-sent opportunity to take a look at our enemy. Our armies are marching into dangerous territory, for no place in India can raise armies the size of the Mahratta forces, and we are precious few in number. We need intelligence, Sharpe, so when we reach them, watch and pray! Keep your eyes skinned. How many battalions? How many guns? What's the state of the guns? How many limbers? Look hard at the infantry. Matchlocks or firelocks? In a month or so we'll be fighting these rogues, so the more we know of them the better.' The Colonel scuffed earth onto the fire, dousing the last small flames that Sharpe had just provoked. 'Now sleep, man. You'll be needing all your strength and wits in the morning.'

Next morning they rode downstream until they found a village next to a vast empty Hindu temple, and in the village were small basket boats that resembled Welsh coracles and McCandless hired a half-dozen of these as ferries. The unsaddled horses were made to swim behind the boats. It was a perilous crossing, for the brown current snatched at the light vessels and whirled them downstream. The horses, white-eyed, swam desperately behind the reed boats that Sharpe noted had no caulking of any kind, but depended on skilful close weaving to keep the water out, and the tug of the horses' leading reins strained the light wooden frames and stretched the weave so that the boats let in water alarmingly. Sharpe used his shako to bail out his coracle, but the boatmen just grinned at his futile efforts and dug their paddles in harder. Once a half-submerged tree almost speared Sharpe's boat, and if the trunk had struck them the boat must surely have been tipped over, but the two boatmen skilfully spun the coracle away, let the tree pass, then paddled on.

It took half an hour to land and saddle the horses. Simone had shared a coracle with McCandless and the brief voyage had soaked the bottom half of her thin linen dress so that the damp weave clung to her legs. McCandless was embarrassed, and offered her a horse blanket for modesty's sake, but Simone shook her head. 'Where do we go now, Colonel?' she asked.

'Towards Aurungabad, Ma'am,' McCandless said gruffly, keeping his eyes averted from her beguiling figure, 'but doubtless we shall be intercepted long before we reach that city. You'll be with your husband by tomorrow night, I don't doubt.'

Sevajee's men rode far ahead now, spread into a picquet line to give warning of any enemy. This land all belonged to the Rajah of Hyderabad, an ally of the British, but it was frontier land and the only friendly troops now north of the Godavery were the garrisons of Hyderabad's isolated fortresses. The rest were all Mahrattas, though Sharpe saw no enemies that day. The only people he saw were peasants cleaning out the irrigation channels in their stubble fields or tending the huge brick kilns that smoked in the sunlight. The brick-workers were all women and children, greasy and sweaty, who gave the travellers scarcely a glance. 'It's a hard life,' Simone said to Sharpe as they passed one half-built kiln where an overseer lazed under a woven canopy and shouted at the children to work faster.

'All life's hard unless you've got money,' Sharpe said, grateful that Simone had at last broken her silence. They were riding a few paces behind the Colonel and kept their voices low so he could not hear them.

'Money and rank,' Simone said.

'Rank?' Sharpe asked.

'They're usually the same thing,' Simone said. 'Colonels are richer than captains, are they not?' And captains are generally richer than sergeants, Sharpe thought, but he said nothing. Simone touched the pouch at her waist. 'I should give you back your diamonds.'

'Why?'

'Because . . .' she said, but then fell silent for a while. 'I do not want you to think . . .' she tried again, but the words would not come.

Sharpe smiled at her. 'Nothing happened, love,' he told her. 'That's what you say to your husband. Nothing happened, and you found the diamonds on a dead body.'

'He will want me to give them to him. For his family.'

'Then don't tell him.'

'He is saving money,' Simone explained, 'so his family can live without work.'

'We all want that. Dream of life without work, we do. That's why we all want to be officers.'

'And I think to myself,' she went on as if Sharpe had not spoken, 'what shall I do? I cannot stay here in India. I must go to France. We are like ships, Sergeant, who look for a safe harbour.'

'And Pierre is safe?'

'He is safe,' Simone said bleakly, and Sharpe understood what she had been thinking for the last two days. He could offer her no security, while her husband could, and although she found Pierre's world stultifying, she was terrified by the alternative. She had dared taste that alternative for one night, but now shied away from it. 'You do not think badly of me?' she asked Sharpe anxiously.

'I'm probably half in love with you,' Sharpe told her, 'so how can I think badly of you?'

She seemed relieved, and for the rest of that day she chattered happily enough. McCandless questioned her closely about Dodd's regiment, how it had been trained and how it was equipped, and though she had taken scant interest in such things, her replies satisfied the Colonel who pencilled notes in a small black book.

They slept that night in a village, and next day rode even more warily. 'When we meet the enemy, Sharpe,' McCandless advised him, 'keep your hands away from your weapon.'

'Yes, sir.'

'Give a Mahratta one excuse to think you're hostile,' the Colonel said cheerfully, 'and he'll use you as an archery butt. They don't make decent heavy horsemen, but as raiders they're unsurpassed. They attack in swarms, Sharpe. A horde of horsemen. Like watching a storm approach. Nothing but dust and the shine of swords. Magnificent!'

'You like them, sir?' Sharpe asked.

'I like the wild, Sharpe,' McCandless said fiercely. 'We've tamed ourselves at home, but out here a man still lives by his weapon and his wits. I shall miss that when we've imposed order.'

'So why tame it, sir?'

'Because it is our duty, Sharpe. God's duty. Trade, order, law, and Christian decency, that's our business.' McCandless was gazing ahead to where a patch of misty white hung just above the northern horizon. It was dust kicked into the air, and maybe it was nothing more than a herd of cattle or a flock of sheep, but the dust smear grew and suddenly Sevajee's men veered sharply away to the west and galloped out of sight.

'Are they running out on us, sir?' Sharpe asked.

'The enemy will likely enough treat you and me with respect, Sharpe,' McCandless said, 'but Sevajee cannot expect courtesy from them. They'd regard him as a traitor and execute him on the spot. We'll meet up with him when we've delivered Madame Joubert to her husband. He and I have arranged a rendezvous.'

The dust cloud drew nearer and Sharpe saw a sliver of reflected sunlight glint in the whiteness and he knew he was seeing the first sign of McCandless's magnificent wild horsemen. The storm was coming.

The Mahratta cavalrymen had spread into a long line as they approached McCandless's small party. There were, Sharpe guessed, two hundred or more of the horsemen and, as they drew nearer, the flanks of their line quickened to form a pair of horns that would encircle their prey. McCandless feigned not to notice the threat, but kept riding gently ahead while the wild horns streamed past in a flurry of dust and noise.

They were, Sharpe noticed, small men on small horses. British cavalry were bigger and their horses were heavier, but these nimble horsemen still looked effective enough. The curved blades of their drawn *tulwars* glittered like their plumed helmets which rose to a sharp point decorated with a crest. Some of the crests were horse-tails, some vultures' feathers and some just brightly coloured ribbons. More ribbons were woven into their horses' plaited manes or were tied to the horn tips of the archers' bows. The horsemen pounded past McCandless, then turned with a swerve, a slew of choking dust, a skid of hooves, a jangle of curb chains and the thump of scabbarded weapons.

The Mahratta leader confronted McCandless who pretended to be surprised to find his path blocked, but nevertheless greeted the enemy with an elaborate and confident courtesy. The cavalry commander was a wildly bearded man with a scarred cheek, a wall eye and lank hair that hung far below his helmet's cloth-rimmed edge. He held his *tulwar* menacingly, but McCandless ignored the blade's threat, indeed he ignored most of what the enemy commander said, and instead boomed his own demands in a voice that showed not the least nervousness. The Scotsman towered over the smaller horsemen and, because he seemed to regard his presence among them as entirely natural, they meekly accepted his version of what was happening. 'I have demanded that they escort us to Pohlmann,' the Scotsman informed Sharpe.

'They probably planned on doing that anyway, sir.'

'Of course they did, but it's far better that I should demand it than that they should impose it,' McCandless said and then, with a lordly gesture, he gave permission for the Mahratta chief to lead the way and the enemy dutifully formed themselves into an escort either side of the three Europeans. 'Fine-looking beggars, are they not?' McCandless asked.

'Wicked, sir.'

'But sadly out of date.'

'They could fool me, sir,' Sharpe said, for though many of the Mahratta horsemen carried weapons that might have been more usefully employed at Agincourt or Crécy than in modern India, all had firelocks in their saddle holsters and all had savagely curved *tulwars*.

McCandless shook his head. 'They may be the finest light

horsemen in the world, but they won't press a charge home and they can't stand volley fire. There's rarely any need to form square against men like these, Sharpe. They're fine for picquet work, unrivalled at pursuit, but chary of dying in front of the guns.'

'Can you blame them?' Simone asked.

'I don't blame them, Madame,' McCandless said, 'but if a horse can't stand fire, then it's of scant use in battle. You don't gain victories by rattling across country like a pack of hunters, but by enduring the enemy's fire and overcoming it. That's where a soldier earns his pay, hard under the enemy muzzles.'

And that, Sharpe thought, was something he had never really done. He had faced the French in Flanders years before, but those battles had been fleeting and rain-obscured, and the lines had never closed on each other. He had not stared at the whites of the enemy's eyes, heard his volleys and returned them. He had fought at Malavelly, but that battle had been one volley and a charge, and the enemy had not contested the day, but fled, while at Seringapatam Sharpe had been spared the horror of going through the breach. One day, he realized, he would have to stand in a battle line and endure the volleys, and he wondered whether he would stand or instead break in terror. Or whether he would even live to see a battle, for, despite McCandless's blithe confidence, there was no assurance that he would survive this visit to the enemy's encampment.

They reached Pohlmann's army that evening. The camp was a short march south of Aurungabad and it was visible from miles away because of the great smear of smoke that hung in the sky. Most of the campfires were burning dried cakes of bullock dung and the acrid smoke caught in Sharpe's throat as he trotted through the lines of infantry shelters. It all looked much like a British camp, except that most of the tents were made from reed matting rather than canvas, but the lines were still neatly arrayed, muskets were carefully stacked in threes and a disciplined ring of picquets guarded the camp's perimeter. They passed some European officers exercising their horses, and one of those men spurred to intercept the newcomers. He ignored McCandless and Sharpe, raising his plumed hat to Simone instead. '*Bonsoir, Madame.*'

Simone did not look at the man, but just tapped her horse's rump with her riding crop. 'That fellow's French, sir,' Sharpe said to McCandless.

'I do speak the language, Sergeant,' the Colonel said.

'So what's a Frog doing here, sir?'

'The same as Lieutenant Dodd, Sharpe. Teaching Scindia's infantry how to fight.'

'Don't they know how to fight, sir? Thought it came natural.'

'They don't fight as we do,' McCandless said, watching the rebuffed Frenchman canter away.

'How's that, sir?'

'The European, Sergeant, has learned to close the gap fast. The closer you are to a man, the more likely you are to kill him; however, the closer you get, the more likely you are to be killed, but it's no use entertaining that fear in battle. Get up close, hold your ranks and start killing, that's the trick of it. But given a chance an Indian will hold back and try to kill at long range, and fellows like Dodd are teaching them how to close the gap hard and fast. You need discipline for that, discipline and tight ranks and good sergeants. And no doubt he's teaching them how to use cannon as well.' The Colonel spoke sourly, for they were trotting beside an artillery park that was crammed with heavy cannon. The guns looked odd to Sharpe, for many of them had been cast with ornate patterns on their barrels, and some were even painted in

155

gaudy colours, but they were neatly parked and all had limbers and full sets of equipment; rammers and wormscrews
and handspikes and buckets. The axles gleamed with grease
and there was not a spot of rust to be seen on the long barrels.
Someone knew how to maintain guns, and that suggested
they also knew how to use them. 'Counting them, Sharpe?'
McCandless asked abruptly.

'No, sir.'

'Seventeen in that park, mostly nine-pounders, but there
are some much heavier brutes at the back. Keep your eyes
open, man. That's why we're here.'

'Yes, sir, of course, sir.'

They passed a line of tethered camels, then a compound
where a dozen elephants were being brought their supper of
palm leaves and butter-soaked rice. Children followed the
men carrying the rice to scavenge what slopped from the
pails. Some of the Mahratta escort had spurred ahead to
spread news of the visitors and curious crowds gathered to
watch as McCandless and his two companions rode still
deeper into the huge encampment. Those crowds became
thicker as they drew close to the camp's centre which was
marked by a spread of large tents. One of the tents was made
of blue-and-yellow-striped canvas, and in front of it were twin
flagpoles, though the wind was slack and the brightly coloured
banners just hung from their tall poles. 'Leave the talking to
me,' McCandless ordered Sharpe.

'Of course, sir.'

Simone suddenly gasped. Sharpe turned and saw she was
staring across the heads of the curious crowd towards a group
of European officers. She looked at Sharpe suddenly and he
saw the sadness in her eyes. She gave him a half-smile.
'Pierre,' she offered in brief explanation, then she shrugged
and tapped her horse with her crop so that it hurried away
from Sharpe. Her husband, a small man in a white coat,

gazed in disbelief, then ran to meet her with a look of pleasure on his face. Sharpe felt oddly jealous of him.

'That's our main duty discharged,' McCandless said happily. 'A disobliging woman, I thought.'

'Unhappy, sir.'

'Doesn't have enough to keep her busy, that's why. The devil likes idle hands, Sharpe.'

'Then he must hate me, sir, most of the time.' He stared after Simone, watching as she slid down from the saddle and was embraced by her shorter husband. Then the crowds hid the couple from him. Someone shouted an insult at the two British horsemen and the other spectators jeered or laughed, but Sharpe, despite their hostility, took some consolation from McCandless's confidence. The Scotsman, indeed, was in a happier mood than he had shown for days, for he revelled being in his enemy's lines.

A group of men emerged from the big striped tent. They were almost all Europeans, and in their forefront was a tall muscled man in shirtsleeves who was attended by a bodyguard of Indian soldiers wearing purple coats. 'That's Colonel Pohlmann,' McCandless said, nodding towards the big red-faced man.

'The fellow who used to be a sergeant, sir?'

'That's him.'

'You've met him, sir?'

'Once, a couple of years back. He's an affable sort of man, Sharpe, but I doubt he's trustworthy.'

If Pohlmann was surprised to see a British officer in his camp, he did not show it. Instead he spread his arms in an expansive gesture of welcome. 'Are you new recruits?' he shouted in greeting.

McCandless did not bother to answer the mocking question, but just slid from his horse. 'You don't remember me, Colonel?'

'Of course I remember you,' Pohlmann said with a smile. 'Colonel Hector McCandless, once of His Majesty's Scotch Brigade, and now in the service of the East India Company. How could I forget you, Colonel? You tried to make me read the Bible.' Pohlmann grinned, displaying tobacco-stained teeth. 'But you haven't answered my question, Colonel. Have you come to join our army?'

'I am the merest emissary, Colonel,' McCandless said, beating dust from the kilt that he had insisted on wearing in honour of meeting the enemy. The garment was causing some amusement to Pohlmann's companions, though they took care not to let their smiles show if McCandless glanced their way. 'I brought you a woman,' McCandless added in explanation.

'How do you say in England, Colonel,' Pohlmann asked with a puzzled frown, 'coals to Newcastle?'

'I offered safe conduct to Madame Joubert,' the Scotsman said stiffly.

'So that was Simone I saw riding past,' Pohlmann said. 'I did wonder. And she'll be welcome, I dare say. We have enough of everything in this army: cannon, muskets, horses, ammunition, men, but there can never really be enough women in any army, can there?' He laughed, then summoned two of his purple-coated bodyguards to take charge of the horses. 'You've ridden a long way, Colonel,' Pohlmann said to McCandless, 'so let me offer you refreshment. You too, Sergeant,' he included Sharpe in his invitation. 'You must be tired.'

'I'm sore after that ride, sir,' Sharpe said, dropping clumsily and gratefully from the saddle.

'You're not used to horses, eh?' Pohlmann crossed to Sharpe and draped a genial arm about his shoulders. 'You're an infantryman, which means you've got hard feet and a soft bum. Me, I never like being on a horse. You know how I go to battle? On an elephant. That's the way to do it, Sergeant. What's your name?'

'Sharpe, sir.'

'Then welcome to my headquarters, Sergeant Sharpe. You're just in time for supper.' He steered Sharpe into the tent, then stopped to let his guests stare at the lavish interior which was carpeted with soft rugs, hung with silk drapes, lit with ornate brass chandeliers and furnished with intricately carved tables and couches. McCandless scowled at such luxury, but Sharpe was impressed. 'Not bad, eh?' Pohlmann squeezed Sharpe's shoulders. 'For a former sergeant.'

'You, sir?' Sharpe asked, pretending not to know Pohlmann's history.

'I was a sergeant in the East India Company's Hanoverian Regiment,' Pohlmann boasted, 'quartered in a rathole in Madras. Now I command a king's army and have all these powdered fops to serve me.' He gestured at his attendant officers who, accustomed to Pohlmann's insults, smiled tolerantly. 'Need a piss, Sergeant?' Pohlmann asked, taking his arm from Sharpe's shoulders. 'A wash?'

'Wouldn't mind both, sir.'

'Out the back.' He pointed the way. 'Then come back and drink with me.'

McCandless had watched this bonhomie with suspicion. He had also smelt the reek of strong liquor on Pohlmann's breath and suspected he was doomed to an evening of hard drinking in which, even though McCandless himself would refuse all alcohol, he would have to endure the drunken badinage of others. It was a grim prospect, and one he did not intend to endure alone. 'Not you, Sharpe,' he hissed when Sharpe returned to the tent.

'Not me what, sir?'

'You're to stay sober, you hear me? I'm not mollycoddling your sore head all the way back to the army.'

'Of course not, sir,' Sharpe said, and for a time he tried to obey McCandless, but Pohlmann insisted Sharpe join him in a toast before supper.

'You're not an abstainer, are you?' Pohlmann demanded of Sharpe in feigned horror when the Sergeant tried to refuse a beaker of brandy. 'You're not a Bible-reading abstainer, are you? Don't tell me the British army is becoming moral!'

'No, sir, not me, sir.'

'Then drink with me to King George of Hanover and of England!'

Sharpe obediently drank to the health of their joint sovereign, then to Queen Charlotte, and those twin courtesies emptied his beaker of brandy and a serving girl was summoned to fill it so that he could toast His Royal Highness George, Prince of Wales.

'You like the girl?' Pohlmann asked, gesturing at the serving girl who swerved lithely away from a French major who was trying to seize her sari.

'She's pretty, sir,' Sharpe said.

'They're all pretty, Sergeant. I keep a dozen of them as wives, another dozen as servants, and God knows how many others who merely aspire to those positions. You look shocked, Colonel McCandless.'

'A man who dwells among the tents of the ungodly,' McCandless said, 'will soon pick up ungodly ways.'

'And thank God for it,' Pohlmann retorted, then clapped his hands to summon the supper dishes.

A score of officers ate in the tent. Half a dozen were Mahrattas, the rest Europeans, and just after the bowls and platters had been placed on the tables, Major Dodd arrived. Night was falling and candles illuminated the tent's shadowed interior, but Sharpe recognized Dodd's face instantly. The sight of the long jaw, sallow skin and bitter eyes brought back sharp memories of Chasalgaon, of flies crawling on Sharpe's eyes and in his gullet, and of the staccato bangs as men stepped over the dead to shoot the wounded. Dodd, oblivious of Sharpe's glare, nodded to Pohlmann. 'I apologize, Colonel Pohlmann, for being late,' he announced with stiff formality.

'I expected Captain Joubert to be late,' Pohlmann said, 'for a man newly reunited with his wife has better things to do than hurry to his supper, if indeed he takes his supper at all. Were you also welcoming Simone, Major?'

'I was not, sir. I was attending to the picquets.'

'Major Dodd's attention to his duty puts us all to shame,' Pohlmann said. 'Do you have the pleasure of knowing Major Dodd, Colonel?' he asked McCandless.

'I know the Company will pay five hundred guineas for Lieutenant Dodd's capture,' McCandless growled, 'and more now, I dare say, after his bestiality at Chasalgaon.'

Dodd showed no reaction to the Colonel's hostility, but Pohlmann smiled. 'You've come for the reward money, Colonel, is that it?'

'I wouldn't touch the money,' McCandless said, 'for it's tainted by association. Tainted by murder, Colonel, and by disloyalty and dishonour.'

The words were spoken to Pohlmann, but addressed to Dodd whose face seemed to tighten as he listened. He had taken a place at the end of the table and was helping himself to the food. The other guests were silent, intrigued by the tension between McCandless and Dodd. Pohlmann was enjoying the confrontation. 'You say Major Dodd is a murderer, Colonel?'

'A murderer and a traitor.'

Pohlmann looked down the table. 'Major Dodd? You have nothing to say?'

Dodd reached for a loaf of flat bread that he tore in half. 'When I had the misfortune to serve in the Company, Colonel,' he said to Pohlmann, 'Colonel McCandless was

well known as the head of intelligence. He did the dishonour-
able job of spying on the Company's enemies, and I've no
doubt that is his purpose here. He can spit all he likes, but
he's here to spy, Colonel.'

Pohlmann smiled. 'Is that true, McCandless?'

'I returned Madame Joubert to her husband, Pohlmann,
nothing more,' McCandless insisted.

'Of course it's more,' Pohlmann said. 'Major Dodd is right!
You're head of the Company's intelligence service, are you
not? Which means that you saw in dear Simone's predicament
a chance to inspect our army.'

'You infer too much,' McCandless said.

'Nonsense, Colonel. Do try the lamb. It's seethed in milk
curds. So what do you wish to see?'

'My bed,' McCandless said curtly, waving away the lamb
dish. He never touched meat. 'Just my bed,' he added.

'And see it you shall,' Pohlmann said genially. The Hanoverian paused, wondering whether to re-ignite the hostility
between McCandless and Dodd, but he must have decided
that each had insulted the other sufficiently. 'But tomorrow,
Colonel, I will provide a tour of inspection for you. You
may see whatever you like, McCandless. You can watch our
gunners at work, you may inspect our infantry, you may go
wherever you wish and talk to whoever you desire. We have
nothing to hide.' He smiled at the astonished McCandless.
'You are my guest, Colonel, so I must show you a proper
hospitality.'

He was as good as his word, and next morning McCandless
was invited to inspect all of Pohlmann's *compoo*. 'I wish there
were more troops here,' Pohlmann said, 'but Scindia is a few
miles northwards with Saleur's and Dupont's *compoos*. I
like to think they're not as able as mine, but in truth they're
both very good units. Both have European officers, of course,
and both are properly trained. I can't say as much for the

Rajah of Berar's infantry, but his gunners are the equal of ours.'

McCandless said very little all morning, and Sharpe, who had learned to read the Scotsman's moods, saw that he was severely discomfited. And no wonder, for Pohlmann's troops looked as fine as any in the Company's service. The Hanoverian commanded six and a half thousand infantry, five hundred cavalry and as many pioneers who served as engineers, and possessed thirty-eight guns. This *compoo* alone outnumbered the infantry of Wellesley's army, and was much stronger in guns, and there were two similar *compoos* in Scindia's service, let alone his horde of cavalry. It was no surprise, Sharpe thought, that McCandless's spirits were falling, and they fell even further when Pohlmann arranged for a demonstration of his artillery and the Scotsman, feigning gratitude to his host, was forced to watch as teams of gunners served a battery of big eighteen-pounder guns with all the alacrity and efficiency of the British army.

'Well-made pieces, too,' Pohlmann boasted, leading McCandless up to the hot guns that stood behind the swathes of burnt grass caused by their muzzle fire. 'A little gaudy, perhaps, for European tastes, but none the worse for that.' The guns were all painted in bright colours and some had names written in a curly script on their breeches. '*Megawati*,' Pohlmann read aloud, 'the goddess of clouds. Inspect them, Colonel! They're well made. Our axletrees don't break, I can assure you.'

Pohlmann was willing to show McCandless even more, but after dinner the Scotsman elected to spend the afternoon in his borrowed tent. He claimed he wished to rest, but Sharpe suspected the Scotsman had endured enough humiliation and wanted some quiet in which to make notes on all he had seen. 'We'll leave tonight, Sharpe,' the Colonel said. 'You can occupy yourself till then?'

'Colonel Pohlmann wants me to ride with him on his elephant, sir.'

The Colonel scowled. 'He likes to show off.' For a moment he seemed about to order Sharpe to refuse the invitation, then he shrugged. 'Don't get seasick.'

The motion of the elephant's howdah was indeed something like a ship, for it swayed from side to side as the beast plodded northwards and at first Sharpe had to grip onto the edge of the basket, but once he had accustomed himself to the motion he relaxed and leaned back on the cushioned seat. The howdah had two seats, one in front of the other, and Sharpe had the rearmost, but after a while Pohlmann twisted in his seat and showed how he could raise his own backrest and lay it flat so that the whole howdah became one cushioned bed that could be concealed by the curtains that hung from the wicker-framed canopy. 'It's a fine place to bring a woman, Sergeant,' Pohlmann said as he restored the backrest to its upright position, 'but the girth straps broke once and the whole thing fell off! It fell slowly, luckily, and I still had my breeches on so not too much dignity was lost.'

'You don't look like a man who worries much about dignity, sir.'

'I worry about reputation,' Pohlmann said, 'which isn't the same thing. I keep my reputation by winning victories and giving away gold. Those men' – he gestured at his purple-coated bodyguards who marched on either flank of the elephant – 'are each paid as much as a lieutenant in British service. And as for my European officers!' He laughed. 'They're all making more money than they dreamed possible. Look at 'em!' He jerked his head at the score of European officers who followed the elephant. Dodd was among them, but riding apart from the others and with a morose expression on his long face as though he resented having to pay court to his commanding officer. His horse was a sway-backed, hard-mouthed mare, a poor beast as ungainly and sullen as her master. 'Greed, Sharpe, greed, that's the best motive for a soldier,' Pohlmann said. 'Greed will make them fight like demons, if our lord and master ever allows us to fight.'

'You think he won't, sir?'

Pohlmann grinned. 'Scindia listens to his astrologers rather more than he listens to his Europeans, but I'll slip the bastards some gold when the time comes, and they'll tell him the stars are propitious and he'll give me the whole army and let me loose.'

'How big is the whole army, sir?'

Pohlmann smiled, recognizing that Sharpe was asking questions on behalf of Colonel McCandless. 'By the time you face us, Sergeant, we should have over a hundred thousand men. And of those, fifteen thousand infantry are first class, thirty thousand infantry are reliable, and the rest are horsemen who are only good for plundering the wounded. We'll also have a hundred guns, all of them as good as any in Europe. And how big will your army be?'

'Don't know, sir,' Sharpe said woodenly.

Pohlmann smiled. 'Wellesley has, maybe, seven and a half thousand men, infantry and cavalry, while Colonel Stevenson has perhaps another seven thousand so together you'll number, what? Fourteen and a half thousand? With forty guns? You think fourteen thousand men can beat a hundred thousand? And what happens, Sergeant Sharpe, if I manage to catch one of your little armies before the other can support it?' Sharpe said nothing, and Pohlmann smiled. 'You should think about selling me your skills, Sharpe.'

'Me, sir?' Sharpe answered lightly.

'You, Sergeant Sharpe,' Pohlmann said forcibly, and the Hanoverian twisted in his seat to stare at Sharpe. 'That's why I invited you this afternoon. I need European officers, Sharpe, and any man as young as you who becomes a sergeant must have a rare ability. I am offering you rank and riches, Sharpe. Look at me! Ten years ago I was a sergeant like you. Now I ride to war on an elephant, need two more to carry my gold and have three dozen women competing to sharpen my sword. Have you ever heard of George Thomas?'

'No, sir.'

'An Irishman, Sergeant, and not even a soldier! George was an illiterate seaman out of the gutters of Dublin, and before he drank himself to death, poor man, he'd become the Begum Somroo's general. I think he was her lover too, though that ain't any distinction with that particular lady, but before he died George needed a whole herd of elephants to haul his gold about. And why? Because the Indian princes, Sergeant, need our skills. Equip yourself with a good European and you win your wars. I captured seventy-two guns at the battle of Malpura and I demanded the weight of one of those guns in pure gold as my reward. I got it, too. In ten years you could be as rich as you want, rich as Benoît de Boigne. You must have heard of him?'

'No, sir.'

'He was a Savoyard, Sergeant, and in just four years he made a hundred thousand pounds and then he went off home and married a seventeen-year-old girl fresh from her father's castle. In only four years! From being a captain in Savoy's army to being governor of half Scindia's territory. There's a fortune to be made here and rank and birth don't come into it. Only ability counts. Nothing but ability.' Pohlmann paused, his eyes on Sharpe. 'I'll make you a lieutenant tomorrow, Sergeant, and you can fight in my *compoo*, and if you're any damn good then you'll be a captain by month's end.' Sharpe looked at the Hanoverian, but said nothing. Pohlmann smiled. 'What are your chances of getting a commission in the British army?'

Sharpe grinned. 'No chance, sir.'

166

'So? I offer you rank, wealth and as many *bibbis* as you can handle.'

'Is that why Mister Dodd deserted, sir?'

Pohlmann smiled. 'Major Dodd deserted, Sharpe, because he faces execution for murder, and because he's sensible, and because he wants my job. Not that he'll admit to that.' The Hanoverian twisted in the howdah. 'Major Dodd!' he shouted.

The Major urged his awkward horse to the elephant's side and looked up into the howdah. 'Sir?'

'Sergeant Sharpe wants to know why you joined us.'

Dodd gave Sharpe a suspicious look, but then shrugged. 'I ran because there's no future in the Company,' he said. 'I was a lieutenant for twenty-two years, Sergeant, twenty-two years! It don't matter to the Company how good a soldier you are, you have to wait your turn, and all the while I watched wealthy young fools buying themselves majorities in the King's ranks and I had to bow and scrape to the useless bastards. Yes, sir, no, sir, three bloody bags full, sir, and can I carry your bags, sir, and wipe your arse, sir.' Dodd had been getting angrier and angrier as he spoke, but now made an effort to control himself. 'I couldn't join the King's army, Sergeant, because my father runs a grist mill in Suffolk and there ain't no money to buy a King's commission. That meant I was only fit for the Company, and King's officers treat Company men like dirt. I can outfight twenty of the bastards, but ability don't count in the Company. Keep your nose clean, wait your turn, then die for the shareholders when the Court of Directors tells you.' He was becoming angry again. 'That's why,' he finished curtly.

'And you, Sergeant?' Pohlmann asked. 'What opportunities will the army offer you?'

'Don't know, sir.'

'You do know,' Pohlmann said, 'you do know.' The

elephant had stopped and the Hanoverian now pointed ahead and Sharpe saw that they had come to the edge of a wood, and a half-mile away was a great city with walls like those the Scots had climbed at Ahmednuggur. The city walls were bright with flags, while its embrasures glinted with the reflection of sunlight from gun barrels. 'That's Aurungabad,' Pohlmann said, 'and everyone inside those walls is pissing themselves in fear that I'm about to start a siege.'

'But you're not?'

'I'm looking for Wellesley,' Pohlmann said, 'and you know why? Because I've never lost a battle, Sharpe, and I'm going to add a British major-general's sword to my trophies. Then I'll build myself a palace, a bloody great marble palace, and I'll line the halls with British guns and hang British colours to shield my bedroom from the sun and I'll bounce my *bibbis* on a mattress stuffed with the hair of British horses.' Pohlmann luxuriated in that dream for a while and then, with a last glance at the city, ordered the mahout to turn the elephant about. 'When is McCandless leaving?' he asked Sharpe.

'Tonight, sir.'

'After dark?'

'Around midnight, sir, I think.'

'That gives you plenty of time to think, Sergeant. To think of your future. To contemplate what the red coat offers you, and what I offer you. And when you have thought about those things, come to me.'

'I'm thinking on it, sir,' Sharpe said, 'I'm thinking on it.' And he was.

CHAPTER 6

Colonel McCandless excused himself from Pohlmann's supper, but did not forbid Sharpe to attend. 'But don't get drunk,' he warned the Sergeant, 'and be at my tent at midnight. I want to be back at the River Godavery by dawn.'

'Yes, sir,' Sharpe said dutifully, then went to Pohlmann's tent where most of the *compoo's* officers had gathered. Dodd was there, and so were a half-dozen wives of Pohlmann's European officers and among them was Simone Joubert, though there was no sign of her husband. 'He is in charge of the army picquets tonight,' Simone explained when Sharpe asked her, 'and Colonel Pohlmann invited me to eat.'

'He invited me to join his army,' Sharpe told her.

'He did?' Her eyes widened as she stared up from her chair. 'And will you?'

'It would mean I'd be close to you, Ma'am,' Sharpe said, 'and that's an inducement.'

Simone half smiled at the clumsy gallantry. 'I think you would not be a good soldier if you changed your loyalty for a woman, Sergeant.'

'He says I'll be an officer,' Sharpe said.

'And is that what you want?'

Sharpe squatted on his heels so that he could be closer to her. The other European wives saw him crouch and pursed their mouths with a disapproval born of envy, but Sharpe was oblivious of their gaze. 'I think I'd like to be an officer,

169

yes. And I can think of one very good reason to be an officer in this army.'

Simone blushed. 'I am a married woman, Sergeant. You know that.'

'But even married women need friends,' Sharpe said, and just then a large hand took unceremonious hold of his clubbed hair and hauled him to his feet.

Sharpe turned belligerently on whoever had manhandled him, then saw that it was a smiling Major Dodd. 'Can't have you stooping to women, Sharpe,' Dodd said before offering an ungainly bow to Simone. 'Good evening, Madame.'

'Major,' Simone acknowledged him coldly.

'You will forgive me, Madame, if I steal Sergeant Sharpe from you?' Dodd asked. 'I want a word with him. Come on, Sharpe.' He plucked Sharpe's arm, guiding him across the tent. The Major was very slightly drunk and evidently intent on becoming more drunk, for he snatched a whole jug of arrack from a servant, then scooped up two beakers from a table. 'Fancy Madame Joubert, do you?' he asked Sharpe.

'I like her well enough, sir.'

'She's spoken for, Sergeant. Remember that if you join us, she's spoken for.'

'You mean she's married, sir?'

'Married?' Dodd laughed, then poured the arrack and gave one beaker to Sharpe. 'How many European officers can you see here? And how many European women? And how many of them are young and pretty like Madame Joubert? Work it out, lad. And you're not jumping the queue.' Dodd smiled as he spoke, evidently meaning his tone to be jocular. 'But you are joining us, aren't you?'

'I'm thinking about it, sir.'

'You'll be in my regiment, Sharpe,' Dodd said. 'I need European officers. I've only got Joubert and he's no damn use, so I've spoken with Pohlmann and he says you can join my Cobras. I'll give you three companies of your own to look after, and God help you if they're not kept in prime condition. I like to look after the men, because come battle they look after you, but God help any officer who lets me down.' He paused to drink half his arrack and pour some more. 'I'll work you hard, Sharpe, I'll work you damned hard, but there'll be plenty of gold washing round this army once we've thrashed Boy Wellesley. Money's your reward, lad, money.'

'Is that why you're here, sir?'

'It's why we're all here, you fool. All except Joubert, who was posted here by his government and is too damned timid to help himself to Scindia's gold. So report to me in the morning. We're marching north tomorrow night, which means you'll have one day to learn my ropes and after that you're Mister Sharpe, gentleman. Come to me tomorrow morning, Sharpe, at dawn, and get rid of that damned red coat.' He poked Sharpe's chest hard. 'I see a red coat,' he went on, 'and I want to start killing.' He grinned, showing yellow teeth.

'Is that what happened at Chasalgaon, sir?' Sharpe asked.

Dodd's grin vanished. 'Why the hell do you ask that?' he growled.

Sharpe had asked because he had been remembering the massacre, and wondering if he could ever serve under a man who had ordered such a killing, but he said none of that. He shrugged instead. 'I heard tales, sir, but no one ever tells us anything proper. You know that, sir, so I just wondered what happened there.'

Dodd considered that answer for a moment, then shrugged. 'I didn't take prisoners, Sharpe, that's what happened. Killed the bastards to the last man.'

And to the last boy, Sharpe thought, remembering Davi Lal. He remained impassive, not letting a hint of memory or hate show. 'Why not take prisoners, sir?'

'Because it's war!' Dodd said vehemently. 'When men fight me, Sergeant, I want them to fear me, because that way the battle's half won before it's started. It ain't kind, I'm sure, but who ever said war was kind? And in this war, Sergeant' – he waved his hand towards the officers clustering about Colonel Pohlmann – 'it's dog eat dog. We're all in competition, and you know who'll win? The most ruthless, that's who. So what did I do at Chasalgaon? I made sure of a reputation, Sharpe. Made a name for myself. That's the first rule of war, Sergeant. Make the bastards fear you. And you know what the second rule is?'

'Don't ask questions, sir?'

Dodd grinned. 'No, lad, the second rule is never to reinforce failure, and the third, lad, is to look after your men. You know why I had that goldsmith thrashed? You've heard of that, haven't you? I'll tell you. It wasn't because he'd cheated me, which he did, but because he cheated some of my men. So I looked after them and let them give him a solid kicking, and the bastard died. Which he deserved to do, rich fat bastard that he was.' The Major turned and scowled at the servants bringing dishes from Pohlmann's cook tent. 'And they're just as bad here, Sharpe. Look at all that food! Enough to feed two regiments there, Sharpe, and the men are going hungry. No proper supply system, see? It costs money, that's why. You don't get issued food in this army, you go out and steal it.' He plainly disapproved. 'I've told Pohlmann, I have. Lay on a commissary, I said, but he won't, because it costs money. Scindia hoards food in his fortresses, but he won't issue it, not unless he's paid, and Pohlmann won't give up a penny of profit, so no food ever comes. It just rots in the warehouses while we have to keep moving, because after a week we've stripped one set of fields bare and have to go on to the next. It's no bloody way to run an army.'

'Maybe one day you'll change the system, sir,' Sharpe said.

'I will!' Dodd said vigorously. 'I bloody will! And if you've any sense, lad, you'll be here helping me. You learn one thing as a miller's son, Sergeant, and that's not just how to grind corn, but that a fool and his money are easily parted. And Scindia's a fool, but given a chance I'll make the bugger into the Emperor of India.' He turned as a servant beat a gong with a muffled stick. 'Time for our vittles.'

It was a strangely subdued supper, though Pohlmann did his best to amuse his company. Sharpe had tried to manoeuvre himself into a seat beside Simone, but Dodd and a Swedish captain beat him to it and Sharpe found himself next to a small Swiss doctor who spent the whole meal quizzing Sharpe about the religious arrangements in British regiments. 'Your chaplains are godly men, yes?'

'Drunken bastards, sir, most of them.'

'Surely not!'

'I hauled two of them out of a whorehouse not a month ago, sir. They didn't want to pay, see?'

'You are not telling me the truth!'

'God's honour, sir. The Reverend Mister Cooper was one of them, and it's a rare Sunday that he's sober. He preached a Christmas sermon at Easter, he was that puzzled.'

Most of the guests left early, Dodd among them, though a few diehards stayed on to give the Colonel a game of cards. Pohlmann grinned at Sharpe. 'You wager, Sharpe?'

'I'm not rich enough, sir.'

Pohlmann shook his head in mock exasperation at the answer. 'I will make you rich, Sharpe. You believe me?'

'I do, sir.'

'So you've made up your mind? You're joining me?'

'I still want to think a bit, sir.'

Pohlmann shrugged. 'You have nothing to think about. You either become a rich man or you die for King George.'

Sharpe left the remaining officers at their cards and walked away into the encampment. He really was thinking, or trying to think, and he sought a quiet place, but a crowd of soldiers were wagering on dog fights, and their cheers, as well as the yelps and snarls of the dogs, carried far through the darkness. Sharpe settled on an empty stretch of ground close to the picketed camels that carried Pohlmann's supply of rockets, and there he lay and stared up at the stars through the mist of smoke. A million stars. He had always thought there was an answer to all life's mysteries in the stars, yet whenever he stared at them the answer slipped out of his grasp. He had been whipped in the foundling home for staring at a clear night's sky through the workshop skylight. 'You ain't here to gawp at the dark, boy,' the overseer had snapped, 'you're here to labour,' and the whip had slashed down across his shoulders and he had dutifully looked down at the great tarry lump of hemp rope that had to be picked apart. The old ropes had been twisted and tightened and tarred into vast knots bigger than Sharpe himself, and they had been used as fenders on the London docks, but when the grinding and thumping of the big ships had almost worn the old fenders through they were sent to the foundling home to be picked apart so that the strands could be sold as furniture stuffing or to be mixed into wall plaster. 'Got to learn a trade, boy,' the master had told him again and again, and so Sharpe had learned a trade, but it was not hemp-picking. He learned the killing trade. Load a musket, ram a musket, fire a musket. And he had not done much of it, not yet, but he liked doing it. He remembered Malavelly, remembered firing the volley at the approaching enemy, and he remembered the sheer exultation as all his unhappiness and anger had been concentrated into his musket's barrel and been gouted out in one explosive rush of flame, smoke and lead.

He did not think of himself as unhappy. Not now. The army had been good to him in these last years, but there was still something wrong in his soul. What that was, he did not know, because Sharpe did not reckon he was any good at thinking. He was good at action, for whenever there was a problem to be solved Sergeant Sharpe could usually find the solution, but he was not much use at simply thinking. But he had to think now, and he stared at the smoke-dimmed stars in the hope that they would help him, but all they did was go on shining. Lieutenant Sharpe, he thought, and was surprised to realize that he saw nothing very odd in that idea. It was ridiculous, of course. Richard Sharpe, an officer? But somehow he could not shake the idea loose. It was a laughable idea, he tried to convince himself; at least in the British army it was, but not here. Not in Pohlmann's army, and Pohlmann had once been a sergeant. 'Bloody hell,' he said aloud, and a camel belched in answer.

The cheers of the spectators greeted the death of a dog, and, nearer, a soldier was playing one of the strange Indian instruments, plucking its long strings to make a sad, plangent music. In the British camp, Sharpe thought, they would be singing, but no one was singing here. They were too hungry, though hunger did not stop a man from fighting. It had never stopped Sharpe. So these hungry men could fight, and they needed officers, and all he had to do was stand up, brush the dirt away and stroll across to Pohlmann's tent and become Lieutenant Sharpe. Mister Sharpe. And he would do a good job. He knew that. Better than Morris, better than most of the army's junior officers. He was a good sergeant, a bloody good sergeant, and he enjoyed being a sergeant. He got respect, not just because of the stripes on his red sleeves, and not just because he had been the man who blew the mine at Seringapatam, but because he was good and tough. He wasn't frightened of making a decision, and that was the key to it, he reckoned. And he enjoyed making decisions, and he enjoyed the respect that decisiveness brought him, and he realized he had been seeking respect all his life. Christ, he thought, but would it not be a joy to walk back into the foundling home with braid on his coat, gold on his shoulders and a sword at his side? That was the respect he wanted, from the bastards in Brewhouse Lane who had said he would never amount to anything and who had whipped him bloody because he was a bastard off the streets. By Christ, he thought, but going back there would make life perfect! Brewhouse Lane, him in a braided coat and a sword, and with Simone on his arm and a dead king's jewels about her neck, and them all touching their hats and bobbing like ducks in a pond. Perfect, he thought, just perfect, and as he indulged himself in that dream an angry shout came from the tents close to Pohlmann's marquee and an instant later a gun sounded.

There was a moment's pause after the gunshot, as if its violence had checked a drunken fight, then Sharpe heard men laughing and the sound of hoofbeats. He was standing now, staring towards the big marquee. The horses went by quite close to him, then the noise of their hooves receded into the dark. 'Come back!' a man shouted in English, and Sharpe recognized McCandless's voice.

Sharpe began running.

'Come back!' McCandless shouted again, and then there was another gunshot and Sharpe heard the Colonel yelp like a whipped dog. A score of men were shouting now. The officers who had been playing cards were running towards McCandless's tent and Pohlmann's bodyguards were following them. Sharpe dodged round a fire, leaped a sleeping man, then saw a figure hurrying away from the commotion. The man had a musket in his hand and he was half crouching as if he did not want to be seen, and Sharpe did not hesitate, but just swerved and ran at the man.

When the fugitive heard Sharpe coming, he quickened his pace, then realized he would be caught and so he turned on his pursuer. The man whipped out a bayonet and screwed it onto the muzzle of his musket. Sharpe saw the glint of moon-light on the long blade, saw the man's teeth white in the dark, then the bayonet lunged at him, but Sharpe had dropped to the ground and was sliding forward in the dust beneath the blade. He wrapped his arms around the man's legs, heaved once and the man fell backwards. Sharpe cuffed the musket aside with his left hand, then hammered his right hand down onto the moon-whitened teeth. The man tried to kick Sharpe's crotch, then clawed at his eyes, but Sharpe caught one of the hooked fingers in his mouth and bit hard. The man screamed in pain, Sharpe kept biting and kept hitting, then he spat the severed fingertip into the man's face and gave him one last thump with his fist. 'Bastard,' Sharpe said, and hauled the man to his feet. Two of Pohlmann's officers had arrived now, one still with a fan of cards in his hand. 'Get his bloody musket,' Sharpe ordered them. The man struggled in Sharpe's hands, but he was much smaller than Sharpe and a good kick between his legs brought him to order. 'Come on, you bastard,' Sharpe said.

One of the officers had picked up the fallen musket and Sharpe reached over and felt the muzzle. It was hot, showing that the weapon had just been fired. 'If you killed my Colonel, you bastard, I'll kill you,' Sharpe said and dragged the man through the campfires to the knot of officers who had gathered about the Colonel's tent.

McCandless's two horses were gone. Both the mare and the gelding had been stolen, and Sharpe realized it was their hoofbeats he had heard go past him. McCandless, woken by the noise of the horse thieves, had come from the tent and fired his pistol at the men, and one of them had fired back and the bullet had buried itself in the Colonel's left thigh. He was lying on the ground now, looking horribly pale, and Pohlmann was bellowing for his doctor to come quickly.

'Who's that?' he demanded of Sharpe, and nodding at the prisoner.

'The bastard who fired at Colonel McCandless, sir. Musket's still hot.'

The man proved to be one of Major Dodd's sepoys, one of the men who had deserted with Dodd from the Company, and he was put into the charge of Pohlmann's bodyguard. Sharpe knelt beside McCandless who was trying not to cry aloud as the newly arrived doctor, the Swiss man who had sat beside Sharpe at dinner, examined his leg. 'I was sleeping!' the Colonel complained. 'Thieves, Sharpe, thieves!'

'We'll find your horses,' Pohlmann reassured the Scotsman, 'and we'll find the thieves.'

'You promised me safety!' McCandless complained.

'The men will be punished,' Pohlmann promised, then he helped Sharpe and two other men lift the wounded Colonel and carry him into the tent where they laid him on the rope cot. The doctor said the bullet had missed the bone, and no major artery was cut, but he still wanted to fetch his probes, forceps and scalpels and try to pull the ball out. 'You want some brandy, McCandless?' Pohlmann asked.

'Of course not. Tell him to get on with it.'

The doctor called for more lanterns, for water and for his instruments, and then he spent ten excruciating minutes looking for the bullet deep inside McCandless's upper thigh. The Scotsman uttered not a sound as the probe slid into his lacerated flesh, nor as the long-necked forceps were pushed down to find a purchase on the bullet. The Swiss doctor was sweating, but McCandless just lay with eyes tight shut and teeth clenched. 'It comes now,' the doctor said and began to pull, but the flesh had closed on the forceps and he had to use almost all his strength to drag the bullet up from the wound. It came free at last, releasing a spill of bright blood, and McCandless groaned.

'All done now, sir,' Sharpe told him.

'Thank God,' McCandless whispered, 'thank God.' The Scotsman opened his eyes. The doctor was bandaging the thigh and McCandless looked past him to Pohlmann. 'This is treachery, Colonel, treachery! I was your guest!'

'Your horses will be found, Colonel, I promise you,' Pohlmann said, but though his men made a search of the camp, and though they searched until morning, the two horses were not found. Sharpe was the only man who could identify them, for Colonel McCandless was in no state to walk, but Sharpe saw no horses that resembled the stolen pair, but nor did he expect to, for any competent horse thief knew a dozen tricks to disguise his catch. The beast would be clipped, its coat would be dyed with blackball, it would be force-fed an enema so that its head drooped, then it would as likely as not be put among the cavalry mounts where one horse looked much like another. Both McCandless's horses had been European bred and were larger and of finer quality than most in Pohlmann's camp, yet even so Sharpe saw no sign of the two animals.

Colonel Pohlmann went to McCandless's tent and confessed that the horses had vanished. 'I shall pay you their value, of course,' he added.

'I won't take it!' McCandless snapped back. The Colonel was still pale, and shivering despite the heat. His wound was bandaged, and the doctor reckoned it should heal swiftly enough, but there was a danger that the Colonel's recurrent fever might return. 'I won't take my enemy's gold,' McCandless explained, and Sharpe reckoned it must be the pain speaking for he knew the two missing horses must have cost the Colonel dearly.

'I shall leave you the money,' Pohlmann insisted anyway, 'and this afternoon we shall execute the prisoner.'

'Do what you must,' McCandless grumbled.

'Then we shall carry you northwards,' the Hanoverian promised, 'for you must stay under Doctor Viedler's care.'

McCandless levered himself into a sitting position. 'You'll not take me anywhere!' he insisted angrily. 'You leave me here, Pohlmann. I'll not depend on your care, but on God's mercy.' He let himself drop back onto the bed and hissed with pain. 'And Sergeant Sharpe can tend me.'

Pohlmann glanced at Sharpe. The Hanoverian seemed about to say that Sharpe might not wish to stay with McCandless, but then he just nodded his acceptance of McCandless's decision. 'If you wish to be abandoned, McCandless, so be it.'

'I have more faith in God than in a faithless mercenary like you, Pohlmann.'

'As you wish, Colonel,' Pohlmann said gently, then backed from the tent and gestured for Sharpe to follow. 'He's a stubborn fellow, isn't he?' The Hanoverian turned and looked at Sharpe. 'So, Sergeant? Are you coming with us?'

'No, sir,' Sharpe said. Last night, he reflected, he had very nearly decided to accept the Hanoverian's offer, but the theft of the horses and the single shot fired by the sepoy had served to change Sharpe's mind. He could not leave McCandless to suffer and, to his surprise, he felt no great disappointment in thus having the decision forced on him. Duty dictated he should stay, but so did sentiment, and he had no regret. 'Someone has to look after Colonel McCandless, sir,' Sharpe explained, 'and he's looked after me in the past, so it's my turn now.'

'I'm sorry,' Pohlmann said, 'truly I am. The execution will be in one hour. I think you should see it, so you can assure your Colonel that justice was done.'

'Justice, sir?' Sharpe asked scornfully. 'It ain't justice, shooting that fellow. He was put up to it by Major Dodd.' Sharpe had no proof of that, but he suspected it strongly. Dodd, he reckoned, had been hurt by McCandless's insults and must have decided to add horse-thieving to his catalogue of crimes. 'You have questioned your prisoner, haven't you, sir?' Sharpe asked. 'Because he must know that Dodd was up to his neck in the business.'

Pohlmann smiled wearily. 'The prisoner told us everything, Sergeant, or I assume he did, but what use is that? Major Dodd denies the man's story, and a score of sepoys swear the Major was nowhere near McCandless's tent when the shots were fired. And who would the British army believe? A desperate man or an officer?' Pohlmann shook his head. 'So you must be content with the death of one man, Sergeant.'

Sharpe expected that the captured sepoy would be shot, but there was no sign of any firing squad when the moment arrived for the man's death. Two companies from each of Pohlmann's eight battalions were paraded, the sixteen companies making three sides of a hollow square with Pohlmann's striped marquee forming the fourth side. Most of the other tents had already been struck ready for the move northwards, but the marquee remained and one of its canvas walls had been brailed up so that the *compoo*'s officers could witness the execution from chairs set in the tent's shade. Dodd was not there, nor were any of the regiment's wives, but a score of officers took their places and were served sweetmeats and drink by Pohlmann's servants.

The prisoner was fetched onto the makeshift execution ground by four of Pohlmann's bodyguards. None of the four carried a musket, instead they were equipped with tent pegs, mallets and short lengths of rope. The prisoner, who wore nothing but a strip of cloth around his loins, glanced from side to side as if trying to find an escape route, but, on a nod from Pohlmann, the bodyguards kicked his feet out from beneath him and then knelt beside his sprawling body and pinioned it to the ground by tying the ropes to his wrists and ankles, then fastening the bonds to the tent pegs. The condemned man lay there, spread-eagled, gazing up at the cloudless sky as the mallets banged the eight pegs home.

Sharpe stood to one side. No one spoke to him, no one even looked at him, and no wonder, he thought, for this was a farce. All the officers must have known that Dodd was the guilty man, yet the sepoy must die. The paraded troops seemed to agree with Sharpe, for there was a sullenness in the ranks. Pohlmann's *compoo* might be well armed and superbly trained, but it was not happy.

The four bodyguards finished tying the prisoner down, then walked away to leave him alone in the centre of the execution ground. An Indian officer, resplendent in silk robes and with a lavishly curved *tulwar* hanging from his belt, made a speech. Sharpe did not understand a word, but he guessed that the watching soldiers were being harangued about the fate which awaited any thief. The officer finished, glanced once at the prisoner, then walked back to the tent and, just as he entered its shade, so Pohlmann's great elephant with its silver-encased tusks and cascading metal coat was led out from behind the marquee. The mahout guided the beast by tugging on one of its ears, but as soon as the elephant saw the prisoner it needed no guidance, but just plodded across to the spread-eagled man. The victim shouted for mercy, but Pohlmann was deaf to the pleas.

The Colonel twisted round. 'You're watching, Sharpe?'

'You've got the wrong man, sir. You should have Dodd there.'

'Justice must be done,' the Colonel said, and turned back to the elephant that was standing quietly beside the victim who twisted in his bonds, thrashed, and even managed to free one hand, but instead of using that free hand to tug at the other three ropes that held him, he flailed uselessly at the elephant's trunk. A murmur ran through the watching sixteen companies, but the jemadars and havildars shouted and the sullen murmur ceased. Pohlmann watched the prisoner struggle for a few more seconds, then took a deep breath. '*Haddah!*' he shouted. '*Haddah!*'

The prisoner screamed in anticipation as, very slowly, the elephant lifted one ponderous forefoot and moved its body slightly forward. The great foot came down on the prisoner's chest and seemed to rest there. The man tried to push the foot away, but he might as well have attempted to shove a mountain aside. Pohlmann leaned forward, his mouth open, as, slowly, very slowly, the elephant transferred its weight onto the man's chest. There was another scream, then the man could not draw breath to scream again, but still he jerked and twitched and still the weight pressed on him, and Sharpe saw his legs try to contract against the bonds at his ankles, and saw his head jerk up, and then he heard the splinter of ribs and saw the blood spill and bubble at the victim's mouth. He winced, trying to imagine the pain as the elephant pressed on down, crushing bone and lung and spine. The prisoner gave one last jerk, his hair flapping, then his head fell back and a great wash of blood brimmed from his open mouth and puddled beside his corpse.

There was a last crunching sound, then the elephant stepped back and a sigh sounded gently through the watching ranks. Pohlmann applauded, and the officers joined in. Sharpe turned away. Bastards, he thought, bastards.

And that night Pohlmann marched north.

Sergeant Obadiah Hakeswill was not an educated man, and he was not even particularly clever unless slyness passed for wits, but he did understand one thing very well, and that was the impression he made on other men. They feared him. It did not matter whether the other man was a raw private, fresh from the recruiting sergeant, or a general whose coat was bright with gold lace and heavy with braid. They all feared him, all but two, and those two frightened Obadiah Hakeswill. One was Sergeant Richard Sharpe, in whom Hakeswill sensed a violence that was equal to his own, while the other was Major General Sir Arthur Wellesley who, when he had been colonel of the 33rd, had always been serenely impervious to Hakeswill's threats.

So Sergeant Hakeswill would have much preferred not to confront General Wellesley, but when his convoy reached Ahmednuggur his enquiries established that Colonel McCandless had ridden north and had taken Sharpe with him, and the Sergeant had known he could do nothing further without Wellesley's permission and so he had gone to the General's tent where he announced himself to an orderly, who had informed an aide, who had commanded the Sergeant to wait in the shade of a banyan tree.

He waited the best part of a morning while the army readied itself to leave Ahmednuggur. Guns were being attached to limbers, oxen harnessed to carts and tents being struck by lascars. The fortress of Ahmednuggur, fearing the same fate as the city, had meekly surrendered after a few cannon shots and, with both the city and its fort safe in his hands, Wellesley was now planning to march north, cross the Godavery and seek out the enemy army. Sergeant Hakeswill had no great wish to take part in that adventure, but he could see no other way of catching up with Sharpe and so he was resigned to his fate.

'Sergeant Hakeswill?' An aide came from the General's big tent.

'Sir!' Hakeswill scrambled to his feet and stiffened to attention.

'Sir Arthur will see you now, Sergeant.'

Hakeswill marched into the tent, snatched off his shako,

184

turned smartly to the left, quick-marched three short paces, then slammed to a halt in front of the camp table where the General was doing paperwork. Hakeswill stood quivering at attention. His face shuddered.

'At ease, Sergeant,' Wellesley, bare-headed, had barely glanced up from his papers as the Sergeant entered.

'Sir!' Hakeswill allowed his muscles to relax slightly. 'Papers for you, sir!' He pulled the warrant for Sharpe's arrest from his pouch and offered it to the General.

Wellesley made no move to accept the warrant. Instead he leaned back in his chair and examined Hakeswill as though he had never seen the Sergeant before. Hakeswill stood rigid, his eyes staring at the tent's brown wall above the General's head. Wellesley sighed and leaned forward again, still ignoring the warrant. 'Just tell me, Sergeant,' he said, his attention already returned to the documents on his desk. An aide was taking whatever sheets the General signed, sprinkling sand on the signatures, then placing more papers on the table.

'I'm ordered here by Lieutenant Colonel Gore, sir. To apprehend Sergeant Sharpe, sir.'

Wellesley looked up again and Hakeswill almost quailed before the cold eyes. He sensed that Wellesley could see right through him, and the sensation made his face quiver in a series of uncontrollable twitches. Wellesley waited for the spasms to end. 'On your own, are you, Sergeant?' the General asked casually.

'Detail of six men, sir.'

'Seven of you! To arrest one man?'

'Dangerous man, sir. I'm ordered to take him back to Hurryhur, sir, so he can . . .'

'Spare me the details,' Wellesley said, looking back to the next paper needing his signature. He tallied up a list of figures. 'Since when did four twelves and eighteen yield a sum of sixty-eight?' he asked no one in particular, then corrected the calculation before signing the paper. 'And since when did Captain Lampert dispose of the artillery train?'

The aide wielding the sand-sprinkler blushed. 'Colonel Eldredge, sir, is indisposed.' Drunk, if the truth was known, which it was, but it was impolitic to say that a colonel was drunk in front of a sergeant.

'Then invite Captain Lampert to supper. We must feed him some arithmetic along with a measure of common sense,' Sir Arthur said. He signed another paper, then rested his pen on a small silver stand before leaning back and looking at Hakeswill. He resented the Sergeant's presence, not because he disliked Sergeant Hakeswill, though he did, but rather because Wellesley had long ago left behind the cares of being the commander of the 33rd and he did not want to be reminded of those duties now. Nor did he want to be in a position to approve or disapprove of his successor's orders, for that would be an impertinence. 'Sergeant Sharpe is not here,' he said coldly.

'So I hear, sir. But he was, sir?'

'Nor am I the person you should be troubling with this matter, Sergeant,' Wellesley went on, ignoring Hakeswill's question. He took up the pen again, dipped it in ink, and crossed a name from a list before adding his signature. 'In a few days,' he continued, 'Colonel McCandless will return to the army and you will report to him with your warrant and I've no doubt he will give the matter its due attention. Till then I shall employ you usefully. I won't have seven men idling while the rest of the army works.' Wellesley turned to the aide. 'Where do we lack men, Barclay?'

The aide considered for a moment. 'Captain Mackay could certainly use some assistance, sir.'

'Very well.' Wellesley pointed the pen's steel nib at Hakeswill. 'You'll attach yourself to Captain Mackay. Captain Mackay commands our bullock train and you will do whatever he desires until Colonel McCandless relieves you of that duty. Dismissed.'

'Sir!' Hakeswill said dutifully, but inwardly he was furious that the General had not shared his indignation about Sharpe. He about-turned, stamped from the tent, and went to find his men. 'Going to the dogs,' he said bitterly.

'Sergeant?' Flaherty asked.

'The dogs. Time was in this army when even a general officer respected sergeants. Now we're to be bullock guards. Pick up your bleeding firelocks!'

'Sharpe ain't here, Sergeant?'

'Of course he ain't here! If he was here we wouldn't be ordered to wipe bullocks' arses, would we? But he's coming back. General's word on it. Just a few days, lads, just a few days and he'll be back with all his glittering stones hidden away.' Hakeswill's fury was abating. At least he had not been ordered to attach himself to a fighting battalion, and he was beginning to realize that any duty attached to the baggage animals would give him a fine chance to fillet the army stores. Pickings were to be made there, and more than just the pickings of stores, for the baggage always travelled with the army's tail of women and that meant more opportunity. It could be worse, Hakeswill thought, so long as this Captain Mackay was no martinet. 'You know what the trouble is with this army?' Hakeswill demanded.

'What?' Lowry asked.

'Full of bleeding Scotchmen.' Hakeswill glowered. 'I hates Scotchmen. Not English, are they? Peasant bleeding Scotchmen. Sawney creatures, they are, sawney! Should have killed them all when we had the chance, but we takes pity on them instead. Scorpions in our bosoms, that's what they are. Says so in the scriptures. Now get a bleeding move on!'

But it would only be a few days, the Sergeant consoled himself, only a few days, and Sharpe would be finished.

* * *

Colonel Pohlmann's bodyguard carried McCandless to a small house that lay at the edge of the encampment. A widow and three children lived there, and the woman shrank away from the Mahratta soldiers who had raped her, stolen all her food and fouled her well with their sewage. The Swiss doctor left Sharpe with strict instructions that the dressing on the Colonel's leg was to be kept damp. 'I'd give you some medicine for his fever, but I have none,' the doctor said, 'so if the fever gets worse just keep him warm and make him sweat.' The doctor shrugged. 'It might help.'

Pohlmann left food and a leather bag of silver coins. 'Tell McCandless that's for his horses,' he told Sharpe.

'Yes, sir.'

'The widow will look after you,' Pohlmann said, 'and when the Colonel's well enough you can move him to Aurungabad. And if you change your mind, Sharpe, you know I'll welcome you.' The Colonel shook Sharpe's hand, then mounted the silver steps to his howdah. A horseman unfurled his banner of the white horse of Hanover. 'I'll spread word that you're not to be molested,' Pohlmann called back, then his mahout tapped the elephant's skull and the great beast set off northwards.

Simone Joubert was the last to say farewell. 'I wish you were staying with us,' she said unhappily.

'I can't.'

'I know, and maybe it's for the best.' She looked left and right to make certain no one was watching, then leaned swiftly forward and kissed Sharpe on the cheek. '*Au revoir*, Richard.'

He watched her ride away, then went back into the hovel which was nothing but a palm thatch roof set above walls made of decayed reed mats. The interior of the hut was blackened by years of smoke, and its only furniture was the rope cot on which McCandless lay. 'She's an outcast,' the Colonel told Sharpe, indicating the woman. 'She refused to jump onto her husband's funeral fire, so her family sent her away.' The Colonel flinched as a stab of pain scythed through his thigh. 'Give her the food, Sergeant, and some cash out of that bag. How much did Pohlmann leave us?'

The coins in Pohlmann's bag were of silver and copper, and Sharpe sorted and counted each different denomination, and McCandless then translated their rough worth into pounds. 'Sixty!' He announced the total bitterly. 'That might just buy one cavalry hack, but it won't buy a horse that can stay over country for days on end.'

'How much did your gelding cost, sir?' Sharpe asked.

'Five hundred and twenty guineas,' McCandless said ruefully. 'I bought him four years ago, when you and I were released from Seringapatam, and I prayed he'd be the last horse I'd ever buy. Except for the mare, of course, but she was just a remount. Even so she cost me a hundred and forty guineas. A bargain, too! I bought her in Madras, fresh off the boat and she was just skin and bones then, but two months of pasture put some muscle on her.'

The figures were almost incomprehensible to Sharpe. Five hundred and twenty guineas for a horse? A man could live his whole life on five hundred and forty-six pounds, and live well. Ale every day. 'Won't the Company replace the horses, sir?' he asked.

McCandless smiled sadly. 'They might, Sharpe, but I doubt it. I doubt it very much.'

'Why not, sir?'

'I'm an old man,' the Scotsman said, 'and my salary is a heavy impost on the Company's debit column. I told you they'd like me to retire, Sharpe, and if I indent for the value of two horses they might well insist on my retirement.' He sighed. 'I knew this pursuit of Dodd was doomed. I felt it in my bones.'

'We'll get you another horse, sir,' Sharpe said.

McCandless grimaced. 'How, pray?'

'We can't have you walking, sir. Not a full colonel. Besides, it was my fault, really.'

'Your fault? Don't be absurd, Sharpe.'

'I should have been with you, sir. But I wasn't. I was off thinking.'

The Colonel looked at him steadily for what seemed a long while. 'I should imagine, Sergeant,' he said at last, 'that you had a lot to think about. How was your elephant ride with Colonel Pohlmann?'

'He showed me Aurungabad, sir.'

'I think he took you to the mountain top and showed you the kingdoms of this world,' the Colonel said. 'What did he offer you? A lieutenancy?'

'Yes, sir.' Sharpe blushed to admit as much, but it was dark inside the widow's hovel and the Colonel did not see.

'He told you of Benoît de Boigne,' McCandless asked, 'and of that rogue George Thomas? And he said you could be a rich man in two or three years, aren't I right?'

'Something like that, sir.'

McCandless shrugged. 'I won't deceive you, Sharpe, he's right. Everything he told you is true. Out there' – he waved towards the setting sun which glinted through the chinks in the reed-mat walls – 'is a lawless society that for years has rewarded the soldier with gold. The soldier, mark me, not the honest farmer or the hard-working merchant. The prince-doms grow fat, Sharpe, and the people grow lean, but there is nothing to stop you serving those princes. Nothing but the oath you took to serve your King.'

'I'm still here, sir, aren't I?' Sharpe said indignantly.

'Yes, Sharpe, you are,' McCandless said, then he closed his eyes and groaned. 'I fear the fever is going to come. Maybe not.'

'So what do we do, sir?'

'Do? Nothing. Nothing helps the fever except a week of shivering in the heat.'

'I meant about getting you back to the army, sir. I could go to Aurungabad and see if I can find someone to take a message.'

'Not unless you speak their language, you won't,' McCandless said, then he lay for a while in silence. 'Sevajee will find us,' he went on eventually. 'News carries far in this countryside, and Sevajee will smell us out in the end.' Again he fell silent, and Sharpe thought he had fallen asleep, but then he saw the Colonel shake his head. 'Doomed,' the Colonel said. 'Lieutenant Dodd is going to be the end of me.'

'We'll capture Dodd, sir, I promise.'

'I pray so, I pray so.' The Colonel pointed to his saddlebags in the corner of the hut. 'Would you find my Bible, Sharpe? And perhaps you'd read to me while there's still a little light? Something from the Book of Job, I think.'

McCandless fell into days of fever and Sharpe into days of isolation. For all he knew the war might have been won or lost, for he saw no one and no news came to the thatched hovel under its thin-leaved trees. To keep himself busy he cleared out an old irrigation ditch that ran northwards across the woman's land, and he hacked at the brush, killed snakes and shovelled earth until he was rewarded by a trickle of water. That done, he tackled the hovel's roof, laying new palm thatch on the old and binding it in place with twists of frond. He went hungry, for the woman had little food other than the grain Pohlmann had left and some dried beans. Sharpe stripped to the waist when he worked and his skin went as brown as the stock of his musket. In the evenings he played with the woman's three children, making forts out of the red soil that they bombarded with stones and, in one memorable twilight, when a toy rampart proved impregnable to thrown pebbles, Sharpe laid a fuse of powder and blew a breach with three of his musket cartridges.

He did his best to tend McCandless, washing the Colonel's face, reading him the scriptures and feeding him spoonfuls of bitter gunpowder diluted in water. He was not sure that the powder helped, but every soldier swore that it was the best medicine for the fever, and so Sharpe forced spoonfuls of the salty mixture down the Colonel's throat. He worried about the bullet wound in McCandless's thigh, for the widow had shyly pushed him aside one day when he was dampening the dressing and had insisted on untying the bandage and putting a poultice of her own making onto the raw wound. There were moss and cobwebs in the poultice, and Sharpe wondered if he had done the right thing by letting her apply the mixture, but as the first week passed the wound did not seem to worsen and, in his more lucid moments, the Colonel claimed the pain was lessening.

Once the irrigation ditch was cleared Sharpe tackled the widow's well. He devised a dredge out of a broken wooden bucket and used it to scoop out handfuls of foul-smelling mud from the base of the well, and all the while he thought about his future. He knew Major Stokes would welcome him back to the Seringapatam armoury, but after a time the regiment would surely remember his existence and want him back and that would mean rejoining the Light Company with Captain Morris and Sergeant Hakeswill, and Sharpe shuddered at that thought. Maybe Colonel Gore would transfer him? The lads said that Gore was a decent fellow, not as chilling as Wellesley, and that was good news, yet even so Sharpe often wondered whether he should have accepted Pohlmann's offer. Lieutenant Sharpe, he muttered it aloud, Lieutenant Sharpe. Why not? And in those moments he would daydream of the joy of going back to the foundling home in Brewhouse Lane. He would wear a sword and a cocked hat, have braid on his jacket and spurs at his heels, and for every lash the bastards had ever laid on small Richard Sharpe he would pay them back tenfold. He felt a terrible anger when he remembered those beatings and he would haul at his makeshift dredge as if he could slake the anger with hard work.

But in all those daydreams he never once returned to Brewhouse Lane in a white coat, or in a purple coat, or in any other coat except a red one. No one in Britain had ever heard of Anthony Pohlmann, and why should they care that a child had gone from the gutters of Wapping to a commission in the Maharajah of Gwalior's army? A man might as well claim to be Colonel of the Moon for all anyone would care. Unless it was a red coat, they would condemn him as a flash bastard, and be done with him, but if he walked back in Britain's scarlet coat then they would take him seriously and that meant he had to become an officer in his own army.

So one night, when the rain was beating on the widow's repaired thatch and the Colonel was sitting on the rope bed declaring that his fever was abating, Sharpe asked McCandless how a man became an officer in Britain's army. 'I mean I know it can be done, sir,' he said awkwardly, 'because we had a Mister Devlin back in England and he came up from the ranks. He'd been a shepherd's boy on the dales before he took the shilling, but he was Lieutenant Devlin when I knew him.'

And was most likely to die as an old and embittered Lieutenant Devlin, McCandless thought, but he did not say as much. Instead he paused before saying anything. He was even tempted to evade the question altogether by pretending that his fever had suddenly taken a turn for the worse, for he understood only too well what lay behind Sharpe's question. Most officers would have mocked the ambition, but Hector McCandless was not a mocker. But he also knew that for a man to aspire to rise from the ranks to the officers' mess was to risk two disappointments: the disappointments of both failure and success. The most likely outcome was failure, for such promotions were as scarce as hens' teeth, but a few men did make the leap and their success inevitably led to unhappiness. They lacked the education of the other officers, they lacked their manners and they lacked their confidence. They were generally disdained by the other officers, and set to work as quartermasters in the belief that they could not be trusted to lead men in battle. And there was even some truth to that belief, for the men themselves did not like their officers to have come from the ranks, but McCandless decided Sharpe knew all that for himself and so he spared him the need to listen to it all over again. 'There are two ways, Sharpe,' McCandless said. 'First you can buy a commission. The rank of ensign will cost you four hundred pounds, but you'll need another hundred and fifty to equip yourself, and even that will only buy a barely adequate horse, a four-guinea sword and a serviceable uniform, and you'll still need a private income to cover your mess bills. An ensign earns close to ninety-five pounds a year, but the army stops some of that for expenses and more for the income tax. Have you heard of that new tax, Sharpe?'

'No, sir.'

'A pernicious thing. Taking from a man what he has honestly earned! It's thievery, Sharpe, disguised as government.' The Colonel scowled. 'So an ensign is lucky to see seventy pounds out of his salary, and even if he lives frugal that won't cover his mess bills. Most regiments charge an officer two shillings for dinner every day, a shilling for wine, though of course you could go without wine well enough and water's free, but there's sixpence a day for the mess servant, another sixpence for breakfast and sixpence for washing and mending. You can't live as an officer without at least a hundred pounds a year on top of your salary. Have you got the money?'

'No, sir,' Sharpe lied. In truth he had enough jewels sewn into his red coat to buy himself a majority, but he did not want McCandless to know that.

'Good,' McCandless said, 'because that isn't the best way. Most regiments won't look at a man buying himself out of the ranks. Why should they? They've got plenty of young hopefuls coming from the shires with their parents' cash hot in their purses, so the last thing they need is some half-educated ranker who can't meet his mess bills. I'm not saying it's impossible. Any regiment posted to the West Indies will sell you an ensign's post cheap, but that's because they can't get anyone else on account of the yellow fever. A posting to the West Indies is a death sentence. But if a man wants to get into anything other than a West-Indies-bound regiment, Sharpe, then he must hope for the second route. He must be a sergeant and he must be able to read and write, but there's a third requirement too. The fellow must perform a quite impossibly gallant act. Leading a Forlorn Hope will do the trick, but any act, so long as it's suicidal, will serve, though of course he must do it under the General's eye or else it's all a waste of time.'

Sharpe sat in silence for a while, daunted by the obstacles that lay in the way of his daydream's fulfilment. 'Do they give him a test, sir?' he asked. 'In reading?' That thought worried him for, although his reading was improving night by night, he still stumbled over quite simple words. He claimed that the Bible's print was too small, and McCandless was kind enough to believe the excuse.

'A test in reading? Good Lord, no! For an officer!' McCandless smiled tiredly. 'They take his word, of course.' The Colonel paused for a second. 'But I've often wondered, Sharpe,' he went on, 'why a man from the ranks would want to be an officer?'

So he could go back to Brewhouse Lane, Sharpe thought,

and kick some teeth in. 'I was just wondering about it, sir,' he said instead. 'Just thinking, sir.'

'Because in many ways,' McCandless said, 'sergeants have more influence with the men. Less formal prestige, perhaps, but certainly more influence than any junior officer. Ensigns and lieutenants, Sharpe, are very insignificant creatures. They're really of very little use most of the time. It's not till a man reaches his captaincy that he begins to be valuable.'

'I'm sure you're right, sir,' Sharpe said lamely. 'I was just thinking.'

That night the Colonel relapsed into fever, and Sharpe sat in the hut doorway and listened to the rain beat on the land. He could not shake the daydream, could not drive away the picture of him ducking through the gate in Brewhouse Lane and seeing the faces he hated. He wanted it, he wanted it terribly, and so he dreamed on, dreaming the impossible, but unable to check the dream. He did not know how, but he would somehow make the leap. Or else die in the attempt.

CHAPTER 7

Dodd called his new gelding Peter. 'Because it's got no balls, Monsewer,' he informed Pierre Joubert, and he repeated the poor joke a dozen times in the next two days just to make certain that its insult was understood. Joubert smiled and said nothing, and the Major would launch himself into a panegyric on Peter's merits. His old horse had whistling lungs, while this one could be ridden all day and still had its head up and a spring in its long stride. 'A thoroughbred, Captain,' he told Joubert, 'an English thoroughbred. Not some screw-backed old French nag, but a proper horse.'

The men in Dodd's Cobras liked to see their Major on his fine big horse. It was true that one man had died in the beast's acquisition, yet the theft had still been a fine piece of banditry, and the men had laughed to see the English Sergeant searching the camp while all the while Major Dodd's Jemadar, Gopal, was hiding the horses a long way to the north.

Colonel Pohlmann was less amused. 'I promised McCandless safe conduct, Major,' he growled at Dodd the first time he saw the Englishman on his new gelding.

'Quite right, sir.'

'And you've added horse-thieving to your catalogue of crimes?'

'I can't think what you mean, sir,' Dodd protested in mock innocence. 'I purchased this beast off a horse trader yesterday, sir. Gypsy-looking fellow from Korpalgaon. Took the last of my savings.'

'And your Jemadar's new horse?' Pohlmann asked, pointing to Gopal who was riding Colonel McCandless's mare.

'He bought her from the same fellow,' Dodd said.

'Of course he did, Major,' Pohlmann said wearily. The Colonel knew it was pointless to chide a man for theft in an army that was encouraged to steal for its very existence, yet he was offended by Dodd's abuse of the hospitality that had been extended to McCandless. The Scotsman was right, Pohlmann thought, Dodd was a man without honour, yet the Hanoverian knew that if Scindia employed none but saints then he would have no European officers.

The theft of McCandless's horses only added more reason for Pohlmann to dislike William Dodd. He found the Englishman too dour, too jealous and too humourless, yet still, despite his dislike, he recognized that the Major was a fine soldier. His rescue of his regiment from Ahmednuggur had been an inglorious operation executed superbly, and Pohlmann, at least, understood the achievement, just as he appreciated that Dodd's men liked their new commanding officer. The Hanoverian was not certain why Dodd was popular, for he was not an easy man; he had no small talk, he smiled rarely, and he was punctilious about details that other officers might let pass, yet still the men liked him. Maybe they sensed that he was on their side, wholly on their side, recognizing that nothing is achieved in war by officers without men, and a good deal by men without officers, and for that reason, if no other, they were glad he was their commanding officer. And men who like their commanding officer are more likely to fight well than men who do not, and so Pohlmann was glad that he had William Dodd as a regimental commander even if he did disdain him as little better than a common thief.

Pohlmann's *compoo* had now joined the rest of Scindia's army, which had already been swollen by the troops of the Rajah of Berar, so that over a hundred thousand men and all their animals now wandered the Deccan Plain in search of grazing, forage and grain. The vast army hugely outnumbered its enemy, but Scindia made no attempt to bring Wellesley to battle. Instead he led his horde in an apparently aimless fashion. They went south towards the enemy, then withdrew north, they made a lumbering surge to the east and then retraced their steps to the west, and everywhere they marched they stripped the farms, slashed down crops, broke into granaries, slaughtered livestock and rifled humble homes in search of rice, wheat or lentils. Every day a score of cavalry patrols rode south to find the enemy armies, but the Mahratta horsemen rarely came close to the redcoats, for the British cavalry counter-patrolled aggressively and each day left dead horses on the plain while Scindia's great host wandered mindlessly on.

'Now that you have such a fine horse,' Pohlmann said to Dodd a week after the Major's theft, 'perhaps you can lead a cavalry patrol?'

'Gladly, sir.'

'Someone has to find out what the British are doing,' Pohlmann grumbled.

Dodd rode south with some of Pohlmann's own cavalry and his patrol succeeded where so many others had failed, but only because the Major donned his old red coat so that it would appear as if his score of horsemen were under the command of a British officer, and the ruse worked, for Dodd came across a much smaller force of Mysore cavalry who rode unsuspecting into the trap. Six enemy escaped, eight died, and their leader yielded a mass of information before Dodd shot him through the head.

'You might have brought him back to us,' Pohlmann remonstrated gently when Dodd returned. 'I could have talked with him myself,' the Colonel added, peering down from his green-curtained howdah. The elephant plodded behind a purple-coated horseman who carried Pohlmann's red flag emblazoned with the white horse of Hanover. There was a girl with Pohlmann, but all Dodd could see of her was a dark languid hand bright with gems hanging over the howdah's edge. 'So tell me what you learned, Major,' Pohlmann ordered.

'The British are back close to the Godavery, sir, but they're still split into two forces and neither has more than six thousand infantry. Wellesley's nearest to us while Stevenson's moving off to the west. I've made a map, sir, with their dispositions.' Dodd held the paper up towards the swaying howdah.

'Hoping to pincer us, are they?' Pohlmann asked, reaching down to pluck the map from the Major's hand. 'Not now, *Liebchen*,' he added, though not to Dodd.

'I imagine they're staying divided because of the roads, sir,' Dodd said.

'Of course,' Pohlmann said, wondering why Dodd was teaching him to suck eggs. The British need for decent roads was much greater than the Mahrattas', for the British carried all their foodstuffs in ox wagons and the cumbersome vehicles could not manage any country other than the smoothest grass plains. Which meant that the two enemy armies could only advance where the ground was smooth or the roads adequate. It made their movements clumsy, and it made any attempt to pincer Scindia's army doubly difficult, though by now, Pohlmann reflected, the British commander must be thoroughly confused about Scindia's intentions. So was Scindia, for that matter, for the Maharajah was taking his tactical advice from astrologers rather than from his European officers which meant that the great horde was impelled to its wanderings by the glimmer of stars, the import of dreams and the entrails of goats.

'If we marched south now,' Dodd urged Pohlmann, 'we could trap Wellesley's men south of Aurungabad. Stevenson's too far away to support him.'

'It does sound a good idea,' Pohlmann agreed genially, pocketing Dodd's map.

'There must be some plan,' Dodd suggested irritably.

'Must there?' Pohlmann asked airily. 'Higher up, *Liebchen*, just there! That's good!' The bejewelled hand had vanished inside the howdah. Pohlmann closed his eyes for an instant, then opened them and smiled down on Dodd. 'The plan,' the Hanoverian said grandly, 'is to wait and see whether Holkar will join us.' Holkar was the most powerful of all the Mahratta chieftains, but he was biding his time, uncertain whether to join Scindia and the Rajah of Berar or whether to sit out the war with his huge forces intact. 'And the next part of the plan,' Pohlmann went on, 'is to hold a durbar. Have you ever attended a durbar, Dodd?'

'No, sir.'

'It is a council, a committee of the old and the wise, or rather of the senile and the talkative. The war will be discussed, as will the position of the stars and the mood of the gods and the failure of the monsoon and, once the durbar is over, if indeed it ever ends, we shall commence our wandering once again, but perhaps a decision of sorts will have been made, though whether that decision will be to retire on Nagpoor, or to advance on Hyderabad, or to choose a battlefield and allow the British to attack us, or simply to march from now until the Day of Judgment, I cannot yet tell you. I shall offer advice, of course, but if Scindia dreams of monkeys on the night before the durbar then not even Alexander the Great could persuade him to fight.'

'But Scindia must know better than to let the two British forces unite, sir?' Dodd said.

'He does, he does, indeed he does. Our lord and master

is no fool, but he is inscrutable. We are waiting for the omens to be propitious.'

'They're propitious now,' Dodd protested.

'That is not for you or me to decide. We Europeans can be relied upon to fight, but not to read the messages of the stars or to understand the meaning of dreams. But when it comes to the battle, Major, you can be sure that the stars and the dreams will be ignored and that Scindia will leave all the decisions to me.' Pohlmann smiled benignly at Dodd, then gazed out at the horde of cavalry that covered the plain. There must have been fifty thousand horsemen in view, but Pohlmann would happily have marched with only a thousand. Most of the Mahratta horsemen were only present for the loot they hoped to steal after victory and, though they were all fine riders and brave fighters, they had no conception of picquet duty and none was willing to charge into the face of an infantry unit. They did not understand that a cavalry troop needed to take horrific casualties if it was to break infantry; instead they reckoned Scindia's great guns and his mercenary infantry would do the shattering and they would then pursue the broken enemy like hornets, and until that happy moment they were just so many useless mouths to feed. If they all went away tomorrow it would make no difference to the war's outcome, for the victory would still be won by the artillery and the infantry. Pohlmann knew that and he imagined lining his guns wheel to wheel in batteries, with his infantry formed just behind and then watching the redcoats walk into a tumult of fire and iron and death. A flail of fire! A storm of metal whipping the air into a gale of bloody ruin amongst which the British would be chopped into butcher's scraps.

'You're hurting me,' the girl said.

'*Liebchen*, I'm so sorry,' Pohlmann said, releasing his grip. 'I was thinking.'

'Sir?' Dodd asked, thinking the Hanoverian was speaking to him.

'I was thinking, Dodd, that it is no bad thing that we wander so aimlessly.'

'It isn't?' Dodd retorted with astonishment.

'Because if we do not know where we are going, then nor will the British, so one day they will march a few miles too far and then we shall pounce on them. Someone will blunder, Dodd, because in war someone always does blunder. It is an immutable rule of war: someone will blunder. We must just have patience.' In truth Pohlmann was just as impatient as Dodd, but the Colonel knew it would not serve any purpose to betray that impatience. In India, he had learned, matters moved at their own pace, as imponderable and unstoppable as an elephant. But soon, Pohlmann reckoned, one of the British forces would make a march too far and find itself so close to the vast Mahratta army that even Scindia could not refuse battle. And even if the two enemy armies joined, what did that matter? Their combined forces were small, the Mahratta horde was vast, and the outcome of their meeting as certain as anything could be in war. And Pohlmann was confident that Scindia would eventually give him command of the army, and Pohlmann would then roll over the enemy like the great Juggernaut of Hindu legend and with that happy prospect he was content.

Dodd looked up to say something more, but the howdah's green curtains had been drawn shut. The girl giggled, while the mahout, seated just in front of the closed howdah, stared impassively ahead. The Mahrattas were on the march, covering the earth like a swarm, just waiting for their enemies to blunder.

Sharpe was tired of being hungry so one day he took his musket and walked in search of game. He reckoned anything would do, even a tiger, but he hoped to find beef. India seemed full of beeves, but that day he saw none, though after four miles he found a herd of goats grazing in a small wood. He drew his bayonet, reckoning it would be easier to cut one of the beast's throats than shoot it and so attract the attention of the herd's vengeful owner, but when he came close to the animals a dog burst out of the trees and attacked him.

He clubbed the dog down with his musket butt, and the brief commotion put the goats to flight and it took him the best part of an hour to find the animals again and by then he could not have cared if he attracted half the population of India and so he aimed and fired, and all he succeeded in doing was wounding one poor beast that started bleating pitifully. He ran to it, cut its throat, which was harder than he had thought, then hoisted the carcass onto his shoulder.

The widow boiled the stringy flesh which tasted foul, but it was still meat and Sharpe wolfed it down as though he had not eaten in months. The smell of the meat roused Colonel McCandless who sat up in his bed and frowned at the pot. 'I could almost eat that,' he said.

'You want some, sir?'

'I haven't eaten meat in eighteen years, Sharpe. I won't start now.' He ran a hand through his lank white hair. 'I do declare I'm feeling better, God be praised.'

The Colonel swung his feet onto the floor and tried to stand. 'But I'm weak as a kitten,' he said.

'Plate of meat will put some strength in you, sir.'

' "Get thee behind me, Satan," ' the Colonel said, then put a hand on one of the posts which held up the roof and hauled himself to his feet. 'I might take a walk tomorrow.'

'How's the leg, sir?'

'Mending, Sharpe, mending.' The Colonel put some

weight on his left leg and seemed pleasantly surprised that it did not buckle. 'God has preserved me again.'

'Thank God for that, sir.'

'I do, Sharpe, I do.'

Next morning the Colonel felt better still. He ducked out of the hut and blinked in the bright sunlight. 'Have you seen any soldiers these last two weeks?'

'Not a one, sir. Nothing but farmers.'

The Colonel scraped a hand across the white bristles on his chin. 'A shave, I think. Would you be so kind as to fetch my box of razors? And perhaps you could heat some water?'

Sharpe dutifully put a pot of water on the fire, then stropped one of the Colonel's razors on a saddle's girth strap. He was just perfecting the edge when McCandless called him from outside the house. 'Sharpe!'

Something in McCandless's voice made Sharpe snatch up his musket, then he heard the beat of hooves as he ducked under the low doorway and he hauled back the musket's cock in expectation of enemies, but McCandless waved the weapon down. 'I said Sevajee would find us!' the Colonel said happily. 'Nothing stays secret in this countryside, Sharpe.'

Sharpe lowered the musket's flint as he watched Sevajee lead his men towards the widow's house. The young Indian grinned at McCandless's dishevelled condition. 'I heard there was a white devil near here, and I knew it would be you.'

'I wish you'd come sooner,' McCandless grumbled.

'Why? You were ill. The folk I spoke to said you would die.' Sevajee slid out of the saddle and led his horse to the well. 'Besides, we've been too busy.'

'Following Scindia, I trust?' the Colonel asked.

'Here, there and everywhere.' Sevajee hauled up a skin of water and held it under his horse's nose. 'They've been south, east, back north again. But now they're going to hold a dur bar, Colonel.'

'A durbar!' McCandless brightened, and Sharpe wondered what on earth a durbar was.

'They've gone to Borkardan,' Sevajee announced happily. 'All of them! Scindia, the Rajah of Berar, the whole lot! A sea of enemies.'

'Borkardan,' McCandless said, summoning a mental map in his head. 'Where's that? Two days' march north?'

'One for a horseman, two on foot,' Sevajee agreed.

McCandless, his shave forgotten, stared northwards. 'But how long will they stay there?'

'Long enough,' Sevajee said gleefully, 'and first they have to make a place fit for a prince's durbar and that will take them two or three days, and then they'll talk for another two or three days. And they need to rest their animals too, and in Borkardan they've found plenty of forage.'

'How do you know?' McCandless asked.

'Because we met some *brindarries*,' Sevajee said with a smile, and turned at the same time to indicate four small, lean and riderless horses that were the trophies of that meeting. 'We had a talk with them,' Sevajee said airily, and Sharpe wondered how brutal that talk had been. 'Forty thousand infantry, sixty thousand cavalry,' Sevajee said, 'and over a hundred guns.'

McCandless limped back into the house to fetch paper and ink from his saddlebag. Then, back in the sunlight, he wrote a despatch and Sevajee detailed six of his horsemen to take the precious news south as fast as they could. They would need to search for Wellesley's army and Sevajee told them to whip their horses bloody because, if the British moved fast, there was a chance to catch the Mahrattas while they were encamped for their durbar and then to attack them before they could form their battle array. 'That would even things up,' McCandless announced happily. 'A surprise attack!'

'They're not fools,' Sevajee warned, 'they'll have a host of picquets.'

'But it takes time to organize a hundred thousand men, Sevajee, a lot of time! They'll be milling about like sheep while we march into battle!'

The six horsemen rode away with the precious despatch and McCandless, tired again, let Sharpe shave him. 'All we can do now is wait,' the Colonel said.

'Wait?' Sharpe asked indignantly, believing that McCandless was implying that they would do nothing while the battle was being fought.

'If Scindia's at Borkardan,' the Colonel said, 'then our armies will have to march this way to reach him. So we might as well wait for them to come to us. Then we can join up again.'

It was time to stop dreaming. It was time to fight.

Wellesley's army had crossed the Godavery and marched towards Aurungabad, then heard that Scindia's forces had gone far to the east before lunging south towards the heartland of Hyderabad, and the report made sense, for the old Nizam had just died and left a young son on the throne and a young ruler's state could make for rich pickings, and so Wellesley had turned his small army and hurried back to the Godavery. They laboriously recrossed the river, swimming the horses, bullocks and elephants to the southern bank, and floating the guns, limbers and wagons across on rafts. The men used boats made from inflated bladders, and it took two whole days to make the crossing and then, after a day's march south towards threatened Hyderabad, more news came that the enemy had turned about and gone back northwards.

'Don't know what they're bleeding doing,' Hakeswill declared.

'Captain Mackay says we're looking for the enemy,' Private Lowry suggested helpfully.

'Looking for his arse, more like. Bloody Wellesley.' Hakeswill was sitting beside the river, watching the bullocks being goaded back into the water to cross once again to the north bank. 'In the water, out the water, up one road, down the next, walk in bleeding circles, then back through the bleeding river again.' His blue eyes opened wide in indignation and his face twitched. 'Arthur Wellesley should never be a general.'

'Why not, Sarge?' Private Kendrick asked, knowing that Hakeswill wanted the opportunity to explain.

'Stands to reason, lad, stands to reason.' Hakeswill paused to light a clay pipe. 'No bleeding experience. You remember that wood outside Seringapatam? Bloody chaos, that's what it was, bloody chaos and who caused it? He did, that's who.' He gestured at Wellesley who, mounted on a tall white horse, had come to the bluff above the river. 'He's a general,' Hakeswill explained, 'because his father's an earl and because his elder brother's the Governor General, that's why. If my father had been a bleeding earl, then I'd be a bleeding general, says so in the scriptures. Lord Obadiah Hakeswill, I'd be, and you wouldn't see me buggering about like a dog chasing fleas up its arse. I'd bleeding well get the job done. On your feet, lads, look smart now!'

The General, with nothing to do except wait while his army crossed the river, had turned his horse up the bank and his path brought him close to where Hakeswill had been seated. Wellesley looked across, recognized the Sergeant and seemed about to turn away, but then an innate courtesy overcame his distaste for speaking with the lower ranks. 'Still here, Sergeant?' he asked awkwardly.

'Still here, sir,' Hakeswill said. He was quivering at attention, his clay pipe thrust into a pocket and his firelock by his side. 'Doing my duty, sir, like a soldier.'

'Your duty?' Wellesley asked. 'You came to arrest Sergeant Sharpe, isn't that right?'

'Sir!' Hakeswill affirmed.

The General grimaced. 'Let me know if you see him. He's with Colonel McCandless, and they both seem to be missing. Dead, probably.' And on that cheerful note the General tugged on his reins and spurred away.

Hakeswill watched him go, then retrieved his clay pipe and sucked the tobacco back to glowing life. Then he spat onto the bank. 'Sharpie ain't dead,' he said malevolently. 'I'm the one who's going to kill Sharpie. Says so in the scriptures.'

Then Captain Mackay arrived and insisted that Hakeswill and his six men help organize the transfer of the bullocks across the river. The animals carried packs loaded with spare round shot for the artillery, and the Captain had been provided with two rafts for that precious ammunition. 'They're to transfer the shot to the rafts, understand? Then swim the beasts over. I don't want chaos, Sergeant. Make them line up decently. And make sure they don't roll the shot into the river to save themselves the bother of reloading it.'

'It isn't a soldier's job,' Hakeswill complained when the Captain was gone. 'Chivvying bullocks? I ain't a bleeding Scotchman. That's all they're good for, chivvying bullocks. Do it all the time, they do, down the green roads to London, but it ain't a job for an Englishman.' But he nevertheless did an effective job, using his bayonet to prod men and animals into the queue which slowly snaked its way down to the water. By nightfall the whole army was over, and next morning, long before dawn, they marched north again. They camped before midday, thus avoiding the worst of the heat, and by mid-afternoon the first enemy cavalry patrols showed in the distance and the army's own cavalry rode out to drive the horsemen away.

They did not move at all for the next two days. Cavalry

scouts tried to discover the enemy's intentions, while Company spies spread gold throughout the north country in search of news, but the gold was wasted, for every scrap of intelligence was contradicted by another. One said Holkar had joined Scindia, another said Holkar was declaring war on Scindia, then the Mahrattas were said to be marching west, or east, or perhaps north, until Wellesley felt he was playing a slow version of blind man's buff.

Then, at last, some reliable news arrived. Six Mahratta horsemen in the service of Syud Sevajee came to Wellesley's camp with a hastily written despatch from Colonel McCandless. The Colonel regretted his absence and explained that he had taken a wound that had been slow to heal, but he could assure Sir Arthur that he had not abandoned his duty and could thus report, with a fair degree of certainty, that the forces of Dowlut Rao Scindia and the Rajah of Berar had finally ceased their wanderings at Borkardan. They planned to stay there, McCandless wrote, to hold a durbar and to let their animals recover their strength, and he estimated those intentions implied a stay in Borkardan of five or six days. The enemy numbered, he reported, at least eighty thousand men and possessed around a hundred pieces of field artillery, many of inferior calibre, but an appreciable number throwing much heavier shot. He reckoned, from his own earlier observations in Pohlmann's camp, that only fifteen thousand of the enemy's infantry were trained to Company standards, while the rest were makeweights, but the guns, he added ominously, were well served and well maintained. The despatch had been written in a hurry, and in a shaky hand, but it was concise, confident and comprehensive.

The Colonel's despatch drove the General to his maps and then to a flurry of orders. The army was readied to march that night, and a galloper went to Colonel Stevenson's force, west of Wellesley's, with orders to march north on a parallel course. The two small armies should combine at Borkardan in four days' time. 'That will give us, what?' Wellesley thought for a second or two. 'Eleven thousand prime infantry and forty-eight guns.' He jotted the figures on the map, then absent-mindedly tapped the numbers with a pencil. 'Eleven thousand against eighty,' he said dubiously, then grimaced. 'It will serve,' he concluded, 'it will serve very well.'

'Eleven against eighty will serve, sir?' Captain Campbell asked with astonishment. Campbell was the young Scottish officer who had thrice climbed the ladder to be the first man into Ahmednuggur and his reward had been a promotion and an appointment as Wellesley's aide. Now he stared at the General, a man Campbell considered as sensible as any he had ever met, yet the odds that Wellesley was welcoming seemed insane.

'I'd rather have more men,' Wellesley admitted, 'but we can probably do the job with eleven thousand. You can forget Scindia's cavalry, Campbell, because it won't manage a thing on a battlefield, and the Rajah of Berar's infantry will simply get in everyone else's way, which means we'll be fighting against fifteen thousand good infantry and rather too many well-served guns. The rest don't matter. If we beat the guns and the infantry, the rest of them will run. Depend on it, they'll run.'

'Suppose they adopt a defensive position, sir?' Campbell felt impelled to insert a note of caution into the General's hopes. 'Suppose they're behind a river, sir? Or behind walls?'

'We can suppose what we like, Campbell, but supposing is only fancy, and if we take fright at fancies then we might as well abandon soldiering. We'll decide how to deal with the rogues once we find them, but the first thing to do is find them.' Wellesley rolled up the map. 'Can't kill your fox till you've run him down. So let's be about our business.'

The army marched that night. Six thousand cavalry, nearly

211

all of them Indian, led the way, and behind them were twenty-two pieces of artillery, four thousand sepoys of the East India Company and two battalions of Scots, while the great clumsy tail of bullocks, wives, children, wagons and merchants brought up the rear. They marched hard, and if any man was daunted by the size of the enemy's army, they showed no sign of it. They were as well trained as any men that had ever worn the red coat in India, they had been promised victory by their long-nosed General, and now they were going for the kill. And, whatever the odds, they believed they would win. So long as no one blundered.

Borkardan was a mere village with no building fit for a prince, and so the great durbar of the Mahratta chiefs was held in an enormous tent that was hastily made by sewing a score of smaller tents together, then lining the canvas with swathes of brightly coloured silk, and it would have made a marvellously impressive structure had the heavens not opened when the durbar began so that the sound of men's voices was half drowned by the beat of rain on stretched canvas and if the hastily made seams had not opened to let the water pour through in streams.

'It's all a waste of time,' Pohlmann grumbled to Dodd, 'but we have to attend.' The Colonel was fixing his newly tied stock with a diamond-studded pin. 'And it isn't a time for any European opinion except mine, understand?'

'Yours?' Dodd, who had rather hoped to make a case for boldness, asked dourly.

'Mine,' Pohlmann said forcibly. 'I want to twist their tails, and I need every European officer nodding like a demented monkey in agreement with me.'

A hundred men had gathered under the dripping silk. Scindia, the Maharajah of Gwalior, and Bhonsla, the Rajah of Berar, sat on *musnuds*, elegant raised platform-thrones that were draped in brocade and sheltered from the intrusive rain by silk parasols. Their Highnesses were cooled by men waving long-handled fans while the rest of the durbar sweltered in the close, damp heat. The high-class brahmins, all in baggy trousers cut from gold brocade, white tunics and tall white turbans, sat closest to the two thrones, while behind them stood the military officers, Indian and European, who were perspiring in their finest uniforms. Servants moved unobtrusively through the crowd offering silver dishes of almonds, sweetmeats or raisins soaked in arrack. The three senior European officers stood together. Pohlmann, in a purple coat hung with golden braid and loops of chain, towered over Colonel Dupont, a wiry Dutchman who commanded Scindia's second *compoo*, and over Colonel Saleur, a Frenchman, who led the infantry of the Begum Somroo. Dodd lingered just behind the trio and listened to their private durbar. The three men agreed that their troops would have to take the brunt of the British attack, and that one of them must exercise overall command. It could not be Saleur, for the Begum Somroo was a client ruler of Scindia's, so her commander could hardly take precedence over her feudal overlord's officers, which meant that it had to be either Dupont or Pohlmann, but the Dutchman generously ceded the honour to the Hanoverian. 'Scindia would have chosen you anyway,' Dupont said.

'Wisely,' Pohlmann said cheerfully, 'very wisely. You're content, Saleur?'

'Indeed,' the Frenchman said. He was a tall, dour man with a badly scarred face and a formidable reputation as a disciplinarian. He was also reputed to be the Begum Somroo's lover, a post that evidently accompanied the command of that lady's infantry. 'What are the bastards talking about now?' he asked in English.

Pohlmann listened for a few seconds. 'Discussing whether to retreat to Gawilghur,' he said. Gawilghur was a hill fort that lay north and east of Borkardan and a group of brahmins were urging the army to retire there and let the British break their skulls against its cliffs and high walls. 'Goddamn brahmins,' Pohlmann said in disgust. 'Don't know a damn thing about soldiering. Know how to talk, but not how to fight.'

But then an older brahmin, his white beard reaching to his waist, stood up and declared that the omens were more suitable for battle. 'You have assembled a great army, dread Lord,' he addressed Scindia, 'and you would lock it away in a citadel?'

'Where did they find him?' Pohlmann muttered. 'He's actually talking sense!'

Scindia said little, preferring to let Surjee Rao, his chief minister, do the talking, while he himself sat plump and inscrutable on his throne. He was wearing a rich gown of yellow silk that had emeralds and pearls sewn into patterns of flowers, while a great yellow diamond gleamed from his pale-blue turban.

Another brahmin pleaded for the army to march south on Seringapatam, but he was ignored. The Rajah of Berar, darker-skinned than the pale Scindia, frowned at the durbar in an attempt to look warlike, but said very little. 'He'll run away,' Colonel Saleur growled, 'as soon as the first gun is fired. He always does.'

Beny Singh, the Rajah's warlord, argued for battle. 'I have five hundred camels laden with rockets, I have guns fresh from Agra, I have infantry hungry for enemy blood. Let them loose!'

'God help us if we do,' Dupont growled. 'Bastards don't have any discipline.'

'Is it always like this?' Dodd asked Pohlmann.

'Good God, no!' the Hanoverian said. 'This durbar is positively decisive! Usually it's three days of talk and a final decision to delay any decision until the next time.'

'You think they'll come to a decision today?' Saleur asked cynically.

'They'll have to,' Pohlmann said. 'They can't keep this army together for much longer. We're running out of forage! We're stripping the country bare.' The soldiers were still receiving just enough to eat, and the cavalrymen made certain their horses were fed, but the camp followers were near starvation and in a few days the suffering of the women and children would cause the army's morale to plummet. Only that morning Pohlmann had seen a woman sawing at what he had assumed was brown bread, then realized that no Indian would bake a European loaf and that the great lump was actually a piece of elephant dung and that the woman was crumbling it apart in search of undigested grains. They must fight now.

'So if we fight,' Saleur asked, 'how will you win?'

Pohlmann smiled. 'I think we can give young Wellesley a problem or two,' he said cheerfully. 'We'll put the Rajah's men behind some strong walls where they can't do any damage, and we three will line our guns wheel to wheel, hammer them hard for their whole approach, then finish them off with some smart volleys. After that we'll let the cavalry loose on their remnants.'

'But when?' Dupont asked.

'Soon,' Pohlmann said, 'soon. Has to be soon. Buggers are eating dung for breakfast these days.' There was a sudden silence in the tent and Pohlmann realized a question had been addressed to him. Surjee Rao, a sinister man whose reputation for cruelty was as widespread as it was deserved, raised an eyebrow to the Hanoverian. 'The rain, Your Serene Excellency,' Pohlmann explained, 'the rain deafened me so I could not hear your question.'

'What my Lord wishes to know,' the minister said, 'is whether we can destroy the British?'

'Oh, utterly,' Pohlmann said as though it was risible to even ask the question.

'They fight hard,' Beny Singh pointed out.

'And they die like other men when fought hard in return,' Pohlmann said dismissively.

Scindia leaned forward and whispered in Surjee Rao's ear. 'What the Lord of our land and the conqueror of our enemy's lands wishes to know,' the minister said, 'is how you will beat the British?'

'In the way that His Royal Highness suggested, Excellency, when he gave me his wise advice yesterday,' Pohlmann said, and it was true that he had enjoyed a private talk with Scindia the day before, though the advice had all been given by Pohlmann, but if he was to sway this durbar then he knew he must let them think that he was simply repeating Scindia's suggestions.

'Tell us, please,' Surjee Rao, who knew full well that his master had no ideas except how to increase the tax yields, asked suavely.

'As we all know,' Pohlmann said, 'the British have divided their forces into two parts. By now both those small armies will know that we are here at Borkardan and, because they are fools eager for death, they will both be marching towards us. Both armies lie to our south, but they are separated by some miles. They nevertheless hope to join together, then attack us, but yesterday, in his unparalleled wisdom, His Royal Highness suggested that if we move eastwards we shall draw the enemy's easternmost column towards us and so make them march away from their allies. We can then fight the two armies in turn, defeat them in turn, and then let our dogs chew the flesh from their carcasses. And when the last enemy is dead, Excellency, I shall bring their General to our ruler's tents in chains and send their women to be his slaves.' More to the point, Pohlmann thought, he would capture

Wellesley's food supplies, but he dared not say that in case Scindia took the words as a criticism. But Pohlmann's bravado was rewarded by a scatter of applause that was unfortunately spoiled as a whole section of the tent roof collapsed to let in a deluge of rain.

'If the British are doomed,' Surjee Rao asked when the commotion had subsided, 'why do they advance on us?'

It was a good question, and one that had worried Pohlmann slightly, though he believed he had found an answer. 'Because, Excellency,' he said, 'they have the confidence of fools. Because they believe that their combined armies will prove sufficient. Because they do not truly understand that our army has been trained to the same level as their own, and because their General is young and inexperienced and too eager for a reputation.'

'And you believe, Colonel, that we can keep their two armies apart?'

'If we march tomorrow, yes.'

'How big is the British General's army?'

Pohlmann smiled. 'Wellesley has five thousand infantry-men, Excellency, and six thousand cavalry. We could lose as many men as that and not even notice they were gone! He has eleven thousand men, but the only ones he relies on are his five thousand infantry. Five thousand men! Five thousand!' He paused, making sure that everyone in the tent had heard the figure. 'And we have eighty thousand men. Five against eighty!'

'He has guns,' the minister observed sourly.

'We have five guns for every one of his. Five against one. And our guns are bigger and they are served just as well as his.'

Scindia whispered to Surjee Rao who then demanded that the other European officers give their advice, but all had been forewarned by Pohlmann to sing his tune. March east, they

217

said, draw one British army into battle, then turn on the other. The minister thanked the foreign officers for their advice, then pointedly turned back to the brahmins for their comments. Some advised that emissaries should be sent to Holkar, begging his help, but Pohlmann's confidence had worked its magic and another man indignantly demanded to know why Holkar should be offered a share in the glory of victory. The tide of the durbar was turning in Pohlmann's favour, and he said nothing more, but nor did he need to.

The durbar talked all day and no course of action was formally agreed, but at dusk Scindia and the Rajah of Berar conferred briefly, then Scindia took his leave between rows of brahmins who bowed as their ruler passed. He paused in the huge tent's doorway while his servants brought the palanquin that would preserve him from the rain. Only when the palanquin was ready did he turn and speak loudly enough for all the durbar to hear. 'We march east tomorrow,' he said, 'then we shall ponder another decision. Colonel Pohlmann will make the arrangements.' He stood for a second, looking up at the rain, then ducked under the palanquin's canopy.

'Praise God,' Pohlmann said, for he reckoned that the decision to march eastwards was sufficient to bring on battle. The enemy was closing all the time, and so long as the Mahrattas did not run northwards, the two sides must eventually meet. And if Scindia's men went eastwards then they would meet on Pohlmann's terms. He rammed on his cocked hat and stalked from the tent, followed by all the European officers. 'We'll march east along the Kaitna!' he said excitedly. 'That's where we'll march tomorrow, and the river bank will be our killing ground.' He whooped like an excited child. 'One short march, gentlemen, and we shall be close to Wellesley's men, and in two or three days we'll fight whether our lords and masters want it or not.'

The army marched early next morning. It covered the earth like a dark swarm that flowed beneath the clearing clouds alongside the muddy River Kaitna which slowly deepened and widened as the army followed it eastwards. Pohlmann gave them a very short march, a mere six miles, so that the leading horsemen had reached Pohlmann's chosen campsite long before dawn and by nightfall the slowest of the Mahratta infantry had reached a small, mud-walled village that lay just two miles north of the Kaitna. Scindia and the Rajah of Berar pitched their lavish tents just outside the village, while the Rajah's infantry was ordered to barricade the streets and make loopholes in the thick mud walls of the outermost houses.

The village lay on the southern bank of the River Juah, a tributary of the Kaitna, and south of the village stretched two miles of open farmland that ended at the steep bank of the River Kaitna. Pohlmann placed his best infantry, his three *compoos* of superbly trained killers, south of the village on the high bluff of the Kaitna's northern bank, and in front of them he ranged his eighty best guns. Wellesley, if he wished to reach Borkardan, must come to the Kaitna and he would find his path blocked by a river, by a fearsome line of heavy guns, by an array of infantry and, behind them, like a fortress, a village crammed with the Rajah of Berar's troops. The trap was laid.

In the fields of a village called Assaye.

The two British armies were close to each other now, close enough for General Wellesley to ride across country to see Colonel Stevenson, the commander of the second army. The General rode with his aides and an escort of Indian cavalry, but they saw no enemy on their way westwards across a long flat plain greened by the previous day's rain. Colonel Stevenson, old enough to be Wellesley's father, was alarmed by his General's high spirits. He had seen such elation in young officers before, and seen it crushed by humiliating defeats brought on by over-confidence. 'Are you sure you're not hurrying too much?' he asked.

'We must hurry, Stevenson, must.' Wellesley unrolled a map onto the Colonel's table and pointed to Borkardan. 'We hear they're likely to stay there, but they won't stay for ever. If we don't close on them now, they'll slip away.'

'If the bastards are that close,' Stevenson said, peering at the map, 'then maybe we should join forces now?'

'And if we do,' the General said, 'it will take us twice as long to reach Borkardan.' The two roads on which the armies advanced were narrow and, a few miles south of the River Kaitna, those roads followed passes through a small but steep range of hills. Every wheeled vehicle in both armies would have to be fed through those defiles in the hills, and if the two small armies combined, the cumbersome business of negotiating the pass would take a whole day, a day in which the Mahrattas might escape northwards.

Instead the two armies would advance separately and meet at Borkardan. 'Tomorrow night,' Wellesley ordered, 'you camp here' – he made a cross on the map at a village called Hussainabad – 'and we'll be here.' The pencil made another cross at a village called Naulniah which lay four miles south of the River Kaitna. The villages were ten miles apart, and both about the same distance south of Borkardan. 'On the twenty-fourth,' Wellesley said, 'we march and join here.' He dashed a circle about the village of Borkardan. 'There!' he added, jabbing the pencil down and breaking its point.

Stevenson hesitated. He was a good soldier with a long experience of India, but he was cautious by nature and it seemed to him that Wellesley was being headstrong and foolish. The Mahratta army was vast, the British armies small, yet Wellesley was rushing into battle. There was a dangerous excitement in the usually cool-headed Wellesley, and Stevenson now tried to rein it in. 'We could meet at Naulniah,' he suggested, thinking it better if the armies combined the day before the battle rather than attempt to make their junction under fire.

'We have no time,' Wellesley declared, 'no time!' He swept aside the weights holding down the map's corners so that the big sheet rolled up with a snap. 'Providence has put their army within striking distance, so let us strike!' He tossed the map to his aide, Campbell, then ducked out of the tent into the day's late sunlight and there found himself staring at Colonel McCandless who was mounted on a small, bony horse. 'You!' Wellesley said with surprise. 'I thought you were wounded, McCandless?'

'I am, sir, but it's healing.' The Scotsman patted his left thigh.

'So what are you doing here?'

'Seeking you, sir,' McCandless answered, though in truth he had come to Stevenson's army by mistake. One of Sevajee's men, scouting the area, had seen the redcoats and McCandless had thought it must be Wellesley's men.

'And what on earth are you riding?' Wellesley asked, pulling himself onto Diomed's back. 'Looks like a gypsy nag, McCandless. I've seen ponies that are bigger.'

McCandless patted the captured Mahratta horse. 'She's the best I can do, sir. I lost my own gelding.'

'For four hundred guineas you can have my spare. Give me a note, McCandless, and he's all yours. Aeolus, he's called, a six-year-old gelding out of County Meath. Good lungs, got a capped hock, but it don't stop him. I'll see you in two days, Colonel,' Wellesley now addressed Stevenson. 'Two days! We'll test our Mahrattas, eh? See if their vaunted infantry can stand some pounding. Good day, Stevenson! Are you coming, McCandless?'

'I am, sir, I am.'

Sharpe fell in beside Daniel Fletcher, the General's orderly. 'I've never seen the General so happy,' Sharpe said to Fletcher.

'Got the bit between his teeth,' Fletcher said. 'He reckons we're going to surprise the enemy.'

'He ain't worried? There are thousands of the buggers.'

'He ain't showing nothing if he is frightened,' Fletcher said. 'Up and at them, that's his mood.'

'Then God help the rest of us,' Sharpe said.

The General talked with McCandless on his way back, but nothing the Scotsman said diminished Wellesley's eagerness, even though McCandless warned him of the effectiveness of the Mahratta artillery and the efficiency of the infantry. 'We knew all that when we declared war,' Wellesley said testily, 'and if it didn't deter us then, why should it now?'

'Don't underestimate them, sir,' McCandless said grimly.

'I rather hope they'll underestimate me!' Wellesley said. 'You want that gelding of mine?'

'I don't have the money, sir.'

'Oh come, McCandless! You on a Company colonel's salary! You must have a fortune stacked away!'

'I've some savings, sir, for my retirement, which is not far off.'

'I'll make it three hundred and eighty guineas, seeing as it's you, and in a couple of years you can sell him for four hundred. You can't go into battle on that thing.' He gestured at the Mahratta horse.

'I'll think on it, sir, I'll think on it,' McCandless said gloomily. He prayed that the good Lord would restore his own horse to him, along with Lieutenant Dodd, but if that did not happen soon then he knew he would have to buy a decent horse, though the prospect of spending such a vast sum grieved him.

'You'll take supper with me tonight, McCandless?' Wellesley asked. 'We have a fine leg of mutton. A rare leg!'

'I eschew meat, sir,' the Scotsman answered.

'You eschew meat? And chew vegetables?' The General decided this was a splendid joke and frightened his horse by uttering a fierce neigh of a laugh. 'That's droll! Very. You eschew meat to chew vegetables. Never mind, McCandless, we shall find you some chewable shrubs.'

McCandless chewed his vegetables that night, and afterwards, excusing himself, went to the tent that Wellesley had lent to him. He was tired, his leg was throbbing, but there had been no sign of the fever all day and for that he was grateful. He read his Bible, knelt in prayer beside the cot, then blew out the lantern to sleep. An hour later he was woken by the thump of hooves, the sound of suppressed voices, a giggle, and the brush of someone half falling against the tent. 'Who is it?' McCandless demanded angrily.

'Colonel?' Sharpe's voice answered. 'Me, sir. Sorry, sir. Lost my footing, sir.'

'I was sleeping, man.'

'Didn't mean to wake you, sir, sorry, sir. Stand still, you bugger! Not you, sir, sorry, sir.'

McCandless, dressed in shirt and breeches, snatched the tent flap open. 'Are you drunk?' he demanded, then fell silent as he gazed at the horse Sharpe was holding. The horse was a gelding, a splendid bay gelding with pricked ears and a quick, nervous energy.

'He's six years old, sir,' Sharpe said. Daniel Fletcher was trying to hammer in the picket and doing a very bad job because of the drink inside him. 'He's got a capped hock, sir, whatever that is, but nothing that'll stop him. Comes from Ireland, he does. All that green grass, sir, makes a good horse. Aeolus, he's called.'

'Aeolus,' McCandless said, 'the god of the wind.'

'Is he one of those Indian idols, sir? All arms and snake heads?'

'No, Sharpe, Aeolus is Greek.' McCandless took the reins from Sharpe and stroked the gelding's nose. 'Is Wellesley lending him to me?'

'Oh no, sir.' Sharpe had taken the mallet from the half-drunk Fletcher and now banged the picket firmly into the soil. 'He's yours, sir, all yours.'

'But . . .' McCandless said, then stopped, not understanding the situation at all.

'He's paid for, sir,' Sharpe said.

'Paid for by whom?' McCandless demanded sternly.

'Just paid for, sir.'

'You're blithering, Sharpe!'

'Sorry, sir.'

'Explain yourself!' the Colonel demanded.

General Wellesley had said much the same thing when, just forty minutes before, an aide had told him that Sergeant Sharpe was begging to see him and the General, who was just bidding goodnight to the last of his supper guests, had reluctantly agreed. 'Make it quick, Sergeant,' he had said, his fine mood disguised by his usual coldness.

'It's Colonel McCandless, sir,' Sharpe said woodenly. 'He's decided to buy your horse, sir, and he sent me with the money.' He stepped forward and tipped a bag of gold onto the General's map table. The gold was Indian, from every state and princedom, but it was real gold and it lay shining like butter in the candle flames.

Wellesley gazed in astonishment at the treasure. 'He said he didn't have the money!'

'He's a Scotsman, sir, the Colonel,' Sharpe had said, as though that explained everything, 'and he's sorry it ain't real money, sir. Guineas. But it's the full price, sir. Four hundred.'

'Three hundred and eighty,' Wellesley said. 'Tell the

Colonel I'll return some to him. But a note would have done just as well! I'm supposed to carry gold on me?'

'Sorry, sir,' Sharpe had said lamely, but he could never have provided a note for the General, so instead he had sought out one of the *bhinjarries* who followed the army, and that merchant had exchanged emeralds for gold. Sharpe suspected he had been cheated, but he had wanted to give the Colonel the pleasure of owning a fine horse and so he had accepted the *bhinjarrie's* price. 'Is it all right, sir?' he had asked Wellesley anxiously.

'Extraordinary way to do business,' Wellesley had said, but he had nodded his agreement. 'A fair sale, Sergeant,' he said, and he had almost held out his hand to shake Sharpe's as a man always shook hands on the sale of a horse, then he remembered that Sharpe was a sergeant and so he had hastily converted his gesture into a vague wave. And after Sharpe had gone and while he was scooping the coins into their bag, the General also remembered Sergeant Hakeswill. Not that it was any of his business, so perhaps it had been sensible not to mention the Sergeant's presence to Sharpe.

McCandless now admired the gelding. 'Who paid for it?'

'Good-looking horse, ain't he, sir?' Sharpe said. 'Good as your other, I'd say.'

'Sharpe! You're blithering again. Who paid for it?'

Sharpe hesitated, but knew he was not going to be spared the interrogation. 'In a manner of speaking, sir,' he said, 'the Tippoo did.'

'The Tippoo? Are you mad?'

Sharpe blushed. 'The fellow that killed the Tippoo, sir, he took some jewels off him.'

'A king's ransom, I should imagine,' McCandless snorted.

'So I persuaded the fellow to buy the horse, sir. As a gift for you, sir.'

McCandless stared at Sharpe. 'It was you.'

'It was me who did what, sir?'

'You killed the Tippoo.' It was almost an accusation.

'Me, sir?' Sharpe asked innocently. 'No, sir.'

McCandless stared at the gelding. 'I can't possibly accept, Sergeant.'

'He's no good to me, sir. A sergeant can't own a horse. Not a proper horse from Ireland, sir. And if I hadn't been daydreaming in Pohlmann's camp, sir, I might have stopped those thieves, so it's only fair that you should let me get you another.'

'You can't do this, Sharpe!' McCandless protested, embarrassed by the generosity of the gift. 'Besides, in a day or two I hope to get my own horse back along with Mister Dodd.'

Sharpe had not thought of that, and for a second he cursed himself for throwing away his money. Then he shrugged. 'It's done anyway, sir. General's got the money and you've got the horse. Besides, sir, you've always been fair to me, so I wanted to do something for you.'

'It's intolerable!' McCandless protested. 'Uncalled for. I shall have to repay you.'

'Four hundred guineas?' Sharpe asked. 'That's the price of an ensign's commission, sir.'

'So?' McCandless stared fiercely at Sharpe.

'So we're going into battle, sir. You on that horse, and me on a Mahratta pony. It's a chance, sir, a chance, but if I do well, sir, real well, I'll need you to talk to the General.' Sharpe blushed as he spoke, amazed at his own temerity. 'That's how you repay me, sir, but that's not why I bought him. I just wanted you to have a proper horse, sir. Colonel like you shouldn't be sitting on a scabby native pony, sir.'

McCandless, appalled at Sharpe's ambition, did not know what to say. He stroked the gelding, felt tears in his eyes and could not tell whether they were for Sharpe's impossible dreams or because he had been so touched by the Sergeant's gift. 'If you do well, Sharpe,' he promised, 'I'll talk to Colonel Wallace. He's a good friend. It's possible he'll have a vacant ensign's post, but don't raise your hopes too high!' He paused, wondering if emotion had driven him to promise far too much. 'How did the Tippoo die?' he asked after a while. 'And don't lie to me, Sharpe, it must have been you who killed him.'

'Like a man, sir. Bravely. Facing front, he was. Never gave up.'

'He was a good soldier,' McCandless said, reflecting that the Tippoo had been beaten by a better one. 'I trust you've still got some of his jewels?'

'Jewels, sir?' Sharpe asked. 'I don't know about jewels, sir.'

'Of course not,' McCandless said. If the Company ever heard that Sharpe was carrying the Tippoo's gems their prize agents would descend on the Sergeant like locusts. 'Thank you, Sharpe,' McCandless said fulsomely, 'thank you very much. I shall repay you, of course, but you've touched me. 'Pon my soul, you have touched me.' He insisted upon shaking Sharpe's hand, then watched the Sergeant walk away with the General's orderly. So much sin there, McCandless thought, and so much goodness. But why had Pohlmann ever put the idea of a commission into Sharpe's head? It was an impossible dream, doomed to disappointment.

Another man also watched Sharpe walk away. It was Private Lowry, of the King's 33rd, who now hurried back to the baggage camp. 'It was him, Sergeant,' he told Hakeswill.

'You sure?'

'Large as life.'

'God bless you, Lowry, God bless you.' And God, Hakeswill thought, had certainly blessed him. He had feared that he would have to endure a battle, but now Sharpe had come and Hakeswill could produce his precious warrant and be on his way south. Let the army fight its battle, and let it win or lose, Hakeswill did not care, for Sergeant Hakeswill had what he wanted and he would be rich.

CHAPTER 8

General Wellesley was like a gambler who had emptied his purse onto the table and now had to wait for the cards to fall. There was still time to scoop the money back and walk away from the game, but if he ever felt that temptation, he did not betray it to his aides, nor to any of the army's senior officers. The colonels in his army were all older than Wellesley, some much older, and Wellesley courteously sought their advice, though he largely ignored it. Orrock, a Company colonel and commander of the 8th Madras Infantry, recommended an extravagant outflanking march to the east, though so far as Wellesley could determine the only ambition of such a manoeuvre was to remove the army as far as possible from the enemy horde. The General was forced to pay more attention to his two Williams, Wallace and Harness, the commanding officers of his two Scottish battalions who were also his brigade leaders. 'If we join Stevenson, sir, we might manage the business,' Wallace opined, his tone making it clear that, even combined, the two British armies would be dangerously outnumbered. 'I've no doubt Harness will agree with me, sir,' Wallace added, though William Harness, the commander of the 78th, seemed surprised to have his opinion sought. 'Your business how you fight them, Wellesley,' he growled. 'Point my men and I warrant they'll fight. The bastards had better fight. I'll flog the scum witless if they don't.'

Wellesley forbore to point out that if the 78th refused to fight then there would be no one left to flog, for there would be no army. Harness would not have listened anyway, for he had taken the opportunity to lecture the General on the ameliorative effects of a flogging. 'My first colonel liked to see one well-scourged back a week, Wellesley,' he said. 'He reckoned it kept the men to their duty. He once flogged a sergeant's wife, I recall. He wanted to know if a woman could take the pain, you see, and she couldn't. The lass was fair wriggling.' Harness sighed, recalling happier days. 'D'you dream, Wellesley?'

'Dream, Harness?'

'When you sleep.'

'At times.'

'A flogging will stop it. Nothing to bring on a good night's sleep like a well-whipped back.' Harness, a tall black-browed man who seemed to wear a constant expression of wide-eyed disapproval, shook his head sadly. 'A dreamless sleep, that's what I dream of! Loosens the bowels too, y'know?'

'Sleep?'

'A flogging!' Harness snapped angrily. 'Stimulates the blood, y'see?'

Wellesley disliked making enquiries about senior officers, but he took care to ride alongside his new aide, Colin Campbell. 'Was there much flogging in the 78th?' he asked the aide who, until the siege of Ahmednuggur, had served under Harness.

'There's been much recent talk of it, sir, but not in practice.'

'Your Colonel seems much enamoured of the practice.'

'His enthusiasms come and go,' Campbell said blandly. 'But until a few weeks ago, sir, he was not a man for enthusiasms. Now, suddenly, he is. He encouraged us to eat snakes in July, though he didn't insist on it. I gather he tried some cobra seethed in milk, but it didn't agree with him.'

'Ah!' the General said, understanding the carefully phrased message. So Harness was going out of his wits? Wellesley chided himself for not guessing as much from the Colonel's fixed glare. 'The battalion has a doctor?'

'You can take a horse to water, sir,' Campbell said carefully.

'Indeed, indeed.' Not that the General could do anything about Harness's incipient madness now, nor had the Colonel done anything that deserved dismissal. Indeed, mad or not, he led a fine battalion and Wellesley would need the Scotsmen when he came to Borkardan.

He thought constantly of Borkardan, though what that place was other than a mark on the map, he did not know. He simply imagined the village as swirls of dust and bellowing noise, a place of galloping horses where big guns would flatten the air with their hot thumps and the sky would be ripped apart with shrieking metal and murderous volleys. It would be Wellesley's first field battle. He had fought skirmishes enough, and led a cavalry charge that rode a bandit army into bloody oblivion, but he had never commanded guns and horse and infantry together, and he had never tried to impose his own will on an enemy general. He did not doubt his ability, nor did he doubt that he would stay calm amidst the dust and smoke and flame and blood, but he did fear that some unlucky shot would kill or maim him and the army would then be in the hands of a man without a vision of victory. Stevenson or Wallace would be competent enough, though Wellesley privately thought them both too cautious, but God help an army guided by Harness's enthusiasms.

The other colonels, all Company men, echoed Wallace's advice to make sure of the junction with Stevenson before battle was joined, and Wellesley recognized the wisdom of that opinion, even while he refused to deflect his army to join Stevenson before they both reached Borkardan. There was no time for such a nicety, so instead whichever army first came to the enemy must engage him first, and the other must join the battle, to which end Wellesley knew he must keep his left flank open, for that was where Stevenson's men would join his own. The General reckoned he must put the bulk of his cavalry on the left and station one of his two Highland regiments to serve as a bulwark on that flank, but beyond that he did not know what he would do once he reached Borkardan except attack, attack and attack again. He reasoned that when a small army faced a great horde then the small army had better keep moving and so destroy the enemy piece by piece, but if the small army stayed still then it risked being surrounded and pulverized into surrender.

Borkardan on the twenty-fourth day of September, that was the goal, and Wellesley marched his men hard. The cavalry vanguard and the infantry picquets of the day were roused at midnight and, an hour later, just as the rest of the army was being stirred into sullen wakefulness, those men would start the northwards march. By two o'clock the whole army was moving. Dogs barked as the cavalry vanguard clattered through the villages, and after the horsemen came heavy guns hauled by oxen, marching Highlanders and long ranks of sepoys under their leather-cased colours. Ten miles to the west Stevenson's army marched parallel to Wellesley's, but ten miles was a half-day's march and if either force was confronted by the enemy then the other could do nothing to help. Everything hinged on their meeting at Borkardan.

Most of the men had little idea of what waited for them. They sensed the sudden urgency and guessed it presaged battle, but though the rumours spoke of the enemy as a numberless horde, they marched confidently. They grumbled, of course, for all soldiers grumble. They complained about being hungry, they swore at being made to tramp through the cavalry's manure, and they cursed the oppressive heat that seemed scarcely alleviated by marching at night. Each march finished by midday when the men would rig their tents and sprawl in the shade while the picquets set guards, the cavalry watered horses and the commissary butchered bullocks to provide ration meat.

The cavalry were the busiest men. Their job was to ride ahead and to the flanks of the army to drive any enemy scouts far away so that Scindia would not know that the two red-coated armies marched to trap him, but each morning, as the eastern horizon turned grey, then flushed with pink, then glowed gold and red before finally exploding into light, the patrols searched in vain for any enemies. The Mahratta horse seemed to be staying home, and some of the cavalry officers feared that their enemy might have slipped away again.

As they were nearing Naulniah which would be Wellesley's last resting place before he marched through the night to Borkardan, the General called his patrols closer to the army, ordering them to ride just a mile or two in front of his column. If the enemy was asleep, he explained to his aides, then it was best to do nothing to wake him. It was Sunday, and if the enemy was still engaged in its durbar, then the next day would bring battle. One day to let fears harass hope, though Wellesley's aides seemed careless enough as they marched the last few miles to Naulniah. Major John Blackiston, an engineer on Wellesley's staff, was needling Captain Campbell by saying that the Scots had no harvest to speak of. 'Oats alone, isn't that it, Captain?'

'You've not seen barley, Major, till you've been to Scotland,' Campbell declared. 'You could hide a regiment in a field of Scottish barley.'

'Can't think why you'd want to do such a thing, but doubtless you have your reasons. But as I understand it, Campbell, you heathen Scots have no order of service to give thanks to God for a harvest?'

'You've not heard of the kirn, Major? The mell feast?'

'Kirn?'

'Harvest-home, you call it, when you scavenge those few weeds in England, then beg us generous Scots to send you food. Which we do, being Christian folk who take pity on those less fortunate than ourselves. And talking of the less fortunate, Major, here's the sick list.' Campbell handed Blackiston a piece of paper on which was tallied the number of men from each regiment who were too sick to march. Those men were now being carried on the ox carts of the baggage train and, routinely, those who were unlikely to recover quickly were sent southwards on returning convoys, but Blackiston knew the General would not want to detach any cavalry to protect a convoy just before a battle.

'Tell Sears the sick can all wait in Naulniah,' Blackiston ordered, 'and warn Captain Mackay to have at least a score of empty wagons ready.' He did not specify why Mackay should prepare empty wagons, but nor did he need to do so. The wagons would carry the men wounded in battle, and Blackiston fervently prayed that no more than a score of ox carts would be needed.

Captain Mackay had anticipated the need for empty wagons and had already put chalk marks on those whose burdens were light and could be transferred to other carts. Once at Naulniah he would have the cargoes rearranged, and he sought out Sergeant Hakeswill to supervise the business, but Obadiah Hakeswill had other plans. 'My criminal's back with the army, sir.'

'And you haven't arrested him already?' Mackay asked in surprise.

'Can't march a man in irons, sir, not at this pace. But if you're establishing a camp, sir, at Naulniah, sir, I can hold my prisoner under guard like my duties say I should.'

'So I shall be losing your services, Sergeant?'

234

'It ain't what I want, sir,' Hakeswill lied, 'but I has my responsibilities, sir, and if we're leaving baggage at Naulniah, sir, then I shall have to stay there with my prisoner. Colonel Gore's orders, sir. Is that Naulniah up ahead, sir?'

'It seems to be,' Mackay said, for the distant village was busy with men laying out the lines for the regiments' tents.

'Then, if you'll forgive, sir, I have to be about my duties.'

Hakeswill had deliberately waited for this moment, reckoning that it would be far too great a bother to keep marching northwards with Sharpe under escort. It would be better to wait until the army had established the baggage camp where Hakeswill could keep Sharpe while the battle was fought, and if one more redcoat died that day, who would miss him? So now, freed from Mackay's baggage guard, the Sergeant hurried his six men up the column to find Colonel McCandless.

McCandless's leg was still throbbing, and the fever had left him weak, but his spirits had recovered, because riding Aeolus had convinced him that no finer horse had ever stepped on earth. The gelding was tireless, McCandless declared, and better schooled than any horse he had ever ridden. Sevajee was amused by the Colonel's enthusiasm. 'You sound like a man with a new woman, McCandless.'

'If you say so, Sevajee, if you say so,' McCandless said, not rising to the Indian's bait. 'But isn't he a beauty?'

'Magnificent.'

'County Meath,' the Colonel said. 'They breed good hunters in County Meath. They have big hedges! Like jumping a haystack.'

'County Meath is in Ireland?' Sevajee asked.

'It is, it is.'

'Another county beneath Britain's heel?'

'For a man beneath my heel, Sevajee,' the Colonel said, 'you look in remarkably fine fettle. Can we talk about tomorrow? Sharpe! I want you to listen.'

Sharpe urged his small Mahratta horse alongside the Colonel's big gelding. Like Wellesley, Colonel McCandless was planning what he would do at Borkardan and, though the Colonel's task was much smaller than the General's, it was no less important to him. 'Let us assume, gentlemen, that we shall win this battle at Borkardan tomorrow,' he said, and waited for the invariable riposte from Sevajee, but the tall Indian said nothing. 'Our task, then,' the Colonel went on, 'is to hunt Dodd among the fugitives. Hunt him and capture him.'

'If he still lives,' Sevajee remarked.

'Which I pray God he does. He must face British justice before he goes to God's condemnation. So when the battle is joined, gentlemen, our task is not to get involved with the fighting, but to search for Dodd's men. It won't be difficult. So far as I know they're the only regiment in white jackets, and once we have them, we stay close. Stay close till they break, then we pursue.'

'And if they don't break?' Sevajee asked.

'Then we march again and fight again,' the Colonel answered grimly. 'But by God's grace, Sevajee, we shall find this man even if we have to hunt him into the deserts of Persia. Britain has more than a heavy heel, Sevajee, it has a long arm.'

'Long arms are easily cut off,' Sevajee said.

Sharpe had stopped listening. He had heard a commotion behind as a group of army wives were thrust off the road and had turned to see who had barged the women aside and, at first, all he had seen was a group of redcoats. Then he had recognized the red facings on the jackets and he had wondered what on earth men of the 33rd were doing here, and then he had recognized Sergeant Hakeswill.

Obadiah Hakeswill! Of all people, Hakeswill! Sharpe stared in horror at his long-time enemy and Obadiah Hakeswill caught his eye and grinned maliciously and Sharpe knew that his appearance boded no good. Hakeswill broke into a lumbering run so that his haversack, pouches, bayonet and musket thumped against his body. 'Sir!' he called up to Colonel McCandless. 'Colonel McCandless, sir!'

McCandless turned and frowned at the interruption, then, like Sharpe, he stared at the Sergeant as though he did not believe his eyes. McCandless knew Hakeswill, for Hakeswill had been imprisoned in the Tippoo Sultan's dungeons at the same time as Sharpe and the Colonel, and what McCandless knew he did not like. The Scotsman scowled. 'Sergeant Hakeswill? You're far from home.'

'As are we all, sir, doing our duties to King and country in an 'eathen land, sir.' Hakeswill slowed to a march, keeping pace with the Scotsman's horse. 'I'm ordered to see you, sir, by the General himself, sir. By Sir Arthur Wellesley, sir, God bless him, sir.'

'I know who the General is, Sergeant,' McCandless said coldly.

'Glad to hear it, sir. Got a paper for you, sir. Urgent paper, sir, what needs your urgent attention, sir.' Hakeswill gave a venomous glance at Sharpe, then held the warrant up to McCandless. 'This paper, sir, what I've been carrying in my pouch, sir, on Colonel Gore's orders, sir.'

McCandless unfolded the warrant. Sevajee had hurried ahead, going to find somewhere to billet his men in the village and, while McCandless read the orders for Sharpe's arrest, Hakeswill fell back so that he was walking beside Sharpe. 'We'll have you off that horse in a quick minute, Sharpie,' he said.

'Go and boil your head, Obadiah.'

'You always did have ideas above your station, Sharpie. Won't do! Not in this army. We ain't the Frogs. We don't wear pretty long red boots like yours, we don't, 'cos we don't have airs and graces, not in this army. Says so in the scriptures.'

Sharpe tugged on his rein so that his small horse swerved into Hakeswill's path. The Sergeant skipped aside. 'Under arrest, you are, Sharpie!' Hakeswill crowed. 'Under arrest! Court-martial offence. Be a shooting job, I dare say.' Hakeswill grinned, showing his yellow teeth. 'Bang bang, you're dead. Taken me a long time, Sharpie, but I'm going to be evens with you. All over for you, it is. Says so in the scriptures.'

'It says nothing of the sort, Sergeant!' McCandless snapped, turning in his saddle and glaring at the Sergeant. 'I've had occasion to speak to you before about the scriptures, and if I hear you cite their authority one more time I shall break you, Sergeant Hakeswill, I shall break you!'

'Sir!' Hakeswill acknowledged. He doubted that McCandless, a Company officer, could break anyone in the King's army, at least not without a deal of effort, but he did not let his scepticism show, for Obadiah Hakeswill believed in showing complete subservience to all officers. 'Never meant to upset you, sir,' he said, 'apologize, sir. No offence meant, sir.'

McCandless read the warrant a third time. Something about the wording worried him, but he could not quite place his concern. 'It says here, Sharpe,' McCandless said, 'that you struck an officer on August the fifth this year.'

'I did what, sir?' Sharpe asked, horrified.

'Assaulted Captain Morris. Here.' And McCandless thrust the warrant towards Sharpe. 'Take it, man. Read it.'

Sharpe took the paper and while he read Sergeant Hakeswill embellished the charge to Colonel McCandless. 'An assault, sir, with a jakes pot, sir. A full one, sir. Liquids and solids, sir, both. Right on the Captain's head, sir.'

'And you were the only witness?' McCandless asked.

'Me and Captain Morris, sir.'

'I don't believe a word of it,' McCandless growled.

'Up to a court to decide, sir, begging your pardon. Your job, sir, is to deliver the prisoner to my keeping.'

'You do not instruct me in my duties, Sergeant!' McCandless said angrily.

'I just knows you will do your duty, sir, like we all does. Except for some as I could mention.' Hakeswill smiled at Sharpe. 'Finding the long words difficult, are we, Sharpie?'

McCandless reached over and took the warrant back from Sharpe, who had, indeed, been finding some of the longer words difficult. The Colonel had expressed his disbelief in the charge, but that was more out of loyalty to Sharpe than from any conviction, though there was still something out of kilter in the warrant. 'Is it true, Sharpe?' McCandless now asked.

'No, sir!' Sharpe said indignantly.

'He was always a good liar, sir,' Hakeswill said helpfully. 'Lies like a rug, sir, he does. Famous for it.' The Sergeant was becoming breathless as he hurried to keep pace with the Scotsman's horse.

'So what do you intend to do with Sergeant Sharpe?' McCandless asked.

'Do, sir? Do my duty, of course, sir. Escort the prisoner back to battalion, sir, as is ordered.' Hakeswill gestured at his six men who marched a few paces behind. 'We'll guard him nice and proper, sir, all the way home and then have him stand trial for his filthy crime.'

McCandless bit his right thumb and shook his head. He rode in silence for a few paces, and when Sharpe protested he ignored the indignant words. He put the warrant in his right hand again and seemed to read it yet another time. Far off to the east, at least a mile away, there was a sudden flurry of dust and the sparkle of sword blades catching the sun. Some enemy horsemen had been waiting in a grove of trees from where they had been watching the British march, but now they were flushed out by a troop of Mysore horsemen who pursued them northwards. McCandless glanced at the distant action. 'So they'll know we're here now, more's the pity. How do you spell your name, Sharpe? With or without an "e"?'

'With, sir.'

'You will correct me if I'm wrong,' McCandless said, 'but it seems to me that this is not your name.' He handed the warrant back to Sharpe who saw that the 'e' at the end of his name had been smeared out. There was a smudge of black ink there, and beneath it the impression of the 'e' made by the steel nib in the paper, but the ink had been diluted and nearly erased.

Sharpe hid his astonishment that McCandless, a stickler for honesty and straight-dealing, had resorted to such a subterfuge. 'Not my name, sir,' Sharpe said woodenly.

Hakeswill looked from Sharpe to McCandless, then back to Sharpe and finally at McCandless again. 'Sir!' The word exploded from him.

'You're out of breath, Sergeant,' McCandless said, taking the warrant back from Sharpe. 'But you will see here that you are expressly ordered to arrest a sergeant whose name is Richard Sharp. No "e", Sergeant. This Sergeant Sharpe uses an "e" on his name so he cannot be the man you want, and I certainly cannot release him to your custody on the authority of this piece of paper. Here.' McCandless held the warrant out, letting it drop a heartbeat before Hakeswill could take it. The paper fluttered down to the dusty road.

Hakeswill snatched the warrant up and peered at the writing. 'Ink's run, sir!' he protested. 'Sir?' He ran after McCandless's horse, stumbling on the uneven road. 'Look, sir! Ink's run, sir.'

McCandless ignored the offered warrant. 'It is clear, Sergeant Hakeswill, that the spelling of the name has been corrected. In all conscience I cannot act upon that warrant. What you must do, Sergeant, is send a message to Lieutenant Colonel Gore asking him to clear up the confusion. A new warrant, I think, would be best, and until such time as I see such a warrant, legibly written, I cannot release Sergeant Sharpe from his present duties. Good day, Hakeswill.'

'You can't do this, sir!' Hakeswill protested.

McCandless smiled. 'You fundamentally misunderstand the hierarchy of the army, Sergeant. It is I, a colonel, who define your duties, not you, a sergeant, who define mine. "I say to a man, go, and he goeth." It says so in the scriptures. I bid you good day.' And with that the Scotsman touched his spurs to the gelding's flanks.

Hakeswill's face twitched as he turned on Sharpe. 'I'll have you, Sharpie, I will have you. I ain't forgotten nothing.'

'You ain't learned nothing either,' Sharpe said, then spurred after the Colonel. He lifted two fingers as he passed Hakeswill, then left him behind in the dust.

He was, for the moment, free.

Simone Joubert placed the eight diamonds on the window ledge of the tiny house where the wives of Scindia's European officers had been quartered. She was alone for the moment, for the other women had gone to visit the three *compoos* that were stationed on the Kaitna's northern bank, but Simone had not wanted their company and so she had pleaded a turbulent stomach, though she supposed she ought to visit Pierre before the battle, if indeed there was to be a fight. Not that Simone cared much. Let them have their battle, she thought, and at the end of it, when the river was dark with British blood, her life would be no better. She gazed at the diamonds again, thinking about the man who had given them to her. Pierre would be angry if he learned she was concealing such wealth, but once his anger had passed he would sell the stones and send the money back to his rapacious family in France.

'Madame Joubert!' A voice hailed her from outside the window and Simone guiltily swept the diamonds into her small purse, though, because she was on an upper floor, no one could see the gems. She peered down from the window and saw a cheerful Colonel Pohlmann in shirtsleeves and braces standing among the straw in the courtyard of the neighbouring house.

'Colonel,' she responded dutifully.

'I am hiding my elephants,' the Colonel said, gesturing at the three beasts which were being led into the courtyard. The tallest carried Pohlmann's howdah, while the other two were burdened with the wooden chests in which the Colonel was reputed to keep his gold. 'Might I leave you to guard my menagerie?' the Colonel asked.

'From what?' Simone asked.

'From thieves,' the Colonel said happily.

'Not the British?'

'They will never reach this far, Madame,' Pohlmann said, 'except as prisoners.' And Simone had a sudden vision of Sergeant Richard Sharpe again. She had been raised to believe that the British were a piratical race, a nation without a conscience who mindlessly impeded the spread of French enlightenment, but perhaps, she thought, she liked pirates.

'I will guard your elephants, Colonel,' she called down.

'And have some dinner with me?' Pohlmann asked. 'I have some cold chicken and warm wine.'

'I have promised to join Pierre,' Simone said, dreading the two-mile ride across the drab fields to where Dodd's Cobras waited beside the Kaitna.

'Then I shall escort you to his side, Madame,' Pohlmann said courteously. Once the battle was over he reckoned he might mount an assault on Madame Joubert's virtue. It would be an amusing diversion, but not, he thought, an especially difficult campaign. Unhappy women yielded to patience and sympathy, and there would be plenty of time for both once Wellesley and Stevenson had been destroyed. And there would be a pleasure, too, in beating Major Dodd to the prize of Simone's virtue.

Pohlmann detailed twenty of his bodyguard to guard the three elephants. He never rode one of the beasts in battle, for an elephant became the target of every enemy gunner, but he looked forward to mounting the howdah for a great victory parade after the campaign. And victory would leave Pohlmann rich, rich enough to start building his great marble palace in which he planned to hang the captured banners of his enemy. From sergeant to princeling in ten years, and the key to that princedom was the gold that he was storing in Assaye. He ordered his bodyguard that no one, not even the Rajah of Berar whose troops were garrisoning the village, should be allowed into the courtyard, then he instructed his servants to detach the golden panels from the howdah and add them to the boxes of treasure. 'If the worst should happen,' he told the subadar who was in charge of the men guarding the treasure, 'I'll join you here. Not that it will,' he added cheerfully.

A clatter of hooves in the alley outside the courtyard announced the arrival of a patrol of horsemen returning from a foray south of the Kaitna. For three days Pohlmann had kept his cavalry on a tight rein, not wanting to alarm Wellesley as the British General marched north towards the trap, but that morning he had released a few patrols southwards and one of those now returned with the welcome news that the enemy was only four miles south of the Kaitna. Pohlmann already knew that the second British army, that of Colonel Stevenson, was still ten miles off to the west, and that meant that the British had blundered. Wellesley, in his eagerness to

243

reach Borkardan, had brought his men to the waiting arms of the whole Mahratta army.

The Colonel thought about waiting for Madame Joubert, then decided he could not afford the time and so he mounted the horse he rode in battle and, with those of his bodyguard not deputed to guard his gold, and with a string of aides surrounding him, he galloped south from Assaye to the Kaitna's bank where his trap was set. He passed the news to Dupont and Saleur, then rode to prepare his own troops. He spoke with his officers, finishing with Major William Dodd. 'I hear the British are making camp in Naulniah,' Pohlmann said, 'so what we should do is march south and hammer him. It's one thing to have Wellesley so close, but it's quite another to bring him to battle.'

'So why don't we march?' Dodd asked.

'Because Scindia won't have it, that's why. Scindia insists we fight on the defensive. He's nervous.' Dodd spat, but made no other comment on his employer's timidity. 'So there's a nasty danger,' Pohlmann went on, 'that Wellesley won't attack us at all, but will retreat towards Stevenson.'

'So we beat them both at once,' Dodd said confidently.

'As we shall, if we must,' Pohlmann agreed drily, 'but I'd rather fight them separately.' He was confident of victory, no soldier could be more confident, but he was no fool and given the chance to defeat two small armies instead of one medium-sized force, he would prefer the former. 'If you have a god, Major,' he said, 'pray that Wellesley is over-confident. Pray that he attacks us.'

It was a fervent prayer, for if Wellesley did attack he would be forced to send his men across the Kaitna which was some sixty or seventy paces broad and flowing brown between high banks that were over a hundred paces apart. If the monsoon had come the river would have filled its bed and been twelve or fifteen feet deep, while now it was only six or seven, though that was quite deep enough to stop an army crossing, but right in front of Pohlmann's position there was a series of fords, and Pohlmann's prayer was that the British would try to cross the fords and attack straight up the road to Assaye. Wellesley would have no other choice, not if he wanted a battle, for Pohlmann had summoned farmers from every village in the vicinity, from Assaye and Waroor, from Kodully, Taunklee and Peepulgaon, and asked them where a man could drive a herd of cattle through the river. He had used the example of a herd of oxen because where such a herd could go so could oxen drawing guns, and every man had agreed that in this season the only crossing places were the fords between Kodully and Taunklee. A man could drive his herds upriver to Borkardan, they told Pohlmann's interpreter, and cross there, but that was a half-day's walk away and why would a man be that foolish when the river provided eight safe fords between the two villages?

'Are there any crossing places downstream?' Pohlmann asked.

A score of dark faces shook in unison. 'No, sahib, not in the wet season.'

'This season isn't wet.'

'There are still no fords, sahib.' They were sure, as sure as only local men who had lived all their lives bounded by the same water and trees and soil could be sure.

Pohlmann had still been unconvinced. 'And if a man does not want to drive a herd, but just wants to cross himself, where would he cross?'

The villagers provided the same answer. 'Between Kodully and Taunklee, sahib.'

'Nowhere else?'

Nowhere else, they assured him, and that meant Wellesley would be forced to cross the river in the face of Pohlmann's waiting army. The British infantry and guns would have to slither down the steep southern bank of the Kaitna, cross a wide expanse of mud, wade through the river, then climb the steep northern bank, and all the while they would be under fire from the Mahratta guns until, when they reached the green fields on the northern shore, they would re-form their ranks and march forward into a double storm of musketry and artillery. Wherever the British crossed the Kaitna, anywhere between Kodully and Taunklee, they would find the same murderous reception waiting, for Pohlmann's three prime *compoos* were arrayed in one long line that fronted that whole stretch of the river. There were eighty guns in that line, and though some threw nothing but a five- or six-pound ball, at least half were heavy artillery and all were manned by Goanese gunners who knew their business. The cannon were grouped in eight batteries, one for each ford, and there was not an inch of ground between the batteries that could not be flailed by canister or beaten by round shot or scorched by shells. Pohlmann's well-trained infantry waited to pour a devastating weight of volley fire into red-coated regiments already deafened and demoralized by the cannon fire that would have torn their ranks into shreds as they struggled across the bloody fords. The numberless Mahratta cavalry were off to the west, strung along the bank towards Borkardan, and there it would wait until the British were defeated and Pohlmann released the horsemen to the joys of pursuit and slaughter.

The Hanoverian reckoned that his battle line waiting at the fords would decimate the enemy and the horsemen would turn the British defeat into a bloody rout, but there was always a small chance that the enemy might survive the river crossing and succeed in gaining the Kaitna's northern bank in good order. He doubted the British could force his three *compoos* back, but in case they did Pohlmann planned to retreat two miles to the village of Assaye and invite the British to waste more men in an assault on what was now a miniature fortress. Assaye, like every other village on the plain, lived in fear of bandit raids and so the outermost houses had high, windowless walls made of thick mud, and the houses were joined so that their walls formed a continous rampart as high as the wall at Ahmednuggur. Pohlmann had blocked the village's streets with ox carts, he had ordered loopholes hacked in the outer wall, he had placed all his smaller guns, a score of two- and three-pounder cannon, at the foot of the wall and then he had garrisoned the houses with the Rajah of Berar's twenty thousand infantrymen. Pohlmann doubted that any of those twenty thousand men would need to fight, but he had the luxury of knowing they were in reserve should anything go wrong at the Kaitna.

He had just one problem left and to solve it he asked Dodd to accompany him eastwards along the river bank. 'If you were Wellesley,' he asked Dodd, 'how would you attack?'

Dodd considered the question, then shrugged as if to suggest that the answer was obvious. 'Concentrate all my best troops at one end of the line and hammer my way through.'

'Which end?'

Dodd thought for a few seconds. He had been tempted to say that Wellesley would attack in the west, at the fords by Kodully, for that would keep him closest to Stevenson's army, but Stevenson was a long way away and Pohlmann was deliberately riding eastwards. 'The eastern end?' Dodd suggested diffidently.

Pohlmann nodded. 'Because if he drives our left flank back he can place his army between us and Assaye. He divides us.'

'And we surround him,' Dodd observed.

'I'd rather we weren't divided,' Pohlmann said, for if Wellesley did succeed in driving back the left flank he might well succeed in capturing Assaye, and while that would still leave Pohlmann's *compoos* on the field, it would mean that the Colonel would lose his gold. So the Colonel needed a good hard anchor at the eastern end of his line to prevent his left flank being turned, and of all the regiments under his command he reckoned Dodd's Cobras were the best. The left flank was now being held by one of Dupont's regiments, a good one, but not as good as Dodd's.

Pohlmann gestured at the Dutchman's brown-coated troops who looked across the river towards the small village of Taunklee. 'Good men,' he said, 'but not as good as yours.'

'Few of them are.'

'But we'd best pray those fellows hold,' Pohlmann said, 'because if I was Wellesley that's where I'd put my sharpest attack. Straight up, turn our flank, cut us off from Assaye. It worries me, it does.'

Dodd could not see that it was overmuch cause for worry, for he doubted that the best troops in the world could survive the river crossing under the massed fire of Pohlmann's batteries, but he did see the left flank's importance. 'So reinforce Dupont,' he suggested carelessly.

Pohlmann looked surprised, as though the idea had not already occurred to him. 'Reinforce him? Why not? Would you care to hold the left, Major?'

'The left?' Dodd said suspiciously. Traditionally the right of the line was the station of honour on a battlefield and, while most of Pohlmann's troops neither cared nor knew about such courtesies, William Dodd certainly knew, which was why Pohlmann had let the Major suggest that the left should be reinforced rather than simply order the touchy Dodd to move his precious Cobras.

'You would not be under Dupont's orders, of course not,' Pohlmann reassured Dodd. 'You'll be your own master, Major, answerable to me, only to me.' Pohlmann paused. 'Of course, if you'd rather not take post on the left I'd entirely

248

understand, and some other fellows can have the honour of defeating the British right.'

'My fellows can do it!' Dodd said belligerently.

'It is a very responsible post,' Pohlmann said diffidently.

'We can do it, sir!' Dodd insisted.

Pohlmann smiled his gratitude. 'I was hoping you'd say so. Every other regiment is commanded by a Frog or a Dutchman, Major, and I need an Englishman to fight the hardest battle.'

'And you've found one, sir,' Dodd said.

I've found an idiot, Pohlmann thought as he rode back to the line's centre, but Dodd was a reliable idiot and a hard-fighting man. He watched as Dodd's men left the line, and as the line closed up to fill the gap, and then as the Cobras took their place on the left flank. The line was complete now, it was deadly, it was anchored firmly, and it was ready. All it needed was the enemy to compound their blunder by trying to attack, and then Pohlmann would crown his career by filling the Kaitna with British blood. Let them attack, he prayed, just let them attack, and the day, with all its glory, would be his.

The British camp spread around Naulniah. Lines of tents sheltered infantry, quartermasters sought out the village headman and arranged that the women of the village would bake bread in return for rupees, while the cavalry led their horses down to drink from the River Purna which flowed just to the north of the village. One squadron of the 19th Dragoons was ordered to cross the river and ride a couple of miles north in search of enemy patrols and those troopers dropped their bags of forage in the village, watered their horses, washed the dust from their faces, then remounted and rode on out of sight.

Colonel McCandless picked a broad tree as his tent. He

had no servant, nor wanted one, so he brushed down Aeolus with handfuls of straw while Sharpe fetched a pail of water from the river. The Colonel, in his shirtsleeves, straightened as Sharpe came back. 'You do realize, Sergeant, that I am guilty of some dishonesty in the matter of that warrant?'

'I wanted to thank you, sir.'

'I doubt I deserve any thanks, except that my deception might have staved off a greater evil.' The Colonel crossed to his saddlebags and brought out his Bible which he gave to Sharpe. 'Put your right hand on the scriptures, Sergeant, and swear to me you are innocent of the charge.'

Sharpe placed his right palm on the Bible's worn cover. He felt foolish, but McCandless's face was stern and Sharpe made his own face solemn. 'I do swear it, sir. I never touched the man that night, didn't even see him.' His voice proclaimed both his indignation and his innocence, but that was small consolation. The warrant might be defeated for the moment, but Sharpe knew such things did not go away. 'What will happen now, sir?'

'We'll just have to make certain the truth prevails,' McCandless said vaguely. He was still trying to decide what had been wrong with the warrant, but he could not identify what had troubled him. He took the Bible, stowed it away, then put his hands in the small of his back and arched his spine. 'How far have we come today? Fourteen miles? Fifteen?'

'Thereabouts, sir.'

'I'm feeling my age, Sharpe, feeling my age. The leg's mending well enough, but now my back aches. Not good. But just a short march tomorrow, God be thanked, no more than ten miles, then battle.' He pulled a watch from his fob pocket and snapped open the lid. 'We have fifteen minutes, Sergeant, so it might be wise to prepare our weapons.'

'Fifteen minutes, sir?'

'It's Sunday, Sharpe! The Lord's day. Colonel Wallace's chaplain will be holding divine service on the hour, and I expect you to come with me. He preaches a fine sermon. But there's still time for you to clean your musket first.'

The musket was cleaned with boiling water which Sharpe poured down the barrel, then sloshed about so that the very last remnants of powder residue were washed free. He doubted the musket needed cleaning, but he dutifully did it, then oiled the lock and put a new flint into the doghead. He borrowed a sharpening stone from one of Sevajee's men and honed the bayonet's point so that the tip shone white and deadly, then he dabbed some oil on the blade before sliding it home into its scabbard. There was nothing else to do now except listen to the sermon, sleep and do the mundane tasks. There would be a meal to cook and the horses to water again, but those commonplace jobs were overshadowed by the knowledge that the enemy was just a short march away at Borkardan. Sharpe felt a shudder of nerves. What would battle be like? Would he stand? Or would he turn out like that corporal at Boxtel who had started to rave about angels and then had run like a spring hare through the Flanders rain?

A half-mile behind Sharpe the baggage train began to trudge into a wide field where the oxen were hobbled, the camels picketed and the elephants tethered to trees. Grass-cutters spread out into the countryside to find forage for the animals which were watered from a muddy irrigation chan-nel. The elephants were fed piles of palm leaves and buckets of rice soaked in butter, while Captain Mackay scurried through the chaos on his small bay horse, making sure that the ammunition was being properly stowed and the animals suitably fed. He suddenly caught sight of a disconsolate Ser-geant Hakeswill and his six men. 'Sergeant! You're still here? I thought you'd have your rogue safely pinioned by now?'

'Problems, sir,' Hakeswill said, standing rigidly to attention. 'Easy, Sergeant, stand easy. No rogue?'

'Not yet, sir.'

'So you're back in my command, are you? That's splendid, just splendid.' Mackay was an eager young officer who did his best to see the good in everybody, and though he found the Sergeant from the 33rd somewhat daunting, he did his best to communicate his own enthusiasm. '*Puckalees*, Sergeant,' he said brightly, '*puckalees*.'

Hakeswill's face wrenched in a series of spasms. '*Puckalees*, sir?'

'Water carriers, Sergeant.'

'I knows what a *puckalee* is, sir, on account of having lived in this heathen land more years than I can count, but begging your pardon, sir, what has a *puckalee* to do with me?'

'We have to establish a collecting point for them,' Mackay said. The *puckalees* were all on the strengths of the individual regiments and in battle their job was to keep the fighting men supplied with water. 'I need a man to watch over them,' Mackay said. 'They're good fellows, all of them, but oddly frightened of bullets! They need chivvying along. I'll be busy enough with the ammunition wagons tomorrow, so can I rely on you to make sure the *puckalees* do their job like the stout fellows they are?' The 'stout fellows' were boys, grandfathers, cripples, the half-blind and the halfwitted. 'Excellent! Excellent!' the young Captain said. 'A problem solved! Make sure you get some rest, Sergeant. We'll all need to be sprightly tomorrow. And if you feel the need for some spiritual refreshment you'll find the 74th are holding divine service any moment now.' Mackay smiled at Hakeswill, then set off in pursuit of an errant group of bullock carts. 'You! You! You with the tents! Not there! Come here!'

'*Puckalees*,' Hakeswill said, spitting, '*puckalees*.' None of his men responded for they knew well enough to leave Sergeant

Hakeswill alone when he was in a more than usually foul mood. 'Could be worse, though,' he said.

'Worse?' Private Flaherty ventured.

Hakeswill's face twitched. 'We has a problem, boys,' he said dourly, 'and the problem is one Scottish Colonel who is attempting to bugger up the good order of our regiment. I won't abide it, I won't. Regimental honour is at stake, it is. He's been wool-pulling, ain't he? And he thinks he's pulled it clean over our eyes, but he ain't, because I've seen through him, I have, I've seen through his Scotch soul and it's as rotten as rotten eggs. Sharpie's paying him off, ain't he? Stands to reason! Corruption, boys, nothing but corruption.' Hakeswill blinked, his mind racing. 'If we're flogging *pukalees* halfway across bleeding India tomorrow, lads, then we will have our moment and the regiment would want us to seize it.'

'Seize it?' Lowry asked.

'Kill the bugger, you blockheaded toad.'

'Kill Sharpie?'

'God help me for leading halfwits,' Hakeswill said. 'Not Sharpie! We wants him private like, where we can fillet him fair and square. You kills the Scotchman! Once Mister bleeding McCandless is gone, Sharpie's ours.'

'You can't kill a colonel!' Kendrick said aghast.

'You points your firelock, Private Kendrick,' Hakeswill said, ramming his own musket's muzzle hard into Kendrick's midriff. 'You cocks your musket, Private Kendrick' – Hakeswill pulled back the doghead and the heavy lock clicked into place – 'and then you shoots the bugger clear through.' Hakeswill pulled his trigger. The powder in the pan exploded with a small crackle and fizz, and Kendrick leaped back as the smoke drifted away from the lock, but the musket had not been charged. Hakeswill laughed. 'Got you, didn't I? You thought I was putting a *goolie* in your belly! But that's what

253

you do to McCandless. A *goolie* in his belly or in his brain or in any other part what kills him. And you do it tomorrow.' The six men looked dubious, and Hakeswill grinned. 'Extra shares for you all if it happens, boys, extra shares. You'll be paying the officers' whores when you get home, and all it will take is one *goolie*.' He smiled wolfishly. 'Tomorrow, boys, tomorrow.'

But across the river, where the blue-coated patrol of the 19th Dragoons was exploring the countryside south of the Kaitna, everything was changing.

Wellesley had dismounted, stripped off his jacket and was washing his face from a basin of water held on a tripod. Lieutenant Colonel Orrock, the Company officer who commanded the picquets that day, was complaining about the two galloper guns that were supposedly attached to his small command. 'They wouldn't keep up, sir. Laggards, sir. I found myself four hundred yards ahead of them! Four hundred yards!'

'I asked you to set a brisk pace, Orrock,' the General said, wishing the fool would go away. He reached for a towel and vigorously scrubbed his face dry.

'But if we'd been challenged!' Orrock protested.

'Gallopers can move briskly when they must,' the General said, then sighed as he realized the prickly Orrock needed placating. 'Who commanded the guns?'

'Barlow, sir.'

'I'll speak to him,' the General promised, then turned as the patrol of 19th Dragoons that had crossed the River Purna to reconnoitre the ground on the far bank came threading through the rising tents towards him. Wellesley had not expected the patrol back this soon and their return puzzled him, then he saw they were escorting a group of *bhinjarries*, the black-cloaked merchants who traversed India buying and selling food. 'You'll excuse me, Orrock,' the General said, plucking his coat from a stool.

'You will talk with Barlow, sir?' Orrock asked.

'I said so, didn't I?' Wellesley called as he walked towards the horsemen.

The patrol leader, a captain, slid off his horse and gestured at the *bhinjarries'* leader. 'We found these fellows a half-mile north of the river, sir. They've got eighteen pack oxen loaded with grain and they reckon the enemy ain't in Borkardan at all. They were planning to sell the grain in Assaye.'

'Assaye?' The General frowned at the unfamiliar name.

'It's a village four or five miles north of here, sir. He says it's thick with the enemy.'

'Four or five miles?' Wellesley asked in astonishment. 'Four or five?'

The cavalry captain shrugged. 'That's what they say, sir.' He gestured at the grain merchants who stood impassively among the mounted troopers.

Dear God, Wellesley thought, four or five miles? He had been humbugged! The enemy had stolen a march on him, and at any moment that enemy might appear to the north and launch an attack on the British encampment and there was no chance for Stevenson to come to his help. The 74th were singing hymns and the enemy was five miles away, maybe less? The General spun round. 'Barclay! Campbell! Horses! Quick now!'

The flurry of activity at the General's tent sent a rumour whipping through the camp, and the rumour was fanned into alarm when the whole of the 19th Dragoons and the 4th Native Cavalry trotted through the river on the heels of the General and his two aides. Colonel McCandless had been walking with Sharpe towards the 74th's lines, but seeing the sudden excitement, he turned and hurried back towards his horse. 'Come on, Sharpe!'

'Where to, sir?'

'We'll find out. Sevajee?'

'We're ready.'

McCandless's party left the camp five minutes after the General. They could see the dust left by the cavalry ahead and McCandless hurried to catch up. They rode through a landscape of small fields cut by deep dry gulches and cactus-thorn hedges. Wellesley had been following the earth road northwards, but after a while the General swerved westwards onto a field of stubble and McCandless did not follow, but kept straight on up the road. 'No point in tiring the horses unnecessarily,' he explained, though Sharpe suspected the Colonel was merely impatient to go north and see what-ever had caused the excitement. The two British cavalry regiments were in sight to the east, but there was no enemy visible.

Sevajee and his men had ridden ahead, but when they reached a crest some two hundred yards in front of McCandless they suddenly wrenched on their reins and swerved back. Sharpe expected to see a horde of Mahratta cavalry come boiling over the crest, but the skyline stayed empty as Sevajee and his men halted a few yards short of the ridge and there dismounted.

'You'll not want them to see you, Colonel,' Sevajee said drily when McCandless caught up.

'Them?'

Sevajee gestured at the crest. 'Take a look. You'll want to dismount.'

McCandless and Sharpe both slid from their saddles, then walked to the skyline where a cactus hedge offered conceal-ment and from where they could stare at the country to the north and Sharpe, who had never seen such a sight before, simply gazed in amazement.

It was not an army. It was a horde, a whole people, a

nation. Thousands upon thousands of the enemy, all in line, mile after mile of them. Men and women and children and guns and camels and bullocks and rocket batteries and horses and tents and still more men until there seemed to be no end to them. 'Jesus!' Sharpe said, the imprecation torn from him.

'Sharpe!'

'Sorry, sir.' But no wonder he had sworn, for Sharpe had never imagined that an army could look so vast. The nearest men were no more than half a mile away, beyond a discoloured river that flowed between steep mud banks. A village lay on the nearer bank, but on the northern side, just beyond the mud bluff, there was a line of guns. Big guns, the same painted and sculpted cannon that Sharpe had seen in Pohlmann's camp. Beyond the guns was the infantry and behind the infantry, and spreading far out of sight to the east, was a mass of cavalry and beyond them the myriad of camp followers. More infantry were posted about a distant village where Sharpe could just see a cluster of bright flags. 'How many are there?' he asked.

'At least a hundred thousand men?' McCandless ventured.

'At least,' Sevajee agreed, 'but most are adventurers come for loot.' The Indian was peering through a long ivory-clad telescope. 'And the cavalry won't help in a battle.'

'It'll be down to these fellows,' McCandless said, indicating the infantry just behind the gun line. 'Fifteen thousand?'

'Fourteen or fifteen,' Sevajee said. 'Too many.'

'Too many guns,' McCandless said gloomily. 'It'll be a retreat.'

'I thought we came here to fight!' Sharpe said belligerently.

'We came here expecting to rest, then march on Borkardan tomorrow,' McCandless said testily. 'We didn't come here to take on the whole enemy army with just five thousand infantry. They know we're coming, they're ready for us and they simply want us to walk into their fire. Wellesley's not a fool, Sharpe. He'll march us back, link up with Stevenson, then find them again.'

Sharpe felt a pang of relief that he would not discover the realities of battle, but the relief was tempered by a tinge of disappointment. The disappointment surprised him, and the relief made him fear he might be a coward.

'If we retreat,' Sevajee warned, 'those horsemen will harry us all the way.'

'We'll just have to fight them off,' McCandless said confidently, then let out a long satisfied breath. 'Got him! There, the left flank!' He pointed and Sharpe saw, far away at the very end of the enemy gunline, a scatter of white uniforms. 'Not that it helps us,' McCandless said wryly, 'but at least we're on his heels.'

'Or he's on ours,' Sevajee said, then he offered his telescope to Sharpe. 'See for yourself, Sergeant.'

Sharpe rested the glass's long barrel on a thick cactus leaf. He moved the lens slowly along the line of infantry. Men slept in the shade, some were in their small tents and others sat in groups and he could have sworn a few were gambling. Officers, Indian and European, strolled behind their men, while in front of them the massive line of guns waited with their ammunition limbers. He moved the glass to the very far left of the enemy line and saw the white jackets of Dodd's men, and saw something else. Two huge guns, much bigger than anything he had seen before. 'They've got their siege guns in the line, sir,' he told McCandless, who trained his own telescope.

'Eighteen-pounders,' McCandless guessed, 'maybe bigger?' The Colonel collapsed his glass. 'Why aren't they patrolling this side of the river?'

'Because they don't want to frighten us away,' Sevajee said. 'They want us to stroll up to their guns and die in the river, but they'll still have some horsemen hidden on this bank, waiting to tell them when we retreat.'

The sound of hooves made Sharpe whip round in expectation of those enemy cavalry, but it was only General Wellesley and his two aides who cantered along the lower ground beneath the crest. 'They're all there, McCandless,' the General shouted happily.

'So it seems, sir.'

The General reined in, waiting for McCandless to come down from the skyline and join him. 'They seem to presume we'll make a frontal attack,' Wellesley said wryly, as though he found the idea amusing.

'They're certainly formed for it, sir.'

'They must assume we're blockheads. What time is it?'

One of his aides consulted a watch. 'Ten minutes of noon, sir.'

'Plenty of time,' the General murmured. 'Onwards, gentlemen, stay below the skyline. We don't want to frighten them away!'

'Frighten them away?' Sevajee asked with a smile, but Wellesley ignored the comment as he spurred on eastwards, parallel with the river. Some troops of Company cavalry were scouring the fields and at first Sharpe thought they were looking for concealed enemy picquets, then he saw they were hunting down local farmers and harrying them along in the General's wake.

Wellesley rode two miles eastwards, a string of horsemen behind him. The farmers were breathless by the time they reached the place where his horse was picketed just beneath a low hill. The General was kneeling on the crest, staring east through a glass. 'Ask those fellows if there are any fords east of here!' he shouted down to his aides.

A hurried consultation followed, but the farmers were quite sure there was no ford. The only crossing places, they insisted, were directly in front of Scindia's army. 'Find a clever one,' Wellesley ordered, 'and bring him up here. Colonel? Maybe you'd translate?'

McCandless picked one of the farmers and led him up the hill. Sharpe, without being asked, followed and Wellesley did not order him back, but just muttered that they should all keep their heads low. 'There' – the General pointed eastwards to a village on the Kaitna's southern bank – 'that village, what's it called?'

'Peepulgaon,' the farmer said, and added that his mother and two sisters lived in the huddle of mud-walled houses with their thatched roofs.

Peepulgaon lay only a half-mile from the low hill, but it was all of two miles east of Taunklee, the village that was opposite the eastern extremity of the Mahratta line. Both villages were on the river's southern bank while the enemy waited on the Kaitna's northern side, and Sharpe did not understand Wellesley's interest. 'Ask him if he has any relatives north of the river,' the General ordered McCandless.

'He has a brother and several cousins, sir,' McCandless translated.

'So how does his mother visit her son north of the river?' Wellesley asked.

The farmer launched himself into a long explanation. In the dry season, he said, she walked across the river bed, but in the wet season, when the waters rose, she was forced to come upstream and cross at Taunklee. Wellesley listened, then grunted in apparent disbelief. He was staring intently through the glass. 'Campbell?' he called, but his aide had gone to another low rise a hundred yards westwards that offered a better view of the enemy ranks. 'Campbell?' Wellesley called again and, getting no answer, turned. 'Sharpe, you'll do. Come here.'

'Sir?'

'You've got young eyes. Come here, and keep low.'

Sharpe joined the General on the crest where, to his surprise, he was handed the telescope. 'Look at the village,' Wellesley ordered, 'then look at the opposite bank and tell me what you see.'

It took Sharpe a moment to find Peepulgaon in the lens, but suddenly its mud walls filled the glass. He moved the telescope slowly, sliding its view past oxen, goats and chickens, past clothes set to dry on bushes by the river bank, and then the lens slid across the brown water of the River Kaitna and up its opposite bank where he saw a muddy bluff topped by trees and, just beyond the trees, a fold of land. And in the fold of land were roofs, straw roofs. 'There's another village there, sir,' Sharpe said.

'You're sure?' Wellesley asked urgently.

'Pretty sure, sir. Might just be cattle sheds.'

'You don't keep cattle sheds apart from a village,' the General said scathingly, 'not in a country infested by bandits.' Wellesley twisted round. 'McCandless? Ask your fellow if there's a village on the other side of the river from Peepulgaon.'

The farmer listened to the question, then nodded. 'Waroor,' he said, then helpfully informed the General that his cousin was the village headman, the *naique*.

'How far apart are those villages, Sharpe?' Wellesley asked

Sharpe judged the distance for a couple of seconds. 'Three hundred yards, sir?'

Wellesley took the telescope back and moved away from the crest. 'Never in my life,' he said, 'have I seen two villages on opposite banks of a river that weren't connected by a ford.'

'He insists not, sir,' McCandless said, indicating the farmer.

'Then he's a rogue, a liar or a blockhead,' Wellesley said cheerfully. 'The latter, probably.' He frowned in thought, his right hand drumming a tattoo on the telescope's barrel. 'I'll warrant there is a ford,' he said to himself.

'Sir?' Captain Campbell had run back from the western knoll. 'Enemy's breaking camp, sir.'

'Are they, by God!' Wellesley returned to the crest and stared through the glass again. The infantry immediately on the Kaitna's north bank were not moving, but far away, close to the fortified village, tents were being struck. 'Preparing to run away, I daresay,' Wellesley muttered.

'Or readying to cross the river and attack us,' McCandless said grimly.

'And they're sending cavalry across the river,' Campbell added ominously.

'Nothing to worry us,' Wellesley said, then turned back to stare at the opposing villages of Peepulgaon and Waroor. 'There has to be a ford,' he said to himself again, so quietly that only Sharpe could hear him. 'Stands to reason,' he said, then he went silent for a long time.

'That enemy cavalry, sir,' Campbell prompted him.

Wellesley seemed startled. 'What?'

'There, sir.' Campbell pointed westwards to a large group of enemy horsemen who had appeared from a grove of trees, but who seemed content to watch Wellesley's group from a half-mile away.

'Time we were away,' Wellesley said. 'Give that lying block-head a rupee, McCandless, then let's be off.'

'You plan to retreat, sir?' McCandless asked.

Wellesley had been hurrying down the slope, but now stopped and stared in surprise at the Scotsman. 'Retreat?'

McCandless blinked. 'You surely don't intend to fight, sir, do you?'

'How else are we to do His Majesty's business? Of course we'll fight! There's a ford there.' Wellesley flung his arm east towards Peepulgaon. 'That wretched farmer might deny it, but he's a blockhead! There has to be a ford. We'll cross it, turn their left flank and pound them into scraps! But we must hurry! Noon already. Three hours, gentlemen, three hours to bring on battle. Three hours to turn his flank.' He ran on down the hill to where Diomed, his white Arab horse, waited.

'Good God,' McCandless said. 'Good God.' For five thousand infantry would now cross the Kaitna at a place where men said the river was uncrossable, then fight an enemy horde at least ten times their number. 'Good God,' the Colonel said again, then hurried to follow Wellesley south. The enemy had stolen a march, the redcoats had journeyed all night and were bone tired, but Wellesley would have his battle.

CHAPTER 9

'There!' Dodd said, pointing.

'I can't see,' Simone Joubert complained.

'Drop the telescope, use your naked eye, Madame. There! It's flashing.'

'Where?'

'There!' Dodd pointed again. 'Across the river. Three trees, low hill.'

'Ah!' Simone at last saw the flash of reflected sunlight from the lens of a telescope that was being used on the far bank of the river and well downstream from where Dodd's Cobras held the left of Pohlmann's line.

Simone and her husband had dined with the Major who was grimly happy in anticipation of a British attack which, he claimed, must inevitably fall hardest on his Cobras. 'It will be slaughter, Ma'am,' Dodd said wolfishly, 'sheer slaughter!' He and Captain Joubert had walked Simone to the edge of the bluff above the Kaitna and shown her the fords, and demonstrated how any men crossing the fords must be caught in the mangling crossfire of the Mahratta cannon, then maintained that the British had no option but to walk forward into that weltering onslaught of canister, round shot and shell. 'If you wish to stay and watch, Madame,' Dodd had offered, 'I can find a place of safety for you.' He gestured towards a low rise of ground just behind the regiment. 'You could watch from there, and I credit no British soldier will come near you.'

'I could not bear to watch a slaughter, Major,' Simone had said feelingly.

'Your squeamishness does you credit, Ma'am,' Dodd had answered. 'War is man's work.' It was then that Dodd had spotted the British soldiers on the opposite bank and had trained his telescope on the distant men. Simone, knowing now where to look, rested the glass on her husband's shoulder and trained its lens on the far hill. She could see two men there, one in a cocked hat and the other in a shako. Both were keeping low. 'Why are they so far down the river?' she asked.

'They're looking for a way round our flank,' Dodd said.

'Is there one?'

'No. They must cross here, Ma'am, or else they don't cross at all.' Dodd gestured at the fords in front of the *compoo*. A band of cavalrymen was galloping through the shallow water, spraying silver from their horses' hooves as they crossed to the Kaitna's south bank. 'And those horsemen,' Dodd explained, 'are going to see whether they will cross or not.'

Simone collapsed the telescope and handed it back to the Major. 'They might not attack?'

'They won't,' her husband answered in English for Dodd's benefit. 'They have too much sense.'

'Boy Wellesley don't have sense,' Dodd said scathingly. 'Look how he attacked at Ahmednuggur? Straight at the wall! A hundred rupees says he will attack.'

Captain Joubert shook his head. 'I do not gamble, Major.'

'A soldier should relish risk,' Dodd said.

'And if they don't cross,' Simone asked, 'there is no battle?'

'There'll be a battle, Ma'am,' Dodd said grimly. 'Pohlmann's gone to fetch Scindia's permission for us to cross the river. If they won't come to us, we'll go to them.'

Pohlmann had indeed gone to find Scindia. The Hanoverian had dressed for battle, donning his finest coat, which was a blue silk jacket, trimmed in scarlet and decorated with loops of gold braid and black aiguillettes. He wore a white silk sash on which was blazoned a star of diamonds and from which hung a gold-hilted sword, though Dupont, the Dutchman, who accompanied Pohlmann to meet Scindia, noted that the Colonel's breeches and boots were old and shabby. 'I wear them for luck,' Pohlmann said, noting Dupont's puzzled glance at his decrepit breeches. 'They're from my old East India Company uniform.' The Hanoverian was in a fine mood. His short march eastwards had achieved all he had desired, for it had brought one of the two small British armies into his lap while it was still far away from the other. All he needed to do now was snap it up like a minnow, then march on Stevenson's force, but Scindia had been insistent that no infantry were to cross the Kaitna's fords without his permission and Pohlmann now needed that permission. The Hanoverian did not plan to cross immediately, for first he wanted to be certain that the British were retreating, but nor did he wish to wait for permission once he heard news of the enemy's withdrawal.

'Our lord and master will be scared at the thought of attacking,' Pohlmann told Dupont, 'so we'll flatter the bugger. Slap on the *ghee* with a shovel, Dupont. Tell him he'll be lord of all India if he lets us loose.'

'Tell him there are a hundred white women in Wellesley's camp and he'll lead the attack himself,' Dupont observed drily.

'Then that is what we shall tell him,' Pohlmann said, 'and promise him that every little darling will be his concubine.'

Except that when Pohlmann and Dupont reached the tree-shaded stretch of ground above the River Juah where the Maharajah of Gwalior had been awaiting his army's victory, there was no sign of his lavish tents. They had been struck, all of them, together with the striped tents of the Rajah of

Berar, and all that remained were the cook tents that even now were being collapsed and folded onto the beds of a dozen ox carts. All the elephants but one were gone, the horses of the royal bodyguards were gone, the concubines were gone and the two princes were gone.

The one remaining elephant belonged to Surjee Rao and that minister, ensconced in his howdah where he was being fanned by a servant, smiled benevolently down on the two sweating and red-faced Europeans. 'His Serene Majesty deemed it safer to withdraw westwards,' he explained airily, 'and the Rajah of Berar agreed with him.'

"They did what?' Pohlmann snarled.

'The omens,' Surjee Rao said vaguely, waving a bejewelled hand to indicate that the subtleties of such supernatural messages would be beyond Pohlmann's comprehension.

'The bloody omens are propitious!' Pohlmann insisted. 'We've got the buggers by the balls! What more omens can you want?'

Surjee Rao smiled. 'His Majesty has sublime confidence in your skill, Colonel.'

'To do what?' the Hanoverian demanded.

'Whatever is necessary,' Surjee Rao said, then smiled. 'We shall wait in Borkardan for news of your triumph, Colonel, and eagerly anticipate seeing the banners of our enemies heaped in triumph at the foot of His Serene Majesty's throne.' And with that hope expressed he snapped his fingers and the mahout prodded the elephant which lumbered away westwards.

'Bastards,' Pohlmann said to Dupont, loudly enough for the retreating minister to hear. 'Lily-livered bastards! Cowards!' Not that he cared whether Scindia and the Rajah of Berar were present at the battle; indeed, given the choice, he would much prefer to fight without them, but that was not true of his men who, like all soldiers, fought better when their rulers were watching, and so Pohlmann was angry for his men. Yet, he consoled himself as he returned southwards, they would still fight well. Pride would see to that, and confidence, and the promise of plunder.

And Surjee Rao's final words, Pohlmann decided, had been more than enough to give him permission to cross the River Kaitna. He had been told to do whatever was necessary, and Pohlmann reckoned that gave him a free hand, so he would give Scindia a victory even if the yellow bastard did not deserve it.

Pohlmann and Dupont cantered back to the left of the line where they saw that Major Dodd had called his men out from the shade of the trees and into their ranks. The sight suggested that the enemy was approaching the Kaitna and Pohlmann spurred his horse into a gallop, clamping one hand onto his extravagantly plumed hat to stop it falling off. He slewed to a stop just short of Dodd's regiment and stared above their heads across the river.

The enemy had come, except this enemy was merely a long line of cavalrymen with two small horse-drawn galloper guns. It was a screen, of course. A screen of British and Indian horsemen intended to stop his own patrols from discovering what was happening in the hidden country beyond. 'Any sign of their infantry?' he called to Dodd.

'None, sir.'

'The buggers are running!' Pohlmann exulted. 'That's why they've put up a screen.' He suddenly noticed Simone Joubert and hastily took off his feathered hat. 'My apologies for my language, Madame.' He put his hat back on and twisted his horse about. 'Harness the guns!' he shouted.

'What is happening?' Simone asked anxiously.

'We're crossing the river,' her husband said quietly, 'and you must go back to Assaye.'

Simone knew she must say something loving to him, for

was that not expected of a wife at a moment such as this? 'I shall pray for you,' she said shyly.

'Go back to Assaye,' her husband said again, noting that she had not given him any love, 'and stay there till it is all over.'

It would not take long. The guns needed to be attached to their limbers, but the infantry were ready to march and the cavalry were eager to begin their pursuit. The existence of the British cavalry screen suggested that Wellesley must be withdrawing, so all Pohlmann needed to do was cross the river and then crush the enemy. Dodd drew his elephant-hilted sword, felt its newly honed edge and waited for the orders to begin the slaughter.

The Mahratta cavalry pursued Wellesley's party the moment they saw that the General was retreating from his observation post above the river. 'We must look to ourselves, gentlemen!' Wellesley had called and driven back his heels so that Diomed had sprung ahead. The other horsemen matched his pace, but Sharpe, on his small captured Mahratta horse, could not keep up. He had mounted in a hurry, and in his haste he could not fit his right boot into the stirrup and the horse's jolting motion made it all the more difficult, but he dared not curb the beast for he could hear the enemy's shouts and the beat of their hooves not far behind. For a few moments he was in a panic. The thud of the pursuing hooves grew louder, he could see his companions drawing ever farther ahead of him and his horse was blowing hard and trying to resist the frantic kicks he gave, and each kick threatened to unseat him so that he clung to the saddle's pommel and still his right boot would not find the stirrup. Sevajee, racing free on the right flank, saw his predicament and curved back towards him. 'You're not a horseman, Sergeant.'

'Never bloody was, sir. Hate the bloody things.'

'A warrior and his horse, Sergeant, are like a man and a woman,' Sevajee said, leaning over and pushing the stirrup iron onto Sharpe's boot. He did it without once checking his own horse's furious pace, then he slapped Sharpe's small mare on the rump and she took off like one of the enemy's rockets, almost tipping Sharpe backwards.

Sharpe clung on to the pommel, while his musket, which was hanging by its sling from his left elbow, banged and thumped his thigh. His shako blew off and he had no time to rescue it, but then a trumpet sounded off to his right and he saw a stream of British cavalrymen riding to head off the pursuit. Still more cavalrymen were spurring north from Naulniah and Wellesley, as he passed them, urged them on towards the Kaitna.

'Thank you, sir,' Sharpe said to Sevajee.

'You should learn horsemanship.'

'I'll stay a foot soldier, sir. Safer. Don't like sitting on things with hooves and teeth.'

Sevajee laughed. Wellesley had slowed now and was patting the neck of his horse, but the brief pursuit had only increased his high spirits. He turned Diomed to watch the Mahratta cavalry spur away. 'A good omen!' he said happily.

'For what, sir?' Sevajee asked.

Wellesley heard the Indian's sceptical tone. 'You don't think we should give battle?'

Sevajee shrugged, seeking some tactful way of expressing his disagreement with Wellesley's decision. 'The battle isn't always to the largest army, sir.'

'Always, no,' Wellesley said, 'but usually, yes? You think I am being impetuous?' Sevajee refused to be drawn and simply shrugged again in answer. 'We shall see, we shall see,' the General said. 'Their army looks fine, I grant you, but once we break the regular *compoos*, the others will run.'

'I do hope so, sir.'

'Depend on it,' Wellesley said, then spurred on.

Sharpe looked at Sevajee. 'Are we mad to fight, sir?'

'Quite mad,' Sevajee said, 'completely mad. But maybe there's no choice.'

'No choice?'

'We blundered, Sergeant. We marched too far and came too close to the enemy, so either we attack him or run away from him, and either way we have to fight. By attacking him we just make the fight shorter.' He twisted in the saddle and pointed towards the now hidden Kaitna. 'Do you know what's beyond that river?'

'No, sir.'

'Another river, Sharpe, and they meet just a couple of miles downstream' – he pointed eastwards towards the place where the waters met – 'and if we cross that ford we shall find ourselves on a tongue of land and the only way out is forward, through a hundred thousand Mahrattas. Death on one side and water on the other.' Sevajee laughed. 'Blundering, Sergeant, blundering!'

But if Wellesley had blundered he was still in high spirits. Once back at Naulniah he ordered Diomed unsaddled and rubbed down, then began issuing commands. The army's baggage would stay at Naulniah, dragged into the village's alleyways which were to be barricaded so that no marauding Mahratta cavalry could plunder the wagons which would be guarded by the smallest battalion of sepoys. McCandless heard that order given, understood its necessity, but groaned aloud when he realized that almost five hundred infantrymen were thus being shorn from the attacking army.

The cavalry that remained in Naulniah were ordered to saddle their horses and ride to the Kaitna, there to form a screen on the southern bank, while the tired infantry, who had marched all morning, were now rousted from their tents and chivvied into ranks. 'No packs!' the sergeants called.

'Firelocks and cartridge boxes only. No packs! Off to a Sunday battle, lads! Save your bleeding prayers and hurry up! Come on, Johnny, boots on, lad! There's a horde of heathens to kill. Look lively, now! Wake yourselves up! On your feet!'

The picquets of the day, composed of a half company from each of the army's seven battalions, marched first. They splashed through the small river north of Naulniah and were met on its far bank by one of the General's aides who guided them onto the farm track that led to Peepulgaon. The picquets were followed by the King's 74th accompanied by their battalion artillery, while behind them came the second battalion of the 12th Madras Regiment, the first battalion of the 4th Madras, the first of the 8th Madras and the first of the 10th Madras, and lastly the kilted Highlanders of the King's 78th. Six battalions crossed the river and followed the beaten-earth track between fields of millet beneath the furnace of an Indian sun. No enemy was visible as they marched, though rumour said the whole of the Mahratta army was not far away.

Two guns fired around one o'clock. The sound was flat and hard, echoing across the heat-shimmering land, but the infantry could see nothing. The sound came from their left, and the battalion officers said there was cavalry somewhere out there, and that doubtless meant that the cavalry's light galloper guns had engaged the enemy, or else the enemy had brought cannon to face the British cavalry, but the fighting did not seem to be ominous, for there was silence after the two shots. McCandless, his nerves strung by the disaster he feared was imminent, galloped Aeolus a few yards westwards as if wanting to find an explanation for the two gunshots, but then he thought better of it and turned his horse back to the road.

More cannon fire sounded a few moments later, but there was nothing urgent in the distant shots which were monotonous, flat and sporadic. If battle had been brewing to the boil the gunshots would have sounded hard and fast, but these shots were almost lackadaisical, as though the gunners were merely practising on Aldershot Heath on a lazy summer's day. 'Their guns or ours, sir?' Sharpe asked McCandless.

'Ours, I suspect,' the Scotsman said. 'Cavalry galloper guns keeping the enemy horse on their toes.' He tugged on Aeolus's rein, moving the gelding out of the path of sixty sepoy pioneers who were doubling down the road's left verge with pick-axes and shovels on their shoulders. The pioneers' task was to reach the Kaitna and make certain that its banks were not too steep for the ox-drawn artillery. Wellesley cantered after the pioneers, riding to the head of the column and trailing a succession of aides. McCandless joined the General's party and Sharpe kicked his horse alongside Daniel Fletcher who was mounted on a big roan mare and leading an unsaddled Diomed by a long rein. 'He'll want him when the bay's tired,' Fletcher told Sharpe, nodding ahead at Wellesley who was now riding a tall bay stallion. 'And the mare's in case both horses get shot,' he added, slapping the rump of the horse he rode.

'So what do you do?' Sharpe asked the dragoon.

'Just stay close until he wants to change horses and keep him from getting thirsty,' Fletcher said. He carried no less than five water canteens on his belt, bulked over a heavy sabre in a metal scabbard, the first time Sharpe had ever seen the orderly carrying a weapon. 'Vicious thing, that,' Fletcher said when he saw Sharpe glance at the weapon, 'a good wide blade, perfect for slicing.'

'Ever used it?' Sharpe asked.

'Against Dhoondiah,' Fletcher answered. Dhoondiah had been a bandit chieftain whose depredations in Mysore had finally persuaded Wellesley to pursue him with cavalry. The resultant battle had been a short clash of horsemen that had been won in moments by the British. 'And I killed a goat with it for the General's supper a week ago,' Fletcher continued, drawing the heavy curved blade, 'and I think the poor bugger died of fright when it saw the blade coming. Took its head clean off, it did. Look at this, Sergeant.' He handed the blade to Sharpe. 'See what it says there? Just above the hilt?'

Sharpe tipped the sabre to the sun. ' "Warranted Never to Fail",' he read aloud. He grinned, for the boast seemed oddly out of place on a thing designed to kill or maim.

'Made in Sheffield,' Fletcher said, taking the blade back, 'and guaranteed never to fail! Good slicer this is, real good. You can cut a man in half with one of these if you get the stroke right.'

Sharpe grinned. 'I'll stick with a musket.'

'Not on horseback, you won't, Sergeant,' Fletcher said. 'A firelock's no good on horseback. You want a blade.'

'Never learned to use one,' Sharpe said.

'It ain't difficult,' Fletcher said with the scorn of a man who had mastered a difficult trade. 'Keep your arm straight and use the point when you're fighting cavalry, because if you bend the elbow the bastards will chop through your wrist as sure as eggs, and slash away like a haymaker at infantry because there ain't bugger all they can do back to you, not once they're on the run. Not that you could use any kind of sword off the back of that horse.' He nodded at Sharpe's small native beast. 'It's more like an overgrown dog, that is. Does it fetch?'

The road reached the high point between the two rivers and Fletcher, mounted high on the General's mare, caught his first glimpse of the enemy army on the distant northern bank of the Kaitna. He whistled softly. 'Millions of the buggers!'

'We're going to turn their flank,' Sharpe said, repeating what he had heard the General say. So far as Sharpe understood, the idea was to cross the river at the ford which no one except Wellesley believed existed, then make an attack on the left flank of the waiting infantry. The idea made sense to Sharpe, for the enemy line was facing south and, by coming at them from the east, the British could well plunge the *compoos* into confusion.

'Millions of the buggers!' Fletcher said again in wonderment, but then the road dropped and took the enemy out of their view. The dragoon orderly sheathed his sabre. 'But he's confident,' he said, nodding ahead at Wellesley who was dressed in his old uniform coat of the 33rd. The General wore a slim straight sword, but had no other weapon, not even a pistol.

'He was always confident,' Sharpe said. 'Cool as you like.'

'He's a good fellow,' Fletcher said loyally. 'Proper officer. He ain't friendly, of course, but he's always fair.' He touched his spurs to the mare's flanks because Wellesley and his aides had hurried ahead into the village of Peepulgaon where the villagers gaped at the foreigners in their red coats and black cocked hats. Wellesley scattered chickens from his path as he cantered down the dusty village street to where the road dropped down a precipitous bluff into the half-dry bed of the Kaitna. The pioneers arrived a moment later and began attacking the bluff to smooth its steep slope. On the river's far bank Sharpe could see the road twist up into the trees that half obscured the village of Waroor. The General was right, he reckoned, and there had to be a ford, for why else would the road show on both banks? But whether the ford was shallow enough for the army to cross no one yet knew.

Wellesley stood his horse at the top of the bluff and drummed the fingers of his right hand on his thigh. It was the only sign of nerves. He was staring across the river, thinking. No enemy was in sight, but nor should they have been for the Mahratta line was now two miles to the west, which

275

meant that Scindia's army was now between him and Stevenson. Wellesley grimaced, realizing that he had already abandoned his first principle for fighting this battle, which had been to secure his left flank so Stevenson could join. Doubtless, the moment the guns began their proper, concentrated work, the sound of their cannonade would bring Stevenson hurrying across country, but now the older man would simply have to join the fight as best he could. But Wellesley had no regrets at posing such difficulties for Stevenson, for the chance to turn the enemy's flank was heaven-sent. So long, that is, as the ford was practicable.

The pioneer Captain led a dozen of his sepoys down towards the river. 'I'll just see to that far bank, sir,' the Captain called up to the General, startling Wellesley out of his reverie.

'Come back!' Wellesley shouted angrily. 'Back!'

The Captain had almost reached the water, but now turned and stared at Wellesley in puzzlement. 'Have to grade that bluff, sir,' he shouted, pointing to where the road climbed steeply to the screen of trees on the Kaitna's northern bank. 'Too steep for guns, sir.'

'Come back!' Wellesley called again, then waited as the dozen men trudged back to the southern bank. 'The enemy can see the river, Captain,' the General explained, 'and I have no wish that they should see us yet. I do not want them knowing our intentions, so you will wait until the first infantry make the crossing, then do your work.'

But the enemy had already seen the pioneers. The dozen men had only been visible in the river's open bed for a few seconds, but someone in the Mahratta gun line was wide awake and there was a sudden and violent plume of water in the river and, almost simultaneously, the sky-battering sound of a heavy gun.

'Good shooting,' McCandless said quietly when the fifteen-foot-high fountain had subsided to leave nothing but a whirling eddy in the river's brown water. The range must have been almost two miles, yet the Mahrattas had turned a gun, trained and fired it in seconds, and their aim had been almost perfect. A second gun fired and its heavy ball ploughed a furrow in the dry, crazed mud beside the river and bounced up to scatter bucket-loads of dry earth from the bluff's face. 'Eighteen-pounders,' McCandless guessed aloud, thinking of the two heavy siege guns that he had seen in front of Dodd's men.

'Damn,' Wellesley said quietly. 'But no real harm done, I suppose.' The first of the infantry were now marching down Peepulgaon's steep street. Lieutenant Colonel Orrock led the picquets of the day, while behind them Sharpe could see the grenadier company of the 74th. The Scottish drums were beating a march rhythm and the sound of the flurries made Sharpe's blood race. The sound presaged battle. It seemed like a dream, but there would be a battle this Sunday afternoon and a bloody one too.

'Afternoon, Orrock,' Wellesley spurred his horse to meet the infantry vanguard. 'Straight across, I think.'

'Has the ford been sounded?' Colonel Orrock, a lugubrious and worried-looking man, asked nervously.

'Our task, I think,' Wellesley said cheerfully. 'Gentlemen?' This last invitation was to his aides and orderly. 'Shall we open proceedings?'

'Come on, Sharpe,' McCandless said.

'You can cross after us, Captain!' Wellesley called to the eager pioneer Captain, then he put his big bay stallion down the slope of the bluff and trotted towards the river. Daniel Fletcher followed close behind with Diomed's leading rein in his hand, while the aides and McCandless and Sevajee and Sharpe all followed. Forty horsemen would be the first men across the Kaitna and the General would be the first of all, and Sharpe watched as Wellesley's stallion trotted into the river. He wanted to see how deep the water was, and he was determined to watch the General all the way through, but suddenly the bang of an eighteen-pounder gun bullied the sky and Sharpe glanced upstream to see a puff of gunsmoke smear the horizon, then he heard a horse screaming and he looked back to see that Daniel Fletcher's mount was rearing at the water's edge. Fletcher was still in the saddle, but the orderly had no head left, only a pulsing spurt of blood from his ragged neck. Diomed's rein was still in the dead man's hand, but somehow the body would not fall from the mare's saddle and she was screaming in fear as her rider's blood splashed across her face.

A second gun fired, but high, and the shot crashed low overhead to tear into the trees on the southern bank. A third ball smashed into the water, drenching McCandless. Fletcher's mare bolted upstream, but was checked by a fallen tree and so she stood, quivering, and still the trooper's decapitated body was in the saddle and Diomed's rein in his dead hand. The grey horse's left flank was reddened with Fletcher's blood. The trooper had slumped now, his headless trunk leaning eerily to drip blood into the river.

To Sharpe it seemed as if time had stopped. He was aware of someone shouting, aware of the blood dripping from the dragoon's collar, aware of his small horse shivering, but the sudden violence had immobilized him. Another gun fired, this one of smaller calibre, and the ball struck the water a hundred yards upstream, ricocheted once, then vanished in a plume of white spray.

'Sharpe!' a voice snapped. Horsemen were wheeling in the river's shallows and reaching for the dead man's bridle. 'Sharpe!' It was Wellesley who shouted. The General was in the middle of the river where the water did not even reach his stirrups, so there was a ford after all and the river could be crossed, but the enemy was hardly going to be taken by surprise now. 'Take over as orderly, Sharpe!' Wellesley shouted. 'Hurry, man!' There was no one else to replace Fletcher, not unless one of Wellesley's aides took over his duties, and Sharpe was the nearest man.

'Go on, Sharpe!' McCandless said. 'Hurry, man!'

Captain Campbell had secured Fletcher's mare. 'Ride her, Sharpe!' the Captain called. 'That little horse won't keep up with us. Just let her go. Let her go.'

Sharpe dismounted and ran to the mare. Campbell was trying to dislodge Fletcher's blood-soaked body, but the trooper's feet were caught in the stirrups. Sharpe heaved Fletcher's left boot free, then gave the booted leg a tug and the corpse slid towards him. He jumped back as the bloody remnants of the neck, all sinew and flesh and tattered scraps, slapped at his face. The corpse fell into the edge of the river and Sharpe stepped over it to mount the General's mare. 'Get the General's canteens,' Campbell ordered him, and an instant later another eighteen-pounder shot hammered low overhead like a clap of thunder. 'The canteens, man, hurry!' Campbell urged Sharpe, but Sharpe was having trouble untying the water bottles from Fletcher's belt, so instead he heaved the body over so that a gush of blood spurted from the neck to be instantly diluted in the shallow water. He tugged at the trooper's belt buckle, unfastened it, then hauled the belt free with its pouches, canteens and the heavy sabre. He wrapped the belt over his own, hastily buckled it, then clambered up into the mare's saddle and fiddled his right foot into the stirrup. Campbell was holding out Diomed's rein.

Sharpe took the rein. 'Sorry, sir.' He apologized for making the aide wait.

'Stay close to the General,' Campbell ordered him, then leaned over and patted Sharpe's arm. 'Stay close, be alert,

279

enjoy the day, Sergeant,' he said with a grin. 'It looks as if it's going to be a lively afternoon!'

'Thank you, sir,' Sharpe said. The first infantry were in the ford now and Sharpe turned the mare, kicked back his heels and tugged Diomed through the water. Campbell was spurring ahead to catch up with Wellesley and Sharpe clumsily kicked the mare into a canter and was almost thrown as she stumbled on the riverbed, but he somehow clung to her mane as she recovered. A round shot thrashed the water white to his left, drenching him with spray. The musket had fallen off his shoulder and was dangling awkwardly from his elbow and he could not manage both it and Diomed's rein, so he let the firelock drop into the river, then wrenched the sword and the heavy canteens into a more comfortable position. Bugger this, he thought. Lost a hat, a horse and a gun in less than an hour!

The pioneers were hacking at the bluff on the northern bank to make the slope less steep, but the first galloper guns, those that accompanied the picquets of the day, were already in the Kaitna. Galloper guns were drawn by horses and the gunners shouted at the pioneers to clear out of their way. The pioneers scattered as the horses came up from the river with water streaming from the leading gun's spinning wheels; a whip cracked over the leader's head and the team galloped up the bluff with the gun and limber bouncing erratically behind. A gunner was thrown off the limber, but he picked himself up and ran after the cannon. Sharpe kicked his horse up the bluff once the second gun was safely past and suddenly he was in low ground, protected from the enemy's cannonade by the rising land to his left.

But where the hell was Wellesley? He could see no one on the high ground that led towards the enemy, and the only men on the road straight ahead were the leading companies of the picquets of the day who continued to march northwards. A slapping sound came from the river and he twisted in his saddle to see that a round shot had whipped through a file of infantry. A body floated downstream in eddies of blood, then the sergeants shouted at the ranks to close up and the infantry kept on coming. But where the hell was Sharpe to go? To his right was the village of Waroor, half hidden behind its trees and for a second Sharpe thought the General must have gone there, but then he saw Lieutenant Colonel Orrock riding up onto the higher ground to the left and Sharpe guessed the Colonel was following Wellesley and so he tugged the mare that way.

The land climbed to a gentle crest across stubble fields dotted by a few trees. Colonel Orrock was the only man in sight and he was forcing his horse up the slope towards the skyline and so Sharpe followed him. He could hear the enemy guns firing, presumably still bombarding the ford that had not been supposed to exist, but as he kicked the mare up through the growing crop the guns suddenly ceased and all he could hear was the thump of hooves, the banging of the sabre's metal scabbard against his boot and the dull sound of the Scottish drums behind.

Orrock had turned north along the skyline and Sharpe, following him, saw that the General and his aides were clustered under a group of trees from where they were gazing westwards through their telescopes. He joined them in the shade, and felt awkward to be in such exalted company without McCandless, but Campbell turned in his saddle and grinned. 'Well done, Sergeant. Still with us, eh?'

'Managing, sir,' Sharpe said, rearranging the canteens that had tangled themselves into a lump.

'Oh, dear God,' Colonel Orrock said a moment later. He was gazing through his own telescope, and whatever he saw made him shake his head before peering through the glass again. 'Dear me,' he said, and Sharpe stood in his stirrups to see what had so upset the East India Company Colonel.

The enemy was redeploying. Wellesley had crossed the ford to bring his small army onto the enemy's left flank, but the Mahratta commander had seen his purpose and was now denying him the advantage. The enemy line was marching towards the Peepulgaon ford, then wheeling left to make a new defence line that stretched clean across the land between the two rivers; a line that would now face head on towards Wellesley's army. Instead of attacking a vulnerable flank, Wellesley would be forced to make a head-on assault. Nor were the Mahrattas making their manoeuvre in a panicked hurry, but were marching calmly in disciplined ranks. The guns were moving with them, drawn by bullocks or elephants. The enemy was less than a mile away now and their steady unhurried redeployment was obvious to the watching officers.

'They anticipate us, sir!' Orrock informed Wellesley, as though the General might not have understood the purpose of the enemy's manoeuvre.

'They do,' Wellesley agreed calmly, 'they do indeed.' He collapsed his telescope and patted his horse's neck. 'And they manoeuvre very well!' he added admiringly, as though he was engaged in nothing more ominous than watching a brigade go through its paces in Hyde Park. 'Your men are through the ford?' he asked Orrock.

'They are, sir, they are,' Orrock said. The Colonel had a nervous habit of jutting his head forward every few seconds as if his collar was too tight. 'And they can reverse themselves,' he added meaningfully.

Wellesley ignored the defeatist sentiment. 'Take them one half-mile up the road,' he ordered Orrock, 'then deploy on the high ground this side of the road. I shall see you before we advance.'

Orrock gazed goggle-eyed at the General. 'Deploy?'

'On this side of the road, if you please, Colonel. You will form the right of our line, Colonel, and have Wallace's brigade on your left. Let us do it now, Colonel, if you would so oblige me?'

'Oblige you . . .' Orrock said, his head darting forward like a turtle. 'Of course,' he added nervously, then turned his horse and spurred it back towards the road.

'Barclay?' the General addressed one of his aides. 'My compliments to Colonel Maxwell and he will bring all Company and King's cavalry to take post to Orrock's right. Native horse will stay south of the river.' There was still enemy cavalry south of the Kaitna and the horsemen from Britain's Indian allies would stay on that bank to keep those enemies at bay. 'Then stay at the ford,' Wellesley went on addressing Barclay, 'and tell the rest of the infantry to form on Orrock's picquets. Two lines, Barclay, two lines, and the 78th will form the left flank here.' The General, who had been gazing at the enemy's calm redeployment, now turned to Barclay who was scribbling in pencil on a scrap of paper. 'First line, from the left. The 78th, Dallas's 10th, Corben's 8th, Orrock's picquets. Second line, from the left. Hill's 4th, Macleod's 12th, then the 74th. They are to form their lines and wait for my orders. You understand? They are to wait.' Barclay nodded, then tugged on his reins and spurred his horse back towards the ford as the General turned again to watch the enemy's redeployment. 'Very fine work,' he said approvingly, 'I doubt we could have manoeuvred any more smartly than that. You think they were readying to cross the river and attack us?'

Major Blackiston, his engineer aide, nodded. 'It would explain why they were ready to move, sir.'

'We shall just have to discover whether they fight as well as they manoeuvre,' Wellesley said, collapsing his telescope, then he sent Blackiston north to explore the ground up to the River Juah. 'Come on, Campbell,' Wellesley said when

Blackiston was gone and, to Sharpe's surprise, instead of riding back to where the army was crossing the ford, the General spurred his horse still further west towards the enemy. Campbell followed and Sharpe decided he had better go as well.

The three men rode into a steep-sided valley that was thick with trees and brush, then up its far side to another stretch of open farmland. They cantered through a field of unharvested millet, then across pastureland, always inclining north towards another low hill crest. 'I'll oblige you for a canteen, Sergeant,' Wellesley called as they neared the crest and Sharpe thumped his heels on the mare's flanks to catch up with the General, then fumbled a canteen free and held it out, but that meant taking his left hand off the reins while his right was still holding Diomed's tether and the mare, freed of the rein, swerved away from the General. Wellesley caught up with Sharpe and took the canteen. 'You might tie Diomed's rein to your belt, Sergeant,' he said. 'It will provide you with another hand.'

A man needed three hands to do Sharpe's job, but once they reached the low crest the General halted again and so gave Sharpe time to fasten the Arab's rein to Fletcher's belt. The General was staring at the enemy who was now only a quarter-mile away, well inside cannon shot, but either the enemy guns were not ready to fire or else they were under orders not to waste powder on a mere three horsemen. Sharpe took the opportunity to explore what was in Fletcher's pouch. There was a piece of mouldy bread that had been soaked when the trooper's body fell into the river, a piece of salted meat that Sharpe suspected was dried goat, and a sharpening stone. That made him half draw the sabre to feel its edge. It was keen.

'A nasty little settlement!' Wellesley said cheerfully.

'Aye, it is, sir!' Campbell agreed enthusiastically.

'That must be Assaye,' Wellesley remarked. 'You think we're about to make it famous?'

'I trust so, sir,' Campbell said.

'Not infamous, I hope,' Wellesley said, and gave his short, high-pitched laugh.

Sharpe saw they were both staring towards a village that lay to the north of the enemy's new line. Like every village in this part of India it was provided with a rampart made of the outermost houses' mud walls. Such walls could be five or six feet in thickness, and though they might crumble to the touch of an artillery bombardment, they still made a formidable obstacle to infantry. Enemy soldiers stood on every rooftop, while outside the wall, in an array as thick as a hedgehog's quills, was an assortment of cannon. 'A very nasty little place,' the General said. 'We must avoid it. I see your fellows are there, Sharpe!'

'My fellows, sir?' Sharpe asked in puzzlement.

'White coats, Sergeant.'

So Dodd's regiment had taken their place just to the south of Assaye. They were still on the left of Pohlmann's line, but now that line stretched southwards from the bristling defences about the village to the bank of the River Kaitna. The infantry were already in place and the last of the guns were now being hauled into their positions in front of the enemy line, and Sharpe remembered Syud Sevajee's grim words about the rivers meeting, and he knew that the only way out of this narrowing neck of land was either back through the fords or else straight ahead through the enemy's army. 'I see we shall have to earn our pay today,' the General said to no one in particular. 'How far ahead of the infantry is their gun line, Campbell?'

'A hundred yards, sir?' the young Scotsman guessed after gazing through his spyglass for a while.

'A hundred and fifty, I think,' Wellesley said.

Sharpe was watching the village. A lane led from its eastern wall and a file of cavalry was riding out from the houses towards some trees.

'They think to allow us to take the guns,' Wellesley guessed, 'reckoning we'll be so pounded by round shot and peppered by canister that their infantry can then administer the *coup de grâce*. They wish to treat us to a double dose! Guns and firelocks.'

The trees where the cavalry had disappeared dropped into a steep gully that twisted towards the higher ground from where Wellesley was observing the enemy. Sharpe, watching the tree-filled gully, saw birds fly out of the branches as the cavalry advanced beneath the thick leaves. 'Horsemen, sir,' Sharpe warned.

'Where, man, where?' Wellesley asked.

Sharpe pointed towards the gully. 'It's full of the bastards, sir. They came out of the village a couple of moments ago. You can't see them, sir, but I think there might be a hundred men hidden there.'

Wellesley did not dispute Sharpe. 'They want to put us in the bag,' he said in seeming amusement. 'Keep an eye out for them, Sharpe. I have no wish to watch the battle from the comfort of Scindia's tent.' He looked back to the enemy's line where the last of the heavy guns were being lugged into place. Those last two guns were the big eighteen-pounder siege guns that had done the damage as the British army crossed the ford, and now the huge pieces were being emplaced in front of Dodd's regiment. Elephants pulled the guns into position, then were led away towards the baggage park beyond the village. 'How many guns do you reckon, Campbell?' the General asked.

'Eighty-two, sir, not counting the ones by Assaye.'

'Around twenty there, I think. We shall be earning our pay! And their line's longer than I thought. We shall have to extend.' He was not so much speaking to Campbell as to himself, but now he glanced at the young Scots officer. 'Did you count their infantry?'

'Fifteen thousand in the line, sir?' Campbell hazarded.

'And at least as many again in the village,' Wellesley said, snapping his telescope shut, 'not to mention a horde of horsemen behind them, but they'll only count if we meet disaster. It's the fifteen thousand in front who concern us. Beat them and we beat all.' He made a pencilled note in a small black book, then stared again at the enemy line beneath its bright flags. 'They did manoeuvre well! A creditable performance. But do they fight, eh? That's the nub of it. Do they fight?'

'Sir!' Sharpe called urgently, for, not two hundred paces away, the first enemy horsemen had emerged from the gully with their *tulwars* and lances bright in the afternoon sun, and now were spurring towards Wellesley.

'Back the way we came,' the General said, 'and fairly briskly, I think.'

This was the second time in one day that Sharpe had been pursued by Mahratta cavalry, but the first time he had been mounted on a small native horse and now he was on one of the General's own chargers and the difference was night and day. The Mahrattas were at a full gallop, but Wellesley and his two companions never went above a canter and still their big horses easily outstripped the frantic pursuit. Sharpe, clinging for dear life to the mare's pommel, glanced behind after two minutes and saw the enemy horsemen pulling up. So that, he thought, was why officers were willing to pay a small fortune for British and Irish horses.

The three men dropped into the valley, climbed its farther side and Sharpe saw that the British infantry had now advanced from the road to form its line of attack along the low ridge that lay parallel to the road, and the redcoat array looked pitifully small compared to the great enemy host less than a mile to the west. Instead of a line of heavy guns, there was only a scatter of light six-pounder cannon and a single battery of fourteen bigger guns, and to face Pohlmann's three *compoos* of fifteen thousand men there were scarcely five thousand red-coated infantry, but Wellesley seemed unworried by the odds. Sharpe did not see how the battle was to be won, indeed he wondered why it was being fought at all, but whenever the doubt made his fears surge he only had to look at Wellesley and take comfort from the General's serene confidence.

Wellesley rode first to the left of his line where the kilted Highlanders of the 78th waited in line. 'You'll advance in a moment or two, Harness,' he told their Colonel. 'Straight ahead! I fancy you'll find bayonets will be useful. Tell your skirmishers that there are cavalry about, though I doubt you'll meet them at this end of the line.'

Harness appeared not to hear the General. He sat on a big horse as black as his towering bearskin hat and carried a huge claymore that looked as if it had been killing the enemies of Scotland for a century or more. 'It's the Sabbath, Wellesley,' he finally spoke, though without looking at the General. '"Remember the Sabbath day, to keep it holy. Six days shalt thou labour, and do all thy work, but the seventh is the Sabbath of the Lord thy God. In it thou shalt not do any work."' The Colonel glowered at Wellesley. 'Are you sure, man, that you want to fight today?'

'Quite sure, Colonel,' Wellesley answered very equably.

Harness grimaced. 'Won't be the first commandment I've broken, so to hell and away with it.' He gave his huge claymore a flourish. 'You'll not need to worry about my rogues, Wellesley, they can kill as well as any man, even if it is a Sunday.'

'I never doubted it.'

'Straight ahead, eh? And I'll lay the lash on any dog who falters. You hear that, you bastards! I'll flog you red!'

'I wish you joy of the afternoon, Colonel,' Wellesley said to Harness, then he rode north to speak with his other five battalion commanders. He gave them much the same instructions as he had given Colonel Harness, though because the Madrassi sepoys deployed no skirmishers, he simply warned them that they had one chance of victory and that was to march straight into the enemy fire and, by enduring it, carry their bayonets into the Mahratta ranks. He told the commanding officers of the two sepoy battalions in the second line that they would now need to join the front line. 'You'll incline right,' he told them, 'forming between Corben's 8th and Colonel Orrock's picquets.' He had hoped to attack in two lines, so that the men behind could reinforce those in front, but the enemy array was too wide and so he would need to throw every infantryman forward in one line. There would be no reserves. The General rode to meet Colonel Wallace who today would command a brigade of his own 74th Highlanders and two sepoy battalions which, with Orrock's picquets, would form the right side of the attacking force. He warned Wallace of the line's extension. 'I'll have Orrock incline right to give your sepoys room,' he promised Wallace, 'and I'm putting your own regiment on Orrock's right flank.' Wallace, because he was commanding the brigade, would not lead his own Highlanders who would be under the command of his deputy, Major Swinton, Colonel McCandless had joined his friend Wallace, and Wellesley greeted him. 'I see your man holds their left, McCandless.'

'So I've seen, sir.'

'But I don't wish to tangle with him early on. He's hard by the village and they've made it a stronghold, so we'll take the right of their line, then swing north and pin the rest against the Juah. You'll get your chance, McCandless, get your chance.'

'I'm depending on it, sir,' McCandless answered. The

Colonel nodded a mute greeting to Sharpe, who then had to follow Wellesley to the ranks of the 74th. 'You'll oblige me, Swinton,' Wellesley said, 'by doubling your fellows to the right and taking station beyond Colonel Orrock's picquets. You're to form the new right flank. I've told Colonel Orrock to move somewhat to his right, so you'll have a good way to go to make your new position. You understand?'

'Perfectly, sir,' Swinton said. 'Orrock will incline right and we double round behind him to form the new flank and sepoys replace us here.'

'Good man!' Wellesley said, then rode on to Colonel Orrock. Sharpe guessed that the General had ordered the 74th to move outside Orrock because he did not trust the nervous Colonel to hold the right flank. Orrock's contingent of half companies was a small but potent force, but it lacked the cohesion of the men's parent battalions. 'You're to lead them rightwards,' Wellesley told the red-faced Colonel, 'but not too far. You comprehend? Not too far right! Because you'll find a defended village on your front right flank and it's a brute. I don't want any of our men near it until we've sent the enemy infantry packing.'

'I go right?' Orrock asked.

'You incline right,' Wellesley said, 'then straighten up. Two hundred paces should do it. Incline right, Orrock, give the line two hundred paces more width, then straighten and march straight for the enemy. Swinton will be bringing his men onto your right flank. Don't wait for him, let him catch you, and don't hesitate when we attack. Just go straight in with the bayonet.'

Orrock jutted his head, scratched his chin and blinked. 'I go rightwards?'

'Then straight ahead,' Wellesley said patiently.

'Yes, sir,' Orrock said, then jerked nervously as one of his small six-pounder cannon, which had been deployed fifty yards in front of his line, fired.

'What the devil?' Wellesley asked, turning to look at the small gun that had leaped back five or six yards. He could not see what the gun had fired at, for the smoke of the discharge made a thick cloud in front of the muzzle, but a second later an enemy round shot screamed through the smoke, twitching it, to bounce between two of Orrock's half companies. Wellesley cantered to his left to see that the enemy guns had opened fire. For the moment they were merely sending ranging shots, but soon the guns would be pouring their metal at the red ranks.

The General cantered back southwards. It was close to mid afternoon now and the sun was burning the world white. The air was humid, hard to breathe, and every man in the British line was sweating. The enemy round shot bounced on the ground in front of them, and one shot ricocheted up to churn a file of sepoys into blood and bone. The sound of the enemy cannon was harsh, banging over the warm ground in successive punches that came closer and closer together as more guns joined the cannonade. The British guns replied, and the smoke of their discharges betrayed their positions, and the enemy gunners levered their pieces to aim at the British cannon which, hugely outnumbered, were having by far the worst of the exchange. Sharpe saw the earth around one six-pounder struck again and again by enemy round shot, each strike kicking up a barrow-load of soil, and then the small gun seemed to disintegrate as a heavy ball struck it plumb on the front of its carriage. Splinters flew to eviscerate the crew that had been ramming the gun. The barrel reared up, its trunnions tearing out of the carriage, then the heavy metal tube slowly toppled onto a wounded man. Another gunner reeled away, gasping for breath, while a third lay on the ground looking as though he slept.

A piper began to play as the General neared the kilted 78th. 'I thought I ordered all musicians to leave their instruments behind, drummers excepted,' Wellesley said angrily.

'Very hard to go into battle without the pipes, sir,' Campbell said reprovingly.

'Hard to save the wounded without orderlies,' Wellesley complained. In battle the pipers' job was to save the wounded, but Harness had blithely disobeyed the order and brought his bagpipers. However, it was too late to worry about that disobedience now. Another round shot found its mark in a sepoy battalion, flinging men aside like broken dolls, while a high ball struck a tall tree, shaking its topmost leaves and provoking a small green parrot to squawk as it fled the branches.

Wellesley reined in close to the 78th. He glanced to his right, then looked back to the eight or nine hundred yards of country that separated his small force from the enemy. The sound of the guns was constant now, its thunder deafening, and the smoke of their cannonade was hiding the Mahratta infantry that waited for his assault. If the General was nervous he showed no sign of it, unless the fingers drumming softly against his thigh betrayed some worry. This was his first proper battle in the field, gun against gun and infantry against infantry, yet he seemed entirely cool.

Sharpe licked dry lips. His mare fidgeted and Diomed kept pricking his ears at the gunfire. Another British gun was hit, this time losing a wheel to an enemy round shot. The gunners rolled a new wheel forward, while the officer commanding the small battery ran forward with a handspike. The infantry waited beneath their bright silk colours, their long line of two ranks tipped with shining bayonets.

'Time to go,' Wellesley said very quietly. 'Forward, gentlemen,' he said, but still not loudly. He took a breath. 'Forward!'

he shouted and, at the same time, took off his cocked hat and waved it towards the enemy.

The British drums began their beat. Sergeants shouted. Officers drew swords. The men began to march.

And the battle had begun.

CHAPTER 10

The redcoats advanced in a line of two ranks. The troops spread out as they walked and sergeants shouted at the files to keep closed. The infantry first had to pass the British gun line that was suffering badly in an unequal artillery duel with the Goanese gunners. The enemy was firing shell as well as solid shot, and Sharpe flinched as a shell exploded among a team of oxen that was picketed a hundred yards behind their gun. The wounded beasts bellowed, and one broke from its picket to limp with a bleeding and trailing leg towards the 10th Madras infantry. A British officer ran and put the beast out of its misery with his pistol and the sepoys stepped delicately about the shuddering corpse. Colonel Harness, seeing that his two small battalion guns would inevitably be destroyed if they stayed in action, ordered his gunners to limber up and follow the regiment forward. 'Do it fast, you rogues! I want you close behind me.'

The enemy gunners, seeing that they had won the fight between the batteries, turned their pieces on the infantry. They were firing at seven hundred yards now, much too far for canister, but a round shot could whip a file into bloody scraps in the blinking of an eye. The sound of the guns was unending, one shot melding into the next and the whole making a thunderous noise of deafening violence. The enemy line was shrouded in grey-white smoke which was constantly lit by flashes of gunfire deep in the smoke's heart. Sometimes a Mahratta battery would pause to let the smoke thin and Sharpe, riding twenty paces behind the General who was advancing just to the right of the 78th, could watch the enemy gunners heave at their pieces, see them back away as the gun captain swung the linstock over the barrel, then the gun would disappear again in a cloud of powder smoke and, an instant later, a ball would plunge down in front of the infantry. Sometimes it would bounce clean over the men's heads, but too often the heavy shots slammed into the files and men would be broken apart in a spray of blood. Sharpe saw the front half of a shattered musket wheel up out of the Highlanders' ranks. It turned in the air, pursued by its owner's blood, then fell to impale its bayonet into the turf. A gentle north wind blew a patch of gunsmoke away from the centre of the enemy line where the guns were almost axle boss to axle boss. Sharpe watched men ram the barrels, watched them run clear, watched the smoke blossom again and heard the shriek of a round shot just overhead. Sometimes Sharpe could see the tongue of dark-red fire streaking towards him in the cloud's heart, and then the lead-grey stroke of a ball arcing towards him in the sky, and once he saw the madly spiralling wisp of smoke left by the burning fuse of a shell, but every time the shots went wide or else fell short to churn up a dusty patch of earth.

'Close the files!' the sergeants shouted. 'Close up!'

The drummer boys beat the advance. There was low ground ahead, and the sooner the attacking line was in that gentle valley, the sooner they would be out of sight of the gunners. Wellesley looked to his right and saw that Orrock had paused in his advance and that the 74th, who should have been forming to the right of Orrock's men, had stopped as well. 'Tell Orrock to go! Tell him to go!' the General called to Campbell who spurred across the advancing line. His horse galloped through a cloud of shell smoke, leaped a broken limber, then Sharpe lost sight of the aide. Wellesley urged his horse closer to the 78th who were now drawing ahead of the sepoys. The Highlanders were taller than the Madrassi battalions and their stride was longer as they hurried to gain the dead ground where the bombardment could not reach them. A bouncing shell came to rest near the grenadier company that was on the right of the 78th's line and the kilted soldiers skipped aside, all but for one man who dashed out of the front rank as the missile spun crazily on the ground with its fuse spitting out a tangle of smoke. He rammed his right boot on the shell to make it still, then struck hard down with the brass butt of his musket to knock the fuse free. 'Am I spared the punishment now, Sergeant?' he called.

'You get in file, John, get in file,' the sergeant answered.

Wellesley grinned, then shuddered as a ball went perilously close to his hat. He looked round, seeking his aides, and saw Barclay. 'The calm before the storm,' the General remarked.

'Some calm, sir.'

'Some storm,' an Indian answered. He was one of the Mahratta chiefs who were allied to the British and whose horsemen were keeping the cavalry busy south of the river. Three such men rode with Wellesley and one had a badly trained horse that kept skittering sideways whenever a shell exploded.

Major Blackiston, the engineer on Wellesley's staff who had been sent to reconnoitre the land north of the army, now galloped back behind the advancing line. 'Broken ground up by the village, sir, cut by gullies,' he reported, 'no place to advance.'

Wellesley grunted. He had no intention of sending infantry near the village yet, so Blackiston's report was not immediately useful. 'Did you see Orrock?'

'He was worried about his two guns, sir. Can't take them forward because the teams have all been killed, but Campbell's chivvying him on.'

Wellesley stood in his stirrups to look north and saw Orrock's picquets at last moving smartly away. They were marching obliquely, without their two small guns, making space for the two sepoy battalions to come into the line. The 74th was beyond them, vanishing into a fold of ground. 'Not too far, Orrock, not too far,' Wellesley muttered, then he lost sight of Orrock's men as his horse followed the 78th into the lower ground. 'Once we have them pinned against the river,' he asked Blackiston, gesturing to show he meant the River Juah to the north, 'can they get away?'

'Eminently fordable, sir, I'm afraid,' Blackiston answered. 'I doubt they can move more than a handful of the guns down the bank, but a man can escape easily enough.'

Wellesley grunted an acknowledgement and spurred ahead, leaving the engineer behind. 'He didn't even ask if I was chased!' Blackiston said to Barclay with mock indignation.

'Were you, John?'

'Damned sure I was. Two dozen of the bastards on those wiry little ponies. They look like children riding to hounds.'

'But no bullet holes?' Barclay asked.

'Not a one,' Blackiston said regretfully, then saw Sharpe's surprised look. 'It's a wager, Sergeant,' the engineer explained. 'Whichever of the General's family ends up with the most bullet holes wins the pot.'

'Do I count, sir?'

'You replace Fletcher, and he didn't have to pay to get in because he claimed he was penniless. We admitted him from the goodness of our hearts. But no cheating now. We can't have fellows poking their coats with swords to win points.'

'How many points does Fletcher get, sir?' Sharpe asked. 'For having his head blown off?'

'He's disqualified, of course, on grounds of extreme carelessness.'

Sharpe laughed. Blackiston's words were not funny, of

course, but the laughter burst out of him, causing Wellesley to turn in his saddle and give him a scowl. In truth Sharpe was fighting a growing fear. For the moment he was safe enough, for the left flank of the attack was now in dead ground and the enemy bombardment was concentrating on the sepoy battalions who had still not reached the valley, but Sharpe could hear the whip-fast rumble of the round shots tearing up the air, he could hear the cannon fire, and every few seconds a howitzer shell would fall into the valley and explode in a puff of flaming smoke. So far the howitzers had failed to do any damage, but Sharpe could see the small bushes bend away from their blasts and hear the scraps of shell casing rip through leaves. In places the dry brush had caught fire.

He tried to concentrate on the small things. One of the canteens had a broken strap, so he knotted it. He watched his mare's ears flicker at every shell burst and he wondered if horses felt fear. Did they understand this kind of danger? He watched the Scots, stolidly advancing through the shrubs and trees, magnificent in their feathered bearskin hats and their pleated kilts. They were a long way from bloody home, he thought, and was surprised that he did not really feel that for himself, but he did not know where home was. Not London, for sure, though he had grown up there. England? He supposed so, but what was England to him? Not what it was to Major Blackiston, he guessed. He wondered again about Pohlmann's offer, and thought what it would be like to be standing in sash and sword behind that line of Mahratta guns. Safe as houses, he reckoned, just standing there and watching through the smoke as a thin line of redcoat enemies marched into horror. So why had he not accepted? And he knew the real reason was not some half-felt love of country, nor an aversion to Dodd, but because the only sash and sword he wanted were the ones that would let him go back to

England and spit on the men who had made his life miserable. Except there would be no sash and sword. Sergeants did not get made into officers, not often, and he was suddenly ashamed of ever having quizzed McCandless about the matter. But at least the Colonel had not laughed at him.

Wellesley had turned to speak to Colonel Harness. 'We'll give the guns a volley of musketry, Harness, at your discretion. That should give us time to reload, but save the second volley for their infantry.'

'I'd already worked out the same for myself,' Harness answered with a scowl. 'And I'll not use skirmishers, not on a Sunday.' Usually the light company went ahead of the rest of the battalion and scattered into a loose line that would fire at the enemy before the main attack arrived, but Harness must have decided that he would rather reserve the light company's fire for the one volley he planned to unload on the gunners.

'Soon be over,' Wellesley said, not contesting Harness's decision to keep his light company in line, and Sharpe decided the General must be nervous, for those last three words were unusually loquacious. Wellesley himself must have decided he had betrayed his feelings, for he looked blacker than ever. His high spirits had vanished ever since the enemy artillery had started firing.

The Scots were climbing now. They were tramping through stubble and at any minute they would cross the brow of the gentle hill and find themselves back in the gunners' sights. The first the gunners would see would be the two regimental standards, then the officers on horseback, then the line of bearskins, and after that the whole red, white and black array of a battalion in line with the glint of their fixed bayonets showing in the sun. And God help us then, Sharpe thought, because every buggering gun straight ahead must be reloaded by now and just waiting for its target, and suddenly the first round shot banged on the crest just a few paces ahead and ricocheted harmlessly overhead. 'That man fired early,' Barclay said. 'Take his name.'

Sharpe looked to his right. The next four battalions, all sepoys, were safe in the dead ground now, while Orrock's picquets and the 74th had vanished among the trees north of the valley. Harness's Scots would climb into view first and, for a moment or two, would have the gunners' undivided attention. Some of the Highlanders were hurrying, as if to get the ordeal over. 'Hold your dressing!' Harness bellowed at them. 'This ain't a race to the tavern! Damn you!'

Elsie. Sharpe suddenly remembered the name of a girl who had worked in the tavern near Wetherby where he had fled after running away from Brewhouse Lane. Why had he thought of her, he wondered, and he had a sudden vision of the taproom, all steaming on a winter night from men's wet coats, and Elsie and the other girls carrying the ale on trays and the fire sputtering in the hearth and the blind shepherd getting drunk and the dogs sleeping under the tables, and he imagined walking back into that smoke-blackened room with his officer's sash and sword, and then he forgot all about Yorkshire as the 78th, with Wellesley's family on its right, emerged onto the flat land in front of the enemy guns.

Sharpe's first surprised reaction was how close they were. The low ground had brought them within a hundred and fifty paces of the enemy guns, and his second reaction was how splendid the enemy looked, for their guns were lined up as though for inspection, while behind them the Mahratta battalions stood in four closely dressed ranks beneath their flags, and then he thought that this was what death must look like, and just as he thought that, so the whole gorgeous array of the enemy army vanished behind a vast bank of smoke, a roiling bank in which the smoke twisted as though it was tortured, and every few yards there was a spear of flame in the whiteness, while in front of the cloud the crops flattened away from the blast of the exploding powder as the heavy round shots tore through the Highlanders' files.

There seemed to be blood everywhere, and broken men falling or sliding in the carnage. Somewhere a man gasped, but no one was screaming. A piper dropped his instrument and ran to a fallen man whose leg had been torn away. Every few yards there was a tangle of dead and dying men, showing where the round shot had snatched files from the regiment. A young officer tried to calm his horse which was edging sideways in fright, its eyes white and head tossing. Colonel Harness guided his own horse round a disembowelled man without giving the dead man a glance. Sergeants shouted angrily for the files to close up, as though it was the Highlanders' fault that there were gaps in the line. Then everything seemed oddly silent. Wellesley turned and spoke to Barclay, but Sharpe did not hear a thing, then he realized that his ears were ringing from the terrible sound of that discharge of gunnery. Diomed pulled away from him and he tugged the grey horse back. Fletcher's blood had dried to a crust on Diomed's flank. Flies crawled all over the blood. A Highlander was swearing terribly as his comrades marched away from him. He was on his hands and knees, with no obvious wound, but then he looked up at Sharpe, spoke one last obscenity and collapsed forward. More flies congregated on the shining blue spill of the disembowelled man's guts. Another man crawled through stubble, dragging his musket by its whitened sling.

'Steady now!' Harness shouted. 'Damn your haste! Ain't running a race! Think of your mothers!'

'Mothers?' Blackiston asked.

'Close up!' a sergeant shouted. 'Close up!'

The Mahratta gunners would be frantically reloading, but this time with canister. The gunsmoke was dissipating, twisting as the small breeze carried it away, and Sharpe could see the misty shapes of men ramming barrels and carrying charges to muzzles. Other men handspiked gun trails to line the recoiled weapons on the Scots. Wellesley was curbing his stallion lest it get too far ahead of the Highlanders. Nothing showed on the right. The sepoys were still in dead ground and the right flank was lost among the scatter of trees and broken ground to the north, so that for the moment it seemed as if Harness's Highlanders were fighting the battle all on their own, six hundred men against a hundred thousand, but the Scotsmen did not falter. They just left their wounded and dead behind and crossed the open land towards the guns that were loaded with their deaths. The piper began playing again, and the wild music seemed to put a new spring in the High-landers' steps. They were walking to death, but they went in perfect order and in seeming calm. No wonder men made songs about the Scots, Sharpe thought, then turned as hooves sounded behind and he saw it was Captain Campbell returning from his errand. The Captain grinned at Sharpe. 'I thought I'd be too late.'

'You're in time, sir. Just in time, sir,' Sharpe said, but for what? he wondered.

Campbell rode on to Wellesley to make his report. The General listened, nodded, then the guns straight ahead started firing again, only raggedly this time as each enemy gun fired as soon as it was loaded. The sound of each gun was a terrible bang, as deafening as a thump on the ear, and the canister flecked the field in front of the Scots with a myriad puffs of dust before bouncing up to snatch men backwards. Each round was a metal canister, crammed with musket balls or shards of metal and scraps of stone, and as it left the barrel the canister was ripped apart to spread its missiles like a giant blast of duckshot.

Another cannon fired, then another, each gunshot pummelling the land and each taking its share of Scotsmen to eternity, or else making another cripple for the parish or a sufferer for the surgeon. The drummer boys were still playing, though one was limping and another was dripping blood onto his drumskin. The piper began playing a jauntier tune, as though this walk into an enemy horde was something to celebrate, and some of the Highlanders quickened their pace. 'Not so eager!' Harness shouted. 'Not so eager!' His basket-hilted claymore was in his hand and he was close behind his men's two ranks as though he wanted to spur through and carry the dreadful blade against the gunners who were flaying his regiment. A bearskin was blown apart by canister, leaving the man beneath untouched.

'Steady now!' a major called.

'Close up! Close up!' the sergeants shouted. 'Close the files!' Corporals, designated as file-closers, hurried behind the ranks and dragged men left and right to seal the gaps blown by the guns. The gaps were bigger now, for a well-aimed barrel of canister could take four or five files down, while a round shot could only blast away a single file at a time.

Four guns fired, a fifth, then a whole succession of guns exploded together and the air around Sharpe seemed to be filled with a rushing, shrieking wind, and the Highlanders' line seemed to twist in that violent gale, but though it left men behind, men who were bleeding and vomiting and crying and calling for their comrades or their mothers, the others closed their ranks and marched stolidly on. More guns fired, blanketing the enemy with smoke, and Sharpe could hear the canister hitting the regiment. Each blast brought a rattling sound as bullets struck muskets, while the Highlanders, like infantry everywhere, made sure their guns' wide stocks covered their groins. The line was shorter now, much shorter, and it had almost reached the lingering edge of the great bank of smoke pumped out by the enemy's guns.

'78th,' Harness shouted in a huge voice, 'halt!'

Wellesley curbed his horse. Sharpe looked to his right and saw the sepoys coming out of the valley in one long red line, a broken line, for there were gaps between the battalions and the passage through the shrub-choked valley had skewed the sepoys' dressing, and then the guns in the northern part of the Mahratta line opened fire and the line of sepoys became even more ragged. Yet still, like the Scots to their left, they pressed on into the gunfire.

'Present!' Harness shouted, a note of anticipation in his voice.

The Scotsmen brought their firelocks to their shoulders. They were only sixty yards from the guns and even a smoothbore musket was accurate enough at that range. 'Don't fire high, you dogs!' Harness warned them. 'I'll flog every man who fires high. Fire!'

The volley sounded feeble compared to the thunder of the big guns, but it was a comfort all the same and Sharpe almost cheered as the Highlanders fired and their crackling volley whipped away across the stubble. The gunners were vanishing. Some must have been killed, but others were merely sheltering behind the big trails of their cannon.

'Reload!' Harness shouted. 'No dallying! Reload!'

This was where the Highlanders' training paid its dividends, for a musket was an awkward brute to reload, and made more cumbersome still by the seventeen-inch bayonet fixed to its muzzle. The triangular blade made it difficult to ram the gun properly, and some of the Highlanders twisted the blades off to make their job easier, but all reloaded swiftly, just as they had been trained to do in hard long weeks at home. They loaded, rammed, primed, then slotted the ramrods back into the barrel hoops. Those who had removed their bayonets refastened them to the lugs, then brought the guns back to the ready.

'You save that volley for the infantry!' Harness warned

them. 'Now, boys, forward, and give the heathen bastards a proper Sabbath killing!'

This was revenge. This was anger let loose. The enemy guns were still not loaded and their crews had been hard hit by the volley, and most of the guns would not have time to charge their barrels before the Scots were on them. Some of the gunners fled. Sharpe saw a mounted Mahratta officer rounding them up and driving them back to their pieces with the flat of his sword, but he also saw one gun, a painted monster directly to his front, being rammed hard by two men who heaved on the rammer, plucked it free then ran aside.

'For what we are about to receive,' Blackiston murmured. The engineer had also seen the gunners charge their barrel.

The gun fired, and its jet of smoke almost engulfed the General's family. For an instant Sharpe saw Wellesley's tall figure outlined against the pale smoke, then he could see nothing but blood and the General falling. The heat and discharge of the gun's gasses rushed past Sharpe just a heart-beat after the scraps of canister had filled the air about him, but he had been directly behind the General and was in his shadow, and it was Wellesley who had taken the gun's blast.

Or rather it was his horse. The stallion had been struck a dozen times while Wellesley, charmed, had not taken a scratch. The big horse toppled, dead before he struck the ground, and Sharpe saw the General kick his feet out from the stirrups and use his hands to push himself up from the saddle as the horse collapsed. Wellesley's right foot touched the ground first and, before the stallion's weight could roll onto his leg, he jumped away, staggering slightly in his hurry. Campbell turned towards him, but the General waved him away. Sharpe kicked the mare on and untied Diomed's reins from his belt. Was he supposed to get the saddle off the dead horse? He supposed so, and thus slid out of his own saddle. But what the hell was he to do with the mare and Diomed while he untangled the saddle from the dead stallion? Then he thought to tie both to the dead horse's bridle.

'Four hundred guineas gone to a penny bullet,' Wellesley said sarcastically, watching as Sharpe unbuckled the girth from the dead stallion. Or near dead, for the beast still twitched and kicked as the flies came to feast on its new blood. 'I'll take Diomed,' Wellesley told Sharpe, then stooped to help, tugging the saddle with its attached bags and holsters free of the dying horse, but then a feral scream made the General turn back to watch as Harness's men charged into the gun line. The scream was the noise they made as they struck home, a scream that was the release of all their fears and a terrible noise presaging their enemies' death. And how they gave it. The Scotsmen found the gunners who had stayed at their posts crouching under the trails and they dragged them out and bayoneted them again and again. 'Bastard,' one man screamed, plunging his blade repeatedly into a dead gunner's belly. 'Heathen black bastard!' He kicked the man's head, then stabbed down with his bayonet again. Colonel Harness backswung his sword to kill a man, then casually wiped the blood off the blade onto his horse's black mane. 'Form line!' he shouted. 'Form line! Hurry, you rogues!'

A scatter of gunners had fled back from the Scots to the safety of the Mahratta infantry who were now little more than a hundred paces away. They should have charged, Sharpe thought. While the Scots were blindly hacking away at the gunners, the infantry should have advanced, but instead they waited for the next stage of the Scots attack. To his right there were still guns firing at the sepoys, but that was a separate battle, unrelated to the scramble as sergeants dragged Highlanders away from the dead and dying gunners and pushed them into their ranks.

'There are still gunners alive, sir!' a lieutenant shouted at Harness.

'Form up!' Harness shouted, ignoring the lieutenant. Sergeants and corporals shoved men into line. 'Forward!' Harness shouted.

'Hurry, man,' Wellesley said to Sharpe, but not angrily. Sharpe had heaved the saddle over Diomed's back and now stooped under the grey horse's belly to gather the girth. 'He doesn't like it too tight,' the General said.

Sharpe buckled the strap and Wellesley took Diomed's reins from him and heaved himself up into the saddle without another word. The General's coat was smeared with blood, but it was horse blood, not his own. 'Well done, Harness!' he called ahead to the Scotsman, then rode away and Sharpe unhitched the mare from the dead horse's bridle, clambered onto her back and followed.

Three pipers played for the 78th now. They were far from home, under a furnace sun in a blinding sky, and they brought the mad music of Scotland's wars to India. And it was madness. The 78th had suffered hard from the gunfire and the line of their advance was littered with dead, dying and broken men, yet the survivors now re-formed to attack the main Mahratta battle line. They were back in two ranks, they held their bloody bayonets in front, and they advanced against Pohlmann's own *compoo* on the right of the enemy line. The Highlanders looked huge, made into giants by their tall bearskin hats with their feather plumes, and they looked terrible, for they were. These were northern warriors from a hard country and not a man spoke as they advanced. To the waiting Mahrattas they must have seemed like creatures from nightmare, as terrible as the gods who writhed on their temple walls. Yet the Mahratta infantry in their blue and yellow coats were just as proud. They were warriors recruited from the martial tribes of northern India, and now they levelled their muskets as the two Scottish ranks approached.

The Scots were terribly outnumbered and it seemed to

Sharpe that they must all die in the coming volley. Sharpe himself was in a half-daze, stunned by the noise yet aware that his mood was swinging between elation at the Scottish bravery and the pure terror of battle. He heard a cheer and looked right to see the sepoys charging into the guns. He watched gunners flee, then saw the Madrassi sepoys tear into the laggards with their bayonets.

'Now we'll see how their infantry fights,' Wellesley said savagely to Campbell, and Sharpe understood that this was the real testing point, for infantry was everything. The infantry was despised for it did not have the cavalry's glamour, nor the killing capacity of the gunners, but it was still the infantry that won battles. Defeat the enemy's infantry and the cavalry and gunners had nowhere to hide.

The Mahrattas waited with levelled muskets. The Highlanders, silent again, marched on. Ninety paces to go, eighty, and then an officer's sword swung down in the Mahratta ranks and the volley came. It seemed ragged to Sharpe, maybe because most men did not fire on the word of command, but instead fired after they heard their neighbour's discharge, and he was not even aware of a bullet going close past his head because he was watching the Scots, terrified for them, but it seemed to him that not a man fell. Some men must have been hit, for he saw ripples where the files opened to step past the fallen, but the 78th, or what was left of the 78th, was intact still and still Harness did not fire, but just kept marching them onward.

'They fired high!' Campbell exulted.

'They drill well, fire badly,' Barclay observed happily.

Seventy paces to go, then sixty. A Highlander staggered from the line and collapsed. Two other men who had been wounded by the canister, but were now recovered, hurried from the rear and pushed their way into the ranks. 'Halt!' Harness suddenly called. 'Present!'

The guns, tipped by their bloodstained steel blades, came up into the Highlanders' shoulders so that the whole line seemed to take a quarter-turn to the right. The Mahratta gunsmoke was clearing and the enemy soldiers could see the Scots' heavy muskets, with hate behind them, and the Highlanders waited a heartbeat so the enemy could also see their death in the levelled muskets.

'You'll fire low, you bastards, or I'll want to know why,' Harness growled, then took a deep breath. 'Fire!' he shouted, and his Highlanders did not fire high. They fired low and their heavy balls ripped into bellies and thighs and groins.

'Now go for them!' Harness shouted. 'Just go for the bastards!' And the Highlanders, unleashed, ran forward with their bayonets and began to utter their shrill war cries, as discordant as the music of the pipes that flayed them onwards. They were killers loosed to the joys of slaughter and the enemy did not wait for its coming, but just turned and fled.

The enemy in the rearward ranks of the *compoo* had room to run, but those in front were impeded by those behind and could not escape. A terrible despairing wail sounded as the 78th struck home and as their bayonets rose and fell in an orgy of killing. An officer led an attack on a knot of standard-bearers who tried desperately to save their flags, but the Scots would not be denied and Sharpe watched as the kilted men stepped over the dead to lunge their blades at the living. The flags fell, then were raised again in Scottish hands. A cheer went up, and just then Sharpe heard another cheer and saw the sepoys charging home at the next section of the enemy line and, just as the first Mahratta troops had run from the Scots, so now the neighbouring battalions fled from the sepoys. The enemy's vaunted infantry had crumpled at the first contact. They had watched the thin line come towards them, and they must have assumed that the red coats would be turned even redder by the heavy fire of the artillery, but the line had taken the guns' punishment and just kept coming, battered and bleeding, and it must have seemed to the Mahrattas that such men were invincible. The huge Scots in their strange kilts had started the rout, but the sepoy battalions from Madras now set about the destruction of all the enemy's centre and right. Only his left still stood its ground.

The sepoys killed, then pursued the fugitives who streamed westwards. 'Hold them!' Wellesley shouted at the nearest battalion commanders. 'Hold them!' But the sepoys would not be held. They wanted to pursue a beaten enemy and they streamed raggedly in his wake, killing as they went. Wellesley wheeled Diomed. 'Colonel Harness!'

'You'll want me to form post here?' the Scotsman asked. Blood dripped from his sword.

'Here,' Wellesley agreed. The enemy infantry might have fled, but there was a maelstrom of cavalry a half-mile away and those horsemen were cantering forward to attack the disordered British pursuers. 'Deploy your guns, Harness.'

'I've given the order already,' Harness said, gesturing towards his two small gun teams that were hurrying six-pounders into position. 'Column of full companies!' Harness shouted. 'Quarter distance!'

The Scots, one minute so savage, now ran back into their ranks and files. The battalion faced no immediate enemy, for there was neither infantry nor artillery within range, but the distant cavalry was a threat and so Harness arranged them in their ten companies, close together, so that they resembled a square. The close formation could defend itself against any cavalry attack, and just as easily shake itself into a line or into a column of assault. Harness's twin six-pounders were unlimbered and now began firing towards the horsemen who, appalled by the wreckage of their infantry, paused rather than attack the redcoats. British and Indian officers were galloping among the pursuing sepoys, ordering them back to their ranks, while Harness's 78th stood like a fortress to which the sepoys could retreat. 'So sanity is not a requisite of soldiering,' Wellesley said quietly.

'Sir?' Sharpe was the only man close enough to hear the General and assumed that the words were addressed to him.

'None of your business, Sharpe, none of your business,' Wellesley said, startled that he had been overheard. 'A canteen, if you please.'

It had been a good start, the General decided, for the right of Pohlmann's army had been destroyed and that destruction had taken only minutes. He watched as the sepoys hurried back to their ranks and as the first *puckalees* appeared from the nearby Kaitna with their huge loads of canteens and waterskins. He would let the men have their drink of water, then the line would be turned to face north and he could finish the job by assaulting Assaye. The General kicked Diomed around to examine the ground over which his infantry must advance and, just as he turned, so all hell erupted at the village.

Wellesley frowned at the dense cloud of gunsmoke that had suddenly appeared close to the mud walls. He heard volley fire, and he could see that it was the surviving Mahratta left wing that did the firing, not his redcoats, and, more ominously, a surge of Mahratta cavalry had broken through on the northern flank and was now riding free in the country behind Wellesley's small army.

Someone had blundered.

The left flank of William Dodd's regiment lay just a hundred paces from the mud walls of Assaye where the twenty guns which defended the village gave that flank an added measure of safety. In front of the Cobras were another six guns, two of them the long-barrelled eighteen-pounders that had bombarded the ford, while Dodd's own small battery of four-pounder guns was bunched in the small gap between his men's right flank and the neighbouring regiment. Pohlmann had chosen to array his guns in front of the infantry, but Dodd expected the British to attack in line and a gun firing straight towards an oncoming line could do much less damage than a gun firing obliquely down the line's length, and so he had placed his cannon wide on the flank where they could work the most havoc.

It was not a bad position, Dodd reckoned. In front of his line were two hundred yards of open killing ground after which the land fell into a steepish gully that angled away eastwards. An enemy could approach in the gully, but to reach Dodd's men they would have to climb onto the flat farmland and there be slaughtered. A cactus-thorn hedge ran across the killing ground, and that would give the enemy some cover, but there were wide gaps in the thorns. If Dodd had been given time he would have sent men to cut down the whole hedge, but the necessary axes were back with the baggage a mile away. Dodd, naturally, blamed Joubert for the missing tools. 'Why are they not here, Monsewer?' he had demanded.

'I did not think. I'm sorry.'

'Sorry! Sorry don't win battles, Monsewer.'

'I shall send for the axes,' Joubert said.

'Not now,' Dodd said. He did not want to send any men back to the baggage camp, for their loss would momentarily weaken his regiment and he expected to be attacked at any moment. He looked forward to that moment, for the enemy would need to expose himself to a withering fire, and Dodd kept standing in his stirrups to search for any sign of an approaching enemy. There were some British and Company cavalry far off to the east, but those horsemen were staying well out of range of the Mahratta guns. Other enemies must have been within the range of Pohlmann's guns, for Dodd could hear them firing and see the billowing clouds of grey-white smoke pumped out by each shot, but that cannonade was well to his south and it did not spread down the line towards him and it slowly dawned on Dodd that Wellesley was deliberately avoiding Assaye. 'God damn him!' he shouted aloud.

'Monsieur?' Captain Joubert asked resignedly, expecting another reprimand.

'We're going to be left out,' Dodd complained.

Captain Joubert thought that was probably a blessing. The Captain had been saving his meagre salary in the hope of retiring to Lyons, and if General Wellesley chose to ignore Captain Joubert then Captain Joubert was entirely happy. And the longer he stayed in India, the more attractive he found Lyons. And Simone would be better off in France, he thought, for the heat of India was not good for her. It had made her restless, and inactivity gave her time to brood and no good ever came from a thinking woman. If Simone was in France she would be kept busy. There would be meals to cook, clothes to mend, a garden to tend, even children to raise. Those things were women's work, in Joubert's opinion, and the sooner he could take his Simone away from India's languorous temptations the better.

Dodd stood in his stirrups again to stare southwards through his cheap glass. 'The 78th,' he grunted.

'Monsieur?' Joubert was startled from his happy reverie about a house near Lyons where his mother could help Simone raise a busy little herd of children.

'The 78th,' Dodd said again, and Joubert stood in his stirrups to gaze at the distant sight of the Scottish regiment emerging from low ground to advance against the Mahratta line. 'And no support for them?' Dodd asked, puzzled, and he had begun to think that Boy Wellesley had blundered very badly, but just then he saw the sepoys coming from the valley.

The attacking line looked very thin and frail, and he could see men being snatched backwards by the artillery fire. 'Why won't they come here?' he asked petulantly.

'They are, Monsieur,' Joubert answered, and pointed eastwards.

Dodd turned and stared. 'Praise God from Whom all blessings flow,' he said softly. 'The fools!' For the enemy was not just coming towards Dodd's position, but approaching in a column of half companies. The enemy infantry had suddenly appeared at the upper edge of the gully, but on Dodd's side of that obstacle, and it was clear that the redcoats must have wandered far out of their position for they were a long way from the rest of the attacking British infantry. Better still, they had not deployed into line. Their commander must have decided that they would make better progress if they advanced in column and doubtless he planned to deploy into line when he launched his attack, but the men showed no sign of deploying yet.

Dodd aimed his telescope and was momentarily puzzled. The leading half company were King's troops in red jackets, black shakoes and white trousers, while the forty or fifty men of the half company behind were in kilts, but the other five half companies were all sepoys of the East India Company. 'It's the picquets of the day,' he said, suddenly understanding the strange formation. He heard a shout as a gun captain ordered his cannon to be levered around to take aim at the approaching men, and he hurriedly shouted to his gunners to hold their fire. 'No one's to fire yet, Joubert,' Dodd ordered, then he spurred his horse northwards to the village.

The infantry and gunners defending the village of Assaye were not under Dodd's command, but he issued them orders anyway. 'You're to hold your fire,' he snapped at them, 'hold your fire. Wait! Wait!' Some of the Goanese gunners spoke a little English, and they understood him and passed the order on. The Rajah's infantry, on the mud walls above the guns, were not so quick and some of those men opened fire on the distant redcoats, but their muskets were far outranged and Dodd ignored them. 'You fire when we fire, understand?' he shouted at the gunners, and some of them understood what he was doing, and they grinned approval of his cunning.

He spurred back to the Cobras. A second British formation had appeared a hundred paces behind the picquets. This second unit was a complete battalion of redcoats advancing in line and, because marching an extended line across country was inevitably slower than advancing in a column of half companies, they had fallen behind the picquets who, in sublime disregard of Assaye's waiting defenders, continued their progress towards the cactus hedge. It seemed to be an isolated attack, far from the clamour in the south that Dodd now ignored. God had given Dodd a chance of victory and he felt the excitement rise in him. It was bliss, pure bliss. He could not lose. He drew the elephant-hilted sword and, as if to give thanks, kissed the steel blade.

The leading half company of picquets had reached the thorn hedge and there they had checked, at last unwilling to continue their suicidal progress towards the waiting Mahrattas. Some artillery from further up the line, which did not lie under Dodd's control, had opened fire on the column, but the white-coated Mahratta forces immediately to the front of the column were silent and the picquets' commanding officer seemed encouraged by that and now urged his men onwards. 'Why doesn't he deploy?' Dodd asked no one, and prayed that they would not deploy, but as soon as the half company of kilted Highlanders had filed through a gap in the cactus thorn they began to spread out and Dodd knew his moment was close. But wait, he told himself, wait for more victims, and sure enough the sepoys pushed through the breaks in the hedge until all the picquets were in front of the cactus and their officers and sergeants began chivvying them forward onto the open pasture where there would be more space for the half companies to deploy into line.

Captain Joubert was worried that Dodd was leaving the command to open fire too late. The second British formation was close to the hedge now, and once they were through the gaps they would add a vast weight of musketry to the attack. But Dodd knew it would take that regiment a long time to manoeuvre through the hedge, and he was concerned solely with the three or four hundred men of the picquets who were now just eighty yards from his gun line and still not properly deployed. His own men were a hundred paces behind the guns, but now he took them forward. 'Regiment will advance,' he ordered, 'at the double!' His interpreter shouted the order and Dodd watched proudly as his men ran smartly forward. They kept their ranks, and checked promptly on his command when they reached the emplaced artillery. 'Thank you, Lord,' he prayed. The picquets, suddenly aware of the horror that awaited them, began to hurry as they spread into line, but still Dodd did not fire. Instead he rode his new horse behind his men's ranks. 'You fire low!' he told his Cobras. 'Make sure you fire low! Aim at their thighs.' Most troops fired high and thus a man who aimed at his enemy's knees would as like as not hit his chest. Dodd paused to watch the picquets who were now advancing in a long double line. Dodd took a deep breath. 'Fire!'

Forty guns and over eight hundred muskets were aimed at the picquets and scarce a gun or a musket missed. One moment the ground in front of the hedge was alive with soldiers, the next it was a charnel house, swept by metal and flayed by fire, and though Dodd could see nothing through the powder smoke, he knew he had virtually annihilated the redcoat line. The volley had been massive. Two of the guns, indeed, had been the eighteen-pounder siege guns and Dodd's only regret was that they had been loaded with round shot instead of canister, but at least they could now reload with canister and so savage the British battalion that had almost reached the cactus hedge.

'Reload!' Dodd called to his men. The smoke was writhing away, thinning as it went, and he could see enemy bodies on the ground. He could see men twitching, men crawling, men dying. Most did not move at all, though miraculously their commanding officer, or at least the only man who had been on horseback, still lived. He was whipping his horse back through the hedge.

'Fire!' Dodd shouted, and a second volley whipped across the killing ground to thrash through the hedge and strike the battalion behind. That battalion was taking even worse punishment from the artillery which was now firing canister, and the blasts of metal were tearing the hedge apart, destroying the redcoats' small cover. The little four-pounder guns, which fired such puny round shot, now served as giant shotguns to spray the redcoats with Dodd's home-made bags of canister. His sepoys loaded and rammed their muskets. The dry grass in front of them flickered with hundreds of small pale flames where the burning wadding had started fires.

'Fire!' Dodd shouted again, and saw, just before the cloud of powder smoke blotted out his view, that the enemy was stepping backwards. The volley crashed out, filling the air with the stench of rotten eggs.

'Reload!' Dodd shouted and admired his men's efficiency. Not one had panicked, not one had fired his ramrod by mistake. Clockwork soldiers, he thought, as soldiers ought to be, while the enemy's return fire was pathetic. One or two of Dodd's men had been killed, and a handful were wounded, but in return they had destroyed the leading British unit and were driving the next one back. 'The regiment will advance!'

he shouted and listened to his interpreter repeat the order.

They marched in line through their own powder smoke and then across the scores of dead and dying enemy picquets. Soldiers stooped to the bodies to filch keepsakes and loot and Dodd shouted at them to keep going. The loot could wait. They reached the remnants of the cactus hedge where Dodd halted them. The British battalion was still going backwards, evidently seeking the safety of the gully. 'Fire!' he shouted, and his men's volley seemed to push the redcoats even further back. 'Reload!'

Ramrods rattled in barrels, dogheads were dragged back to the full. The British line was retreating fast now, but from the north, from the land hard by the river, a mass of Mahratta cavalry was riding south to join the slaughter. Dodd wished the cavalry would stay out of it, for he had an idea that he could have pursued this British battalion clear down the tongue of land to where the rivers met and the last of their men would die in the Kaitna's muddy shallows, but he dared not fire another volley in case he hit the cavalry. 'The regiment will advance!' he told his interpreter. He would let the cavalry have their moment, then go on with the slaughtering himself.

The British battalion commander saw the cavalry and knew his retreat must stop. His men were still in line, a line of only two ranks, and cavalrymen dreamed of encountering infantry in line. 'Form square!' their commanding officer shouted, and the two wings of the line dutifully withdrew towards the centre. The double rank became four, the four ranks wheeled and dressed, and suddenly the cavalry faced a fortress of redcoats, muskets and bayonets. The front rank of the square knelt and braced their muskets on the ground while the other three readied their muskets for the coming horsemen.

The cavalry should have sheered away at the sight of the square, but they had seen the earlier slaughter and thought

318

to add to it, and so they dipped their pennanted lances, raised their *tulwars* and screamed their war cries as they galloped straight towards the redcoats. And the redcoats let them come, let them come perilously close before the order was shouted and the face of the square nearest the cavalry exploded in flame and smoke and the horses screamed as they were hit and died. The surviving horsemen swerved aside and received another killing volley as they swept past the sides of the square. More horses tumbled, dust spewing from their sliding bodies. A *tulwar* spun along the ground, its owner shrieking as his trapped leg was ground into bloody ruin by the weight of his dying horse.

'Reload!' a Scots voice shouted from inside the square and the redcoats recharged their muskets.

The cavalry charged on into open country and there wheeled about. Some of the horses were riderless now, others were bloody, but all came back towards the square.

'Let them come close!' a mounted British officer shouted inside the square. 'Let them come close. Wait for it! Fire!'

More horses tumbled, their legs cracking as the bones shattered, and this time the cavalry did not sheer away to ride down the square's lethal flanks, but instead wheeled clean about and spurred out of range. Two lessons were sufficient to teach them caution, but they did not go far away, just far enough to be out of range of the redcoats' muskets. The cavalry's leaders had seen Dodd's regiment come through the cactus hedge and they knew that their own infantry, attacking in line, must overwhelm the square with musketry and, when the square shattered, as it must under the infantry's assault, the horsemen could sweep back to pick off the survivors and pluck the great gaudy banners as trophies to lay before Scindia.

Dodd could scarcely believe his luck. At first he had resented the cavalry's intrusion, believing that they were about to steal his victory, but their two impotent charges had forced the enemy battalion to form square and mathematics alone dictated that a battalion in square could only use one quarter of its muskets against an attack from any one side. And the British battalion, which Dodd now recognized from its white facings as the 74th, was much smaller than Dodd's Cobras, probably having only half the numbers Dodd possessed. And, in addition to Dodd's men, a ragged regiment of the Rajah of Berar's infantry had poured out of Assaye to join the slaughter while a battalion from Dupont's *compoo*, which had been posted immediately on Dodd's right, had also come to join the killing. Dodd resented the presence of those men whom he feared might dilute the glory of his victory, but he could scarcely order them away. The important thing was to slaughter the Highlanders. 'We're going to kill the bastards with volley fire,' he told his men, then waited for his translator to interpret. 'And then we'll finish them off with bayonets. And I want those two colours! I want those flags hanging in Scindia's tent tonight.'

The Scots were not waiting idly for the attack. Dodd could see small groups of men dashing out of the square and at first he thought they were plundering the dead cavalrymen, and then he saw they were dragging the bodies of men and horses back to make a low rampart. The few survivors of the picquets were among the Scots, who were now caught in a terrible dilemma. By staying in square they would keep themselves safe from any attack by the cavalry which still hovered to the south, though the square made them into an easy target for the enemy's muskets, but if they deployed into line, so that they could use all their muskets against the enemy's infantry line, they made themselves into cavalry bait. Their commanding officer decided to stay in square. Dodd reckoned he would do the same if he was ever so foolish as to be trapped like these fools were trapped. They still had to be finished off, and that promised to be grim work, for the 74th was a notoriously tough regiment, but Dodd had the advantage of numbers and the advantage of position and he knew he must win.

Except that the Scotsmen did not agree with him. They crouched behind their barricade of dead men and horses and poured a blistering fire of musketry at the white-coated Cobras. A lone piper, who had disobeyed the order to leave his instrument at Naulniah, played in the square's centre. Dodd could hear the sound, but he could not see the piper, nor, indeed, the square itself, which was hidden by a churning fog of dark powder smoke. The smoke was illuminated by the flashes of musket fire, and Dodd could hear the heavy balls thumping into his men. The Cobras were no longer advancing, for the closer they got to the deadly smoke the greater their casualties and so they had paused fifty yards from the square to let their own muskets do the work. They were reloading as fast as their enemies, but too many of their bullets were being wasted on the barricade of corpses. All four faces of the square were firing now, for the 74th was surrounded. To the west they fired at Dodd's attacking line, to the north they fired at the Rajah's infantry, while to the east and south they kept the cavalry at bay. The Mahratta horsemen, scenting the Scottish regiment's death, were prowling ever closer in the hope that they could dash in and take the colours before the infantry.

Dodd's Cobras, together with the battalion from Dupont's *compoo*, began to curl about the southern flank of the trapped regiment. It should take only three or four volleys, Dodd thought, to end the business, after which his men could go in with the bayonet. Not that his men were firing volleys any longer; instead they were firing as soon as their muskets were charged and Dodd felt their excitement and sought to curb it. 'Don't waste your fire!' he shouted. 'Aim low!' William

Dodd had no desire to lead a charge through the stinking smoke to find an unbroken formation of vengeful Highlanders waiting with bayonets. Dodd might dislike the Scots, but he had a healthy fear of fighting them with cold steel. Thin the bastards first, he thought, batter them, bleed them, then massacre them, but his men were too excited at the prospect of imminent victory and far too much of their fire was either going high or else being wasted on the barricade of the dead. 'Aim low!' he shouted again. 'Aim low!'

'They won't last,' Joubert said. Indeed the Frenchman was amazed that the Scots still survived.

'Awkward things to kill, Scotsmen,' Dodd said. He took a drink from his canteen. 'I do hate the bastards. All preachers or thieves. Stealing Englishmen's jobs. Aim low!' A man was thrown back near Dodd, blood bright on his white coat. 'Joubert?' Dodd called back to the Frenchman.

'Monsieur?'

'Bring up two of the regiment's guns. Load with canister.' That would end the bastards. Two gouts of canister from the four-pounders would blow great gaps in the Scottish square and Dodd could then lead his men into those gaps and fillet the dying regiment from its inside out. He would be damned if the cavalry would take the flags. They were his! It was Dodd who had fought these Highlanders to a standstill and Dodd who planned to carry the silk banners to Scindia's tent and there fetch his proper reward. 'Hurry, Joubert!' he called.

Dodd drew his pistol and fired over his men's ranks into the smoke that hid the dying square. 'Aim low!' he shouted. 'Don't waste your fire!' But it would not be long now. Two blasts of canister, he reckoned, and then the bayonets would bring him victory.

Major Samuel Swinton stood just behind the western face of the square which looked towards the white-coated infantry.

He could hear an English voice shouting orders and encouragement in the enemy lines and, though Swinton himself was an Englishman, the accent angered him. No English bastard was going to destroy the 74th, not while Major Swinton commanded, and he told his men that a Sassenach was their enemy and that seemed to add zest to their efforts. 'Keep low!' he told them. 'Keep firing!' By staying low the Scots kept behind the protection of their makeshift barricade, but it also made their muskets much more difficult to reload and some men took the risk of standing after each shot. Their only protection then was the mask of smoke that hid the regiment from its enemies. And thank God, Swinton thought, that the enemy had brought no artillery forward.

The square was swept by musket fire. Much of it, especially from the north, flew high, but the white-coated regiment was better trained and their musketry was having an effect, so much so that Swinton took the inside rank of the eastern face and added it to the west. The sergeants and corporals closed the ranks as the enemy bullets hurled men back into the bloody interior of the shrinking square where the Major stepped among the Scottish dead and wounded. Swinton's horse had died, struck by three musket balls and put out of its misery by the Major's own pistol. Colonel Orrock, who had first led the picquets to disaster, had also lost his horse. 'It wasn't my fault,' he kept telling Swinton, and Swinton wanted to hit the bastard every time he spoke. 'I obeyed Wellesley's orders!' Orrock insisted.

Swinton ignored the fool. Right from the beginning of the advance Swinton had sensed that the picquets were going too far to the right. Orrock's orders had been clear enough. He was to incline right, thus making space for the two sepoy battalions to come into the line, then attack straight ahead, but the fool had led his men ever more northwards and Swinton, who had been trying to loop about the picquets to come up on their right, never had a chance to get into position. He had sent the 74th's adjutant to speak with Orrock, pleading with the East India Company Colonel to turn ahead, but Orrock had arrogantly brushed the man off and kept marching towards Assaye.

Swinton had a choice then. He could have ignored Orrock and straightened his own attack to form the right of the line that Wellesley had taken forward, but the leading half company of Orrock's picquets were fifty men from Swinton's own regiment and the Major was not willing to see those fifty men sacrificed by a fool and so he had followed the picquets on their errant course in the hope that his men's fire could rescue Orrock. It had failed. Only four of the fifty men of the half company had rejoined the regiment, the rest were dead and dying, and now the whole 74th seemed to be doomed. They were encompassed by noise and smoke, surrounded by enemies, dying in their square, but the piper was still playing and the men were still fighting and the regiment still lived, and the two flags were still lifted high, though by now the fringed squares of silk were ripped and tattered by the blast of bullets.

An ensign in the colour party took a musket ball in his left eye and fell backwards without a sound. A sergeant gripped the staff in one hand and in his other was a halberd with a wicked blade. In a moment, the sergeant knew, he might have to fight with the halberd. The square would end with a huddle of bloodied men around the colours and the enemy would fall on them and for a few moments it would be steel against steel, and the sergeant reckoned he would give the flag to a wounded man and do what harm he could with the heavy, long-shafted axe. It was a pity to die, but he was a soldier, and no one had yet devised a way a man could live for ever, not even those clever bastards in Edinburgh. He thought of his wife in Dundee, and of his woman in the camp at Naulniah, and he regretted his many sins, for it was not good for a man to go to his God with a bad conscience, but it was too late now and so he gripped the halberd and hid his fear and determined he would die like a man and take a few other men with him.

The muskets banged into Highlanders' shoulders. They bit the tips from new cartridges and every bite added salty gunpowder to their mouths so that they had no spittle, only bone-dry throats that breathed filthy smoke, and the regiment's *puckalees* were far away, lost somewhere in the country behind. The Scots went on firing, and the powder sparks from the pan burned their cheeks, and they loaded and rammed and knelt and fired again, and somewhere beyond the smoke the enemy's fire came flashing in to shudder the corpses of the barricade or else to snatch a man back in a spray of blood. Wounded men fought alongside the living, their faces blackened by powder, their mouths parched, their shoulders bruised, and the white facings and cuffs of their red coats were spattered with the blood of men now dead or dying.

'Close up!' the sergeants shouted and the square shrank another few feet as dying men were hauled back to the square's centre and the living closed the files. Men who had started the day five or six files apart were neighbours now.

'It wasn't my fault!' Orrock insisted.

Swinton had nothing to say. There was nothing to say, and nothing more to do except die, and so he picked up the musket of a dead man, took the cartridge box from the corpse's pouch, and pushed into the square's western face. The man to his right was drunk, but Swinton did not care, for the man was fighting. 'Come to do some proper work, Major?' the drunken man greeted Swinton, with a toothless grin.

'Come to do some proper work, Tam,' Swinton agreed.

He bit the end from a cartridge, charged the musket, primed the lock and fired into the smoke. He reloaded, fired again, and prayed he would die bravely.

Fifty yards away William Dodd watched the cloud of smoke made by the Scottish muskets. The cloud was getting smaller, he thought. Men were dying there and the square was shrinking, but it was still spitting flame and lead. Then he heard the jingle of chains and turned to see the two four-pounder guns being hauled towards him. He would let the guns fire one blast of canister each, then he would have his men fix bayonets and he would lead them across the rampart of corpses into the heart of the smoke.

And then the trumpet called.

CHAPTER 11

Colonel McCandless had stayed close to his friend Colonel
Wallace, the commander of the brigade which formed the
right of Wellesley's line. Wallace had seen the picquets and
his own regiment, the 74th, vanish somewhere to the north,
but he had been too busy bringing his two sepoy battalions
into the attacking line to worry about Orrock or Swinton.
He did charge an aide to keep watching for Orrock's men,
expecting to see them veering back towards him at any
moment, then he forgot the errant picquets as his men
climbed from the low ground into the fire of the Mahratta
gun line. Canister shredded Wallace's ranks, it beat like hail
on his men's muskets and it swept the leaves from the scattered trees through which the Madrassi battalions marched,
but, just like the 78th, the sepoys did not turn. They walked
doggedly on like men pushing into a storm, and at sixty
paces Wallace halted them to pour a vengeful volley into the
gunners and McCandless could hear the musket balls clanging
off the painted gun barrels. Sevajee was with McCandless
and he stared in awe as the sepoys reloaded and went forward
again, this time carrying their bayonets to the gunners. For
a moment there was chaotic slaughter as Madrassi sepoys
chased Goanese gunners around limbers and guns, but Wallace was already looking ahead and could see that the vaunted
enemy infantry was wavering, evidently shaken by the easy
victory of the 78th, and so the Colonel shouted at his sepoys

to ignore the gunners and re-form and push on to attack the infantry. It took a moment to re-form the line, then it advanced from the guns. Wallace gave the enemy infantry one volley, then charged, and all along the line the vaunted Mahratta foot fled from the sepoy attack.

McCandless was busy for the next few moments. He knew that the assault had gone nowhere near Dodd's regiment, but nor had he expected it to, and he was anticipating riding northwards with Wallace to find the 74th, the regiment McCandless knew was nearest to his prey, but when the sepoys lost their self-control and broke ranks to pursue the beaten enemy infantry, McCandless helped the other officers round them up and herd them back. Sevajee and his horsemen stayed behind, for there was a possibility that they would be mistaken for enemy cavalry. For a moment or two there was a real danger that the scattered sepoys would be charged and slaughtered by the mass of enemy cavalry to the west, but its own fleeing infantry was in the cavalry's way, the 78th stood like a fortress on the left flank, and the Scottish guns were skipping balls along the cavalry's face, and the Mahratta horsemen, after a tentative move forward, thought better of the charge. The sepoys took their ranks again, grinning because of their victory. McCandless, his small chore done, rejoined Sevajee. 'So that's how Mahrattas fight.' The Colonel could not resist the provocation.

'Mercenaries, Colonel, mercenaries,' Sevajee said, 'not Mahrattas.'

Five victorious redcoat regiments now stood in ranks on the southern half of the battlefield. To the west the enemy infantry was still disordered, though officers were trying to re-form them, while to the east there was a horror of bodies and blood left on the ground across which the redcoats had advanced. The five regiments had swept through the gun line and chased away the infantry and now formed their ranks some two hundred paces west of where the Mahratta infantry had made their line so that they could look back on the trail of carnage they had caused. Riderless horses galloped through the thinning skeins of powder smoke where dogs were already gnawing at the dead and birds with monstrous black wings were flapping down to feast on corpses. Beyond the corpses, on the distant ground where the Scots and sepoys had started their advance, there were now Mahratta cavalrymen, and McCandless, gazing through his telescope, saw some of those cavalrymen harnessing British artillery that had been abandoned when its ox teams had been killed by the bombardment that had opened the battle.

'Where's Wellesley?' Colonel Wallace asked McCandless.

'He went northwards.' McCandless was now staring towards the village where a dreadful battle was being fought, but he could see no details, for there were just enough trees to obscure the fight, though the mass of powder smoke rising above the leaves was as eloquent as the unending crackle of musketry. McCandless knew his business was to be where that battle was being fought, for Dodd was surely close to the fight if not involved, but in McCandless's path was the stub of the Mahratta defence line, that part of the line which had not been attacked by the Scots or the sepoys, and those men were turning to face southwards. To reach that southern battle McCandless would have to loop wide to the east, but that stretch of country was full of marauding bands of enemy cavalry. 'I should have advanced with Swinton,' he said ruefully.

'We'll catch up with him soon enough,' Wallace said, though without conviction. It was clear to both men that Wallace's regiment, the 74th, had marched too far to the north and had become entangled in the thicket of Mahratta defences about Assaye and their commanding officer, removed from them to lead the brigade, was plainly worried.

'Time to turn north, I think,' Wallace said, and he shouted at his two sepoy battalions to wheel right. He had no authority over the remaining two sepoy battalions, nor over the 78th, for those were in Harness's brigade, but he was ready to march his two remaining battalions towards the distant village in the hope of rescuing his own regiment.

McCandless watched as Wallace organized the two battalions. This part of the battlefield, which minutes before had been so loud with screaming canister and the hammer of volleys, was now strangely quiet. Wellesley's attack had been astonishingly successful, and the enemy was regrouping while the attackers, left victorious on the Kaitna's northern bank, drew their breath and looked for the next target. McCandless thought of using Sevajee's handful of horsemen as an escort to take him safely towards the village, but another rush of Mahratta cavalry galloped up from the low ground. Wellesley and his aides had ridden northwards and they seemed to have survived the milling enemy horsemen, but the General's passing had attracted more horsemen to the area and McCandless had no mind to run the gauntlet of their venom and so he abandoned the idea of a galloping dash northwards. It was just then that he noticed Sergeant Hakeswill, crouching by a dead enemy with the reins of a riderless horse in one hand. A group of redcoats was with him, all from his own regiment, the 33rd. And just as McCandless saw the Sergeant, so Hakeswill looked up and offered the Scotsman a glance of such malevolence that McCandless almost turned away in horror. Instead he spurred his horse across the few yards that separated them. 'What are you doing here, Sergeant?' he asked harshly.

'My duty, sir, as is incumbent on me,' Hakeswill said. As ever, when addressed by an officer, he had straightened to attention, his right foot tucked behind his left, his elbows back and his chest thrust out.

'And what are your duties?' McCandless asked.

'*Puckalees*, sir. In charge of *puckalees*, sir, making sure the scavenging little brutes does their duty, sir, and nothing else, sir. Which they does, sir, on account of me looking after them like a father.' He unbent sufficiently to give a swift nod in the direction of the 78th where, sure enough, a group of *puckalees* was distributing heavy skins of water they had brought from the river.

'Have you written to Colonel Gore yet?' McCandless asked.

'Have I written to Colonel Gore yet, sir?' Hakeswill repeated the question, his face twitching horribly under the shako's peak. He had forgotten that he was supposed to have the warrant reissued, for he was relying instead on McCandless's death to clear the way to Sharpe's arrest. Not that this was the place to murder McCandless, for there were a thousand witnesses within view 'I've done everything what ought to be done, sir, like a soldier should,' Hakeswill answered evasively.

'I shall write to Colonel Gore myself,' McCandless now told Hakeswill, 'because I've been thinking about that warrant. You have it?'

'I do, sir.'

'Then let me see it again,' the Colonel demanded.

Hakeswill unwillingly pulled the grubby paper from his pouch and offered it to the Colonel. McCandless unfolded the warrant, quickly scanned the lines, and suddenly the falsity in the words leaped out at him. 'It says here that Captain Morris was assaulted on the night of August the fifth.'

'So he was, sir. Foully assaulted, sir.'

'Then it could not have been Sharpe who committed the assault, Sergeant, for on the night of the fifth he was with me. That was the day I collected Sergeant Sharpe from Seringapatam's armoury.' McCandless's face twisted with distaste as he looked down at the Sergeant. 'You say you were a witness to the assault?' he asked Hakeswill.

Hakeswill knew when he was beaten. 'Dark night, sir,' the Sergeant said woodenly.

'You're lying, Sergeant,' McCandless said icily, 'and I know you are lying, and my letter to Colonel Gore will attest to your lying. You have no business here, and I shall so inform Major General Wellesley. If it was up to me then your punishment would take place here, but that is for the General to decide. You will give me that horse.'

'This horse, sir? I found it, sir. Wandering, sir.'

'Give it here!' McCandless snapped. Sergeants had no business having horses without permission. He snatched the reins from Hakeswill. 'And if you do have duties with the *puckalees*, Sergeant, I suggest you attend to them rather than plunder the dead. As for this warrant . . .' The Colonel, before Hakeswill's appalled gaze, tore the paper in two. 'Good day, Sergeant,' McCandless said and, his small victory complete, turned his horse and spurred away.

Hakeswill watched the Colonel ride away, then stooped and picked up the two halves of the warrant which he carefully stowed in his pouch. 'Scotchman,' he spat.

Private Lowry shifted uncomfortably. 'If he's right, Sergeant, and Sharpie wasn't there, then we shouldn't be here.'

Hakeswill turned savagely on the private. 'And since when, Private Lowry, did you dispose of soldiery? The Duke of York has made you an officer, has he? His Grace put braid on your coat without telling me, did he? What Sharpie did is no business of yours, Lowry.' The Sergeant was in trouble, and he knew it, but he was not broken yet. He turned and stared at McCandless who had given the horse to a dismounted officer and was now in deep conversation with Colonel Wallace. The two men glanced towards Hakeswill and the Sergeant guessed they were discussing him. 'We follows that

Scotchman,' Hakeswill said, 'and this is for the man who puts him under the sod.' He fished a gold coin from his pocket and showed it to his six privates.

The privates stared solemnly at the coin, then, all at once, they ducked as a cannonball screamed low over their heads. Hakeswill swore and dropped flat. Another gun sounded, and this time a barrelful of canister flecked the grass just south of Hakeswill.

Colonel Wallace had been listening to McCandless, but now turned eastwards. Not all the gunners in the Mahratta line had been killed and those who survived, together with the cavalry which had been looking for employment, were now manning their guns again. They had turned the guns to face west instead of east and were now firing at the five regiments who were waiting for the battle to begin again. Except the gunners had surprised them, and the captured British guns, fetched from the east, now joined the battery to pour their shot, shell and canister into the red-coated infantry. They fired at three hundred paces, point-blank range, and their missiles tore bloodily through the ranks.

For the Mahrattas, it seemed, were not beaten yet.

William Dodd could smell victory. He could almost feel the sheen of the captured silk colours in his hands, and all it would take was two blasts of canister, a mucky slaughter with bayonets, and then the 74th would be destroyed. Horse Guards in London could cross the first battalion of the regiment off the army list, all of it, and mark down that it had been sacrificed to William Dodd's talent. He snarled at his gunners to load their home-made canister, watched as the loaders rammed the missiles home, and then the trumpet sounded.

The British and Company cavalry had been posted in the northern half of the battlefield to guard against enemy horsemen sweeping about the infantry's rear, but now they came to the 74th's rescue. The 19th Dragoons emerged from the gully behind the Highlanders and their charge curved northwards out of the low ground towards the 74th and the village beyond. The troopers were mostly recruits from the English shires, young men brought up to know horses and made strong by farm work, and they all carried the new light cavalry sabre that was warranted never to fail. Nor did it.

They struck the Mahratta horse first. The English riders were outnumbered, but they rode bigger horses and their blades were better made, and they cut through the cavalry with a maniacal savagery. It was hacking work, brutal work, screaming and fast work, and the Mahrattas turned their lighter horses away from the bloody sabres and fled northwards, and once the enemy horsemen were killed or fleeing, the British cavalry raked back their spurs and charged at the Mahratta infantry.

They struck the battalion from Dupont's *compoo* first, and because those men were not prepared for cavalry, but were still in line, it was more an execution than a fight. The cavalry were mounted on tall horses, and every man had spent hours of sabre drill learning how to cut, thrust and parry, but all they had to do now was slash with their heavy, wide-bladed weapons that were designed for just such butchery. Slash and hack, scream and spur, then push on through panicking men whose only thought was flight. The sabres made dreadful injuries, the weight of the blade gave the weapons a deep bite and the curve of the steel dragged the newly sharpened edges back through flesh and muscle and bone to lengthen the wound.

Some Mahratta cavalry bravely tried to stem the charge, but their light *tulwars* were no match for Sheffield steel. The 74th were standing and cheering as they watched the English horsemen carve into the enemy who had come so terribly close, and behind the Englishmen rode Company cavalry, Indians on smaller horses, some carrying lances, who spread the attack wider to drive the broken Mahratta horsemen northwards.

Dodd did not panic. He knew he had lost this skirmish, but the helpless mass of Dupont's battalion was protecting his right flank and those doomed men gave Dodd the few seconds he needed. 'Back,' he shouted, 'back!' and he needed no interpreter now. The Cobras hurried back towards the cactus-thorn hedge. They did not run, they did not break ranks, but stepped swiftly backwards to leave the enemy's horse room to sweep across their front, and, as the horsemen passed, those of Dodd's men who still had loaded muskets fired. Horses stumbled and fell, riders sprawled, and still the Cobras went backwards.

But the regiment was still in line and Dupont's panicked infantry were now pushing their way into Dodd's right-hand companies, and the second rank of dragoons rode in among that chaos to slash their sabres down onto the white-coated men. Dodd shouted at his men to form square, and they obeyed, but the two right-hand companies had been reduced to ragged ruin and their survivors never joined the square which was so hastily made that it was more of a huddle than an ordered formation. Some of the fugitives from the two doomed companies tried to join their comrades in the square, but the horsemen were among them and Dodd shouted at the square to fire. The volley cut down his own men with the enemy, but it served to drive the horsemen away and so gave Dodd time to send his men back through the hedge and still further back to where they had first waited for the British attack. The Rajah of Berar's infantry, who had been on Dodd's left, had escaped more lightly, but none had stayed to fight. Instead they ran back to Assaye's mud walls. The gunners by the village saw the cavalry coming and fired

335

canister, killing more of their own fugitives than enemy cavalry, but the brief cannonade at least signalled to the dragoons that the village was defended and dangerous.

The storm of cavalry passed northwards, leaving misery in its wake. The two four-pounder cannon that Joubert had taken forward were abandoned now, their teams killed by the horsemen, and where the 74th had been there was now nothing but an empty enclosure of dead men and horses that had formed the barricade. The survivors of the beleaguered square had withdrawn eastwards, carrying their wounded with them, and it seemed to Dodd that a sudden silence had wrapped about the Cobras. It was not a true silence, for the guns had started firing again on the southern half of the battlefield, the distant sound of hooves was neverending and the moaning of the nearby wounded was loud, but it did seem quiet.

Dodd spurred his horse southwards in an attempt to make some sense of the battle. Dupont's *compoo* next to him had lost one regiment to the sabres, but the next three regiments were intact and the Dutchman was now turning those units to face southwards. Dodd could see Pohlmann riding along the back of those wheeling regiments and he suspected that the Hanoverian would now turn his whole line to face south. The British had broken the far end of the line, but they had still not broken the army.

Yet the possibility of annihilation existed. Dodd fidgeted with the elephant hilt of his sword and contemplated what less than an hour before had seemed an impossibility: defeat. God damn Wellesley, he thought, but this was no time for anger, just for calculation. Dodd could not afford to be captured and he had no mind to die for Scindia and so he must secure his line of retreat. He would fight to the end, he decided, then run like the wind. 'Captain Joubert?'

The long-suffering Joubert trotted his horse to Dodd's side. 'Monsieur?'

Dodd did not speak at once, for he was watching Pohlmann come nearer. It was clear now that the Hanoverian was making a new battle line, and one, moreover, that would lie to the west of Assaye with its back against the river. The regiments to Dodd's right, which had yet to be attacked, were now pulling back and the guns were going with them. The whole line was being redeployed, and Dodd guessed the Cobras would move from the east side of the mud walls to the west, but that was no matter. The best ford across the Juah ran out of the village itself, and it was that ford Dodd wanted. 'Take two companies, Joubert,' he ordered, 'and march them into the village to guard this side of the ford.'

Joubert frowned. 'The Rajah's troops, surely . . .' he began to protest.

'The Rajah of Berar's troops are useless!' Dodd snapped. 'If we need to use the ford, then I want it secured by our men. You secure it.' He jabbed at the Frenchman with a finger. 'Is your wife in the village?'

'*Oui, Monsieur.*'

'Then now's your chance to impress her, Monsewer. Go and protect her. And make sure the damn ford isn't captured or clogged up with fugitives.'

Joubert was not unhappy to be sent away from the fighting, but he was dismayed by Dodd's evident defeatism. Nevertheless he took two companies, marched into the village, and posted his men to guard the ford so that if all was lost, there would still be a way out

Wellesley had ridden north to investigate the furious fighting that had erupted close to the village of Assaye. He rode with a half-dozen aides and with Sharpe trailing behind on the last of the General's horses, the roan mare. It was a furious ride, for the area east of the infantry was infested with Mahratta horsemen, but the General had faith in the size and speed of his big English and Irish horses and the enemy was easily outgalloped. Wellesley came within sight of the beleaguered 74th just as the dragoons crashed in on their besiegers from the south. 'Well done, Maxwell!' Wellesley shouted aloud, though he was far out of earshot of the cavalry's leader, and then he curbed his horse to watch the dragoons at work.

The mass of the Mahratta horsemen who had been waiting for the 74th's square to collapse, now fled northwards and the British cavalry, having hacked the best part of an enemy infantry regiment into ruin, pursued them. The cavalry's good order was gone now, for the blue-coated troopers were spurring their horses to chase their broken enemy across country. Men whooped like fox hunters, closed on their quarry, slashed with sabre, then spurred on to the next victim. The Mahratta horsemen were not even checked by the River Juah, but just plunged in and spurred their horses through the water and up the northern bank. The British and Indian cavalry followed so that the pursuit vanished in the north. The 74th, who had fought so hard to stay alive, now marched out of range of the cannon by the village and Wellesley, who had smelt disaster just a few minutes before, breathed a great sigh of relief. 'I told them to stay clear of the village, did I not?' he demanded of his aides, but before anyone could answer, new cannon fire sounded from the south. 'What the devil?' Wellesley said, turning to see what the gunfire meant.

The remaining infantry of the Mahratta line were pulling back, taking their guns with them, but the artillery which had stood in front of the enemy's defeated right wing, the same guns that had been overrun by the red-coated infantry, were now coming alive again. The weapons had been turned and were crashing back on their trails and jetting smoke from their muzzles, and behind the guns was a mass of enemy cavalry ready to protect the gunners who were flaying the five battalions that had defeated the enemy infantry. 'Barclay?' Wellesley called.

'Sir?' The aide spurred forward.

'Can you reach Colonel Harness?'

The aide looked at the southern part of the battlefield. A moment before it had been thick with Mahratta horsemen, but those men had now withdrawn behind the revived guns and there was a space in front of those guns, a horribly narrow space, but the only area of the battlefield that was now free of enemy cavalry. If Barclay was to reach Harness then he would have to risk that narrow passage and, if he was very lucky, he might even survive the canister. And dead or alive, Barclay thought, he would win the lottery of bullet holes in his coat. The aide took a deep breath. 'Yes, sir.'

'My compliments to Colonel Harness, and ask him to retake the guns with his Highlanders. The rest of his brigade will stay where they are to keep the cavalry at bay.' The General was referring to the mass of cavalry that still threatened from the west, none of which had yet entered the battle. 'And my compliments to Colonel Wallace,' the General went on, 'and his sepoy battalions are to move northwards, but are not to engage the enemy until I reach them. Go!' He waved Barclay away, then twisted in his saddle. 'Campbell?'

'Sir?'

'Who's that?' The General pointed eastwards to where one single cavalry unit had been left out of the charge that had rescued the 74th, presumably in case the dragoons had galloped into disaster and needed a rescue.

Campbell peered at the distant unit. '7th Native Cavalry, sir.'

'Fetch them. Quick now!' The General drew his sword as Campbell galloped away. 'Well, gentlemen,' he said to his remaining aides, 'time to earn our keep, I think. Harness can drive the wretches away from the southernmost guns, but we shall have to take care of the nearer ones.' For a moment Sharpe thought the General planned to charge the guns with just the handful of men who remained with him, then he realized Wellesley was waiting for the 7th Native Cavalry to arrive. For a few seconds Wellesley had considered summoning the survivors of the 74th, but those men, who had retreated back across the gully, were still recovering from their ordeal. They were collecting their wounded, taking the roll call and reorganizing ten broken companies into six. The 7th Native Cavalry would have to beat down the guns and Campbell brought them across the battlefield, then led their commanding officer, a red-faced major with a bristling moustache, to Wellesley's side. 'I need to reach our infantry, Major,' the General explained, 'and you're going to escort me to them, and the quickest way is through their gun line.'

The Major gaped at the guns with their crowd of attendant cavalry. 'Yes, sir,' he said nervously.

'Two lines, if you please,' the General ordered brusquely. 'You will command the first line and drive off the cavalry. I shall ride in the second and kill the gunners.'

'You'll kill the gunners, sir?' the Major asked, as though he found that idea novel, then he realized his question was dangerously close to insubordination. 'Yes, sir,' he said hurriedly, 'of course, sir.' The Major stared at the gun line again. He would be charging the line's flank, so at least no gun would be pointing at his men. The greater danger was the mass of Mahratta cavalry that had gathered behind the guns and which far outnumbered his troopers, but then, sensing Wellesley's impatience, he spurred his horse back to his men and shouted at his troopers. 'Two lines by the right!' The Major commanded a hundred and eighty men and Sharpe saw them grin as they drew their sabres and spurred their horses into formation.

'Ever been in a cavalry charge, Sergeant?' Campbell asked Sharpe.

'No, sir. Never wanted to be, sir.'

'Nor me. Should be interesting.' Campbell had his claymore drawn and he gave the huge sword a cut in the air which almost took his horse's ears off. 'You might find it more enjoyable, Sergeant,' he said helpfully, 'if you drew your sabre.'

'Of course, sir,' Sharpe said, feeling foolish. He had somehow imagined that his first battle would be spent in an infantry battalion, firing and reloading as he had been trained to do, but instead it seemed that he was to fight as a cavalry trooper. He drew the heavy weapon which felt unnatural in his hand, but then this whole battle seemed unnatural. It swung from moments of bowel-loosening terror to sudden calm, then back to terror again. It also ebbed and flowed, flaring in one part of the field, then dying down as the tide of killing passed to another patch of dun-coloured farmland.

'And our job is to kill the gunners,' Campbell explained, 'to make sure they don't fire at us again. We'll let the experts look after their cavalry and we just slaughter whatever they leave us. Simple.'

Simple? All Sharpe could see was a mass of enemy horsemen behind the huge guns that were bucking and rearing as they crashed out smoke, flame and death, and Campbell thought it was easy? Then he realized that the young Scots officer was just trying to reassure him, and he felt grateful. Campbell was watching Captain Barclay ride through the artillery barrage. It seemed the Captain must be killed, for he went so close to the Mahratta guns that at one point his horse vanished in a cloud of powder smoke, but a moment later he reappeared, low in his saddle, his horse galloping, and Campbell cheered when he saw Barclay swerve away towards Harness's brigade.

'A canteen, Sergeant, if you please?' Wellesley demanded, and Sharpe, who had been watching Barclay, fumbled to loosen one of the canteen straps. He gave the water to the General, then opened his own canteen and drank from it. Sweat was pouring down his face and soaking his shirt. Wellesley drank half the water, stoppered it and gave the canteen back, then trotted his horse into a gap in the right-hand side of the second line of the cavalry. The General drew his slim sword. The other aides also found places in the line, but there seemed no space for Sharpe and so he positioned himself a few yards behind the General. 'Go!' Wellesley shouted to the Major.

'Forward line, by the centre,' the Major shouted. 'Walk! March!'

It seemed an odd order, for Sharpe had expected the two lines to start at the gallop, but instead the leading line of horsemen set off at a walk and the second line just waited. Leaving the wide gap made sense to Sharpe, for if the second line was too close to the first then it could get entangled with whatever carnage the leading line made, whereas if there was a good distance between the two lines then there was space for the second to swerve around obstacles, but even so, walking a horse into battle seemed idiocy to Sharpe. He licked his lips, already dry again, then wiped his sweaty hand on his trousers before regripping the sabre's hilt.

'Now, gentlemen!' Wellesley said and the second line started forward at the same sedate pace as the first. Curb chains jingled and empty scabbards flapped. After a few seconds the Major in the first line called out an order and the two lines went into the trot. Dust swirled away from the hooves. The troopers' black hats had tall scarlet plumes that tossed prettily, while their curved sabres flashed with reflected sunlight. Wellesley spoke to Blackiston beside him and Sharpe saw the Major laugh, then the trumpeter beside the Major

342

blew a call and the twin lines went into the canter. Sharpe tried to keep up, but he was a bad rider and the mare kept swerving aside and tossing her head. 'Keep going!' Sharpe snarled at her. The Mahrattas had seen the attack coming now and the gunners were desperately trying to lever the northernmost gun about to face the threat while a mass of enemy cavalrymen was spurring forward to confront the charge.

'Go!' the Major shouted and his trumpeter sounded the full charge and Sharpe saw the sabres of the leading line drop so that their points were jutting forward like spears. This was more like it, he thought, for the horses were galloping now, their hooves making a furious thunder as they swept on to the enemy.

The leading line crashed into the oncoming enemy cavalry. Sharpe expected to see the line stop, but it hardly seemed to check. Instead there was the flash of blades, an impression of a man and horse falling and then the Major's line was through the cavalry and riding over the first gun. Sabres rose and fell. The second line was swerving to avoid the fallen horses, then they too were among the enemy and closing on the first line which was at last being slowed by the enemy's resistance.

'Keep going!' Wellesley shouted at the foremost riders. 'Keep going! Get me to the infantry!'

The cavalry had charged so that their right flank would overrun the guns, while the rest of the attack would face the cavalry to the east of the gun line. Those easternmost men were making good progress, but the right-flank troopers were being held up by the big ammunition limbers that were parked behind the guns. The Indian troopers slashed at the Goanese gunners who dived beneath their cannon for shelter. One gunner swung a rammer and swept a trooper off a horse. Muskets banged, a horse screamed and fell in a tangle of flailing hooves. An arrow flicked towards Sharpe, missing him by a hair's breadth. Sabres slashed and bit. Sharpe saw one tall trooper standing in his stirrups to give his swing more room. The man screamed as he hacked down, then wrenched his blade free from his victim and spurred on to find another. Sharpe clung desperately to the saddle as the mare swerved to avoid a wounded horse, then he was among the guns himself. Two lines of cavalry had ridden over these weapons, but still some of the gunners lived and Sharpe swung at one man with the sabre, but at the last moment the mare's motion unbalanced him and the blade went far above the enemy's head. It was all bloody chaos now. The cavalry was fighting its way up the line, but some of the enemy horsemen were galloping around the first line's flank to attack the second line, and groups of gunners were fighting back like infantry. The gunners were armed with muskets and pikes, and Sharpe, kicking his horse behind Wellesley, saw a group of them appear from the shelter of a painted eighteen-pounder gun and run towards the General. He tried to shout a warning, but the sound that emerged was more like a scream for help.

Wellesley was isolated. Major Blackiston had wheeled left to chop down at a tall Arab wielding a massive blade, while Campbell was loose on the right where he was racing in pursuit of a fugitive horseman. The Indian troopers were all in front of the General, sabring gunners as they spurred ahead, while Sharpe was ten paces behind. Six men attacked the General, and one of them wielded a long, narrow-bladed pike that he thrust up at Wellesley's horse. The General sawed on Diomed's reins to wheel him out of the man's path, but the big horse was going too fast and ran straight onto the levelled pike.

Sharpe saw the man holding the pike twist aside as the horse's weight wrenched the staff out of his hands. He saw the white stallion falling and sliding, and he saw Wellesley thrown forward onto the horse's neck. He saw the half-dozen enemy closing in for the kill and suddenly the chaos and terror of the day all vanished. Sharpe knew what he had to do, and knew it as clearly as though his whole life had been spent waiting for just this moment.

He kicked the roan mare straight at the enemy. He could not reach the General, for Wellesley was still in the saddle of the wounded Diomed who was sliding on the ground and trailing the pikestaff from his bleeding chest, and the threat of the horse's weight had driven the enemy aside, three to the left and three to the right. One fired his musket at Wellesley, but the ball flew wide, and then, as Diomed slowed, the Mahrattas closed in and it was then that Sharpe struck them. He used the mare as a battering ram, taking her perilously close to where the General had fallen from the saddle, and he drove her into the three gunners on the right, scattering them, and at the same time he kicked his feet from the stirrups and swung himself off the horse so that he fell just beside the dazed Wellesley. Sharpe stumbled as he fell, but he came up from the ground snarling with the sabre sweeping wide at the three men he had charged, but they had been driven back by the mare's impact, and so Sharpe whipped back to see a gunner standing right over the General with a bayonet raised, ready to strike, and he lunged at the man, screaming at him, and felt the sabre's tip tear through the muscles of the gunner's belly. Sharpe pushed the sabre, toppling the gunner back onto Diomed's blood-flecked flank.

The sabre stuck in the wound. The gunner was thrashing, his musket fallen, and one of his comrades was climbing over Diomed with a *tulwar* in his hand. Sharpe heaved on the sabre, jerking the dying man, but the blade would not free itself of the flesh's suction and so he stepped over Wellesley, who was still dizzied and on his back, put his left boot on the gunner's groin and heaved again. The man with the *tulwar* struck down, and Sharpe felt a blow on his left shoulder, but then his own sabre came free and he swung it clumsily at his new attacker. The man stepped back to avoid the blade and tripped on one of Diomed's rear legs. He fell. Sharpe turned, his sabre sweeping blindly wide with drops of blood flicking from its tip as he sought to drive back any enemies coming from his right. There were none. The General said something, but he was still scarcely conscious of what was happening, and Sharpe knew that he and the General were both going to die here if he did not find some shelter fast.

The big painted eighteen-pounder gun offered some small safety, and so Sharpe stooped, took hold of Wellesley's collar, and unceremoniously dragged the General towards the cannon. The General was not unconscious, for he clung to his slim straight sword, but he was half stunned and helpless. Two men ran to cut Sharpe off from the gun's sanctuary and he let go of the General's stiff collar and attacked the pair. 'Bastards,' he screamed as he fought them. Bugger the advice about straight arm and parrying, this was a time to kill in sheer rage and he went for the two gunners in a berserk fury. The sabre was a clumsy weapon, but it was sharp and heavy and he almost severed the first man's neck and the subsequent backswing opened the second man's arm to the bone, and Sharpe turned back to Wellesley, who was still not recovered from the impact of his fall, and he saw an Arab lancer spurring his horse straight at the fallen General. Sharpe bellowed an obscenity at the man, then leaped forward and slashed the sabre's heavy blade across the face of the lancer's horse and saw the beast swerve aside. The lance blade jerked up into the air as the Arab tried to control his pain-maddened horse, and Sharpe stooped, took Wellesley's collar again, and hauled the General into the space between the gun's gaudy barrel and one of its gigantic wheels. 'Stay there!' Sharpe snapped to Wellesley, then turned around to see that the Arab had been thrown from his horse, but was now leading a charge of gunners. Sharpe went to meet them. He swept the lance aside with the sabre's blade, then rammed the weapon's bar hilt into the Arab's face. He felt the man's nose break, kicked him in the balls, shoved him back, hacked down with the sabre, then turned to his left and sliced the blade within an inch of a gunner's eyes.

The attackers backed away, leaving Sharpe panting. Wellesley at last stood, steadying himself with one hand on the gunwheel. 'Sergeant Sharpe?' Wellesley asked in puzzlement.

'Stay there, sir,' Sharpe said, without turning round. He had four men in front of him now, four men with bared teeth and bright weapons. Their eyes flicked from Sharpe to Wellesley and back to Sharpe. The Mahrattas did not know they had the British General trapped, but they knew the man beside the gun must be a senior officer, for his red coat was bright with braid and lace, and they came to capture him, but to reach him they first needed to pass Sharpe. Two men came from the gun's far side, and Wellesley parried a pike blade with his sword, then stepped away from the gun to stand beside Sharpe and immediately a rush of enemy came to seize him. 'Get back!' Sharpe shouted at Wellesley, then stepped into the enemy's charge.

He grabbed a pike that was reaching for the General's belly, tugged it towards him, and met the oncoming gunner with the sabre's tip. Straight into the man's throat, and he twisted the blade free and swung it right and felt the steel jar on a man's skull, but there was no time to assess the damage, just to step left and stab at a third man. His shoulder was bleeding, but there was no pain. He was keening a mad noise as he fought and it seemed to Sharpe at that instant as though he could do nothing wrong. It was as if the enemy had been magically slowed to half speed and he had been quickened. He was much taller than any of them, he was much stronger, and he was suddenly much faster. He was even enjoying the fight, had he known anything of what he felt, but he sensed only the madness of battle, the sublime madness that blots out fear, dulls pain and drives a man close to ecstasy. He was screaming obscenities at the enemy, begging them to come and be killed.

He moved to his right and slashed the blade in a huge downward cut that opened a man's face. The enemy had retreated, and Wellesley again came to Sharpe's side and so invited the attackers to close in again, and Sharpe again pushed the General back into the space between the tall gunwheel and the huge painted barrel of the eighteen-pounder. 'Stay there,' he snapped, 'and watch under the barrel!' He turned away to face the attackers. 'Come on, you bastards! Come on! I want you!'

Two men came, and Sharpe stepped towards them and used both his hands to bring the heavy sabre down in a savage cut that bit through the hat and skull of the nearest enemy. Sharpe screamed a curse at the dying man, for his sabre was trapped in his skull, but he wrenched it free and sliced it right, a grey jelly sliding off its edge, to chase the second man back. That man held up his hands as he retreated, as if to suggest that he did not want to fight after all, and Sharpe cursed him as he slashed the blade's tip through his gullet. He spat on the staggering man and spat dry-mouthed again at the enemies who were watching him. 'Come on! Come on!' he taunted them. 'Yellow bastards! Come on!'

There were at last horsemen riding back to help now, but more Mahrattas were closing in on the fight. Two men tried to reach Wellesley across the cannon barrel and the General stabbed one in the face, then slashed at the arm of the other as he reached beneath the gun barrel. Behind him Sharpe was screaming insults at the enemy and one man took up the challenge and ran at Sharpe with a bayonet. Sharpe shouted in what sounded like delight as he parried the lunge and then punched the sabre's hilt into the man's face. Another man was coming from the right and so Sharpe kicked his first assailant's legs out from under him, then slashed at the newcomer. Christ knows how many of the bastards there were, but Sharpe did not care. He had come here to fight and God had given him one screaming hell of a battle. The man parried Sharpe's cut, lunged, and Sharpe stepped past the lunge and hammered the sabre's bar hilt into the man's eye. The man screamed and clutched at Sharpe, who tried to throw him off by punching the hilt into his face again. The other attackers were vanishing now, fleeing from the horsemen who spurred back towards Wellesley.

But one Mahratta officer had been stalking Sharpe and he now saw his opportunity as Sharpe was held by the half-blinded man. The officer came from behind Sharpe and he swung his *tulwar* at the back of the redcoat's neck.

The stroke was beautifully aimed. It hit Sharpe plumb on the nape of his neck, and it should have cut through his spine and dropped him dead to the bloody ground in an instant, but there was a dead king's ruby hidden in the leather bag around which Sharpe's hair was clubbed and the big ruby stopped the blade dead. The jolt of the blow jerked Sharpe forward, but he kept his feet and the man who had been clutching him at last released his grip and Sharpe could turn. The officer swung again and Sharpe parried so hard that the Sheffield steel slashed clean through the *tulwar's* light blade and the next stroke cut through the blade's owner. 'Bastard!' Sharpe shouted as he tugged the blade free and he whirled around to kill the next man who came near, but instead it was Captain Campbell who was there, and behind him were a dozen troopers who spurred their horses into the enemy and hacked down with their sabres.

For a second or two Sharpe could scarcely believe that he was alive. Nor could he believe that the fight was over. He wanted to kill again. His blood was up, the rage was seething in him, and there was no more enemy and so he contented himself by slashing the sabre down onto the Mahratta officer's head. 'Bastard!' he shouted, then booted the man's face to jolt the blade free. Then, suddenly, he was shaking. He turned and saw that Wellesley was staring at him aghast and Sharpe was certain he must have done something wrong. Then he remembered what it was. 'Sorry, sir,' he said.

'You're sorry?' Wellesley said, though he seemed scarcely able to speak. The General's face was pale.

'For pushing you, sir,' Sharpe said. 'Sorry, sir. Didn't mean to, sir.'

'I hope you damn well did mean to,' Wellesley said forcibly, and Sharpe saw that the General, usually so calm, was shaking too.

Sharpe felt he ought to say something more, but he could not think what it was. 'Lost your last horse, sir,' he said instead. 'Sorry, sir.'

Wellesley gazed at him. In all his life he had never seen a man fight like Sergeant Sharpe, though in truth the General could not remember everything that had happened in the last two minutes. He remembered Diomed falling and he remembered trying to loosen his feet from the stirrups, and he remembered a blow on the head that was probably one of Diomed's flailing hooves, and he thought he remembered seeing a bayonet bright in the sky above him and he had known that he must be killed at that moment, and then everything was a dizzy confusion. He recalled Sharpe's voice, using language that shocked even the General, who was not easily offended, and he remembered being thrust back against the gun so that the Sergeant could face the enemy alone, and Wellesley had approved of that decision, not because it spared him the need to fight, but because he had recognized that Sharpe would be hampered by his presence.

Then he had watched Sharpe kill, and he had been astonished by the ferocity, enthusiasm and skill of that killing, and Wellesley knew that his life had been saved, and he knew he must thank Sharpe, but for some reason he could not find the words and so he just stared at the embarrassed Sergeant whose face was spattered with blood and whose long hair had come loose so that he looked like a fiend from the pit. Wellesley tried to frame the words that would express his gratitude, yet the syllables choked in his throat, but just then a trooper came trotting to the gun with the reins of the roan mare in his hand. The mare had survived unhurt, and now the trooper offered the reins towards Wellesley who, as if in a dream, walked out of the sheltered space inside the gun's tall wheel to step across the bodies Sharpe had put onto the ground. The General suddenly stooped and picked up a stone. 'This is yours, Sergeant,' he said to Sharpe, holding out the ruby. 'I saw it fall.'

'Thank you, sir. Thank you.' Sharpe took the ruby.

The General frowned at the ruby. It seemed wrong for a sergeant to have a stone that size, but once Sharpe had closed his fingers about the stone, the General decided it must have been a blood-soaked piece of rock. It surely was not a ruby?

'Are you all right, sir?' Major Blackiston asked anxiously.

'Yes, yes, thank you, Blackiston.' The General seemed to shake off his torpor and went to stand beside Campbell who had dismounted to kneel beside Diomed. The horse was shaking and neighing softly. 'Can he be saved?' Wellesley asked.

'Don't know, sir,' Campbell said. 'The pike blade's deep in his lung, poor thing.'

'Pull it out, Campbell. Gently. Maybe he'll live.' Wellesley looked around him to see that the 7th Native Cavalry had scoured the gunners away and driven the remaining Mahratta horsemen off, while Harness's 78th had again marched into canister and round shot to capture the southern part of the Mahratta artillery. Harness's adjutant now cantered through the bodies scattered around the guns. 'We've nails and mauls if you want us to spike the guns, sir,' he said to Wellesley.

'No, no. I think the gunners have learned their lesson, and we might take some of the cannon into our own service,' Wellesley said, then saw that he was still holding his sword. He sheathed it. 'Pity to spike good guns,' he added. It could take hours of hard work to drill a driven nail out of a touchhole, and so long as the enemy gunners were defeated then the guns would no longer be a danger. The General turned to an Indian trooper who had joined Campbell beside Diomed. 'Can you save him?' he asked anxiously.

The Indian very gently pulled at the pike, but it would not move. 'Harder, man, harder,' Campbell urged him, and laid his own hands on the pike's bloodied shaft.

The two men tugged at the pike and the fallen horse screamed with pain. 'Careful!' Wellesley snapped.

'You want the pike in or out, sir?' Campbell asked.

'Try and save him,' the General said, and Campbell shrugged, took hold of the shaft again, put his boot on the horse's red wet chest, and gave a swift, hard heave. The horse screamed again as the blade left his hide and as a new rush of blood welled down to soak his white hair.

'Nothing more we can do now, sir,' Campbell said.

'Look after him,' Wellesley ordered the Indian trooper, then he frowned when he saw that his last horse, the roan mare, still had her trooper's saddle and that no one had thought to take his own saddle off Diomed. That was the orderly's job and Wellesley looked for Sharpe, then remembered he had to express his thanks to the Sergeant, but again the words would not come and so Wellesley asked Campbell to change the saddles, and once that was done he climbed onto the mare's back. Captain Barclay, who had survived his dash across the field, reined in beside the General. 'Wallace's brigade is ready to attack, sir.'

'We need to get Harness's fellows into line,' Wellesley said. 'Any news of Maxwell?'

'Not yet, sir,' Barclay said. Colonel Maxwell had led the cavalry in their pursuit across the River Juah.

'Major!' Wellesley shouted at the commander of the 7th Native Cavalry. 'Have your men hunt down the gunners here. Make sure none of them live, then guard the guns so they can't be retaken. Gentlemen?' He spoke to his aides. 'Let's move on.'

Sharpe watched the General ride away into the thinning skein of cannon smoke, then he looked down at the ruby in his hand and saw that it was as red and shiny as the blood that dripped from his sabre tip. He wondered if the ruby had been dipped in the fountain of Zum-Zum along with the Tippoo's helmet. Was that why it had saved his life? It had done bugger all for the Tippoo, but Sharpe was alive when he should have been dead, and so, for that matter, was Major General Sir Arthur Wellesley.

The General had left Sharpe alone by the gun, all but for the dead and dying men and the trooper who was trying to staunch Diomed's wound with a rag. Sharpe laughed suddenly, startling the trooper. 'He didn't even say thank you,' Sharpe said aloud.

'What, sahib?' the trooper asked.

'You don't call me sahib,' Sharpe said. 'I'm just another bloody soldier like you. Good for bloody nothing except fighting other people's battles. And ten to one the buggers won't thank you.' He was thirsty so he opened one of the General's canteens and drank from it greedily. 'Is that horse going to live?'

The Indian did not seem to understand everything Sharpe

said, but the question must have made some sense for he pointed at Diomed's mouth. The stallion's lips were drawn back to reveal yellow teeth through which a pale pink froth seeped. The Indian shook his head sadly.

'I bled that horse,' Sharpe said, 'and the General said he was greatly obliged to me. Those were his very words, "greatly obliged". Gave me a bloody coin, he did. But you save his life and he doesn't even say thank you! I should have bled him, not his bloody horse. I should have bled him to bloody death.' He drank more of the water and wished it were arrack or rum. 'You know what the funny thing is?' he asked the Indian. 'I didn't even do it because he was the General. I did it because I like him. Not personally, but I do like him. In a strange sort of way. I wouldn't have done it for you. I'd have done it for Tom Garrard, but he's a friend, see? And I'd have done it for Colonel McCandless, because he's a proper gentleman, but I wouldn't have done it for too many others.' Sharpe sounded drunk, even to himself, but in truth he was stone cold sober in a battlefield that had suddenly gone silent beneath the westering sun. It was almost evening, but there was still enough daylight left to finish the battle, though whether Sharpe would have anything to do with the finishing seemed debatable, for he had lost his job as the General's orderly, had lost his horse, had lost his musket and was stranded with nothing but a dented sabre. 'That ain't really true,' he confessed to the uncomprehending Indian, 'what I said about liking him. I want him to like me, and that's different, ain't it? I thought the miserable bugger might make me an officer! Sod that for a hope, eh? No sash for me, lad. It's back to being a bloody infantryman.' He used the bloody sabre to cut a strip of cloth from the robes of a dead Arab, and he folded the strip into a pad that he pushed under his jacket to staunch the blood from the *tulwar* wound on his left shoulder. It was not a serious injury, he decided, for he could feel no broken bones and his left arm was unhindered. He tossed the dented sabre away, found a discarded Mahratta musket, tugged the cartridge box and bayonet off the dead owner's belt, then went to find someone to kill.

It took half an hour to form the new line from the five battalions that had marched through the Mahratta gunfire and put Pohlmann's right to flight, but now the five battalions faced north towards Pohlmann's new position which rested its left flank on Assaye's mud walls then stretched along the southern bank of the River Juah. The Mahrattas had forty guns remaining, Pohlmann still commanded eight thousand infantry and innumerable cavalry, and the Rajah of Berar's twenty thousand infantrymen still waited behind the village's makeshift ramparts. Wellesley's infantry numbered fewer than four thousand men, he had only two light guns that were serviceable and scarcely six hundred cavalrymen mounted on horses that were bone weary and parched dry. 'We can hold them!' Pohlmann roared at his men. 'We can hold them and beat them! Hold them and beat them.' He was still on horseback, and still in his gaudy silk coat. He had dreamed of riding his elephant across a field strewn with the enemy's dead and piled with the enemy's captured weapons, but instead he was encouraging his men to a last stand beside the river. 'Hold them,' he shouted, 'hold them and beat them.' The Juah flowed behind his men, while in front of them the shadows stretched long across Assaye's battle-littered farmlands.

Then the pipes sounded again, and Pohlmann turned his horse to look at the right-hand end of his line and he saw the tall black bearskins and the swinging kilts of the damned Scottish regiment coming forward again. The sun caught their white crossbelts and glinted from their bayonets. Beyond them, half hidden by the trees, the British cavalry was threatening, though they seemed to be checked by a battery of cannon on the right of Pohlmann's line. The Hanoverian knew the cavalry was no danger. It was the infantry, the unstoppable red-jacketed infantry, that was going to beat him, and he saw the sepoy battalions starting forward on the High-landers' flank and he half turned his horse, thinking to ride to where the Scottish regiment would strike his line. It would hit Saleur's *compoo*, and suddenly Pohlmann could not care less any more. Let Saleur fight his battle, because Pohlmann knew it was lost. He stared at the 78th and he reckoned that no force on earth could stop such men. 'The best damned infantry on earth,' he said to one of his aides.

'Sahib?'

'Watch them! You'll not see better fighting men while you live,' Pohlmann said bitterly, then sheathed his sword as he gazed at the Scots who were once again being battered by cannon fire, but still their two lines kept marching forward. Pohlmann knew he should go west to encourage Saleur's men, but instead he was thinking of the gold he had left behind in Assaye. These last ten years had been a fine adven-ture, but the Mahratta Confederation was dying before his eyes and Anthony Pohlmann did not wish to die with it. The rest of the Mahratta princedoms might fight on, but Pohlmann had decided it was time to take his gold and run.

Saleur's *compoo* was already edging backwards. Some of the men from the rearward ranks were not even waiting for the Scots to arrive, but were running back to the River Juah and wading through its muddy water that came up to their chests. The rest of the regiments began to waver. Pohlmann watched. He had thought these three *compoos* were as fine as any infantry in the world, but they had proved to be brittle. The British fired a volley and Pohlmann heard the heavy balls thump into his infantry and he heard the cheer from the redcoats as they charged forward with the bayonet, and suddenly there was no army opposing them, just a mass of men fleeing to the river.

Pohlmann took off his gaudily plumed hat that would mark him as a prize capture and threw it away, then stripped off his sash and coat and tossed them after the hat as he spurred towards Assaye. He had a few minutes, he reckoned, and those minutes should be enough to secure his money and get away. The battle was lost and, for Pohlmann, the war with it. It was time to retire.

CHAPTER 12

Assaye alone remained in enemy hands, for the rest of Pohlmann's army had simply disintegrated. The great majority of the Mahratta horsemen had spent the afternoon as spectators, but now they turned and spurred west towards Borkardan while to the north, beyond the Juah, the remnants of Pohlmann's three *compoos* fled in panic, pursued by a handful of British and Company cavalry on tired horses. Great banks of gunsmoke lay like fog across the field where men of both armies groaned and died. Diomed gave a great shudder, lifted his head a final time, then rolled his eyes and went still. The sepoy trooper, charged with guarding the horse, stayed at his post and waved the flies away from the dead Diomed's face.

The sun reddened the layers of gunsmoke. There was an hour of daylight left, a few moments of dusk, and then it would be night, and Wellesley used the last of the light to turn his victorious infantry towards the mud walls of Assaye. He summoned gunners and had them haul captured enemy cannon towards the village. 'They won't stand,' he told his aides. 'A handful of round shot and the sight of some bayonets will send them packing.'

The village still held a small army. The Rajah of Berar's twenty thousand men were behind its thick walls, and Major Dodd had succeeded in marching his own regiment into the village. He had seen the remainder of the Mahratta line crumple, he had watched Anthony Pohlmann discard his hat and coat as he fled to the village and, rather than let the panic infect his own men, Dodd had turned them eastwards, ordered the regiment's cumbersome guns to be abandoned, then followed his commanding officer into the tangle of Assaye's narrow alleys. Beny Singh, the Rajah of Berar's warlord and the Killadar of the village's garrison, was glad to see the European. 'What do we do?' he asked Dodd.

'Do? We get out, of course. The battle's lost.'

Beny Singh blinked at him. 'We just go?'

Dodd dismounted from his horse and steered Beny Singh away from his aides. 'Who are your best troops?' he asked.

'The Arabs.'

'Tell them you're going to fetch reinforcements, tell them to defend the village, and promise that if they can hold the place till nightfall then help will come in the morning.'

'But it won't,' Beny Singh protested.

'But if they hold,' Dodd said, 'they cover your escape, sahib.' He smiled ingratiatingly, knowing that men like Beny Singh could yet play a part in his future. 'The British will pounce on any fugitives leaving the village,' Dodd explained, 'but they won't dare attack men who are well drilled and well commanded. I proved that at Ahmednuggur. So you're most welcome to march north with my men, sahib. I promise they won't be broken like the rest.' He climbed back into his saddle and rode back to his Cobras and ordered them to join Captain Joubert at the ford. 'You're to wait for me there,' he told them, then shouted for his own sepoy company to follow him deeper into the village.

The battle might be lost, but Dodd's men had not failed him and he was determined they should have a reward and so he led them to the house where Colonel Pohlmann had stored his treasure. Dodd knew that if he did not give his

359

men gold then they would melt away to find another warlord who would reward them, but if he paid them they would stay under his command while he sought another prince as employer.

He heard the sonorous bang of a great gun being fired beyond the village and he reckoned that the British had begun to pound Assaye's mud wall. Dodd knew that wall could not last long, for every shot would crumble the dried mud bricks and collapse the roof beams of the outermost houses so that in a few minutes there would be a wide breach leading into Assaye's heart. A moment later the redcoats would be ordered into the dusty breach and the village's alleys would be clogged by panic and filled with screams and bayonets.

Dodd reached the alley leading to the courtyard where Pohlmann had placed his elephants and he saw, as he had expected, that the big gate was still shut. Pohlmann was undoubtedly inside the courtyard, readying to escape, but Dodd could not wait for the Hanoverian to throw open the gates, so instead he ordered his men to fight their way through the house. He left a dozen men to block the alley, gave one of those men his horse to hold, then led the rest of the sepoys towards the house. Pohlmann's bodyguard saw them coming and fired, but fired too early and Dodd survived the panicked volley and roared his men on. 'Kill them!' he shouted as, sword in hand, he charged through the musket smoke. He kicked the house door open and plunged into a kitchen crowded with purple-coated men. He lunged with his sword, driving the defenders back, and then his sepoys arrived to carry their bayonets to Pohlmann's men. 'Gopal!' Dodd shouted.

'Sahib?' the Jemadar said, tugging his *tulwar* from the body of a dead man.

'Find the gold! Make sure it's loaded on the elephants, then open the courtyard gate!' Dodd snapped the orders, then went on killing. He was consumed with a huge anger. How could any fool have lost this battle? How could a man, given a hundred thousand troops, be beaten by a handful of redcoats? It was Pohlmann's fault, all Pohlmann, and Dodd knew Pohlmann had to be somewhere in the house or court-yard and so he hunted him and vented his rage on Pohlmann's guards, pursuing them from room to room, slaughtering them mercilessly, and all the while the great guns hammered the sky with their noise and the round shot thumped into the village walls.

Most of the Rajah of Berar's infantry fled. Those on the makeshift ramparts could see the redcoats massing beyond the smoke of the big cannon and they did not wait for that infantry to attack, but instead ran northwards. Only the Arab mercenaries stayed, and some of those men decided caution was better than bravery and so joined the other infantry that splashed through the ford where Captain Joubert waited with Dodd's regiment.

Joubert was nervous. The village's defenders were fleeing, Dodd was missing, and Simone was still somewhere in the village. It was like Ahmednuggur all over again, he thought, only this time he was determined that his wife would not be left behind and so he kicked back his heels and urged his horse towards the house where she had taken refuge.

That house was hard by the courtyard where Dodd was searching for Pohlmann, but the Hanoverian had vanished. His gold was all in its panniers, and Pohlmann's bodyguard had succeeded in strapping the panniers onto the two pack elephants before Dodd's men attacked, but there was no sign of Pohlmann himself. Dodd decided he would let the bastard live, and so, abandoning the hunt, he sheathed his sword then lifted the locking bar from the courtyard gates, 'Where's my horse?' he shouted to the men he had left guarding the alley.

'Dead, sahib!' a man answered.

Dodd ran down the alley to see that his precious new gelding had been struck by a bullet from the one volley fired by Pohlmann's bodyguard. The beast was not yet dead, but it was leaning against the alley wall with its head down, dulled eyes and blood dripping from its mouth. Dodd swore. The big guns were still firing beyond the village, showing that the redcoats were not advancing yet, but suddenly they went silent and Dodd knew he had only minutes left to make his escape, and just then he saw another horse turn into the alley. Captain Joubert was in the saddle, and Dodd ran to him. 'Joubert!'

Joubert ignored Dodd. Instead he cupped his hands and shouted up at the house where the wives had been sheltered during the fighting. 'Simone!'

'Give me your horse, Captain!' Dodd demanded.

Joubert still ignored the Major. 'Simone!' he called again, then spurred his horse on up the alley. Had she already gone? Was she north of the Juah? 'Simone?' he shouted.

'Captain!' Dodd screamed behind him.

Joubert turned, summoned the courage to tell the Englishman to go to hell, but as he turned he saw that Dodd was holding a big pistol.

'No!' Joubert protested.

'Yes, Monsewer,' Dodd said, and fired. The ball snatched Joubert back against the alley wall and he slid down to leave a trail of blood. A woman screamed from a window above the alley as Dodd pulled himself into the Frenchman's saddle. Gopal was already leading the first elephant out of the gate. 'To the ford, Gopal!' Dodd shouted, then he spurred into the courtyard to make certain that the second elephant was ready to leave.

While outside, in the alleys, there was a sudden silence. Most of the village's garrison had fled, the dust drifted from its broken walls, and then the order was given for the redcoats to advance. Assaye was doomed.

Colonel McCandless had watched Dodd's men retreat into the village and he doubted that the traitor was leading his men to reinforce the doomed garrison. 'Sevajee!' McCandless called. 'Take your men to the far side!'

'Across the river?' Sevajee asked.

'Watch to see if he crosses the ford,' McCandless said.

'Where will you be, Colonel?'

'In the village.' McCandless slid from Aeolus's back and limped towards the captured guns that had started to fire at the mud walls. The shadows were long now, the daylight short and the battle ending, but there was still time for Dodd to be trapped. Let him be a hero, McCandless prayed, let him stay in the village just long enough to be caught.

The big guns were only three hundred paces from the village's thick wall and each shot pulverized the mud bricks and started great clouds of red dust that billowed thick as gunsmoke. Wellesley summoned the survivors of the 74th and a Madrassi battalion and lined them both up behind the guns. 'They won't stand, Wallace,' Wellesley said to the 74th's commander. 'We'll give them five minutes of artillery, then your fellows can take the place.'

'Allow me to congratulate you, sir,' Wallace said, taking a hand from his reins and holding it towards the General.

'Congratulate me?' Wellesley asked with a frown.

'On a victory, sir.'

'I suppose it is a victory. 'Pon my soul, so it is. Thank you, Wallace.' The General leaned across and shook the Scotsman's hand.

'A great victory,' Wallace said heartily, then climbed out of his saddle so that he could lead the 74th into the village.

McCandless joined him. 'You don't mind if I come, Wallace?'

'Glad of your company, McCandless. A great day, is it not?'

'The Lord has been merciful to us,' McCandless agreed. 'Praise His name.'

The guns ceased, their smoke drifted northwards and the dying sun shone on the broken walls. There were no defenders visible, nothing but dust and fallen bricks and broken timbers.

'Go, Wallace!' Wellesley called, and the 74th's lone piper hoisted his instrument and played the redcoats and the sepoys forward. The other battalions watched. Those other battalions had fought all afternoon, they had destroyed an army, and now they sprawled beside the Juah and drank its muddy water to slake their powder-induced thirst. None crossed the river, only a handful of cavalry splashed through the water to chase the laggard fugitives on the farther bank.

Major Blackiston brought Wellesley a captured standard, one of a score that had been abandoned by the fleeing Mahrattas. 'They left all their guns too, sir, every last one of them!'

Wellesley acknowledged the standard with a smile. 'I'd rather you brought me some water, Blackiston. Where are my canteens?'

'Sergeant Sharpe still has them, sir,' Campbell answered, holding his own canteen to the General.

'Ah yes, Sharpe.' The General frowned, knowing there was unfinished business there. 'If you see him, bring him to me.'

'I will, sir.'

Sharpe was not far away. He had walked north through the litter of the Mahratta battle line, going to where the guns fired on the village and, just as they stopped, so he saw McCandless walking behind the 74th as it advanced on the village. He hurried to catch up with the Colonel and was rewarded with a warm smile from McCandless. 'Thought I'd lost you, Sharpe.'

'Almost did, sir.'

'The General released you, did he?'

'He did, sir, in a manner of speaking. We ran out of horses, sir. He had two killed.'

'Two! An expensive day for him! It sounds as if you had an eventful time!'

'Not really, sir,' Sharpe said. 'Bit confusing, really.'

The Colonel frowned at the blood staining the light infantry insignia on Sharpe's left shoulder. 'You're wounded, Sharpe.'

'A scratch, sir. Bastard with – sorry, sir – man with a *tulwar* tried to tickle me.'

'But you're all right?' McCandless asked anxiously.

'Fine, sir.' He raised his left arm to show that the wound was not serious.

'The day's not over yet,' McCandless said, then gestured at the village. 'Dodd's there, Sharpe, or he was. I'm glad you're here. He'll doubtless try to escape, but Sevajee's on the far side of the river and between us we might yet trap the rogue.'

Sergeant Obadiah Hakeswill was a hundred paces behind McCandless. He too had seen the Colonel following the 74th and now Hakeswill followed McCandless, for if McCandless wrote his letter, then Hakeswill knew his sergeantcy was imperilled. 'It ain't that I like doing it,' he said to his men as he stalked after the Colonel, 'but he ain't giving me a choice. No choice at all. His own fault. His own fault.' Three of his men were following him, the others had refused to come.

A musket fired from Assaye's rooftops, showing that not all the defenders had fled. The ball fluttered over Wallace's head and the Colonel, not wanting to expose his men to any other fire that might come from the village, shouted at his men to double. 'Just get in among the houses, boys,' he called. 'Get in and hunt them down! Quick now!'

More muskets fired from the houses, but the 74th were running now, and cheering as they ran. The first men scrambled over the makeshift breach blown by the big guns, while others hauled aside a cart that blocked an alleyway and, with that entrance opened, a twin stream of Scotsmen and sepoys hurried into the village. The Arab defenders fired their last shots, then retreated ahead of the redcoat rush. A few were trapped in houses and died under Scottish or Indian bayonets.

'You go ahead, Sharpe,' McCandless said, for his wounded leg was making him limp and he was now far behind the Highlanders. 'See if you can spot the man,' McCandless suggested, though he doubted Sharpe would. Dodd would be long gone by now, but there was always a chance he had waited until the end and, if men of the 74th had trapped Dodd, then Sharpe could at least try and make sure that the wretch was taken alive. 'Go, Sharpe,' the Colonel ordered, 'hurry!'

Sharpe dutifully ran on ahead. He clambered up the dust of the breach and jumped down into the pitiful wreckage of a room. He pushed through the house, stepped over a dead Arab sprawled in the outer door, edged about a dungheap in the courtyard, then plunged into an alleyway. Shots sounded from the river and so he headed that way past houses that were being looted of what little remained after the Mahratta occupation. A sepoy emerged from one house with a broken pot while a Highlander had found a broken brass weighing-scale, but the plunder was nothing like the riches that had been taken in Ahmednuggur. Another volley sounded ahead and Sharpe broke into a run, turned a corner and then stopped above the village's ford.

Dodd's regiment was on the far side of the river where

two white-coated companies had formed a rearguard. It was just like Ahmednuggur, where Dodd had guarded his escape route with volley fire, and now the Major had done it again. He was safely over the river with Pohlmann's two elephants, and his men had been firing at any redcoats who dared show on the ford's southern bank, but then, just as Sharpe arrived at the ford, the rearguard about-turned and marched north.

'He got away,' a man said, 'the bastard got clean away,' and Sharpe looked at the speaker and saw an East India Company sergeant in a doorway a few yards away. The man was smoking a cheroot and appeared to be standing guard over a group of prisoners in the house behind him.

Sharpe turned to watch Dodd's regiment march into the shadow of some trees. 'The bastard,' Sharpe spat. He could see Dodd on his horse just ahead of the two rearguard companies, and he was tempted to raise his musket and try one last shot, but the range was much too great and then Dodd vanished among the shadows. His rearguard followed him. Sharpe could see Sevajee off to the west, but the Indian was helpless. Dodd had five hundred men in ranks and files, and Sevajee had but ten horsemen. 'He bloody got away again,' Sharpe said, and spat towards the river.

'With my gold,' the East India Company sergeant said miserably, and Sharpe looked again at the man.

'Bloody hell,' Sharpe said in astonishment, for he was looking at Anthony Pohlmann who had donned his old sergeant's uniform. Pohlmann's 'prisoners' were a small group of his bodyguard.

'A pity,' Pohlmann said, spitting a scrap of tobacco from between his teeth. 'Ten minutes ago I was one of the richest men in India. Now I suppose I'm your prisoner?'

'I couldn't care less about you, sir,' Sharpe said, slinging the musket on his shoulder.

'You don't want to march me to Wellesley?' the Hanoverian asked. 'It would be a great feather in your cap.'

'That bastard doesn't give feathers,' Sharpe said. 'He's a stuck-up, cold-hearted bastard, he is, and I'd rather fillet him than you.'

Pohlmann grinned. 'So I can go, Sergeant Sharpe?'

'Do what you bloody like,' Sharpe said. 'How many men have you got there?'

'Five. That's all he left me. He slaughtered the rest.'

'Dodd did?'

'He tried to kill me, but I hid under some straw. A shameful end to my career as a warlord, wouldn't you say?' Pohlmann smiled. 'I think you did well, Sergeant Sharpe, to turn down my commission.'

Sharpe laughed bitterly. 'I know my place, sir. Down in the gutter. Officers don't want men like me joining them. I might scratch my arse on parade or piss in their soup.' He walked to the small house and peered through the open door. 'Better tell your fellows to take their coats off, sir. They'll be shot otherwise.' Then he went very still for, crouching at the back of the small room, was a woman in a shabby linen dress and a straw hat. It was Simone. Sharpe pulled off his shako. 'Madame?'

She stared at him, seeing only his silhouette against the dazzle of the day's last sun.

'Simone?' Sharpe said.

'Richard?'

'It's me, love.' He grinned. 'Don't tell me you got left behind again!'

'He killed Pierre!' Simone cried. 'I watched him. He shot him!'

'Dodd?'

'Who else?' Pohlmann asked behind Sharpe.

Sharpe stepped into the room and held his hand towards

368

Simone. 'You want to stay here,' he asked her, 'or come with me?'

She hesitated a second, then stood and took his hand. Pohlmann sighed. 'I was hoping to console the widow, Sharpe.'

'You lost, sir,' Sharpe said, 'you lost.' And he walked away with Simone, going to find McCandless to give him the bad news. Dodd had escaped.

Colonel McCandless limped up the breach and into Assaye. He sensed that Dodd was gone, for there was no more fighting in the village, though some shots still sounded from the river bank, but even those shots ended as the Scotsman edged past the dead man in the house doorway and through the court-yard into the street.

And perhaps, he thought, it did not really matter any longer, for this day's victory would echo throughout all India. The redcoats had broken two armies, they had ruined the power of two mighty princes, and from this day on Dodd would be hunted from refuge to refuge as the British power spread northwards. And it would spread, McCandless knew. Each new advance was declared to be the last, but each brought new frontiers and new enemies and so the redcoats marched again, and maybe they would never stop marching until they reached the great mountains in the very north. And maybe it was there, McCandless thought, that Dodd would at last be trapped and shot down like a dog.

And suddenly McCandless did not care very much. He felt old. The pain in his leg was terrible. He was still weak from his fever. It was time, he thought, to go home. Back to Scotland. He should sell Aeolus, repay Sharpe, take his pension, and board a ship. Go home, he thought, to Lochaber and to the green slopes of Glen Scaddle. There was work to be done in Britain, useful work, for he was corresponding with men in London and Edinburgh who wished to establish a society to spread Bibles throughout the heathen world and McCandless decided he could find a small house in Lochaber, hire a servant, and spend his days translating God's word into the Indian languages. That, he thought, would be a job worth doing, and he wondered why he had waited so long. A small house, a large fire, a library, a table, a supply of ink and paper and, with God's help, he could do more for India from that one small house than he could ever achieve by hunting down one traitor.

The thought of the great task cheered him, then he turned a corner and saw Pohlmann's great elephant wandering free in an alleyway. 'You're lost, boy,' he said to the elephant and took hold of one of its ears. 'Someone left the gate open, didn't they?'

He turned the elephant which followed him happily enough. They walked past a dead horse, and then McCandless saw a dead European in a white jacket, and for an instant he thought it must be Dodd, then he recognized Captain Joubert lying on his back with a bullet hole in his breast. 'Poor man,' he said, and he guided the elephant through the gate into the courtyard. 'I'll make sure you're brought some food,' he told the beast, then he turned and barred the gate.

He left the courtyard through the house, picking his way across the welter of bodies in the kitchen. He pushed open the outer door and found himself staring into Sergeant Hakeswill's blue eyes.

'I've been looking for you, sir,' Hakeswill said.

'You and I have no business, Sergeant,' McCandless said.

'Oh, but we does, sir,' Hakeswill said, and his three men blocked the alley behind him. 'I wanted to talk to you, sir,' Hakeswill said, 'about that letter you ain't going to write to my Colonel Gore.'

McCandless shook his head. 'I have nothing to say to you, Sergeant.'

'I hates the bleeding Scotch,' Hakeswill said, his face twitching. 'All prayers and morals, ain't you, Colonel? But I ain't cumbered with morals. It's an advantage I have.' He grinned, then drew his bayonet and slotted it onto the muzzle of his musket. 'They hanged me once, Colonel, but I lived 'cos God loves me, He does, and I ain't going to be punished again, not ever. Not by you, Colonel, not by any man. Says so in the scriptures.' He advanced on McCandless with the bayonet. His three men hung back and McCandless reckoned they were nervous, but Hakeswill showed no fear of this confrontation.

'Put up your weapon, Sergeant,' McCandless snapped.

'Oh, I will, sir, I'll put it up inside you unless you promises me on the holy word of God that you won't write no letter.'

'I shall write the letter tonight,' McCandless said, then drew his claymore. 'Now put up your weapon, Sergeant.'

Hakeswill's face twitched. He stopped three paces from McCandless. 'You'd like to strike me down, wouldn't you, sir? 'Cos you don't like me, sir, do you? But God loves me, sir, he does. He looks after me.'

'You're under arrest, Sergeant,' McCandless said, 'for threatening an officer.'

'Let's see who God loves most, sir. Me or you.'

'Put up your weapon!' McCandless roared.

'Bloody Scotch bastard,' Hakeswill said, and pulled his trigger. The bullet caught McCandless in the gullet and blew out through the back of his spine, and the Colonel was dead before his body touched the floor. The elephant in the nearby courtyard, startled by the shot, trumpeted, but Hakeswill ignored the beast. 'Scotch bastard,' he said, then stepped through the doorway and knelt to the body which he searched for gold. 'And if any one of you three says a bleeding word,' he threatened his men, 'you'll join him in heaven. If he's gone there, which I doubt, on account of God not wanting to clutter paradise with Scotchmen. Says so in the scriptures.' He found gold in McCandless's sporran and turned to show the coins to his men. 'You want it?' he asked. 'Then you keeps silent about it.'

They nodded. They wanted gold. Hakeswill tossed them the coins, then led them deeper into the house to see if there was anything worth plundering in its rooms. 'And once we're done,' he said, 'we'll find the General, we will, and have him give us Sharpie. We're almost there, lads. It's been a long road, it has, and hard in places, but we're almost there.'

Sharpe searched the village for Colonel McCandless, but could not find him in any of the alleys. He took Simone with him as he searched some of the larger houses and, from one high window, he found himself staring down into the court-yard where Pohlmann's great elephant was penned, but there was no sign of McCandless and Sharpe decided he was wasting his time. 'I reckon we'll give up, love,' he told Simone. 'He'll look for me, like enough, probably down by the river.' They walked back to the ford. Pohlmann had vanished and Dodd's men had long disappeared. The sun was at the horizon now and the farmlands north of the Juah were stained black by long shadows. The men who had captured the village were filling their canteens from the river, and the first few campfires glittered in the dusk as men boiled water to make themselves tea. Simone clung to him and kept talking of her husband. She felt guilty because she had not loved him, yet he had died because he had gone back into the village to find her, and Sharpe did not know how to console her. 'He was a soldier, love,' he told her, 'and he died in battle.'

'But I killed him!'

'No, you didn't,' Sharpe said, and he heard hooves behind him and he turned, hoping to see Colonel McCandless, but instead it was General Wellesley and Colonel Wallace and a score of aides riding up to the ford. He straightened to attention.

'Sergeant Sharpe,' Wellesley said, sounding embarrassed.

'Sir,' Sharpe said woodenly.

The General slid from his saddle. His face was red, and Sharpe supposed that was the effect of the sun. 'I have been remiss, Sergeant,' the General said awkwardly, 'for I believe I owe you my life.'

Sharpe felt himself blushing and was glad that the sun was low and the roadway where he stood was in deep shadow. 'Just did my best, sir,' he muttered. 'This is Madame Joubert, sir. Her husband was killed, sir, fighting for Colonel Pohlmann.'

The General took off his hat and bowed to Simone. 'My commiserations, Madame,' he said, then looked back to Sharpe whose long black hair still spilled over his collar. 'Do you know where Colonel McCandless is?' he asked.

'No, sir. I've been looking for him, sir.'

Wellesley fidgeted with his hat, paused to take a deep breath, then nodded. 'Colonel McCandless managed to have a long talk with Colonel Wallace this afternoon,' the General said. 'How they found time to have a conversation in battle, I don't know!' This was evidently a jest, for the General smiled, though Sharpe stayed straight-faced, and his lack of reaction disconcerted Wellesley. 'I have to reward you, Sharpe,' Wellesley said curtly.

'For what, sir?'

'For my life,' the General said in a tone of irritation.

'I'm just glad I was there, sir,' Sharpe said, feeling as awkward as Wellesley himself evidently felt.

'I'm rather glad you were there too,' the General said, then

373

took a step forward and held out his hand. 'Thank you, Mister Sharpe.'

Sharpe hesitated, astonished at the gesture, then made himself shake the General's hand. It was only then that he noticed what Wellesley had said. 'Mister, sir?' he asked.

'It is customary in this army, Mister Sharpe, to reward uncommon bravery with uncommon promotion. Wallace tells me you desire a commission, and he has vacancies in the 74th. God knows he has too many vacancies, so if you're agreeable, Sharpe, you can join the Colonel's regiment as an ensign.'

For a second Sharpe did not really comprehend what was being said, then he suddenly did and he smiled. There were tears in his eyes, but he reckoned that must be because of the powder smoke that lingered in the village. 'Thank you, sir,' he said warmly, 'thank you.'

'There, that's done,' Wellesley said with relief. 'My congratulations, Sharpe, and my sincere thanks.' His aides were all smiling at Sharpe, not Sergeant Sharpe any longer, but Ensign Sharpe of the King's 74th. Captain Campbell even climbed down from his saddle and offered his hand to Sharpe who was still smiling as he shook it.

'It'll turn out badly, of course,' Wellesley said to Campbell as he turned away. 'It always does. We promote them beyond their station and they inevitably take to drink.'

'He's a good man, sir,' Campbell said loyally.

'I doubt that too. But he's a good soldier, I'll say that. He's all yours now, Wallace, all yours!' The General pulled himself into his saddle, then turned to Simone. 'Madame? I can offer you very little, but if you care to join me for supper I would be honoured. Captain Campbell will escort you.'

Campbell held his hand out to Simone. She looked at Sharpe, who nodded at her, and she shyly accepted Campbell's arm and followed the General back up the street.

Colonel Wallace paused to lean down from his horse and shake Sharpe's hand. 'I'll give you a few minutes to clean yourself up, Sharpe, and to get those stripes off your arm. You might like to chop off some of that hair, while you're about it. And I hate to suggest it, but if you walk a few paces east of the village you'll find plenty of red sashes on corpses. Pick one, help yourself to a sword, then come and meet your fellow officers. They're few enough now, I fear, so you'll surely be welcome. Even the men might be glad of you, despite your being English.' Wallace smiled.

'I'm very grateful to you, sir,' Sharpe said. He was still scarcely able to believe what had happened. He was Mister Sharpe! Mister!

'And what do you want?' Wallace suddenly asked in an icy tone, and Sharpe saw that his new Colonel was staring at Obadiah Hakeswill.

'Him, sir,' Hakeswill said, pointing at Sharpe. 'Sergeant Sharpe, sir, what is under arrest.'

Wallace smiled. 'You may arrest Sergeant Sharpe, Sergeant, but you will certainly not arrest Ensign Sharpe.'

'Ensign?' Hakeswill said, going pale.

'Mister Sharpe is a commissioned officer, Sergeant,' Wallace said crisply, 'and you will treat him as such. Good day.' Wallace touched his hat to Sharpe, then turned his horse and rode away.

Hakeswill gaped at Sharpe. 'You, Sharpie,' he said, 'an officer?'

Sharpe walked closer to the Sergeant. 'That's not how you address a King's officer, Obadiah, and you know it.'

'You?' Hakeswill's face twitched. 'You?' he asked again in horror and amazement.

Sharpe thumped him in the belly, doubling him over. 'You call me "sir", Obadiah,' he said.

'I won't call you "sir",' Hakeswill said between gasps for

breath. 'Not till hell freezes, Sharpie, and not even then.'

Sharpe hit him again. Hakeswill's three men watched, but did nothing. 'You call me "sir",' Sharpe said.

'You ain't an officer, Sharpie,' Hakeswill said, then yelped because Sharpe had seized his hair and was dragging him up the street. The three men started to follow, but Sharpe snarled at them to stay where they were, and all three obeyed.

'You'll call me "sir", Sergeant,' Sharpe said, 'just you watch.' And he pulled Hakeswill up the street, going back to the house from where he had seen the elephant. He dragged Hakeswill through the door and up the stairs. The Sergeant screamed at him, beat at him, but Hakeswill had never been a match for Sharpe who now snatched the musket from Hakeswill's hand, threw it away, then took him to the window that opened just one floor above the courtyard. 'See that elephant, Obadiah?' he asked, holding the Sergeant's face in the open window. 'I watched it trample a man to death not long ago.'

'You won't dare, Sharpie,' Hakeswill squealed, then yelped as Sharpe took hold of the seat of his pants.

'Call me "sir",' Sharpe said.

'Never! You ain't an officer!'

'But I am, Obadiah, I am. I'm Mister Sharpe. I'll wear a sword and a sash and you'll have to salute me.'

'Never!'

Sharpe heaved Hakeswill onto the window ledge. 'If you ask me to put you down,' he said, 'and if you call me "sir", I'll let you go.'

'You ain't an officer,' Hakeswill protested. 'You can't be!'

'But I am, Obadiah,' Sharpe said, and he heaved the Sergeant over the ledge. The Sergeant screamed as he fell into the straw below, and the elephant, made curious by this strange irruption into this already strange day, plodded over to inspect him. Hakeswill beat feebly at the animal which had him cornered. 'Goodbye, Obadiah,' Sharpe called, then he used the words he remembered Pohlmann shouting when Dodd's sepoy had been trampled to death. '*Haddah!*' Sharpe snapped. '*Haddah!*'

'Get the bastard off me!' Hakeswill screamed as the elephant moved still closer and raised a forefoot.

'That won't do, Obadiah,' Sharpe said.

'Sir!' Hakeswill called. 'Please, sir! Get it off me!'

'What did you say?' Sharpe asked, cupping a hand to his ear.

'Sir! Sir! Please, sir! Mister Sharpe, sir!'

'Rot in hell, Obadiah,' Sharpe called down, and walked away. The sun was gone, the village was stinking with powder smoke, and two armies lay in ragged ruin on the bloody fields outside Assaye, but that great victory was not Sharpe's. It was the voice calling from the courtyard, calling frantically as Sharpe ran down the wooden stairs and walked down the alleyway. 'Sir! Sir!' Hakeswill shouted, and Sharpe listened and smiled, for that, he reckoned, was his real victory. It was Mister Sharpe's triumph.

Historical Note

The background events to *Sharpe's Triumph,* the siege of Ahmednuggur and the battle of Assaye, both happened much as described in the novel, just as many of the characters in the story existed. Not just the obvious characters, like Wellesley, but men like Colin Campbell, who was the first man over the wall at Ahmednuggur, and Anthony Pohlmann who truly was once a sergeant in the East India Company, but who commanded the Mahratta forces at Assaye. What happened to Pohlmann after the battle is something of a mystery, but there is some evidence that he rejoined the East India Company army again, only this time as an officer. Colonel Gore, Colonel Wallace and Colonel Harness all existed, and poor Harness was losing his wits and would need to retire soon after the battle. The massacre at Chasalgaon is a complete invention, though there was a Lieutenant William Dodd who did defect to the Mahrattas just before the campaign rather than face a civilian trial for the death of the goldsmith he had ordered beaten. Dodd had been sentenced to six months' loss of pay and Wellesley, enraged by the leniency of the court martial, persuaded the East India Company to impose a new sentence, that of dismissal from their army, and planned to have Dodd tried for murder in a civilian court. Dodd, hearing of the decision, fled, though I doubt that he took any sepoys with him. Nevertheless desertion was a problem for the Company at that time, for many sepoys knew that the Indian states would pay well for British-trained troops. They would pay even more for competent European (or American) officers, and many such made their fortunes in those years.

The city of Ahmednuggur has grown so much that most traces of its wall have now been swallowed by new building, but the adjacent fortress remains and is still a formidable stronghold. Today the fort is a depot of the Indian Army, and something of a shrine to Indians, for it was within the vast circuit of its red stone ramparts that the leaders of Indian independence were imprisoned by the British during the Second World War. Visitors are welcome to explore the ramparts with their impressive bastions and concealed galleries. The height of the fort's wall was slightly greater than the city's defences, and the fort, unlike the city, had a protective ditch, but the ramparts still offer an idea of the obstacle Wellesley's men faced when they launched their surprise escalade on the morning of 8 August 1803. It was a brave decision, and a calculated one, for Wellesley knew he would be heavily outnumbered in the Mahratta War and must have decided that a display of arrogant confidence would abrade his enemy's morale. The success of the attack certainly impressed some Indians. Goklah, a Mahratta leader who allied himself with the British, said of the capture of Ahmednuggur, 'These English are a strange people, and their General a wonderful man. They came here in the morning, looked at the *pettah* wall, walked over it, killed all the garrison, and returned to breakfast! What can withstand them?' Goklah's tribute was apt, except that it was Scotsmen who 'walked over the wall' and not Englishmen, and the celerity of their victory helped establish Wellesley's reputation for invincibility. Lieutenant Colin Campbell of the 78th was rewarded for his bravery with a promotion and a place on Wellesley's staff. He eventually became Sir Colin Campbell, governor of Ceylon.

The story of Wellesley deducing the presence of the ford at Peepulgaon by observation and common sense is well attested. To use the ford was an enormously brave decision, for no one knew if it truly existed until Wellesley himself spurred into the river. His orderly, from the 19th Dragoons, was killed as he approached the River Kaitna and nowhere is it recorded who took his place, but some soldier must have picked up the dragoon's duties, for Wellesley did have two horses killed beneath him that day and someone was close at hand on both occasions with a remount. Both horses died as described in the novel, the first during the 78th's magnificent assault on Pohlmann's right, and Diomed, Wellesley's favourite charger, during the scrappy fighting to retake the Mahratta gun line. It was during that fight that Wellesley was unhorsed and surrounded momentarily by enemies. He never told the tale in detail, though it is believed he was forced to use his sword to defend himself, and it was probably the closest he ever came to death in his long military career. Was his life saved by some unnamed soldier? Probably not, for Wellesley would surely have given credit for such an act that could well have resulted in a battlefield commission. Wellesley was notorious for disliking such promotions from the ranks ('they always take to drink'), though he did promote two men for conspicuous bravery on the evening of Assaye.

Assaye is not the most famous of Arthur Wellesley's battles, but it was the one of which he was most proud. Years later, long after he had swept the French out of Portugal and Spain, and after he had defeated Napoleon at Waterloo, the Duke of Wellington (as Arthur Wellesley became) was asked what had been his finest battle. He did not hesitate. 'Assaye,' he answered, and so it surely was, for he outmanoeuvred and outfought a much larger enemy, and did it swiftly, brutally and brilliantly. He did it, too, without Colonel Stevenson's help. Stevenson tried to reinforce Wellesley, but his local guide misled him as he hurried towards the sound of the guns, and Stevenson was so upset by the guide's error that he hanged the man.

Assaye was one of the costliest of Wellesley's battles: 'the bloodiest for the numbers that I ever saw,' the Duke recalled in later life. Pohlmann's forces had 1200 killed and about 5000 wounded, while Wellesley suffered 456 dead (200 of them Scottish) and around 1200 wounded. All the enemy guns, 102 of them, were captured and many were discovered to be of such high quality that they were taken into British service, though others, mostly because their calibres did not match the British standard artillery weights, were double-shotted and blown up on the battlefield where some of their remnants still lie.

The battlefield remains virtually unchanged. No roads have been metalled, the fords look as they did, and Assaye itself is scarcely larger now than it was in 1803. The outer walls of the houses are still ramparts of mud bricks, while bones and bullets are constantly ploughed out of the soil ('they were very big men', one farmer told me, indicating the ground where the 74th suffered so much). There is no memorial at Assaye, except for a painted map of the armies' dispositions on one village wall and the grave of a British officer which has had its bronze plate stolen, but the inhabitants know that history was made in their fields, are proud of it and proved remarkably welcoming when we visited. There ought to be some marker on the field, for the Scottish and Indian troops who fought at Assaye gained an astonishing victory. They were all extraordinarily brave men, and their campaign was not yet over, for some of the enemy have escaped and the war will go on as Wellesley and his small army pursue the remaining Mahrattas towards their great hill fastness at Gawilghur. Which means that Mister Sharpe must march again.

'Sharpe' now has its own fan club which encompasses the books and TV series. If you would like further details on membership, please write to the following address:

Sharpe Appreciation Society
PO Box 14
Lowdham
Notts
NG14 7HU